SEA STATE

J. M. Simpson

ISBN: 9798760995520
Independently published.

Authors Note.
I have taken a degree of literary license when depicting the wonderful work and crew members of the Royal National Lifeboat Institution (RNLI). I have embellished various aspects and fictionalised others to get the story right. So all mischaracterizations are fictional, and any procedural errors are mine.

The RNLI is an outstanding organisation whose volunteer lifeboat crews provide a 24-hour rescue service in the UK and Ireland, and their seasonal lifeguards look after people on busy beaches.

RNLI crews and lifeguards have saved over 143,500 lives since 1824. They influence, supervise and educate people. Their Community Safety teams explain the risks and share safety knowledge with anyone going out to sea or to the coast. And their international team work with like-minded organisations to help tackle drowning in communities at risk all around the world. As a charity they rely on kindness and generosity so if you'd like to donate please visit https://rnli.org/support-us

For my Crew – You are my true north.

For all the lifeboat heroes of the sea.
Past, present, and future.

The Sea washes away all the ills of men.

Euripides

PROLOGUE

She was dying. She knew it. She was absolutely and irrevocably sure of it. Unable to move, she felt like something invisible was pinning her to the floor. She seemed to be watching herself from above. Watching as he kicked and punched her repeatedly and screamed obscenities at her. A sensation of wetness suddenly flooded over her and, looking down, she realised it was blood. Was it hers? It was all over him too, but he didn't seem to notice. Icy coldness crept in, enfolding her, and black spots danced in front of her eyes. *This is what it must feel like to be dying*, she thought, as she watched him lay another vicious kick to her head. *How can anyone possibly survive this?*

CHAPTER 1

Leslie Cotton felt the familiar rush of rage that drove her to do the work she did. Swearing quietly, she flicked through the graphic photographs of the injured woman, held together with a paperclip in the worn brown folder with the annoying curly edges. She focused on one of the pictures, inspecting it closely, wincing at the injury. Entering the observation room, which smelt suspiciously of curry, despite the 'No food or drink allowed' sign she approached the one-way mirror to look at the woman.

In an effort to create a 'relaxed and comfortable environment' in the police interview room, someone in the higher echelons of purchasing had decided that two uncomfortable blue sofas were the answer. Leslie had spent hours in these rooms and could categorically conclude that the environment was neither relaxed nor comfortable.

A woman sat on one of the sofas, a wheelchair by her side. She was in her mid-thirties, with dark hair. Her eyes were barely visible in her swollen, black and purple face, with its discoloured split lips and a large dressing down one side. Both arms and lower legs were in casts. Chaotic blue, purple and yellow bruising was visible on her body through her thin white V-neck T-shirt.

Leslie's straight-talking northern colleague had described her as 'looking like hammered shit.'

The woman sat still, eyes closed, body tense. She wore a deep frown, as if remembering something unpleasant. In each corner of the room two CCTV cameras were fixed, their small red lights blinking. The strip lighting was hospital-like, fluorescent and unforgiving, giving the woman a slightly yellow tinge.

Leslie watched as Emily, a young PC, entered the room, placed a glass of water on the table in front of the woman and touched her arm softly.

'Jesse?'

The woman on the sofa started, looking panicked, recoiling from Emily's touch.

'It's OK,' Emily said softly. 'You're safe here. I just wanted to say DS Cotton is on her way.'

The woman managed a wan smile. Leslie watched Emily leave and a few seconds later she opened the door to the observation room.

'God, it stinks of curry in here,' she announced as she poked her head in and wrinkled her nose. 'It's showtime.'

'Thanks ... She OK?' Leslie asked as she gathered up the file and grabbed her water.

Emily shrugged. 'Think so. She's well jumpy though.'

'Thanks for getting her.' Leslie grabbed the open door from Emily and headed for the interview room. She pushed the door open with her shoulder and entered, smiling warmly.

'Jesse ... good to see you again. How are you doing?'

The woman looked up. 'Hi Leslie, I'm OK, how are you?'

Leslie sat down opposite Jesse, placing her file on the table. 'I'm good, thanks. So, how are you feeling about today?'

Jesse looked down at her hands, which were fiddling with a crumpled tissue. Her voice trembled. 'Err ... how do I feel? Nervous, anxious, terrified ... pick whichever word fits ... All of the above really.'

'It'll be OK.' Leslie leant across and placed a hand on Jesse's arm. 'Let's get started, so we don't have to think about it too much. Sometimes that's worse, isn't it? Thinking rather than doing? Anything you need before we make a start?'

2

Jesse shook her head. Leslie picked up the file.

'Ok Jesse. So, this is a record of what you remember, the night you were attacked. We're going to go through it. Everything is relevant. We need to collect as much evidence as we can ... OK? I know this is hard and it'll be really difficult and really painful, but we can take a break whenever you want. You do need to be aware though, that if the CPS deem it necessary, you'll be called to give evidence in Court.'

Jesse's eyes filled with tears.

'OK, so we need to do this, Jesse…while it's still fresh,' Leslie said authoritatively.

Jesse nodded, tears rolling down her cheeks.

'To be clear, we're recording this. So, for the purposes of the recording, Jesse, as you know, I'm Detective Sergeant Leslie Cotton from the Directorate of Professional Standards and you're Jesse Stevens. The date is the twenty-first of September 2018. This is a video record of your evidence concerning the attack you suffered at the hands of Police Officer Christopher Cherry on the twenty-seventh of August 2018, who is now in custody. Just for the record, I'm obliged to ask you formally to confirm to me, Jesse, you feel well enough to continue, given your very severe injuries.'

Jesse nodded.

'For the recording, Jesse,' prompted Leslie.

'Yes, I'm OK to continue,' Jesse said in a low tone.

'So, in your own time, tell me what happened on the night of the twenty-seventh of August 2018. You can stop anytime, we can take a break.' Leslie looked up from her notes. 'OK?'

Jesse closed her eyes. She was quiet for so long that Leslie was just about to lean forwards and touch her arm when suddenly Jesse opened her eyes and whispered, 'He called me.' Her voice shook. She looked over Leslie's shoulder into the distance, remembering. 'He was so angry. I'd never heard him that angry before.'

Leslie leant forwards to catch Jesse's words as they were so faint.

'He said … he said … "Are you ready, bitch?" … I said … "For what? What are you talking about …?" and he said … "For the overdue beating you need, you fucking bitch." Then he told me I was going to die.'

Jesse looked up at Leslie and took a deep breath.

3

'He said I was going to die. That he was going to kill me and enjoy every single second of it ... And I believed him.'

CHAPTER 2

He was dying. He was going to drown, and in that moment the irony was not lost on him. He felt the panic of not being able to breathe and tried to control it, remembering the training. He felt the crushing weight of his lungs, desperate for air; he was sure they were going to burst. He couldn't see a way out, couldn't feel a way out in the blackness. More time, he needed more time. He struggled, his strength waning. White light appeared. This was it, he thought. Time's up.

Doug woke suddenly, drawing in a huge breath. He lay in the dark bedroom for a moment, clutching onto the bedclothes as if they were the only thing anchoring him to the bed. He was trembling and sweating profusely. He saw the other side of the bed, empty and unslept in.

He struggled to sit up, wincing at the sharp pain in his side. He gingerly rubbed a hand over his face, feeling the sore cuts and the tender bruising, the stitches along his jawline.

Doug was forty, tall and trim, with dark blond hair and a tanned face from being in close proximity to the sea and sun. People told him his eyes were his best feature, an exceptionally light blue – wolf-like in some lights. Direct and unforgiving, or soft and warm, depending on how he felt.

He turned painfully to his bedside table which sported a variety of bottles of pills and awkwardly shook out a few, slugging them down with some water. He closed his eyes and lay back down again, trying to control the waves of nausea that threatened to engulf him.

He'd looked at himself in the bathroom mirror and decided he had looked better. His appearance had genuinely shocked him. He'd made a poor attempt at shaving, but the area on his face where the stiches were remained covered in stubble. His hand was too shaky to navigate around these areas.

He swore softly to himself as he struggled across the bedroom with the crutches. He slowly managed to open the curtains, pain shooting through him as he overstretched. The day had dawned bright and sunny.

He'd managed, with some difficulty, to get on a pair of black trousers and a white shirt, but was irritated that his bandage was visible through his shirt and that the wound on his torso had seeped more blood. His black tie hung loosely around his neck, as he had given up trying to tie it with his shaking hands. Exhausted and dizzy, he sat down again slowly, wincing once more as he sat.

A tall, blonde-haired, slim woman in a black dress and high heels marched into the bedroom, heading straight for the mirror. She fiddled with her hair, then turned to look at Doug with a disparaging expression.

'You're up. Finally. Christ, you look awful.'

Doug regarded her stoically. 'Is that a medical opinion?'

Claire grabbed him under the arm, yanking him upwards, making him stand. Doug inhaled sharply as the pain hit.

'It's a medical opinion,' she said briskly. 'You look pale.' She stood back slightly. 'And green. Are you going to throw up?'

'… Thinking about it,' he said through gritted teeth.

'Well, don't do it over me. This is a new dress,' she said, brushing a spec of something non-existent off her skirt and smoothing it over her hips. She stepped back, viewing him critically.

'Come on. Let's get this damn thing over with. You know I can't stand funerals. You shouldn't even be out of hospital, but as usual you think you know best.' She marched out of the room calling to Doug in an authoritative tone, 'Leaving in five, Douglas. Be ready. Now's the time to throw up.'

Claire drove, the RNLI truck jerking and the engine roaring with her angry gear changes. Doug was sitting in the passenger seat, thinking about how awful he felt and how he'd prefer to actually die than face today. He also paused for a moment of sympathy for his beloved truck.

'I hate this bloody tank. I absolutely hate it. Douglas, I need today like I need a hole in the bloody head. I'm going straight into work afterwards. You can make your own way home with the kids? I see absolutely no point in hanging around with you or your cronies and moping about.'

Doug muttered, 'Forever the supportive wife.'

Claire brought the truck to an abrupt halt in the harbour car park with a squeal of tyres, throwing Doug painfully forwards in his seat. She switched off the engine and turned on him angrily.

'Don't give me that crap, Douglas. I've been busy trying to hold down a job while you get back on your feet.'

She snapped down the visor and applied lipstick.

'I mean, I do wonder, while we're on the subject, whether this hasn't prompted you to do something different with your life, so it's not me and the children standing over a coffin on the bandstand at some point in the future. You know, something a bit more useful perhaps.'

Doug stared at Claire in disbelief. 'A bit more useful?'

'You know what I mean.'

'Are we really doing this today?' Doug stared at Claire.

She snorted derisively. 'Well, when is a good time, Douglas? I'm serious, I think you should think about doing something else. Something different. God forbid I have to be the grieving widow.'

'God forbid,' Doug muttered.

A tap on the window made them both jump and they turned to see a tall, handsome, dark-haired man with a neat dark beard in his twenties, also in dress uniform standing by the truck.

Claire turned to Doug. 'Your cronies await. Let's get this over with. I have patients to see.' She opened the door, climbed out and slammed it.

'Mike,' she said, walking away.

Mike said to her departing back. 'Claire.'

Doug opened the car door slowly.

'You alright, Skipper?' Mike asked, looking at Claire's retreating back, then back to Doug. 'Skip, no disrespect and all that, but you look like hell. You should still be in hospital.'

Doug sighed. 'I have to do it. I have to be here. For them.'

The Victorian bandstand sat proudly below the castle, overlooking the sandy bay. The old bandstand was a stark contrast to the contemporary design of the lifeboat station, which stood nearby, silently guarding the sea. On the raised bandstand, two coffins lay, draped in RNLI flags, surrounded by men in dress uniform, heads bowed. Surrounding the bandstand were people dressed in black who had come to pay their respects to their lost loved ones.

Doug stopped. He could hear the local mayor on the bandstand getting to the end of reading Tennyson's 'Crossing the Bar'. He saw the four steps up to his destination and it might well have been the north face of the Eiger. He felt like he could lie down and sleep, or even better, die, right where he stood, then it would all be over. He felt exhausted, sick and sweaty. He felt a hand on his shoulder as he turned to see two of his crew standing next to him.

'You OK, Skip?' asked Dan softly, a regular crew member also in his early twenties. He was handsome with longer hair and much-ribbed designer stubble. He was standing next to Mike, both of them looking concerned.

'Do you need a hand up, Skip?' Mike asked quietly.

Doug shook his head and breathed deeply. He climbed the four steps and moved awkwardly past the mayor and coffins, nodding to people as he shuffled past.

For a dreadful moment, Doug thought his body would betray him and throw up. He took a huge breath and adjusted his stance to rest a hand on one of the coffins.

The weight of his own personal grief was threatening to overwhelm him; he could feel it building like a tidal wave of crashing emotion. He cleared his throat and spoke, his Scottish accent always much more pronounced when he was emotional.

'Thank you … All of you … For coming and paying your respects, for your support over the last few weeks … since …' His voice cracked and his eyes filled with tears; he struggled to get control. 'It means a lot to us. All of us.' He paused for a moment and looked out to sea, fighting the lump in his throat. 'Courage is not the absence of fear, but rather the judgement that something else is more important than fear. Jeff and Gavin, you showed enormous strength and courage and showed no fear.'

Doug looked down at the two coffins. 'I heard a song on the radio this morning. The song said fear was for the brave, cowards never stare it in the eye, and I thought of you two and your incredible bravery. You gave your lives to save others and we'll always be grateful for that. This community will forever be grateful. Jeff and Gav ... our friends. Our family. You'll be missed.'

Doug looked across the sea of faces, seeing Claire at the back of the crowd fully engrossed in her phone, the anger he felt steeled him to refocus and get his emotions under control.

'You've both left a huge hole that can never be filled. You paid the ultimate price. Your courage, sacrifice and bravery meant that others could live. You'll be missed, but you'll never be forgotten.'

Doug turned and nodded to the crew who had stepped forward to carry the coffins. They picked the coffins up and carried them slowly to the waiting hearses in the harbour car park. Doug followed, struggling down the steps slowly.

A small blonde woman, dressed in black and crying softly, stepped forward.

'Doug,' she said quietly.

Doug looked up at her. His eyes filled with tears and he shook his head. He struggled to form a sentence. 'Anna ... I ... I'm ... I'm sorry ...'

She smiled at him and reached up a hand to touch his face. 'Doug, it wasn't your fault, everyone knows it wasn't your fault. No one thinks it was. You mustn't blame yourself. He wouldn't have wanted that. He loved you, you were his best friend. He would have walked through fire for you.'

Tears streamed down Doug's face, but he made no effort to wipe them away. He kept shaking his head, looking down at his feet.

'Doug. Gavin will always be with us. He'll always be part of you.'

She placed a gentle hand on his face, wiping away a tear and walked away, following the coffins.

Doug stood there, huge sobs silently wracking his body. Behind him, Claire was walking away from the crowd in the opposite direction, laughing into her phone.

Doug arrived at the harbour as the coffins were being lowered into the back of the hearses. He was out of breath, and black spots were dancing in his eyes and clouding his vision. He was still fighting back huge waves of nausea.

The crew were still with heads bowed. They fell into line behind him. Doug looked up the high street that stretched up towards the church and wondered whether he would make it up the hill.

The hearses moved slowly as they climbed the high street. Doug promised himself he could die later if he could just get through the day.

People lined the streets and standing respectfully to the side as the funeral procession passed by the shops and restaurants in the town. Some muttered condolences and prayers, some sobbed for lost friends, and some threw flowers onto the slow-moving cars.

To Doug, the road seemed endless.

Doug wanted a drink and then he wanted to either sleep or die. He didn't care which came first. He was vaguely aware of being in his RNLI truck.

'Skip ... Wakey, wakey.' Mike shook Doug's arm gently as he swung the truck into Doug's driveway.

'Thanks, mate.'

'I'll bring the kids in,' Mike said. 'Come on you two. Your palace awaits.'

The two kids yawned and climbed out of the truck. Doug struggled towards the front door, digging in his pocket for his key, while juggling his crutches. He opened the front door and turned to wait for the kids. Jude was bleary eyed. At eleven, he was tall for his age with light brown curly hair and his father's very light blue eyes. Christy was small and petite for eight, with bright blonde hair and the bright cornflower blue eyes of her mother.

Mike stood for a moment on the doorstep, handing the truck keys to Doug. The kids waved at Mike and disappeared into the dark house. Doug turned to the kids. 'Straight up and into bed, OK?'

The kids shuffled upstairs.

Mike gestured to the dark house. 'Mate, where's Claire? You shouldn't be on your own with the kids in your state. Do you want me to stick around?'

Doug smiled gratefully, thinking what a great bunch of lads he had on his crew. 'She's at work. I'll be fine. I can always call Nessie next door. Thanks for everything today. I was proud of you all.'

Mike started to head out of the drive 'Call me if you need anything? It's no trouble.'

'Don't you want to take the truck?' Doug called.

'Nah, I'm good, I'll call in tomorrow, see how you are.'

'Night, mate,' Doug called.

Doug entered the kitchen and leant his crutches against the worktop. He opened the fridge, the light brightening the dark kitchen. Doug tutted as he saw the contents. Milk, a small packet of cheese and a sliced loaf. Taking out his phone he called a number while staring into the fridge. The phone went straight to voicemail.

'Claire, it's me. So, it's nearly nine. Hope you're OK. Let me know when you might be home. I'm hoping you'll have eaten.'

Doug slammed the fridge door shut. He picked up a bottle of whisky from the worktop, grabbed a glass and sat painfully down at the kitchen table in the dark. Silence pervaded the kitchen apart from the gentle hum of the fridge.

He stared at the bottle for a long time, lost in his thoughts. Slowly he unscrewed the cap and poured out a measure, his hand shaking, liquid splashing over the side of the glass. He drank deeply. Then he leant forward, his head in his hands, and huge silent sobs wracked his shoulders.

He was drowning. Again. The darkness. The panic. The black water closing in. Can't see a way out. Lungs bursting. Screaming underwater, no one to hear. Thumping and pushing at an immovable object, there's no way out. Panic. Can't see them, can't get to them. Can't save them. No time, no time! The white light. Game Over. Time's up.

Doug awoke in a panic, the norm since the accident. He lay in bed, breathing hard, gulping in air like a man trying to stop himself from drowning. He lay with his eyes closed trying to regulate his terror by listening to sounds outside the bedroom.

He gingerly swung his legs over the side of the bed. His limbs felt like lead.

The bedroom door opened, and Claire appeared, in a navy blue and white dress, her short blonde hair immaculate as ever.

'You look absolutely dreadful.'

Doug acknowledged her words with a nod. 'Didn't think you were here.'

Claire inspected her watch and tutted. 'I'm not. I'm just going. The kids are sorted, so I'm off. I assume it all went well yesterday? I couldn't bear it anymore, so I left before the church service.'

'I noticed.'

'So, it went off well then?'

'It wasn't a fucking wedding, Claire. What time did you get in last night?'

Claire inspected her face in the mirror, touching her perfect hair. 'It was this morning. I grabbed a few hours on the sofa as you were thrashing about here, and I can't abide that. You looked like you were having dreams. I think you should speak to someone. Douglas? Are you listening?'

'Someone?'

'Not me obviously,' Claire said.

'Obviously not,' muttered Doug.

'You know, someone that knows what they're doing, poking around in people's minds – ughh can't stand the idea myself, I much prefer surgery – cut out the problem and be done with it. So, you'll do it … today?'

'Do what today?'

'You know, speak to someone, sort yourself out.'

'Sort myself out?'

'Don't look at me like that, Douglas. You need to get your head back in the game. Stop moping around.'

Doug stared at her, not really believing what she was saying. 'Moping around?'

'Don't be obtuse, Douglas.'

Doug heaved in a breath and struggled to stand. He faced her, his face like thunder, his wolfish blue eyes cold with anger.

'Claire, I've been home from hospital for two days. Yesterday, I buried two of my closest friends. My best friends, whose deaths were …' His words caught in his throat. 'Their deaths were my fault and I have to live with that … knowing that. They died because of me. Does that even register with you?'

Claire tried to answer, but Doug held a hand up to silence her.

'So, Claire, apologies if you think that the funeral yesterday was "moping around". I'm letting you know it might just take me a few more days to get my head back in the game. If this doesn't fit in exactly with Dr Claire Brodie's prescribed quick-fix recovery plan, then I apologise in advance. As for my mental health, I'll go at my own pace and not be pushed into anything because it suits you and your busy schedule. Am I being clear enough?'

Claire opened her mouth as if to say something and then closed it again. She turned and strode towards the bedroom door where she stopped and faced Doug.

'You should be a little more gracious in accepting help and support, Douglas, when it's offered. I'm going to work, I'll be late. Don't wait up. I'll drop the children off. You can sort them out later; it'll give you something to do. Stop you moping.'

Her heels clattered as she stomped angrily down the wooden stairs. Doug heard the front door slam and sat back down on the bed wondering what the hell had just happened and what he had done for her to be so angry with him all the time.

13

EIGHTEEN MONTHS LATER

CHAPTER 3

Jesse crunched the gears of the Luton van, chuckling at how everybody seemed to let large white vans out at junctions. She was thoroughly enjoying herself, a rare thing these days. She tickled the ears of the border collie next to her.

'Nearly there, boy,' she said lovingly, as he licked her hand.

'Here we go. Number 12.' She pulled the van over. 'Come on.' She opened the door and he jumped down and followed at her heels. She fished a key out of her pocket and opened the bright blue front door of her new home.

Jesse stood in the kitchen and surveyed her work. She was pleasantly exhausted. Hopefully, it meant she'd sleep and not dream. Most days she tried to wear herself out so she would fall into a dreamless sleep, but every now and again the dreams returned. They crept in like an unwanted prowler and shook her to the core.

The kitchen and the dining room were unpacked; her bed was made upstairs; everything else could wait. She picked up a small box from a kitchen chair and saw the corner of a photo frame. She pulled it from the bubble wrap. Jesse and a blonde-haired woman were laughing together and the writing on the frame said. Best friends forever'. Her eyes filled with tears.

'Miss you,' she whispered.

The microwave dinged. She gently placed the photo on a shelf. She dumped her meal out onto a plate and sat down opposite two large glass doors which opened out onto the garden. She ate watching the birds dart in and out of the trees.

She put her plate in the sink and enjoyed the feeling she could wash it up later – it didn't have to be done now, this minute, dried and put away to avoid an argument. She looked at the dog who sensed a question. He turned his head on its side and pricked up his ears.

'Walkies?' she asked softly.

The dog rushed off down the hall and returned with a lead hanging from his mouth.

'Come on, then,' she said, grinning.

Dusk was settling in, leaving a chilly nip in the spring air. She stood by the castle that overlooked the town. The harbour was bustling with activity; lights were on in the pretty coloured houses that stretched up the hill and along the cliff tops. A group of teenage boys in canoes were being bossed about by a woman with red hair. She was in a canoe, calling instructions to them as they arrived back in the harbour, with a few of them capsizing their small boats while trying to get out.

Jesse moved around to look down at the lifeboat station and sat down on a bench. The dog jumped up next to her. She placed an arm around him and pulled him close.

'Fresh start here, boy, this is home now … for a while anyway.'

She watched two men leave the RNLI station. One was older, she guessed early sixties, with close cropped grey hair, a tan-weathered face and a slight limp. The younger man was in his late thirties or early forties, with dark blond hair and an attractive tanned face. He was tall and fairly lean. He was talking. The older man threw his head back and laughed, clapping the younger man on the back. Jesse watched them as they walked around the harbour. She assumed them to be part of her new crew. Suddenly she was nervous about meeting them all and being the new girl. She felt the panic rising in her chest; the dog, sensing her change in mood, nudged against her. Her hand went to him automatically

16

and she stroked his soft ears, feeling the process relax her. She had to begin again. A new life. She couldn't go back. Didn't want to go back. Too many memories. Too much darkness.

Night had fallen while she had been lost in her thoughts. Jesse rose from the bench and walked through the streets, now almost deserted. The dog trotted quietly beside her. She cut down a small alley, stopping abruptly at the sound of a door slamming and a bottle smashing. Jesse's heart thumped, terrified instantly by the noise. She moved from the shadows and began walking again, faster this time. She unlocked the door to her cottage and quickly bolted the door and double-locked the latch. She felt ridiculous to be frightened like this. She was angry with herself. The dog pawed her leg as if to remind her he was there, and she slid down, back to the door to pet him, burying her face in his soft fur.

'It's OK, boy, we're safe here.'

I see her in the distance. I see her carrying boxes into the small white house with the bright blue door. She's healed well. The scar looks good. I like it ... WE like it. The dog is at her heels all the time, he's new. She must have got him when we lost her. Now we've found her again. We are very happy we've found her. We thought she was lost. She looks well. Healthy. This is clearly home now. She struggled with the big stuff on her own, but she persevered, we like that too ... they used to call it gumption. We watch her slam the blue front door and climb into the van with the dog sat beside her. We see her pull away slowly, and we pull out to follow. Not too close ... not too close.

CHAPTER 4

Doug had decided he was going to say something. Enough was enough; he couldn't be walking on eggshells every day. He knew they'd drifted apart since the accident. She seemed so distant, so angry, so ... he searched for the word as he drove ... so absent, that was it. Time for action, he thought, as he pulled into the driveway. Time to mend and build bridges.

He pushed open the bedroom door and watched Claire with amusement as she angrily dried her hair and muttered. She threw the hairdryer down and selected a pair of earrings, not noticing Doug in the doorway. She started to apply make-up, swearing as she watched the clock.

Doug strolled into the room smiling. He wore a navy RNLI polo shirt and jeans. His forehead sported a large scar, but he looked healthy and well.

'Hello, how was your day?' he asked amiably.

Claire glared at him in the mirror. 'You're late!'

Doug looked surprised. 'Hello to you too. Is there a problem?'

'Did you get my message?'

Doug looked blank. 'Message?'

'Jesus bloody Christ. WHAT is the point of you having a bloody mobile phone if you never use the bloody thing?'

Doug looked confused 'Sorry, it's been a bit of a busy day, I haven't had a chance to check ...'

Claire said with contempt. 'Oh please, Douglas. You don't know the meaning of the word busy ...'

This wasn't what he had hoped would happen this evening. He took a deep breath.

'What was it? The message?'

Claire rolled her eyes. 'I said I had a function tonight in Carmarthen and an early surgery tomorrow morning, so I see no point in coming home later.'

Doug opened his mouth to say something, and then changed his mind.

'Nope, no point at all.'

Claire glanced at him suspiciously. 'What? What is it? What were you going to say?'

'I just ...'

'Good God, just what? Just what?' Claire said impatiently, rolling her eyes.

Doug sighed. 'I just thought it would be good to talk ... you know, sort of re-connect.'

'Talk? Re-connect? She laughed mockingly. 'Who on earth have you been talking to?'

Doug shrugged. 'We never ... you know ... talk, spend time together. I just get a sense we need to. We don't see each other that much, the kids are noticing ... I ... want to try—'

Claire interrupted him. 'I see, so it's my fault for working too much, is it?'

Doug ignored her comment. He persisted calmly. 'So, I wondered whether perhaps we should go out, you know, have dinner or something. Talk about things.'

'What things exactly?' Claire asked in a dangerous tone.

'Things. Us. The kids.'

'Go out to talk about you and me?'

'And other stuff ...'

Claire placed her hairbrush down very precisely on the dressing table. 'Oh, there's other stuff is there? Such as?'

'I just think we could do with a bit of time out together. It might be nice. Make the effort, you know, like those days when it was us against the world?'

'Are you suggesting I don't make the effort?'

Doug frowned. 'No … Claire.'

Claire sighed. 'OK. If you insist, I'll look at my schedule and see what I can do.'

She picked up a wrap and small handbag from the dressing table. Doug caught her wrist as she drew level with him.

'You look beautiful,' he said softly. 'Look, I just want to spend some time together, that's all.'

'OK, I'll look at my schedule. Of course, all of this "effort" and "re-connecting" will be completely redundant if you get a shout, won't it? That's the thing that takes priority over everything, isn't it? Almost not worth bothering in a way, is it? Cut out the disappointment. The children need feeding by the way, I haven't had the time.'

She left Doug standing in the bedroom looking annoyed, half wishing he hadn't bothered.

Doug's pager buzzed insistently on the bedside table. He dragged himself awake and sprang into action. He frowned at the empty bed, then remembered that Claire was away. He threw on jeans and a polo shirt, shoved his feet into a pair of Dude deck shoes and quietly slipped down the stairs. A gentle knocking on the front door made him smile. He opened it to see a white-haired lady standing on the step, clutching a knitting bag.

'I heard the pager,' she said. 'Figured missy wouldn't be here so I'll sit with the kids and get them up and out if you're not back.'

Doug dropped a kiss on the top of her head. 'Nessie, they broke the mould when they made you. You sure?'

'Away with you. People to save.'

'I'd be lost without you.'

She made a shooing gesture with her bag. 'You mind how you go, or you'll have me to answer to.'

'Yes, boss. See you later. Give the kids a kiss from me.'

Doug drove towards the harbour; the wind was strong tonight, he thought ruefully as he noticed waves crashing in over the harbour wall. He gripped the steering wheel. For a moment, panic and uncertainty overwhelmed him. What if he lost more crew? What if he couldn't cope? Went to pieces? They'd not had a big shout in these conditions since the accident.

He pulled into a parking space and took a deep breath. He set off, running towards the lifeboat station. He unlocked the door, flicked on the lights and pressed the button to raise the massive roller doors to the boat ramp. The other crew arrived out of breath, hurrying to the changing room and emerging wearing their trademark yellow gear. Dan appeared from the control room, looking at a piece of paper.

'What is it?' Doug asked

'Jesus. Cruise liner, way off course, engine trouble, near the rocks, possible fire.'

'Launch in two,' Doug shouted, starting the engines. 'Helmets on, it's going to be a rough ride. Tie on, hold on.'

The shrill station alarm sounded, and the boat started moving down the steep causeway, rushing into the water with a large whoosh as it hit the ocean with a spectacular splash. The engines roared and the boat fought against the waves as it headed off into the night.

In the distance the outline of the rugged coastline was silhouetted. Looming large was a small cruise liner listing to one side, the boat stark white against the dark cliffs behind. The ships alarm blasted shrilly. The lights on the liner were flickering on and off and the sounds of screaming were carried through the wind.

Doug registered the size of the liner and his guts churned.

'Jesus Christ,' he said softly. 'There must be two hundred people on there.'

He turned.

'Dan, get onto the coastguard. We're going to need all the help we can get. Get the word out to the local fishermen too, they'll need to help us bring all these people back safely once we can get them out of danger.'

Doug saw the faces of the crew with him, all looking shocked at the size of the vessel. He gestured them closer to him and shouted, his words difficult to hear with the wind.

'This is about getting people out of the water and to safety. No one goes on board. AT ALL. Under no circumstances. We want people out of the water. Looks like an oil spill over there and we don't want that going up with people in the water. Everyone clear?'

The crew nodded. As the lifeboat drew nearer the liner, the spotlights cast light over a large, jagged hole; water was gushing in and out as the waves crashed over the liner.

Inside Doug was a mess. He looked out at the carnage before him and heard the screams. He was swamped by a wave of panic. He couldn't run this rescue – he wasn't ready. He couldn't be responsible for all these people. He looked down at his shaking hands and tried to swallow. He felt a strong hand on his shoulder. Bob, the oldest and longest serving member of the crew, looked at him as if he understood him perfectly.

'Stop overthinking it. It's just another day at the office.'

Doug looked at his friend, it was like he had read his mind. He nodded to Bob. Another day at the office had been one of Gavin's mantras. It had been the last thing Gavin had said to Doug as he had winked and disappeared below decks, the night that had robbed him of his life.

Doug coughed constantly from the thick black smoke. His throat felt raw and he would happily have sold his soul for a drink of cold water. He wiped his stinging eyes, trying to focus through the smoke to see if the lifeboats were being lowered down the side of the liner. He needed to see them to make sure that people were getting to safety.

As he heaved yet another traumatised passenger onto the deck, heavy and soaking wet, Doug told them they were safe now. He looked around and saw with relief that his crew were hooking in survivors, many of whom were struggling in wet evening gowns or dinner jackets. No one with lifejackets on.

His next problem was where to put everyone before it became too dangerous to carry on and affected the boats overall stability. He shouted down into the bridge.

'Dan. We need more boats to offload these passengers, get a mayday out to all the fisherman locally. Stress it's retrieval, not rescue. They'll come.'

'Skip.' A voice floated up.

The coastguard chopper arrived and was training searchlights onto the liner and the water's surface. Doug watched in frustration as he saw people jumping in the water and swimming towards the laden lifeboats, waving at the chopper, with some being lost in the swell.

'Jesus Christ,' he murmured. From the corner of his eye, he saw the fire taking hold in the crippled liner and people jumping from the deck screaming, some on fire. He looked at the liner and then back to the circling chopper and shouted back down to the bridge.

'Radio the chopper, that fire is going to go soon, so they need to be clear of the boat in case the fuel tanks catch.' He leant towards Mike who was steering the lifeboat.

'Mike, we need to get away from the boat, a good distance. That fire is taking hold. Let's sweep around and do a wider pick up and get to the people nearest that oil spill pronto, just in case it catches.'

'Yes Skip.'

The wind had changed direction momentarily and whipped the smoke away from the liner towards the coastline. Two other large lifeboats appeared from the nearby coastal towns, and he waved an arm in greeting.

Suddenly there was a large explosion. For a moment it seemed to Doug that everything was quiet, as if the explosion had sucked the noise out of the air for a split second.

Mike powered the boat further away just as the rear of the liner exploded in a fireball, leaving a gaping hole at the back of the boat, which was rapidly filling with water.

Doug looked back over his shoulder as they sped away. The water was full of people thrashing and screaming, trying to stay afloat in their heavy clothes. The air was filled with smoke.

Doug squinted. He could just about make out some passengers still on the liner, looking desperately for a way off the burning ship, their only escape being the sharp rocks below. Doug's own boat was over maximum capacity and sitting low in the water with the weight of the extra passengers. He couldn't endanger lives by trying to pick anyone else up.

'Dan,' he barked. 'Update on the mayday. Any extra boats?'

'Checking now, Skip,' came the calm reply.

In the dawn light, the fire was almost out. The sea was calmer. The liner was on its side, still smoking. Doug closed his tired, gritty eyes for a second.

The fishing fleet had come; there must have been thirty boats buzzing around helping the lifeboats, who were still picking up survivors to decant them and take them to safety.

He was beyond shattered. His arms ached from pulling people into the boat; his stomach muscles were screaming in agony and his throat felt like he had swallowed broken glass.

He looked at his crew, still pulling people out of the water. Doug felt sorrow for the casualties as he heaved yet another body into the boat, gently passing it over to the crew members who were checking for life signs. Fishing boats were helping take the dead and injured back to land from the lifeboats.

Doug gestured to the skippers on a pod of smaller fishing boats, and they came and encircled the larger RNLI boat, each boat carefully taking people off.

He looked up and saw the body of a woman, her lips tinged with blue in a long green sequined dress, her blonde hair fanned out by the sea. She was lying wedged against some rocks and was being gently moved by the motion of the waves. For a moment Doug thought she looked like a peaceful mermaid lying there.

Over on the beach nearby Doug saw the row of orange body bags lined up on the sand. There were at least thirty bags, and people in high visibility jackets were busy preparing more bags as the bodies of the drowned were delivered solemnly by the busy boats.

Hours later, Doug and the team returned to the station. They were exhausted, dirty, quiet and solemn. There was no chat, just silence. They moved quietly into the locker room and started to take their gear off.

Doug looked around at the crew and felt he ought to say something. He cleared his throat.

'Well done. Tough night. You all look shattered. Go home and get some kip. I don't know about you guys but I'm no use to anyone now. Let's do food, sleep and I plan to go out again in a few hours.' Doug looked around expectantly. 'Look I understand if no one can face it again, no one's judging anyone. If you're here, then great. No problem if not. Go on home.'

The crew nodded to Doug as they passed him on their way out, a couple of them clapping him on the shoulder as a gesture of comfort. He turned and watched them go.

Doug walked slowly to his truck. He'd not been this tired since … well, since early on in his recovery. Starting the engine, the news was on the radio.

… at a devastating scene that has been going on all through the night. Around 10.30 p.m. last night the coastguard received a mayday from the Lady Magdellan Explorer, *a small cruise liner carrying 150 passengers and 70 crew members, which had been blown off course with serious engine trouble. The ship had been carried too close to the shore where it ran into the rocks. A fire broke out and quickly took hold around the ship and then in the early hours of the morning there was a large explosion. Rescue services and coastguard were launched and many local fishing boats have been providing assistance. Some of the rescued passengers remain in critical condition, while others have life-changing injuries. The crews are still working to recover the bodies of the passengers who didn't survive …*

Doug turned off the radio. He couldn't listen to that now. He just wanted to get home and sleep. He knew that Nessie would have got the kids up and walked them to school. She was an angel, that one. He remembered how she had announced after the death of her husband, a lifelong RNLI crew member, she would be keeping his pager so she could continue to help whoever needed it. No one had argued with the bright-eyed feisty old lady, who took everyone under her wing and ran the RNLI shop with a rod of iron.

Doug pulled into his drive and entered the silent house. In the kitchen was a large sandwich covered in cling film, with a post-it note in spidery handwriting.

'Eat this, then sleep. Kids OK. I'll get them from school. Nessie.'

Doug smiled, picked up the sandwich and went through to the lounge, sitting down on the sofa. He was asleep before he'd even wrestled the cling film off.

CHAPTER 5

Jesse's stomach was churning. She asked herself why she had agreed to this. The building she was looking for loomed into view as if taunting her. It was too late to change her mind and she pulled into the car park.

She sat in the car checking the letter again, wishing she had the wrong date or was miles away from her destination. The letter was right, this was the right building. She pondered just driving off and pretending this wasn't happening. But she told herself she should do it. She needed to do it. At least once anyway. She sighed and got out of the car, the dog following closely at her heels.

She pushed the door open and approached a reception desk with a pretty blonde girl sat behind it.

'Hi there, can I help you?' she asked with a twang of what sounded like an Australian accent.

'Hi,' Jesse said awkwardly, looking around what seemed to be a waiting area. 'Err, I've got an appointment. I'm a little late.'

The receptionist chuckled softly. 'That's fine. You're not the only one to be late to a first appointment, trust me. You must be Jesse, yes? And who is this gorgeous creature?' She cooed. 'My folks back home have got collies on the farm, four of them. My dad always maintains they're more reliable and loyal than people.'

'I like the sound of your dad.'

The receptionist smiled. 'I'm Nat … Natasha, it's good to meet you, and who is this?' she asked.

'This is Brock,' said Jesse.

'Hello there, Brockie,' Nat whispered. 'Have you had him since he was a pup?'

'No, I've had him about 18 months now, give or take. He was a rescue dog, in a bad way, needed a bit of TLC.'

'Don't we all?' Nat said, laughing. At that moment, the buzzer on her desk sounded, loud and insistent.

'She's ready for you, go on in, but she doesn't allow dogs in there.' Nat said. 'Leave him here. I'll have him with me. You don't mind, do you Brockie?'

She looked at the dog who turned his head on one side as if listening and then trotted underneath Nat's desk and lay down with a large sigh. Jesse leaned over the desk where the dog looked up at her.

'Judas,' she said smiling lovingly at him.

Nat pointed to a white door. 'Through there, go straight in, it's OK. She's nice, not scary at all,' she said, grinning.

Jesse walked towards the door, feeling the absence of Brock at her heels. She got to the door and knocked.

'Come in!' a voice called.

Dr Emma Marshall was in her early forties. She was trim, attractive and well dressed with reddish hair and startling green eyes. She was sitting at the desk reading a file on her laptop. When Jesse stepped in, she closed the laptop lid quickly.

Jesse was nervous; for a split second she felt the need to run away. Flight mode they used to call it, she remembered. She took a deep breath. She'd done too much of that she thought, she couldn't spend her life running away from everything that frightened her.

She focused on the woman walking towards her with her hand outstretched. She was smiling and looked vaguely familiar to Jesse, but she couldn't place her. Jesse stepped into the room and shut the door behind her.

28

'Jesse. Very good to meet you,' Emma said warmly. 'Please come in and sit down, make yourself comfortable. Thanks for coming. It's a great sign you've come, so already it's good progress. Please call me Emma. OK?'

Jesse perched on the corner of the sofa and sat with her arms tightly folded defensively.

'Look,' she blurted out. 'I was told to come really. I didn't feel like I had a choice particularly.'

Emma nodded. 'OK, well it's important to remember you do have a choice. You're the one in control, Jesse. All we really do here is chat. It can be about what you want to talk about, about what you feel comfortable talking about. Nothing too major, no pressure, nothing to worry about. We go at your pace. You control it all.'

Jesse watched her silently for a few moments and then said, 'Do I? Have control? I was told to come by Leslie … well, DS Cotton. She said I really should come. That it would really help me to move on and deal with it. My attack. I didn't really feel I had an option to say no, not to her anyway. I know she was really trying to help. Her team, the Police Professional Standards team, sorted it all out. For what it's worth, my mother thinks this is an excellent idea and will lead to some sort of closure,' she added wryly. 'So, tell me how this works exactly? We talk and you take notes and eventually give a report to … who?'

Emma smiled reassuringly. 'All I do is report on progress generally. I don't talk specifically about anything. Just that you're attending sessions and progressing with your treatment. The police are paying the bill, but you're my client and we're bound by strict confidentiality.'

She shifted forward in her seat. 'Look Jesse, I've seen your file. Read the notes and seen the pictures. I know what you do for a living and what you've had to give up coming here and starting again. I can assure you I won't break confidences.'

Jesse continued to look uncomfortable. 'I still don't know how I feel about this,' she muttered while looking out of the window.

Emma looked at her questioningly. 'In what way, Jesse?'

'Well, considering it was one of their own people who put me in hospital and made me leave my home, my friends and everything I know … it feels weird to me. Why would they do this? I mean what would they gain from it?' Jesse raked her fingers through her hair. 'I … I just don't know, I can't get my head around it. It just seems weird to me.'

'OK,' Emma said briskly. 'Let's not focus too much on this aspect, Jesse. It's not at all unusual that this happens. In my experience, the police nearly always recommend some form of counselling after highly traumatic events. Different forces have different approaches. So let's not get bogged down in the whats and why it's happening. Let's look at it this way instead, they want to try to help you. To help you get your life back on track.'

Jesse pursed her lips. 'Umm …'

'Perhaps look at it this way then. It's a free gig for a bit and might help you through something. What's to lose? Try to accept it for what it is. Time is marching on so let's start slowly and with something easy. Tell me, how long have you been in Wales now?'

Jesse regarded Emma from under her lashes; she saw through the attempt to get her talking. She shrugged. 'I got here a few days ago. Got a house sorted. I start work tomorrow.'

Emma consulted her notes. 'I have to say I kind of expected to see you a while ago. My file said you were due a few months ago.'

Jesse stared off into the distance. 'I know. I was staying with a friend. I was there longer than I thought I'd be.'

'Why was that? Did you not feel ready to make the move?'

Jesse continued to look out of the window, anything was better than looking into the unforgiving green-eyed gaze of the doctor.

'I didn't feel ready to do anything if the truth be known,' Jesse said distantly.

'And how do you feel now, Jesse?' Emma probed.

Jesse avoided eye contact. She thought for a moment and sighed deeply, sounding resigned to the conversation that was about to unfold.

'I feel … unsettled. Nervous, anxious, like I can't cope. Can't breathe sometimes. It comes in huge waves. One minute I feel OK and the next minute it's like a wave that crashes in over me and leaves me feeling that way. I'm terrified in here.' She pressed a hand to her breastbone. 'But more often than not, I feel … how can I put it? Cast adrift, like I'm lost … I constantly have that awful feeling you get when you're nervous about something … kind of like I'm sitting a really big exam tomorrow, that awful feeling in your chest and gut.'

30

Emma made more notes. 'OK, Jesse. It's good you're aware of how you feel and are being honest about it.'

Jesse picked her fingers. 'I feel on edge all the time. I feel no peace at all, and I struggle with that. I lurch from being completely terrified to being slightly less terrified. Every single day.'

Emma nodded thoughtfully. 'Good ...'

'How's that good?' Jesse said, frowning.

'Well, good you're aware of how you feel. Do you think things will get better in time? Can you see yourself having a different life? Free from the attack?'

Jesse's breathing was shaky as she looked back out of the window.

'I don't know in all honesty ... I don't know how I feel about any of it.' She frowned. 'But isn't this what this is all about? Being honest to a stranger, saying how I really feel? Not being judged? Off-loading and getting "closure" in a non-judgemental environment?'

'That's an interesting comment, Jesse. Are you worried about being judged then?'

Jesse exhaled loudly and raked her hands through her hair.

'Am I worried about being judged? Damn right I am. You saw what he did to me.' She struggled to control herself. 'He tried to kill me and left me for dead. I almost died. It took me three months to be able to walk again, two months to be able to write my name again after he smashed my hand by stamping on it. I'll never have kids now. NEVER. All because of him. So, yes, I'm worried about being judged. Someone will judge me. Fucking damn right they will. Someone in a suit that costs more than I earn in a year, in a courtroom will say that somehow I asked for it and persuade a group of twelve people it was my fault and he is in fact the victim. I'm worried about being judged wrongly and that fucker never ever paying for what he did to me.'

'So ... you feel angry because you feel justice won't be done and he won't somehow pay for it?'

Jesse viewed her with disbelief. 'Seriously? How would you feel in my position?'

'My feelings are irrelevant. Is he in prison?'

'Yes.'

'So in a way he's paying for what he did already, isn't he?' Emma held up a hand. 'Look, Jesse. I know you're angry. Any normal person would be. I get it. I understand. For me, I have to help you find a way through this so that anger isn't the main emotion you feel.'

Jesse snorted and folded her arms. 'Good luck with that. What's so bad about being angry about it? If you sit there and start banging on about finding it in my heart to forgive him, you're way out of luck, that's never going to happen.'

'I'm not suggesting that, at this stage. I just want to help try and deal with your feelings, so you aren't carrying all this anger about. I want to help you to live a normal life, Jesse.'

Jesse refused to meet Emma's eye. 'A normal life? Jesus, what even is that? I don't get to have a normal life, not now. I know how I'd feel better. If he was dead. I'd happily fucking kill him given the opportunity. The way I feel … this rage. I want him to die. Quite simply, then I would feel a whole lot better.'

'We're going to try and help you deal with this and get rid of the rage, Jesse,' Emma said softly.

Jesse struggled not to cry. 'I just don't know how bringing it all up again and again, and re-hashing it isn't going to help. Talking endlessly about it. It won't change anything. It's still my fault I went back. I'm trying to get on with my life and not think about what happened. If there was a magic bullet that would make it all go away, bring it on … but there isn't. So, I have to just keep getting up in the morning every day and getting on with it.'

'There isn't a magic solution, Jesse. It's time. Time, and learning to accept the decisions you made and that what happened was not in your control.'

Jesse sniffed. 'I just want to be in a place where I don't have to think about it. Move on from it.'

Emma proffered a tissue. 'How's that working out for you currently, Jesse? I'll bet you dream about the attack, fairly regularly, wake up terrified? How many dreams have you had? Do you wake in the middle of the night and think he's there? Look Jesse, you never know, I might be able to help you … help you deal with all this. Don't dismiss it without trying.'

Jesse looked up at the ceiling, tears in her eyes. 'It's too raw. I feel like I'm clinging on by my fingernails and if I lose focus for a moment then that's it.'

'What will happen if you let go, Jesse?'

'I'm too frightened to think about it. I don't want to be too frightened to go out. I've spent too long being that way. I can't let him win. If I become too scared to do anything then he's won, hasn't he?'

'Not necessarily. The fact you recognise all of these things means you're better than you think, which is good. Take comfort. Trust me. Look, we're going to leave the heavy stuff for now and we're going to change the subject a bit. Let's get into the now, tell me about daily life at the moment, tell me about this Jesse here,' she said, gesturing towards Jesse and smiling as she tried to relieve the tension.

Jesse sniffed. 'I'm sorting out a new place at the moment, doing a bit of decorating and lots of long walks with the dog.'

Emma looked interested. 'A dog? Is this a new thing?'

'Not really. I've had him ages now since I got out of … He needed a new home … I expect there's some Freudian explanation for us both needing stability and all that old crap.'

Emma smiled. 'I expect there is … What about work? When do you meet the new team, or have you met them yet?'

Jesse looked out of the window, replying absently. 'Crew … Not team … Crew. I meet them tomorrow.'

'How do you feel about it?' Emma asked, making a note.

'Umm, nervous, anxious, a bit out of control.'

Emma frowned. 'In what way out of control?'

'In every way. It's like starting again. Crews are tight. Really tight. It'll be hard starting again. Fitting in.'

'Everyone feels that way on day one of a new job. OK. So let's make some decisions. How often are we going to see you, Jesse?'

'Don't know, what are they paying for?'

Emma consulted her notes. 'They're paying for four sessions a month for six months to start with. Now we can do it weekly, or we can double it up fortnightly. What's best for you?'

Jesse looked cornered. 'Uhh. Don't know really.'

'Let's do it weekly for the first few, then take a view. OK? So, what days suit you? Same time as today?'

'I don't know my schedule yet with work.'

'OK, book in with Natalie when you know. I'll look forward to hearing about the crew and how that went. Use this time. It might help.

Even if you come in and sit in silence you're still coming, and we can work from there. I think you underestimate even the progress we've made today. So I'll see you next week?' she asked brightly.

Jesse stood. 'Suppose so.' She said opening the door. 'Bye then.'

Emma smiled. 'Take care, Jesse. Have a good week.'

CHAPTER 6

Doug sat on the wall outside Maggie's beach café, waiting for his coffee. He was bone tired. His whole body ached from the liner shout a few days before and he could still taste smoke.

He sighed. It would have been Gav's birthday yesterday and his dreams last night had been full of Gavin and Jeff struggling to get out of the water.

A sharp scream from the beach jolted him back to reality. He relaxed when he saw a young couple chasing each other. They looked young, carefree and very much in love.

Doug smiled, thinking back to when he and Claire had enjoyed each other's company. His efforts the other night to take some time out had not been met with the enthusiasm he'd hoped for. In fact, since then she'd been even more absent.

'Here you go, gorgeous.' Maggie appeared. She was a short woman, in her late fifties with a penchant for bright red lipstick and very tight T-shirts that read 'Maggie's beach café' across her ample chest. She handed him a coffee. 'You look miles away, my love. Are you OK?'

'Fine thanks, Mags,' said Doug absently.

She patted him on the shoulder and walked back inside. He strolled back towards the station. By the time he had got there he had decided he would really make an effort with Claire. He would employ what Gavin used to call, 'An essential charm offensive.'

Doug was annoyed. Really annoyed. The good mood he'd started the day with had disappeared rapidly, as had his warm and nostalgic feelings towards Claire. All achieved with a simple phone call.

'Well, Claire. I'm here until about 6.30 unless we're out on a shout, but you know that. Are you out again?' He listened, his face like thunder. 'Fuck's sake, Claire. You have to stop doing this. If I know, I can plan for it and it's easier on everyone.'

Doug ended the call and looked out of the window to the sea, swearing softly. He made a call to ask Helen the childminder to pick up the kids again.

There was a knock at the office door, and he turned to see an attractive dark-haired woman, with a noticeable scar on her face, standing in the doorway. Still caught up in his grumpiness, he said shortly, 'The volunteers' office is upstairs if you're here for the shop?'

'Err, I'm Jesse Stevens.' She stepped forward and held out her hand. 'New mechanic here …?' She faltered.

'Oh! Christ yes!' Doug smiled and his whole face changed. 'Christ! Hardly a good start, is it? I hadn't forgotten, honestly. I was miles away. Sorry, come in and sit down. I'm Doug Brodie.' He gestured to a chair. 'Coffee?'

'Umm, thanks, black's fine.' Jesse said perching on a chair. 'So, there are worse views from the office, huh?' she said, gesturing towards the window.

'Lovely, isn't it?' said Doug, handing her a mug of coffee. 'Two dolphins out there yesterday.'

'Wow, I'd never get any work done if this was my office. So, what do you prefer to be called? Skipper? Douglas, Brodie?'

'Certainly not Douglas. My wife calls me that when she's annoyed with me, which seems to be most of the time.' He paused. 'I like to think I earn people calling me Skipper but call me whatever you're comfortable with as long as it's fairly polite.'

'OK.' She took a sip of coffee and coughed.

'Bit strong?' Doug asked, watching her.

'It'll put hairs on my chest, as my dad used to say.'

Doug smiled. 'So, welcome to Castleby Station. How long have you been here? You've moved up from the south, haven't you?'

'Uh huh. Got here a few days ago. I'm getting my bearings, enjoying the beach.'

Doug remembered the file, all very cloak and dagger. He'd have to remind himself and read it properly, he thought, if he could find it.

'Have you met anyone here yet?

Jesse looked surprised. 'What? Oh, you mean here at the station?'

Doug nodded.

'Umm, the guy who showed me to your office. Young guy, holding a broom; he seemed nice. Oh, and two guys arguing quite vocally over the last biscuit as I walked past.' She laughed. 'I think they were going to settle it with an arm wrestle.'

Doug rolled his eyes. 'Of course they were. So, the two arguing over the biscuits are Ben and Paul, brothers and fairly inseparable, despite appearances. The young guy with the broom is Tom. He's a good lad, bit of a player with that face, so watch out.' Doug said lightly and then looked serious.

'Right, so don't take this the wrong way but they all need to get their heads around this. We've not had a mechanic for well over a year now, since Billy … everything needs a bit of TLC here. We've been using one of the local mechanics, but he's not got the time or the brains to do too much. Billy was big shoes to fill. He was part of the furniture.'

'Did Billy not make it then? I heard there was a bad shout.'

Doug hadn't been prepared to answer questions on the subject; it was all still too raw. He hadn't had to talk about it because everyone knew about it, so it was always there, but never said. He felt grief and guilt rising up inside him.

Abruptly he stood and fiddled about with something on the top of the filing cabinet trying to get himself under control before he faced her again.

'He was injured at the rescue, but he wasn't on the trawler trying to get the guys out.'

Jesse frowned. 'Oh, I read two guys didn't make it and one more was badly injured. Was that not Billy then?'

'No, Billy was on the main boat. The sea was so rough, lots of the gear had been washed overboard and he was having to pull some of the survivors in from the water. He pulled his shoulder clean out of the socket. The same time as he pulled the last guy in, a blood vessel popped in his head and he had a massive stroke. He's still alive ... well, if you can call it that.'

'Oh God, that's awful. I'm so sorry. So how was the other guy that was badly injured, did he make it?'

Doug couldn't look at her. 'Yup. He's OK.' In a clumsy attempt to deflect the subject he asked. 'So, Jesse, how did you get into being a mechanic?'

'I was always fascinated by boats. As a kid I used to go into the local chandlery as much as I could. Growing up in the west country careers were fairly limited for girls. It seemed to be either train as a cook or go to secretarial college. I wanted something different.'

Jesse looked off into the distance as she remembered. 'At the time, the Marine Police Service were really the only people offering apprenticeships. I was the only woman to apply, but I got through. I was there for nearly ten years and then a job came up in Hastings with the RNLI. They'd rescued a friend of mine who nearly drowned, so I wanted to give something back in a way. She owed her life to the lads on that shout.'

She looked at Doug as if she'd forgotten he was there. 'Sorry,' she said, smiling. 'Rambling on.'

'It's OK.' Doug glanced at his watch. 'Look, we've got a meeting in about ten minutes. Most of the lads are here for it. I'll show you around and then introduce you to them all. OK?'

Jesse pulled a face and said wryly, 'Gotta do it sometime.'

Most of the crew had come in and were crammed into the small meeting space, some on chairs, some standing and others sitting on tables. Jesse sat at the back.

Doug began. 'Thanks for coming in today, folks. We've got a few things to cover. Firstly, as we all know, Billy won't be back ...'

A few murmurs came from the gathered crew. Doug held up a hand.

'I know, I know. But! We finally have a replacement full-time mechanic starting immediately, so I'd like you all to meet Jesse Stevens.

Jesse, give us a wave from the back there. Jesse's got lots of experience in a similar size station and has come from the south coast, but we won't hold that against her. I know I don't have to say it, but I'd like you all to make her feel welcomed into the crew. We look out for each other, so welcome to the family.'

Jesse looked up to see a sea of faces in front of her, smiling, nodding and saying hi.

'Jesse, do you want to say a few words?'

Jesse stood, the colour rising in her face. 'Umm ... Hi everyone. So as Doug said, I'm Jesse or Jess, and I've been in another crew for the last ten years or so. A similar boat to this, so I like to think I know what I'm doing. If anyone has any concerns with any of the boats, even the ribs, then let me know. I'll be starting from scratch here, stripping it all back and giving it a going-over, so don't be afraid to come and have a chat. So, er, I think that's it, look forward to working with you all ... thanks.'

She sat down again. The two brothers whom she had seen arguing over the biscuits gave her a thumbs up.

An older guy stood up. His face was very brown and weathered. He pointed at Jesse but addressed Doug directly. 'We don't want her here. It's bloody unlucky to have a woman in the crew.' He looked at Jesse. 'Go back to where you came from – you're not welcome here.'

There was an instant chorus of disapproval from the rest of the crew and Doug raised his voice, his Scottish accent sharp with anger. 'Jesus, Bob. Enough! You're out of bloody order.'

Bob was shaking with anger and looking at Doug with utter contempt. 'It'll be the end of Bill if he finds out we've replaced him, especially with a bloody woman. It'll kill him. He'll give up hope.'

Doug said quietly, 'Bob, that happened a while ago. He can't come back here, you know that. Blaming Jesse isn't going to make a blind bit of difference to his situation.'

'I can't believe you've replaced him with a bloody woman. I won't have it. I bloody well won't.'

Bob went out, slamming the door. Silence sat heavily in the room. Doug took a breath and said dryly, 'So, Jesse, you've met Bob. He's in charge of our equal opportunities policy and welcoming all new starters here.'

39

Doug was relieved when there was a ripple of laughter from the crew; he was also pleased to see Jesse laughing too. 'Seriously, though, Jesse, ignore that. Bob and the Billy situation – not your problem. It's bigger than the role of mechanic. Trust me.'

There was a ripple of agreement from the lads in the room.

'So, back to business. Everyone here on call this weekend? Check your phones and pagers are working … that means you, Tom … especially you, Tom.'

This comment elicited much nudging and jeering from the lads in the room. Jesse looked at Doug questioningly. Tom looked sheepishly at Doug.

'Yes, Skip.'

Doug chuckled. 'Jesse, Tom here is our wee town Casanova; he tends to forget he's part of the crew when he's engaged in activities with a lady. So he's off having a great time, oblivious to a phone, pager and even the town alarm. We're all geared up and waiting and who finally appears just as we're about to launch, just wearing his underwear and a smile? Hopping down the high street trying to put his trousers on by all accounts.'

Tom shrugged. 'Just taking one for the team, Skip. Keeping up local relations and all that. Can't blame a man for trying.'

'I don't think her husband thought that way,' someone shouted. More laughter filled the room.

'OK, OK. Seriously. The weekend is upon us and that means silly bugger season, so keep your wits about you, keep your mobiles and pagers on. The town council said we can use the town alarm for a bad shout so be aware of that too, but that'll probably just be in the summer months. Also, there's more training needed on some of the new equipment so sign up for it; the list is on the notice board. OK, off you go.'

The room emptied, with a few of the crew introducing themselves to Jesse as they left.

Jesse said lightly, 'Well, Bob's quite the charmer.'

'Ach, pay no mind to him. He's Billy's oldest mate. He can be a pain in the arse, but he's solid. He's got outdated ideas sometimes. He's not what you'd call a new-age man, by his own admission.'

Jesse smiled wryly. 'A new best friend for me then. Winning hearts and minds already.'

'They're a good bunch here. We've got a mix of occupations, but we do have a core of around six guys that tend to go out on most shouts because they happen to get here first. Bob's always here doing something. Mike, the young guy that was sat by the door, and Tom tend to be here a lot as they work around the corner in the pub and climbing centre. Dan, the guy in his whites, works around the corner, he's a chef. Ben and Paul, the two brothers, one's a plumber and the other's a plasterer, but they're always pretty local. Now, are you sticking around for the rest of the day or are you in tomorrow now?'

Jesse looked around. 'I'm going to go and have a poke around downstairs and see how the land lies with the gear and the engines. Have you got some keys for me?'

Doug nodded and held the door open for her.

'Your workshop awaits,' he said with a grin as she walked past him.

We've seen her enter the lifeboat station. She looked worried. This is her first day. We've been watching, taking pictures, enjoying the view. We know where she lives, where she works. We keep well back. We can't be seen. Can't be seen. She looks good. She's been on the beach with the dog a lot. She looks happy when she's with him. We don't like dogs; this one is a bit too alert for us too. We have to keep our distance. Still, silver linings. We have her now. We know where she is. We can watch and wait. We can plan. We like to watch.

CHAPTER 7

Jesse was having an excellent day, considering everything. The only downside was she was missing the dog. Things seemed out of kilter if he wasn't by her side. Still, it felt good to be working again. She had spent hours tidying up the workshop and sworn like a scaffolder when she found a box of screws and various items that were labelled 'spare bits from big lifeboat engine'. This made her nervous to say the least.

She found an outboard motor propped up in a corner, with a scribbled note that read 'broken'. Not to be outwitted by a chunk of metal and moving parts, she took it to pieces so she could work her magic. She had grimy hands and a smudge of grease on the scar on her face. She'd also found a radio and it was loudly blaring out, accompanied, fairly tunelessly, by Jesse to an old Queen song. Jesse was content and, unusually for her, completely oblivious to her surroundings.

Doug appeared in the workshop, which was located in the bowels of the station. He had been upstairs fighting with paperwork, heard her singing along and chuckled at her enthusiasm.

'Jesse,' he said. She carried on oblivious.

'Jesse,' he said loudly. Still nothing from her, except another chorus of the Queen track. He stepped forward and touched her shoulder.

'JESUS!' Jesse jumped sideways. The tool she was holding clattered to the floor as her hand flew up in front of her, catching on the sharp engine casing.

'Shit!' She said, blood oozing from the cut.

Doug backed away. 'Christ, I'm sorry. I just wanted to see if you wanted a cup of tea.'

Jesse was breathing heavily. As she eyed Doug, she calmed down a bit and started to look embarrassed. 'Sorry, you frightened the life out of me …'

Doug regarded her from a distance. 'I saw that. Sorry. Sooo … yes or no?'

'To what?'

'Tea?'

'Oh … yes please, white without.'

Doug stepped forward slowly, reluctant to make any sudden moves. 'Should we see to that hand?'

Jesse looked down at her hand. 'Oh. It's OK, I'll sort it.' She turned and used the process as an excuse to try and control her thudding heart. She opened a cupboard door and took the first aid kit out, trying to regulate her breathing.

Doug watched her. 'Are you sure you're OK?'

Jesse nodded and Doug left the room. Jesse closed her eyes and took a minute to calm down properly. She mopped up her hand, cleaned the cut and put a plaster on it.

'Here you go,' Doug said as he returned with a cup of tea. 'You need to do the colour chart in the kitchen.'

Jesse looked perplexed. 'The what?'

'In the kitchen, there's a paint colour chart in there for browns. The whole range. You pick which colour you like your tea and write your name on it, then everyone knows how you have it.'

'Genius.' She murmured, now feeling ridiculously embarrassed. 'Thanks. Look, sorry about just now, you scared me.'

'Look, Jesse, are you sure you're OK? I mean I know I'm no oil painting, but I've not been known to scare women quite so much. Anything I can do?'

Jesse thought what a genuinely nice guy Doug seemed. He was watching her with such concern she almost broke down in tears. She tried to laugh but couldn't quite manage it.

'I'm OK, sorry. I feel like a bit of an idiot. I'm just a bit jumpy sometimes.' She turned her back on Doug to avoid eye contact. 'You just surprised me. I didn't hear you coming. That's all. No big deal.'

Doug opened his mouth to speak and his phone rang loudly. He looked at the screen and his whole face changed as if he was already resigned to what was coming. He turned to Jesse. 'Sorry.'

'Claire, what can I do for you?' Doug listened to the call. 'Overnight? … Again?'

Jesse watched him with interest. This was Doug clearly annoyed with whoever was calling him. She noticed a muscle twitching in his jaw and his eyes had got colder instantly.

'Right … so I'll just see you when you turn up then. Will you be ringing the kids later? Perhaps you can squeeze that in?'

Doug ended the call. He hung his head for a moment, forgetting Jesse was there and she heard him swear softly.

Jesse said tentatively. 'Everything OK?'

Doug shook himself out of it and gave her a thin smile. 'Fine. Domestic bliss, that's all.' Doug picked up his tea to leave the room. He turned before he climbed the stairs. 'That hand OK?'

Jesse gave him a thumbs up.

Jesse was pleased. Despite her sore hand she managed to put the engine back together and it was making all the right noises. She was annoyed she had embarrassed herself in front of Doug when the poor man was only asking her if she wanted a cup of tea. She tutted, stood back, and surveyed her work with a nod of satisfaction.

The shrill alarm went off in the station, making her jump. Jesse ran to the locker room as Doug raced out of his office and the others started to arrive.

'Leaving in five,' shouted Doug as the roller clattered upwards. 'Helmets on. What have we got?'

'Boy swept in off the rocks. Friend has lost sight of him. He's on the cliffs above. He called it in.'

The lifeboat surged through the swell of the ocean, the crew on deck were straining to see if they could spot the missing boy through their binoculars. As the boat approached the rocky cliffs it slowed. Doug trained his binoculars on the cliff and saw a boy in a red jacket stood looking over the edge. He dialled the number the coastguard had given him.

'Hello, is that Joe? This is Doug, I'm the skipper of the lifeboat. The coastguard gave me your number. Am I looking at you in the red jacket on the cliff? Can you wave your arm at me?' Doug spoke clearly and quickly to try and get the boy to focus.

The figure on the cliff waved an arm. Doug returned the gesture as the boat stopped and sat idle in the water.

'How you doing there, Joe?' Doug asked.

'Gareth is missing,' cried Joe. 'I can't see him anymore. He's just gone. I ... I told him to be careful ... not to go down there ... but he carried on and now I can't see him anymore.'

Doug covered the phone with his hand and turned to Mike. 'Tell the others to be aware and everyone out with eyes on the surface ... the boy's been washed out so he could be anywhere. Last thing we need is to hit him with the boat.'

Doug turned his attention back to the phone. 'OK, Joe. Now I need you to keep calm and focus for me. OK? Did Gareth fall in or was he swept in? Right ... so he was swept in, below where you're standing? Have you seen him since? What colour top was he wearing, Joe?'

Joe was pacing around. 'I saw him at first. He was about twenty metres out, to your right near those big rocks, he was shouting and waving but I couldn't hear him, and he got further away. He'd hit his head, I think, there was blood on it. He's in a blue top.'

Doug experienced the usual dread he felt when dealing with children being lost in the water.

'Joe,' he said firmly. 'I need you to focus and think about how long ago it was since you last saw Gareth.'

'It was about ... half an hour ago, I think ... maybe a bit longer ... oh god ...'

Doug took the phone from his ear and spoke softly to Dan, who was standing by his side scanning the sea with binoculars.

'Dan. Call the local nick and tell them to send someone up there to get him and take him back to the station, ours or theirs, and we'll talk to him later. If it's that long ago since he's seen him, we'll likely be recovering a body,' Doug said grimly.

Dan went below decks.

'Joe?' Doug said. 'I've radioed for a chopper to come and help us look as they've got a better view, so that should be here soon. I want you to wait there, OK? Someone will be up to get you. You can't do anything else here now.'

'What? I can't leave, I need to stay, to help,' Joe said, sobbing.

'Joe, listen to me. We need to get you somewhere safe where we can look after you and keep an eye on you. So Joe, I need to go now and look for Gareth. You stay there. Someone will be out to get you.'

Doug ended the call and gave the instruction to get going. As the engines roared and the boat peeled away, Doug waved at the figure on the cliffs from the deck.

Doug scanned the water. He had a bad feeling. He knew the sea. He knew in his bones she had claimed this boy for her own. He vowed he would search until he physically couldn't do it anymore. He didn't want her to win and take the boy completely. He needed to take something back from her. He grabbed the radio control and radioed the coastguard helicopter, which had joined the search.

'Come in Rescue 206. This is the lifeboat below … receiving? Over.'

There was a crackle of static and a tinny voice responded. 'Rescue 206 receiving. Over.'

'How long do you want to do this for, boys? We've been looking for hours now. I think you guys should go, we'll carry on for a while. I think we're recovering a body, though. Before you go can you sweep down the inlets and shallow coves. He might have floated in there, easier for you guys to look. Over.'

'Roger that, last sweep. Will be in touch. Over.'

On deck, the crew spaced out at intervals, all scanning the sea using their binoculars for any sign of the boy. The sky was getting darker and the time ticked by. The radio crackled.

'Come in, lifeboat. Over.'

Dan reached for the radio mike. 'Lifeboat here. What've you got, Rescue 206? Over.'

'Doing a last sweep around by Shrinkle Haven and there's something floating in the water. Flashes of blue visible. Sound like your boy? Are you affirmative to attend? Over.'

Doug looked over and nodded to Dan, who replied. 'Able to attend Rescue 206. Safe Travels. Over.'

Doug leant down and spoke into the lower bridge. 'Shrinkle Haven quickly. Chopper thinks he's in the water.'

The lifeboat surged off at full power. The crew on the deck moved to the side of the boat to try and get the best view of the coastline through their binoculars. Dan pointed.

'Skip. Over there by the rocks … near the church doors?' Doug took the binoculars from Dan. The beautiful granite forms of what the locals named the church doors, due to their shape, sat proudly behind a series of jagged rocks. Wedged against those rocks was what looked like the body of a young boy with a blue top clearly visible.

'Launch the Y and get him back here, careful on those rocks,' Doug said quietly.

The lifeboat slowed and waited. The rear lifted up and a small rib, the Y boat, launched. Dan and Mike climbed in and headed off. Doug watched them go, sadness filling him to the brim. Another young life lost. He watched the small boat draw alongside the boy. Carefully, the two men pulled the body into the boat.

'Jesus,' said Doug softly as the Y returned to the lifeboat. The face of the dead boy was pale, his eyes shut like he was asleep. Bob stepped forward placing a hand on Doug's shoulder.

'Doesn't get any bloody easier, does it?' he said in a gruff way, and approached the rear of the boat, bending to carefully take the body from Dan. Jesse appeared and tried to help him bring the boy into the deck from the smaller boat, but he waved her away dismissively. Bob laid down the boy on the deck and Dan and Mike checked again for signs of life. Doug stepped forward and squeezed Mike's shoulder.

'He's gone … a while ago I'd say. Let's get him back.'

Jesse appeared and covered the boy with a dry blanket. Dan was shaking his head and he looked over at Doug, frowning.

'Bloody waste, isn't it? Couple of lads just out fishing for the day and look what happens.'

Mike stood slowly. 'I just don't know when people will learn ... you never turn your back on the sea in a situation like that ... she'll have you. First chance she gets. She'll have you.'

'Aye. Such a loss,' Doug said sadly. 'Come on, let's get him back.'

Doug turned to Jesse who was looking at the boy sadly.

'Some first shout with us, eh?' He said quietly. Jesse nodded and held onto the rail as the lifeboat engines roared and the boat surged back towards the station in the darkening skies.

The lifeboat arrived back at the station. Standing on the upper gantry watching the proceedings was a paramedic in his trademark green uniform. Mike greeted him.

'Hi, Phil. How you doing, mate?' Phil raised his mug in greeting.

'Alright, Mike? Saw you Saturday night at the Stowaway, it was a good set. The missus was well impressed. Been told to pick up your poor guest there and take him back to the hospital morgue. You did well to find him in that swell. I'll go and grab the stretcher.'

Phil disappeared off and returned a little while later with a short blonde woman. Mike was stood on deck and looked genuinely happy to see her. 'Hey, Liz,' he called. 'How are you? How come you missed out on a cuppa?'

Liz chortled. 'Hello, my love. He got to come in here and I got to have a cuppa with Fishy John out in the harbour, so I didn't miss out. Now where's this poor soul? I can't bear it when they're kids.'

Mike gestured to the top deck. 'I'll lift him down if you put the stretcher there.'

Liz and Phil moved the stretcher nearer to the boat and Mike carefully negotiated the steps down and placed the body on the stretcher. The paramedics strapped him on and ensured the blanket was still covering him. A door crashed open and Joe ran out wide-eyed, followed by a young police officer who was trying to hold him back.

'Gareth? Gareth?'

Joe stopped and gave a horrified look at the two paramedics. He pointed with a shaky finger.

'Is that ...?'

Mike stepped forward. 'I'm sorry, mate. We looked for hours ...'

Doug appeared. He swiftly stepped off the boat and stood between Joe and the stretcher.

'Joe. I'm Doug. We spoke on the phone while we were out on the rescue. I'm so sorry about your friend. We did everything we could to find him'

'Where was he?' Joe croaked.

Doug placed a hand on Joe's shoulder.

'He'd been swept around to Shrinkle Haven. We found him in the rocks there ...'

Joe hiccupped a sob out. 'Was ... he ...'

'I'm sorry, Joe. When we found him it looked like Gareth had drowned.'

Joe looked at the stretcher and then at the paramedics with suspicion. 'Where are they taking him?'

'The hospital have to check a few things and they can look after him there. Now I need you to go back in the room with the policeman for a while, so we can take Gareth off. Can you do that? I'll make sure he's safe.'

Joe was led away, looking like he was in a trance. Doug turned to the paramedics.

'Are we good to go?' Phil and Liz nodded and wheeled the stretcher around the corner to the ambulance. They loaded Gareth into the back. Phil remained in the back of the ambulance while Liz jumped out to drive. She stood next to Doug and squeezed his arm.

'Take care, Doug,' she said.

Doug saluted a farewell and returned slowly back to the station. He found Jesse in the mess sat with Joe and the police officer. Doug sat down in front of the young boy.

'Joe. I need you to listen to me. The police will need you to tell them what happened today. Are your parents about?'

The PC said, 'They're at the station now so we need to go.'

Joe stared at Doug; the boy was pale and shocked, and visibly struggling not to cry.

Doug said: 'Joe. If you ever have any questions about today, or you want to talk it through ... come and find me, OK?'

Joe nodded, his bottom lip trembling. The policeman helped Joe to his feet.

'Doug, we'll need a statement from you too if that's OK?' the policeman said quietly.

'No problem mate.'

The PC ushered Joe out of the door.

Doug stood at the station door watching. Joe's small shoulders heaved with sobs as he walked. Doug closed the door to the station; all he wanted to do was get home and see the kids.

CHAPTER 8

The house was in darkness. The outside streetlights broke though the thin lounge curtains, casting a slight orange glow. The silence was broken by a soft scraping at the back door. A figure dressed in black stepped in carefully, listening for any sounds of activity in the dark house.

The figure crept to the bottom of the stairs, looking upwards. He carefully climbed. He paused at the top, and gently pushed open the door to the bedroom. He stood for a moment, watching the room.

Jesse lay asleep in the bed, with the black and white dog sprawled alongside her, fast asleep. The figure approached the bed and leant forwards, gently lifting the covers.

'What made you think you could ever escape me, Jesse?'

Jesse screamed and sat upright in bed. She was covered in sweat. The dog woke up and barked loudly. Jesse quickly turned on the light, looking around the room in panic.

She threw herself backwards in bed and lay, breathing heavily. Brock nuzzled her hand, confused at her upset.

'Christ alive. It's OK boy ... it's only a dream.'

* * *

Dr Emma Marshall was standing looking out of the window when the knock came.

'Come in,' she called. Jesse stepped into the room and Emma smiled warmly. 'Jesse. Do you want some coffee? There's some in the pot.'

'Please.'

'Milk or sugar?'

'No thanks.' Jesse took the cup and sat down.

Emma came to sit opposite her.

'So, how are things with you?'

Jesse sipped her coffee. 'OK ... I'm OK.'

Emma nodded encouragingly. 'How did your first day at work go?'

'It was OK. It was ... um ... eventful.'

Emma raised her eyebrows.

'One of the crew has issues with me being a woman and taking someone's job. But the rest of the guys seem nice. The skipper's nice. Seems a really solid guy. The guys worship him. That says to me he's a good one.'

'A good one? What does that mean?'

Jesse relaxed slightly. 'It's something we say about a skipper. If the guys worship a skipper, then it means they're firm but fair, and fearless in a rescue. Someone to aspire to. To trust.'

'And you think your new skipper is like that?'

'We've been out a few times and he's very cool and controlled. The crew seem a good bunch of lads, not idiots. They gel well. They trust his judgement implicitly, which in my experience says he's very good at what he does.'

'Is that important to you then? For the skipper to be good at what he does?'

Jesse frowned. 'Of course, it's crucial. When you go out on a rescue, you put your life at risk. You have to have a skipper who watches your back and is the voice of reason when everything else is going to pot. When the sea is after blood and the wind is wailing and the waves are so high you're sure you're going to die right there, he's the one that stays level-headed. He's the one that keeps you safe. He's the voice you listen to.'

Jesse looked over Emma's shoulder, out of the window. 'We had a nasty rescue couple of shifts back. We lost a boy, he got swept in. The skipper was fantastic with his friend who saw it all happen. He calmed down the boy just by talking to him. He's a good one I think.'

'I'm interested to know how you feel when you're on the boat or at the station? Do you feel different there to how you feel anywhere else?'

Jesse shifted in her seat. 'Jumping right in today, aren't we?'

Emma smiled. 'Yes I am. Let's get going.'

Jesse sighed. 'How do I feel? I don't know really. I think I feel safe on a rescue in the sense I'm with the crew and we watch out for each other, but we're totally focused on other stuff there, so perhaps I just don't think about it. I couldn't really say whether I feel safer there than at home. I've not given it any real thought.'

'OK. Think about it now for a minute. Who do you feel safest around at the moment, or perhaps where, that might be easier to pin down?'

Jesse looked around the room, thinking. 'Erm ... I think I mostly feel safe at my house. That's probably because of the dog, though. I don't know if I feel safe at the station. I don't know if safe is the right word. I feel sort of happy ... content in some ways.'

'Ok, so ... do you feel protected by the crew, and also the dog?'

Jesse shrugged. 'Yes, I suppose I do.'

Emma nodded encouragingly. 'So if the dog wasn't at home, would you feel safe?'

'Probably not.'

'Why not?'

'I don't know really.'

'Do you think your attacker would come to your house?'

Jesse shifted in her chair. 'I don't want to think about that.'

'If it's a fear of yours we should explore that.'

'I don't want to.'

'OK. Bit soon maybe. So, have you made friends yet?'

'Early days, I think. Some of the guys are nice, inclusive, you know? That's the nature of a crew, though, you become part of a family really quickly. It's a leap of faith in some ways. You put your faith in them, they in you.'

'You mentioned one was difficult?'

'Umm ... there is always someone ... someone who has an issue that isn't really to do with you ... you just happen to be in the wrong place, or your face doesn't fit. It'll get easier.'

'Well, that all sounds pretty good. Are you still sorting out your house?'

'Yeah. A lot to do and I'm spending more time at the station sorting things out there. Lots of TLC needed there – those boats have been neglected.'

'You said last time you felt no peace. Is that still the case?'

Jesse thought for a minute. 'Nothing's really changed. Why do you ask?'

Emma finished making a note. 'I think it's important to have peace. It grounds you. Helps with perspective.'

'I'm not really sure what peace is or what it looks like. I've spent so long without it.'

'You look tired. How are you sleeping?'

Jesse inhaled sharply. 'Some nights are better than others.'

'That says last night was not a good night?' Emma probed.

Jesse closed her eyes. 'It was another bad dream. He was in the house while I slept. He leant over and asked whether I thought I could really escape him.'

'And what happens then?'

'I wake up screaming.'

'And how do you feel when this is happening, Jesse?'

'Utterly terrified, like my heart is going to stop. When I realise it's a dream, I calm down. But then I think it could happen. He could get out and find me.'

'Jesse, what would you do if he found you?' Emma asked softly.

'I … I …' she struggled for words, panic rising in her chest and threatening to engulf her.

'Jesse? I said, what would you do if he found you?' Emma persisted.

Jesse was spiralling, struggling to breathe. She had to get out. She needed to go. 'I can't do this … I can't think …' She leapt to her feet and rushed out. The dog attached himself to her heels as she ran past Natalie's desk and out of the door. Natalie looked up in surprise.

Emma watched Jesse run across the car park.

'Interesting,' she murmured to herself.

Jesse got in the car, slamming the door and locking it instantly, checking over her shoulder for anyone sitting in the back seat. Only when she was safely locked in did the tears come. She felt shattered. Exhausted emotionally. She craved the beach, the freedom of the sea, the expanse of space.

Jesse walked along the sand and wondered whether this was what therapy was supposed to do. Well, if it was, they could keep it, she thought. This was her therapy. The beach and the dog, that's all she needed. Brock was in his element; he'd found a long stick and liked to spend his time whacking Jesse on the back of the legs with it as he ran past her. It was absolutely his favourite game.

She thought as she walked. She thought about talking to Emma; was she supposed to feel worse before she felt better, she wondered? Perhaps she was supposed to talk about what scared her the most. Was that what therapy was all about? She had no idea. She did know she didn't want to think about HIM. She tried to shake the feeling off, laughing as the dog ran past her; she chased after him, laughing, oblivious to who else was on the beach.

* * *

Doug was having the day from hell. He'd had yet another run in with Claire, who'd said she couldn't pick up the children and as usual she'd left it until the last minute to tell him. Head office had been on at him to get a load of paperwork back to them and when he'd been looking for a file in his desk drawer, he'd found the picture. The world got dark as he remembered. He'd craved solitude and the sea. He had practically abandoned the car and almost run to the beach for some time alone. To think.

He sat on the sand, remembering the night when Jeff and Gavin had been lost. He blamed himself. He realised he was still angry with Jeff, even now; he remembered telling them not to go down together, and to rope up; but Jeff was the worst for doing his own thing. Jeff's nickname was 'Maverick' for that very reason. He should have called them back and insisted. He looked at the picture, crumpled in his hand; him and two other men, arms around each other, smiling and laughing. Doug looked up at the sky, his face wet with tears.

God, he missed Gavin; he missed them both. It was so painful some days. Gavin was his best mate; they were so close they could almost read each other's minds. Gav always said the right things when invariably

Doug said the wrong thing; but together they were brilliant. Doug wiped his face. He had to get himself together. He couldn't let the kids see him upset and it was time to get them. He stood and walked slowly along the beach and up the hill, looking like he had the weight of the world on his shoulders.

CHAPTER 9

The town was quiet in the early morning, apart from the odd seagull and the row that had started in Jimmy Ryan's small cottage.

'Jesus, Jimmy, how many more times?'

'Marie, I know you need the money, but I just haven't got it. You know the boat needs repairs and I need the boat to make money.'

'Always that bloody boat! I can't pay for everything all the time. We've got nothing now, we've gotta pay the bloody rent! What are you going to do about it?'

Jimmy thumped his fist on the table. 'What do you think I'm trying to do?'

Marie snorted. 'Perhaps you need to spend less time in the bloody pub and more time on the bloody boat!'

'I can't talk to you when you're like this!' He yanked open the door, marching off down the road with a thunderous look on his face. Jimmy, in his mid-thirties, was tall, wiry and surfer-blond, with a deep tan. Jimmy operated a lobster boat and had done for years.

Marie hung over the yellow stable door and yelled after him.

'That's right, proper grown up! Just walk out and sulk. I've had enough of this, Jimmy Ryan, I can bloody tell you. Get your act together!'

The top of the stable door slammed and quiet was restored in the street.

Jimmy had gone to his boat which had eventually started. As he left the harbour, he passed another boat.

The man in the boat waved over and shouted: 'Jim! Alright? How long you going out for?'

Jimmy raised his chin in greeting. 'Alright, Alan. I'm getting the pots and maybe some mackerel, be back later.'

'OK. Maybe see you later for a pint?' Alan shouted.

Jimmy gave him the thumbs up and headed out towards Kirby Island.

Marie was worried; the clock said nearly four p.m. Even if he'd gone to the pub he was always back by now. She found her mobile.

'Jimmy? Can you call me when you get this please? Come on, you big lump, you can't still be sulking. I'm getting worried now ... where are you?'

She wondered what to do next.

Inside the lifeboat station, the sound of the phone echoed through the building. Doug appeared and ducked into his office, picking up the phone.

'Lifeboat,' he said briskly. 'Hey, Marie. You OK?' He frowned as he listened. 'No, I've not seen him. When did he go? ... He's in his boat? Well if I see anything, I'll let you know. Have you tried some of the other guys that were night fishing, they might have passed him on their way in?' He listened again. 'OK. Calm down a wee bit here. Will you feel better if I send a couple of the boys out? Aye no problem, speak to you later, Marie.'

Doug hung up and shouted out of the door. 'Lads, who's around here for a wee bit?'

Tom, Ben, Mike and Jesse appeared from various doorways.

'Who's mates with Jimmy Ryan here?'

Mike raised his hand. 'I am, we jam together sometimes, he's not bad actually.'

Tom weighed in. 'We're mates, but not close. Why, what's up?'

'Marie's just been on the phone. She's worried he's not appeared home. He stormed off early this morning but he's always back by now.

59

She says he went out on the boat, but she can't get hold of him. Anyone seen him?'

The crew shook their heads and Ben said, 'I'll go and see if he's on the radio.'

Jesse asked. 'Who's Jimmy? Is he a fisherman?'

Mike answered. 'Yeah, he mostly does lobster, crab and mackerel, does some trips too. He's not been doing too well lately. Been really short of cash. He's worried about his boat too, just can't afford to fix it.'

Jesse looked interested. 'What's up with it?'

Mike shrugged. 'Don't know. Temperamental, I think. Think he said it was kicking out crap. Couldn't start it sometimes.'

'I could look at it for him,' Jesse said.

Mike grinned at her. 'He couldn't afford you.'

'I wouldn't expect to be paid … perhaps the odd lobster.'

'I'll tell him that when I see him. So, what did he storm out about this morning, Skip, did she say?'

'No, she just said they had a row and he stomped off.'

Ben returned. 'No answer, Skip. But I rang Alan as he often comes in early from night fishing and he says he saw him leaving the harbour early this morning … said he was getting his pots and mackerel.'

Doug looked thoughtful. 'When was this?'

'Around six, I think.'

Doug glanced at his watch. 'Um, so it's four now, where are his pots? Where might he be, Mike?'

'He drops the pots off Kirby Island, he says the best lobster is there.'

'OK, Ben, radio Wyn on the ferry. See if he's spotted him; they know each other. I think a couple of us should take out the small rib and have a wee scout around Kirby and see what we can see, just in case he's got into trouble.'

Ben headed off again. Mike stepped forward.

'I'll go, Skip. I'll take Ben too. Jesse, do you fancy a tour of Kirby Island?'

Jesse, Ben and Mike headed off in the small rib towards the island. Ben turned to wave at the ferry passing by full of people, with Wyn's Welsh border collie stood on the front of the boat, enjoying the wind in his face.

Mike nudged Ben. 'Did Wyn say he'd seen Billy?'

'He said he hadn't seen him all day'

The rib bumped its way across the bay towards the island. Jesse turned to Mike. 'What does Jimmy's boat look like?'

'It's a lobster boat, open deck, bright yellow.'

Jesse pointed. 'Like that one in the distance?'

'Just like that one.'

The lifeboat rib pulled up alongside the boat. Mike tied the two boats together and looked around the small deck.

'Jim?' he called out, opening the small door to the wheelhouse and poking his head in.

'Nothing here, except his phone. There's loads of missed calls. All the baskets are still down. No sign of Jimmy, though.'

Jesse peered at the shore. 'Could he have swum to shore? It's not that far.'

Ben stepped back into the rib to radio Doug. 'Come in, Skip. We've found Jimmy's boat, but no sign of Jimmy. Over.'

Doug's voice sounded tinny. 'Check around, under the boat too? Remember that old guy we found. See if maybe he's on the shore or around there?'

'Will do, Skip. Over.'

'Check under the boat? What old guy?' Jesse said.

'Really sad, we found a boat very much like this, no sign of anyone, but we found the old guy had got his leg caught in a line, gone over and then the line had got caught up on the prop shaft and almost wedged him under the boat. He'd been dead a while when we found him.'

Jesse peered over the side. 'Poor guy. The water is pretty clear here, I don't see anything.'

'Me neither.' Ben said peering over the side. 'You don't think he would have done anything stupid, do you Mike?'

'I don't know … his fags are here, his keys. Let's check in with Doug – see what he thinks.'

Ben radioed Doug again. 'There's nothing here, Skip. Just his phone, keys and fags.'

Doug was firm. 'I want to be clear he's not in the water. Do a slow scoot around along Kirby edges, check anywhere where he might have floated or swum to. Do a good sweep and then come back. I'll notify the coastguard to keep eyes and ears open. Over.'

'OK, Skip. Over.'

Jesse and the boys spent the next hour slowly circling the coastline gullies. After finding nothing, Mike called it a day. The three of them entered the station and Ben went into Doug's office.

'Skip, we've left his boat there as we found it. We've looked everywhere but no sign. If he's not back by tomorrow morning perhaps we should check with Marie it's OK to bring his boat back in and notify the coastguard.'

Doug picked up his phone. 'I'll call her now, stay around for a minute.' Doug put the speaker phone on.

Marie answered breathlessly. 'Doug?'

'Marie? Heard anything?'

Marie sighed, 'No.'

'Look Marie, you're on speaker phone and I've got Ben with me. We found Jimmy's boat off Kirby Island. It was empty, no sign of him, but his phone, keys and ciggies were there. The pots were all still down too. We've checked all around. Now we've left the boat where it is, but if he's not back by tomorrow morning, can we go and bring the boat back please as it's not the best place for it to be left?'

'What? No sign of him at all?' she said doubtfully.

'Nothing. Do you think he would have swum off somewhere maybe? Or gone off in another boat?'

'I've no idea, Doug. I'm really worried now. The boat was anchored properly though, yes? He wouldn't have left it floating around, the boat is everything to him.'

'He's anchored it, but the wheelhouse was unlocked.'

'Yeah, the lock's broken. He's been meaning to fix it. He wouldn't just go off like this. He was pissed off yes, but not in a state to do anything silly.'

'Marie, now don't think the worst. With your permission we'll go and bring the boat back tomorrow. But I have to call the coastguard to inform them that there is a person missing, but I'm sure he'll be fine, he might just be cooling off somewhere.'

Marie sniffed. 'OK, so what … I just wait?'

'Looks that way – sorry, Marie. Anyone with you?'

'No, I'm going to go to work anyway, we need the money. I'll try and take my mind off fretting about it. Thanks for ringing, Doug.'

'No bother, I'll be in touch.' Doug ended the call and looked at Ben. 'What do you reckon?'

'I don't know what to think.'

Doug exhaled loudly. 'Are you here tomorrow, Ben?'

Ben shook his head. 'No, Skip, working all day, sorry.'

Doug went to the door of his office. 'Mike? Tom? Either of you around tomorrow first thing?'

Mike appeared in the doorway of the kitchen, cup of tea in hand. 'I am, Skip. I'm doing a few bits here before I go to work, I've got a class at eleven. What do you need?'

'Are you OK to go and get Jimmy's boat in the morning?'

'Yeah, no problem, as long as it's first thing. Are we going to leave it moored in the harbour?'

'Yup. Soon as we do, let me know and I'll tell Marie it's back.'

* * *

Jimmy was pumped. Finally, some cash on the horizon. He stood on the deck of the larger black trawler as it pulled alongside his boat and then jumped down onto it and tied it to the larger one. He quickly loaded three large fishing crates onto his boat and covered them with a large old blue tarp. Dawn was a way off and his running lights weren't working so he needed to be off the sea as quickly as possible. A large, tattooed man poked his head out of the window of the wheelhouse of the large trawler. His voice had a thick Eastern European accent. 'We will call when next one due? You wait for call to pick up and get your money.'

Jimmy nodded. 'When's he going to call?'

The tattooed man shrugged. 'Few days … keep it safe, key and lock. Yes?'

Jimmy untied the trawler from his boat. The large boat chugged away. He went into the wheelhouse and picked up his mobile and saw the missed calls. He shook his head and swore. He quickly brought up the lobsters and packed the deck neatly, hiding the stash. He made a call as he tried to start the boat. The engine chugged reluctantly into life after the fourth attempt, and he heard the phone ringing.

Marie answered it breathlessly. 'Jimmy?'

'Hey, it's me.'

'Jesus, Jimmy! Where the hell have you been? I've had the lifeboat out looking for you!'

Jimmy rolled his eyes. 'Jesus. Calm down, I'm fine. I'm on my way back in, just got to stop off and offload some lobsters. I've gotta go, phones about to die.'

He ended the call and rubbed his face while he steered. Doug had been out looking for him? Christ, that's all he needed. He pushed the throttle forward hoping to get back before either the coastguard found him, or the engine packed up for good. He banged the wheel in frustration. He was torn about what he was doing. Although he wasn't averse to the odd joint every now and again, he hated hard drugs. He was desperate for cash, though, and fishing just wasn't bringing it in. He had bills piling up and no way to pay them. He decided he would only do this until he got back on his feet, then he would stop. He didn't like it, but needs must, and needing cash took priority over his principles as far as he could see.

* * *

Doug woke up alone in bed. He looked over and picked up his mobile phone, reading the text message sent in the early hours of the morning from his wife informing him she wouldn't make it back that night. He got up and headed to the bathroom shouting as he went.

'KIDS! Time to get up …'

Doug was running late, which was the one thing he hated most. He juggled the kids' breakfast things and tried to make a call, accidentally scattering cereal over the work surface. Swearing at his incompetence, he dialled and quickly checking the kids were still upstairs, pushed the kitchen door shut. He felt a burst of anger when his call went to answer phone.

'Claire. It's me. Come on. Can you try and make it home at some point? You're down to pick up the kids later so if that changes, I'll need to know and not at the last bloody minute. I can't keep dumping them on Helen with no notice.'

Doug was just about to hang up and then felt guilty about his grumpiness. 'Look, sorry. I didn't mean to sound grumpy … It would be really nice to see you sometime, you know … after what we talked about the other day. Hopefully see you later.'

He looked at his watch again and swore.

'Hurry up' he bellowed up the stairs.

Doug arrived in the harbour and parked. He struggled for a moment to control his emotions when he saw Gareth's boat sat idle and unloved where he'd left it before he'd gone on the shout that had cost him his life. God, he missed his mate. He would have talked to him about Claire, and Gareth would have told him what to do. Gareth always knew what to do.

He headed off around the corner to the station. Mike was on his way in.

'Morning, Skip, you alright?'

Doug smiled. 'I'm good. You?'

'Good, is Jesse here yet?' Mike turned and yelled 'Jesse? You here?'

Jesse appeared from the kitchen, coffee in hand. 'What's up? You want coffee? She asked them both. Doug shook his head and disappeared into his office.

'I'm good ta. You OK to come and get Jimmy's boat? Mike asked.

'I'm guessing he didn't make it home then?' Jesse asked.

'I've just checked the harbour for his boat and it's not there.'

'OK, but can we take the small rib please? The engine is running a bit rich and I want to see how it sounds.'

Mike nodded. 'No probs, you good to go now?'

Jesse put her cup down and gestured for him to leave in front of her.

Jesse liked Mike; he seemed a solid, genuine guy. She liked people who didn't pretend to be something they weren't. She therefore didn't mind being out alone with him. They were heading towards the island where Jimmy's boat was. Jesse slowed the engine and looked around; there was no sign of the boat anywhere.

Mike looked perplexed. 'Where the hell is it? It was here yesterday.'

'Perhaps he's back then. Radio Doug and see what he knows.'

Mike picked up the radio. 'Skip. Come in. Jimmy's boat's not here. You heard anything. Over?'

Doug's voice came back. 'I've not heard from Marie at all. Sit tight and I'll call her and get back to you. Over.'

'Roger that. Over.'

Jesse turned to open her toolbox. She turned off the engine and took the casing off.

'I'll give this a tweak while we're here,' she said.

Mike sat back watching her. 'So,' he said slowly.

'Can you pass me that spanner please?' Jesse was engrossed in the engine. 'The little one.'

'This one?'

Jesse held out her hand. 'Ta.'

'So …'

'And pass me those long nose pliers please?'

These? So …'

'Why do you keep saying, "so …"?'

'I was starting to try and make conversation, but you keep getting me to pass you things.'

'Oh … OK, pass me that flat screwdriver? The one with the orange handle?'

Mike looked exasperated. 'So … as I was saying … I was trying to make conversation with you, find out a bit more about you.'

'Why's that?'

'Why's what?'

'Why are you trying to find out more about me?'

Mike looked at her like she was a moron. 'I'm making conversation – it's what people do.'

'Is it? Can you pass me the lubricant?'

Mike looked around. 'This squirty stuff?'

'Bingo. What's with all the questions?'

Mike sighed. 'I'm not being nosey, I'm just chatting.'

'Ah … so this is "chatting", but not in a nosey way then?'

'That's right … so let's start small.'

Jesse was slightly entertained by him. 'Must we?'

'Yes, please play along. You must try and look interested and answer my questions like friendly people chatting do, that aren't being nosey.'

Jesse was not convinced. 'Umm.'

'So, Jesse … I hear you're from the south coast.'

Jesse decided to indulge him. 'Yes. Hello, Mike. My name is Jesse, I'm 35 and I'm from the south coast. I'm a Gemini and—'

'I don't think you're taking this seriously.'

Jesse pretended to look horrified. 'Mike, of course I'm taking this seriously. This is important stuff, right? Friendly people chatting, but not being nosey?'

Mike held up his hands in surrender, laughing. 'OK, OK.'

'I'm very boring, nothing to know at all.'

Mike regarded her closely. 'Hmm. Are you here alone? Partner? Husband? Enormous hordes of small children you keep locked under the stairs, Harry Potter style?'

Jesse smiled at him. 'None of the above … I've got a tiny family, mum, dad and a sister who all live in the West Country. Here alone apart from my dog.'

Mike brightened up at the mention of a dog. 'What sort of dog?'

'Border collie.'

'Ah, lovely dogs, how old is it?'

'He's six.'

'You should bring him into the station. Doug loves dogs. He's cool with them being around too. Gav, one of the guys … who died … used to bring in his dog. He was gorgeous.'

'The dog?'

Mike chortled. 'Yeah … he died not long after Gav. We reckon he missed him so much he couldn't go on. Doug will be cool with you bringing in yours … what's his name?'

'Brock. Don't ask.'

The sound of the radio broke the silence with its crackle. 'Come in, Mike. Over.'

Mike picked up the radio. 'Skip? Any news?'

'I got hold of Marie. She says she had a call from Jimmy early this morning – says he was on his way back in, but he's not back yet. Over.'

Mike frowned, 'Weird we didn't pass him then. Did he say where he'd been?'

'No … Come back in guys. Over.'

'OK, Skip. Soon as Jesse's rebuilt the engine, she's got it in pieces.'

Doug chuckled over the radio. 'Really?'

Jesse raised her voice. 'I'm tweaking.'

Mike laughed. 'Apparently she's only tweaking. We'll see you in a bit. Over.'

Jesse struck while the iron was hot, still focused on the engine. 'So ... as we're in chatty mode.'

Mike interrupted. 'That would be friendly chatty mode, that isn't being nosey.'

Jesse nodded straight-faced. 'Absolutely. Were you on the shout the night that the guys died?'

'No, I was playing at a wedding that night. Heard all about it, though. Sounded the most God-awful night. Poor Jeff and Gav, and then Billy, that was an awful twist of fate. You know Jeff was Ben and Paul's uncle, didn't you?'

Jesse stopped tweaking the engine.

'No, I'd no idea. Poor guys. So who was the other crewman who got really badly injured?'

'It was Doug. He almost died too.'

Jesse was shocked. 'Jesus. So what happened?'

Mike exhaled loudly. 'Blimey. OK, so you know it was a Norwegian trawler that was in trouble? It was an absolute bitch of a night anyway. The sea, well, she was out for a good old fight. They'd got nearly everyone out, but their skipper and one of the new guys was missing – the skipper was last seen below decks looking for the newbie.

'Doug was busy helping the crew into the lifeboat, so he sent Jeff and Gav down to check and told them to rope up and stick together. Off they went. By all accounts Jeff didn't rope up and went mavericking off, and Gav followed trying to keep him safe. Anyway, the weather was so bad the chopper couldn't come out, so they had to do what they could. We think Jeff and Gav were below decks when something massive hit the hull. I mean it must have been huge and probably smashed a hole through it.

'They didn't stand a chance by all accounts. The water came in too quickly and it was so cold. I still don't know why they'd gone in without roping up. Doug is a stickler for it for this very reason. The crew got all the trawler men off and managed to get them into the main boat, which almost rolled. Doug was the last one left on the boat as it was going down. He was looking for a way to try and get Jeff and Gav out, then he heard someone shout and he went down through the galley and found the newbie hiding under the table. He grabbed the kid who was gibbering like an idiot and stepped back into the galley and, basically, half the boat tore off and was dragged under.'

Jesse's eyes were like saucers. 'Jesus! What happened then?'

'Well, as the bottom half of the boat was dragged down, an enormous shard of metal whipped up and cut Doug almost straight down his middle, clean through all the gear. He says he remembers looking down and not understanding what was happening. He still managed to get the kid up to the deck to safety, though. Don't know how he did it, even put a lifesaver on him in case he went in, which he did, as they were washed off the deck and into the sea.'

Jesse couldn't believe it. 'My God. How did they get back?'

Mike looked proud. 'The lads went back for him. Bob took control and gave the orders. Doug had roped up before he went down on his lifesaver and they managed to get him out using that rope. If he hadn't done that he'd have been long gone. He held onto that newbie with such a vice-like grip that even when he passed out from the pain, they had to prise his hands off the kid. That kid owes his life to Doug, no one else would have gone back for him … he's a bloody hero to have got him out.'

Jesse was looking genuinely shocked. 'So … he … Doug was badly hurt then?'

Mike looked incredulous. 'Shit yes! He was touch and go for ages. Intensive care for a good week. As I remember it, they couldn't get hold of Claire anywhere for that time either, she was off on a course or something. We all thought it was weird we couldn't find her. It took them ages to sew him back together – something like eighteen hours of surgery. It did some real damage. He's got scars everywhere, a real patchwork. It's a wonder he made it really.'

'He seems well … is he OK now?' Jesse asked.

Mike made a rueful face. 'Yeah, he's OK physically anyway. Blames himself though and lives with it. But do you know what? The funeral was a few weeks after the shout because they wanted to find the bodies. Doug only went and checked himself out of hospital the day before and went to the funeral. He said some words there and spent the whole day on his feet. I don't know how he managed that, he looked awful. I took him home that night to an empty house, no Claire anywhere to be seen. In that state too, I ask you. You wouldn't leave anyone that had been that ill to cope on their own, let alone look after two kids. Anyway, I don't know how you ever get over being that close to death, whether it stays with you or not. What do you reckon?'

Jesse turned her back to Mike, her eyes filling with tears, confused about how affected she was to hear that Doug had nearly died. She fiddled with the engine and replaced the cover of the outboard motor.

'I don't know. I guess you have to try and live with it and think that there must be a reason why you're still around. You good to go?' she asked, restarting the engine.

'Yeah … suppose that's one way of seeing it.'

'So poor Billy's stroke did a lot of damage?' Jesse probed.

'Yeah. He's up on the hill at that care home, trapped inside this body that won't work. He hates it. It's like his internal light has gone off, he was always at the station doing something, always pottering around. It was his life.'

'A bad night for everyone that night then. So which care home was it?'

Mike struggled to remember. 'Err … oh what's it called … oh … Belvedere House I think, something like that. Bob goes up often and reads the paper to him, they're lifelong mates those two, one doesn't work properly without the other.'

Jesse snorted. 'Really? Bob didn't strike me as the caring type.'

'Don't be fooled. Bill's his oldest friend – he loves him. Probably why he was such an arse to you. Anyway, does the engine sound better now you've taken it apart?'

Jesse looked frustrated. 'I didn't take it apart, I tweaked it. It's much better. Can't you tell?'

Mike shrugged. 'If it was a guitar yes … an engine no.'

Doug had decided to stroll down to the harbour, to look for a boat. Jimmy's boat to be precise. It irked him that the lads had been sent out twice to look for him. Doug stood for a moment to look over the boats and then spied Jimmy and wandered over.

Jimmy, who had been frantically unpacking his boat, panicked at seeing Doug making a beeline for him. He covered the crates, with a tarpaulin just as Doug arrived at the quayside.

'Jimmy. You had us all a wee bit worried.'

Jimmy looked uncomfortable. 'Yeah. I'm sorry about that, Doug. I can't believe she phoned you, silly mare.'

Doug frowned. 'She was worried. I was worried, we wondered where you'd gone, leaving all your stuff in the boat like that.'

'I swam to the beach and was just too tired to swim back.'

Doug didn't believe a word of it. 'So why would you do that, Jimmy?'

Jimmy stammered. He'd always been a terrible liar. 'I just wanted a break, you know? From the constant earache and the moaning about money. It gets on top of me, you know? You must get earache from your missus, surely?'

'Ach my missus is never around long enough to give me earache. Look I had the guys out looking for you yesterday and this morning. I've a mind to charge you.'

Jimmy looked horrified. 'Look, I'm sorry mate … it won't happen again, I promise.'

Doug fixed him with the stare again. 'Make sure it doesn't. I'll have to go and tell the coastguard you're accounted for now.'

'Sorry again, mate.' Jimmy said, desperate for Doug to go so he could crack on.

'No bother. Do you need a hand up with those crates? They'll go off, if they're fish, soon enough?'

Jimmy stood in front of the crates. 'No, no … it's fine thanks … It's just bait for the pots.'

Doug looked down at him thoughtfully. 'OK, see you later, Jimmy,' he said smiling. 'Take care of yourself.' Doug turned and wandered off along the quayside.

Jimmy almost cried with relief at Doug's departure. He liked Doug and hated lying to him. He was a good bloke, an anchor pin of the community, despite him being Scottish. Jimmy hurried to collect his truck, carefully reversing it down into the harbour area as close to the boat as possible so he could load his three crates into the back.

Jimmy drove carefully. He was sweating like he'd run a marathon, hoping to God he wouldn't be pulled by the police, today of all days. If he took it easy, he'd be fine. He let out a breath as his lock-up came into view, and he turned off the main road to a collection of ramshackle wooden garages surrounded by old rotting lobster pots and a couple of half-rotten small wooden dinghies. He pulled up outside one of the garages and got out, looking around furtively. He unlocked the padlock and quickly unloaded the crates, covering them with the tarpaulin. He carefully relocked the door and drove off smiling. Some cash was finally on the horizon.

* * *

Doug arrived home that evening, surprised he hadn't received a phone call from Claire informing him he needed to pick up the children at the last minute. He let himself in quietly and stood for a moment, listening. There were a variety of sounds coming from the kitchen, low murmurings and then a loud burst of laughter. Doug strolled towards the kitchen and found the kids laying the table.

Christy squealed, 'Daddy!' and rushed over for a hug.

Jude grinned at him. 'Pizza for tea, Dad,' he said proudly. 'We've made it from scratch with Mum.'

Claire appeared from the garden, looking relaxed and happy in jeans and an old, faded Cambridge University T-shirt, with a large smudge of flour across her cheek. For a moment, she could have passed for the twenty-year-old that Doug had fallen head over heels in love with almost instantly.

'Perfect timing,' she said, leaning to kiss him on the cheek. 'Jude, check on them, they must be nearly ready.'

Jude peered into the oven. 'Bit longer I reckon, the cheese hasn't melted yet.'

Doug leant against the worktop and folded his arms, accepting a glass of red wine from Claire.

'Well, this is very nice,' he said, sipping it and smiling at Claire. 'It's really good to see you here. What prompted all this?'

Claire waved her hand dismissively, not meeting his eye. 'I thought about what you said. We do need some time together as a family.'

Surprised by her sudden change, Doug said. 'Well, it smells delicious. I'm starving.'

'God, me too,' moaned Jude. 'I'm so hungry I think I'll pass out soon.'

Claire rolled her eyes. 'Five more minutes, I reckon,' she said, looking in the oven. 'Do you think you'll be able to last that long, Jude?'

Claire pushed herself up onto the counter to sit next to Doug; it was closer than they'd been for months.

'So how was your day?' she asked, smiling at him.

Doug looked at her and his stomach did the familiar flip that happened when she turned her intense cornflower blue eyes on him. Part of him desperately wished she was like this all the time. He raised a hand and softly brushed flour off her face with his thumb.

'Good. It was a good day. You've got the ingredients all over your face.' He smiled and his stomach lurched again when she turned her head and kissed his hand.

Claire spoke very softly so only Doug could hear. 'I'm sorry about how I've been ...'

'Pizza's ready!' Jude shouted excitedly staring into the oven. 'Come on!'

Claire grabbed the oven gloves and expertly transferred the pizzas onto each plate.

'Let's eat!' she said sitting at the table. 'These look great!'

Doug couldn't recall the last time they'd done this. To him, the evening couldn't have been more perfect. The family dinner was full of laughter and jokes and, later, the two of them had packed the children off to bed and shared the rest of the bottle of wine. They talked and Claire had promised to try and be home more. They eventually abandoned the clearing up and went to bed.

As Claire lay in Doug's arms, she murmured. 'I can't remember the last time we did that.'

Doug smiled in the darkness; he was on the very edge of falling asleep. 'Made pizzas?'

She giggled. 'That too.'

She cuddled up to him and gave a small sigh of contentment.

'Mm, we should think about doing that more often, maybe?'

Doug gently kissed the top of her blonde head. 'I'm game if you are,' he said quietly. 'Love pizza.'

But Claire had already fallen asleep.

CHAPTER 10

The brothers, Ben and Paul, had engineered a day off together and had decided to spend the day jet skiing. The day had dawned bright and sunny, and the boys had been in a state of excitement about spending the day with each other to do boys' things – a rare treat. They'd met at the beach car park, donned wet suits, unloaded the jet skis and headed off at high speed across the bay. They were both flat out neck and neck, trying to beat each other.

Suddenly Ben's jet ski flew up into the air, breaking apart into pieces and throwing Ben into the air too. Paul circled to a halt, horrified, and yelled for his brother.

'Ben! BEN!'

Ben broke up out of the water, coughing, with a bloody gash on his forehead. Paul almost cried with relief and steered the jet ski over to him.

'Jesus, mate. Scared the bloody hell out of me! What happened?'

Ben was gasping and grabbed onto Paul's jet ski. 'I hit something!' he gulped. 'There's something in the water.'

Paul hauled Ben onto the back of the jet ski. They headed off slowly towards the debris.

Ben pointed. 'There! What's that?'

The boys approached and saw the corner of what looked like a bit of metal sticking up from the sea.

'Looks like a container.' Paul frowned as he looked closely.

'Jesus, look at the size of this thing ... this could've killed me.'

Paul re-aligned the jet ski alongside the container. 'Let's have a closer look.'

'Hold it steady,' Ben said, scrambling from the jet ski onto the container. He balanced carefully on the slightly submerged surface and walked about gingerly on it. It moved very slightly under him.

'Jesus, I think this is a full-size container.' Ben stared at Paul in amazement. 'This genuinely could have killed one of us.'

Paul looked worried. 'Look, that cut on your head is bad and we can't just leave this here. What if another boat hits it? It'll sink a wooden boat in a heartbeat. We should tell Doug.'

'Look, there's a hole in the corner where the metal has buckled.' Ben knelt and leant forwards to try and look into the container, recoiling and gagging. 'Oh my God that's so bad ... that smell!'

Paul kept the jet ski steady. 'Can you see anything?' he called.

Ben shook his head. 'I can't see anything. It's gotta be meat or something like that that's gone off.'

Paul looked over at Ben. 'Maybe it was one of those refrigerated ones.'

Ben got to his feet. 'Either way, it's rank. We need to call this in and somehow mark this so that people can see it.' He looked around. 'Let's use one of our life jackets – at least it's bright and can be spotted.'

Ben arranged it on the corner of the container and climbed on the back of the jet ski.

'Come on, the quicker we can report this the better.'

Doug was reading an incredibly boring report on safety equipment. He kept drifting off and thinking about Claire and how she had seemed her old self the other night.

Intruding on his daydreaming was the sound of his name being shouted and he was up out of his chair almost as soon as he'd heard it.

Paul and Ben were running up the ramp yelling for Doug. He appeared up on the upper gantry.

'What's up? Jesus, what's happened to your head, Ben?'

Ben couldn't get his words out quickly enough. 'We were out past Long Beach, and I hit something in the water and it's a bloody metal container! Massive it is! It totaled my jet ski. I went flying off.'

Doug looked at Ben's head with concern as he came down the stairs towards the pair. 'Let's have a quick look at that head.'

'No, I'm more bothered about that container floating in the way of everyone. Doug, we need to get back out to it, in case something hits it.' He bounced on each foot impatiently.

Doug held up his hands to try and calm him down. 'We'll go and take care of it. Paul, go and call the coastguard and tell them what you found, and that we're going to go and do a reccy and make it visible. We'll radio them with an update.'

'Skip.' Paul ran off to make the call.

'Ben, come and get your face fixed while he does that.'

Doug shouted for Jesse and she appeared, wiping her hands on an oily rag.

'Jesus, what happened to your face, Ben?'

Doug turned to her. 'The boys hit a container in the sea while they were out on their jet skis. We've got to go back and make it visible, it's a major hazard. We'll take the small rib – you up for a trip? Can you sort out Ben's head please, before we go?'

Jesse took Ben into the kitchen.

Paul re-appeared. 'Skip, coastguard says co-ordinates please and to anchor it somehow, or see whether we think we can tow it back.'

He passed Doug a handful of high visibility vests and some inflatable buoys he'd grabbed from the locker room and headed off for more. Jesse and Ben, with Steri-Strips on his forehead, re-appeared and they loaded the gear into the smaller rib and headed off.

They spotted the boys' efforts at making the container visible easily and pulled alongside it.

'Paul, radio this location to the coastguard.'

Doug turned to the brothers, his face serious. 'Jesus Christ guys, this thing could have killed you.'

Ben climbed out onto the container again. He turned and motioned for Doug to join him. Paul kept the rib steady and alongside. Doug and Paul were inspecting the container, chatting quietly. Jesse was looking at it. There was something bothering her, but she didn't know what.

76

She raised her hands and said loudly. 'WAIT! Everyone quiet.' She strained to hear, head on one side.

Doug said softly, 'Did you hear something?'

Jesse nodded. 'Did you hear that? I could have sworn I heard a faint knocking on the metal. Paul, cut the engine.'

Jesse scrabbled about and produced a metal torch; she threw it to Ben.

'Ben, tap this on the container loudly and say hello, then everyone quiet ...'

Ben moved to the corner poking out of the water and tapped loudly on the container with the metal sound clearly ringing out. The crew strained to hear; there was a very faint knocking.

Ben looked horrified. 'It's coming from in there! There's fucking someone in there!'

Doug's face paled. 'Jesus Christ.' He grabbed his radio. 'Coastguard, this is the inshore lifeboat, Castleby. We can hear sounds of knocking from inside the container. There's a gap in the top edge – we now can't tow it back in case it fills with water and affects whoever's in there. Over.'

The static reply was difficult to make out, but Doug spoke sharply into the radio. 'No, we can't see inside, but the smell is God-awful. We need to get a chopper here and airlift it out to somewhere where we can get it open quickly. Over.' He listened to what sounded like more static. 'What about the RAF? OK ... do it quickly though? Over.'

Doug turned to the crew. 'They don't think their chopper can lift this. They're going to buzz the RAF for a Chinook, there's one fairly locally.'

Ben was still balanced on the container. 'I'm going to see if I can see what else is in there.'

He lay down near the hole, wriggling towards it. He grimaced, switched on the torch and peered in. He looked away and gagged again. 'Christ it's awful, that smell.'

'Did you see anything?' Doug asked.

Ben shook his head and wriggled into a better position and he looked away to breathe a few times. He looked again for a long time and then turned to face the rest of the crew, his face ashen white.

'Ben? What is it?'

Ben looked stunned. 'It's full of people ... dead ... oh my God, is there someone in there alive ... in that lot?'

Doug stood on the gently rocking container staring at it in disbelief. Ben beckoned him to look into the open hole. Doug peered into the space with the torch and looked up at the others who were watching silently.

'He's right. I think ... there's a hand moving in there ... my God, imagine being in there with those bodies. Jesus, we've got to get them out.'

Doug grabbed the radio. 'This is the inshore Castleby. This container is full of people ... do you get me? Yes people. Lots of them are dead. Did you hear that? DEAD. But we can see someone alive. Can you please put a rocket up whoever's bureaucratic arse you need to put one up and get this out of the water? Over.'

There was a burst of static and a disembodied voice said. 'Helicopter en route to your location, ETA 20 minutes. Stand by. Over.'

The team waited, silent and shocked. Ben had shouted in through the hole that help was coming. In the distance, they heard the Chinook before it was visible. As the helicopter approached, a frogman in scuba gear dropped into the sea and waited for four large metal hooks to be winched down. He attached the hooks to each corner eye and also attached a chain-like sling around the container. He swam away and lifted his arm, making a circular motion to the winchman. The frogman reached the inshore lifeboat, and Doug pulled him in.

The Chinook's downdraft was causing the sea to get choppy. Doug was worried that the container would fill up with water. He was very relieved when, finally, the container was lifted clear. The helicopter seemed to initially struggle, and water poured out of the holes in the container leaving a rancid pool of scum on the ocean surface. The Chinook swung off towards Castleby, carrying its dripping cargo.

In the harbour, Doug watched the Chinook as it circled towards him. They were ready. The area was being cleared by police, and the place seemed full of people in high visibility jackets. The police helped to guide the container down and into position, releasing the hooks, the downdraft from the Chinook rocking the boats moored in the harbour. People were gathering around the harbour's upper pathways and filming with mobile phone cameras.

Doug, Jesse, Ben and Paul approached the police officers near the container. Doug knew the local police inspector well and shook his hand. 'How you doing, Steve?'

Steve looked worried and kept scratching his head. 'Doug, is this a crime scene or what? What the hell do you think you've found in there?'

Doug said in a low voice, 'People are in there. Loads of them, mostly dead, we think at least one alive. Surely forensics will need to come down and shield it off otherwise it's a free for all? First thing, though, we need to get this open and find anyone alive.'

Doug stopped talking and looked around, seeing the crowds gathered on the walls above the harbour.

He turned and raised his voice so that the emergency workers around him could hear. 'Guys, listen up. We need everyone in gloves and face masks if the paramedics have got any spare. Prepare yourself, the smell is bad. We think there are people alive in there. We're going to have to find them somehow ... so ... let's clear this area and lay a tarp down. Steve, have you got any spare blankets?'

Steve nudged a colleague beside him, who headed back to the squad car. Doug spotted a fisherman in the doorway to one of the arches that served as lock-ups in the harbour wall.

'Rhys! Can you help us?'

The fisherman looked over at Doug. 'Course mate, what do you need?'

Doug called, 'You still got those old sails that were ripped a while back?'

Rhys shouted. 'They're in the back of the lock-up.'

Doug gave him a thumbs up. 'Then can you grab that Heras fencing over there and drape the sails over it and line up the fencing so whoever we pull out isn't all over social media?' he said, gesturing to the crowds filming.

Rhys looked up and nodded grimly. 'Happy to help, mate.'

Doug stood next to Steve in front of the container and the crew and others gathered around. Doug glanced at the faces surrounding him.

'Everyone ready?' he asked, grabbing the handle and sliding the lock gently free.

As the huge doors were unlocked, and Doug and Paul swung them open. Bodies fell forward, tumbling out with fetid water, grey faces, eyes open, lips blue. The crew and others all collectively stepped back gasping with shock and coughing, as the smell assaulted their senses. A young police officer turned and threw up.

'Christ alive. There's so many.' Doug mentally shook himself. 'OK guys, check them all for life signs and move them out.'

The helpers checked for signs of life, laying the bodies gently on the tarpaulins. The police forensics team arrived and busied themselves making the area more private.

Up on the harbour wall, the local news outside broadcasting truck had turned up and started filming. Doug took a moment to look for his team but couldn't see Jesse anywhere. He spotted her finally. She was wearing a police baseball cap pulled low over her eyes and had a mask on as she was in the container helping to bring bodies out. The body count was mounting, Women, children, teenagers and some older men were all being brought out and laid on the tarpaulins.

Jesse yelled, 'Here! Over here!'

Jesse was cradling a small child with dark hair; her skin tinged a light blue. Jesse looked hopefully at the paramedic who was checking her over.

'I felt something and I think her eyes moved.'

'You're right … it's faint, but it's there. Good shout.' The paramedic said, strapping the girl onto a stretcher and quickly rigging up a drip.

Doug shouted, 'Wait!'

He was kneeling down next to a young man in his late teens. The boy was thin, dirty and pale with a large bruise on his head. The paramedic ran over and checked him carefully.

'He's got a very weak pulse and looks badly dehydrated. I'm not happy with that head bump either. Let's get him in the rig. I'll radio for another one to come.'

Doug helped the paramedic lift the boy onto a stretcher and into the ambulance.

'Keep us posted, yes?' Doug asked.

The paramedic drove off, sirens blaring and lights flashing. The news teams scrambled to film the ambulance leaving, only to be pushed back by police officers.

Daylight was fading and the forensic teams had set up a small generator and floodlights. To the dismay of the news crews, the forensic team had erected a series of large white tents to preserve the dignity of the dead. So now the only thing to look at was a wall of white.

The container had been emptied and the forensics team were busy inside, looking for evidence of origin. Doug and the team were together, watching.

Shirley, the owner of the harbour drink and donut kiosk, took pity on them and passed out a large tray of cups of tea. They took them gratefully and stood sipping their drinks, all of them looking hollow-eyed and shattered.

Doug couldn't quite believe that the day had morphed into this. It seemed like a lifetime ago he was reading the boring safety report.

'Jesus. What a day,' he said quietly to no one in particular.

Jesse made a noise of agreement. She asked quietly. 'Anyone know how many were there roughly, in the end?'

Doug exhaled loudly. 'About forty, I think. I just can't tell.'

Jesse rubbed her eyes. 'I can't bear it ... there were kids ... young kids ... who would do that? Why would they do that?'

Paul threw his empty cup into a nearby bin. 'The police don't know whether they were just trying to get into the country, and this was a new way of doing it or whether it was some sort of trafficking op. I'm inclined to think it's some sort of trafficking. But who knows?'

Ben sighed. 'That picture of them all tumbling out ... it keeps going around in my head.'

'I've never seen anything like this... this sort of thing stays with you, I think.' Paul said quietly.

Jesse turned to Doug. 'What else can we do here?

'Nothing. Steve has said he'll type up your statements and you'll just need to go and sign them, but tomorrow is fine. They need us out of here – they're going to section it off. They're going to store the bodies in the fish market temporarily as it's cold. They need to get forensics on it to try and find out more. I need to go back and write this up, no doubt there will be a procession of government suits down here wanting to know everything.'

Jesse looked troubled. 'This is going to sound awful. But what if this isn't the only one? What if there are more containers? I mean where did it come from? Was it a container ship? A smaller vessel? What if there are more floating about?'

'We should have a chat with the coastguard. Maybe we can assess a rough area of where it might have come from or drifted from. They'll have a good idea of currents and should know which boats have passed through this way … perhaps we need to work backwards.'

Paul chipped in. 'Perhaps it's a better idea to do an aerial search to try and look for any more that might be floating?'

'Good idea,' Doug said. 'I've got to put a call into the coastguard in a minute anyway, so I'll discuss it with them.'

Jesse touched Doug on the arm. 'Doug, I'm going to whip the rib back around to the station, I need to work on it. Can one of you guys give me a hand pulling it in please?'

Ben moved to stand beside Jesse. Doug and Paul looked up towards the exit of the harbour.

'We're gonna get mobbed if we head up that way anyway,' Doug said grimly.

The crew walked through the throng of activity and climbed into the rib, heading back out of the harbour towards the station, leaving the flashing blue lights and sounds of activity behind them.

We are in the crowd of people on the wall above the harbour, all hoping for a view of the activity below. We are trying to see, but not draw attention to ourselves. We want to see her. We need to see her. Where is she? We can't see her. She must be behind the Heras fencing, behind all the ambulances and cars. We are jostled by people wanting to see, but we have the greater need. We want to see her. We keep moving around people pushing them out of the way. Finally, we see her. There she is! We spy her and we stand still and watch her as she stands sipping a tea. She looks tired. She's found a police baseball cap and pulled it low on her head. But we know it's her. We know. We know how she walks, holds herself. We know. We'll watch for a while longer … Just a little longer. Can't be seen, can't be seen.

CHAPTER 11

Doug was so tired he felt like he was wearing lead boots. He locked the station and walked towards his car, fishing his phone from his pocket as he dug out his keys. His heart sank when he saw eight missed calls. Two from school and six from Claire. He dialled Claire's mobile, tutting as it went straight to answerphone.

As he drove home, he recognised a familiar feeling in the pit of his stomach, a dread of whether Claire was likely to kick off or not. He remembered pizza night and reflected on how completely different she'd been. Like her old self. He was fairly sure that the Claire he'd see tonight would not be the one he saw the other night. He wished again that his mate Gav was around to talk to.

'Miss you, mate,' he said out loud to the empty car. 'Could do with you being around.'

Doug arrived home and turned off the engine. He rested his head on the steering wheel, closing his eyes. On the brink of drifting off to sleep, he started awake and got out of the car.

He heard the TV from the lounge and poked his head in the door. Both children were splayed out in front of the TV, with Jude watching upside down from his position on the sofa. Both acknowledged Doug with a wave and Christy blew him a kiss. Doug returned the kiss, then followed the sounds coming from the kitchen.

Claire was crashing pots and pans about, visibly annoyed. 'Oh, so you've finally decided to make it home.'

Doug leant against the worktop, forgoing the idea of giving her a kiss in greeting. 'Hello to you too.'

Claire threw a saucepan down loudly. 'Where the bloody hell have you been? I'm supposed to be at a work thing tonight. I can't believe I got called by the school at work and had to leave! It's beyond embarrassing!'

'Claire, you were down to pick them up anyway. Did I get that wrong?'

Claire stood hands on her hips looking furious.

Doug frowned. 'Claire, did you think you could just not turn up and hope that I'd sort it out? That's what usually happens, isn't it?' He went to touch her arm. 'Come on Claire, I thought we were past this ... the other night ...'

Claire brushed his hand away. 'What? A family dinner and a bunk up has made it all better, has it? Don't be so bloody naïve, Douglas.'

Doug felt winded. He couldn't believe she could speak to him with such malevolence after the other night. He said as he left the kitchen, 'I'm going for shower.'

Claire marched after him, standing at the foot of the stairs. 'Don't you walk away from me.'

Doug stopped halfway up and turned. 'Please don't talk to me like that Claire. I'm not one of your junior doctor flunkies.' He stopped and took a breath trying to control his temper. Why did everything have to be a battle with this woman he thought? 'I'm not in the mood for this today, not after what I've seen. I'm going for a shower.'

Claire was in full swing now. 'Let me guess, you pulled a pensioner out of a dingy? Seriously Douglas? What? Some teenager break a nail on his surfboard?'

Doug moved to the bathroom and she seemed set to follow him in.

'Douglas. I'm serious, I want an explanation.'

'Just leave it Claire ...'

'No! I won't bloody leave it! I want to know where you were and why the bloody hell you couldn't get the kids!'

85

Doug knew he was rapidly approaching a point of no return on the temper front. He hooked a foot around the door and kicked it shut. Claire hammered on the door.

'You have no idea about my life at work, the level of commitment they need from me ...'

Doug rested his hands on the bathroom sink. He saw a flash of the bodies tumbling out of the container. The eyes open and staring ...

'Douglas. Why can't you come and have a bloody conversation with me?'

'Give me a minute ... just give me a minute,' he called.

Jude shouted loudly from the lounge. 'MUM! Dad's on the TV!'

Doug heard Claire going back down the stairs and reluctantly followed. Claire and the children were watching the television news footage of the container. Doug and the crew were moving about in the bustle of emergency services. Someone had managed to take some film of the bodies laid out on the tarpaulins.

Jude was bouncing about on the sofa. 'Oh my God, Dad! That's *so* cool! What happened?'

Claire looked at Doug. 'You were in this thing with the container?'

'The lads found it and it was me that opened it.'

Claire sighed loudly. 'Well, it looks horrible. Although I still don't understand why you couldn't at least have called Helen to sort out the kids.'

Doug looked at the woman he thought he knew up until that moment. 'Seriously, Claire? That's what you think of? Nearly forty dead bodies, some of them kids the same age as ours, and you're busting me because I didn't get the kids when you couldn't be bothered.'

Claire raised her chin in defiance. 'Two minutes! That's all you needed for a quick phone call, then we could have both done what we wanted to.'

'I just can't do this now.'

Doug brushed past Claire, picking up the keys as he went. He couldn't get the door open quick enough to get away from her.

What the hell is she on? When did she get so unfeeling?

Doug drove to the lifeboat station. His sanctuary. He unlocked the front door, stepping in with relief at the familiar smells and quiet stillness of the building.

Doug flopped down in his office chair, closed his eyes and then opened them again instantly when he heard the clatter of metal dropped on concrete. Suddenly alert, he headed out to investigate.

Creeping down the stairs quietly, he saw Jesse lying on the floor underneath the big boat. He moved towards the light switch, flicking the light on and off twice.

'What the …?'

Doug called out. 'It's me, didn't want to scare you. I just wanted to let you know I was here.'

Jesse's head appeared. 'I thought you went home.'

Doug smiled wryly. 'You know, paperwork to do.'

Jesse regarded him quietly. 'Uh huh, I didn't want to go home either.'

'Ok. Well, I'll be upstairs then.'

Doug went back up to his office, hearing his mobile phone ringing. He looked at the display. Claire. He ignored it. He couldn't bring himself to talk to her. He grabbed a quick shower and then sat in his chair to watch the setting sun.

Jesse wandered up the stairs towards Doug's office. He had looked so sad when he came back, she wondered what the issue was. She stood for a moment outside his office. He was sat in his chair looking out to sea, lost in thought.

'Hey,' she said softly. 'You eaten yet?'

He blinked, trying to bring himself back in the moment. 'Not really hungry. Are you?'

Jesse plonked herself in one of the chairs by Doug's desk. 'No, but I feel like I ought to eat, like I'm running on empty.'

'I'm not really hungry, thanks.'

'Look. I'm going to ring that pizza place on the high street. Pete's, is it? Do you want to share? Come on, take pity on me, I can't eat alone.'

'OK, as it's Pete's. As long as it's not Hawaiian or anything that has no business whatsoever being on a pizza.'

Jesse laughed and raised an eyebrow. 'Oh God, are you one of those really old school people who think meat and three veg is adventurous?'

Doug looked amused. 'No, but I have standards … come on … chicken tikka on a pizza … fruit on a pizza? Must I go on?'

Jesse laughed. 'Point taken. I'll go and call Pete's.'

Doug's phone rang again, and he ignored it.

Jessie turned. 'Oh, I've been hearing a phone going. I just assumed that one of the guys had left one in their locker.'

'It's mine.'

'And you're not going to answer it?'

'Nope.'

Jesse headed off, re-appearing with a small bottle of wine, and two mugs.

'I found this in the cupboard. Pizza's on its way. Let's sit out on the deck.'

They sat outside in silence, watching the sea. Jesse poured them wine and they sipped in silence. The bell rang and Jesse disappeared, returning with the box of pizza.

She lifted the lid and Doug peered doubtfully at the pizza.

'What is it?'

'Pepperoni – figured that wasn't too weird for you.'

Doug helped himself. They ate in silence until Doug's phone rang again.

'Someone's keen to talk to you. Do you want me to give you a minute?'

Doug stared straight ahead. 'Nope.'

'That sounds pretty final.'

'Yup.'

'Not talking about it then?'

'Nope.'

Jesse decided to tease him a little. 'Not even a tiny bit?'

'Nope.'

Jesse left it a few minutes and then said. 'What about now?'

Doug smiled. 'Nope.'

'You know someone could feel overwhelmed with this level of chat here, you babbling on.'

Doug shook his head. 'Won't work.'

Jesse held up her hands in mock surrender. 'OK, OK. You really don't want to talk about this, do you?'

'Not a jot. You're quick on the uptake, though. I like that.'

Jesse raised the mug as if accepting a compliment.

'OK, Miss Chatty. Tell me more about you. You seem to be settling in well, part of the crew …'

Jesse giggled. 'With the obvious exception of Bob.'

'Well… Bob IS Bob.'

'Oh yes he is,' she said dryly.

Doug held out his mug for a top up. 'So, apart from Bob, who is clearly your biggest fan … tell me about you, I don't know anything about you at all.'

Up until that point, Jesse had been enjoying herself. Now she shifted in her seat, tensing up.

'Nothing to tell,' she said dismissively. 'I'm very boring really.'

Doug turned to look at her, but she refused to meet his eyes. 'Well, it seems to me you and I have more in common than we first thought.'

Jesse looked confused. 'How so?'

'Well, neither of us wants to talk much about our shit home lives.'

Jesse looked uncomfortable. 'It's not I don't want to talk about it, it *is* genuinely boring. *I'm* genuinely very boring.'

Doug viewed her with his unusually light lupine eyes. 'Umm, so you keep saying. So, what's at home?'

'What do you mean?'

'You know, what, who … anyone at home for you?'

Jesse began to shift about. 'No, no one at home, except … Well, I've been meaning to ask you … I have a dog, he's lovely. Ben was talking about another dog you used to have around the station, and I wondered if it would be OK to bring him into work sometimes. He wouldn't be any trouble …' She trailed off.

'It's fine, it'll be nice. Jeff used to bring his in, he became part of the family there, a black Labrador called Brindley. Lovely fella. So what's yours then?'

'Border collie, he's about six. He's lovely. I wouldn't necessarily put him in charge of sheep though.'

'It'll be lovely to have a dog around the place again. Bring him in.' He watched her for a moment. 'Surprised it took you this long to ask.'

Jesse smiled happily. 'Thank you. I really appreciate it.'

The phone rang again, and Doug glanced at it. He pushed the call to answer phone.

Jesse looked sideways at him. 'Still not feeling chatty then?'

'Nope.'

'I couldn't help but see. Claire is your wife, isn't she?'

'Yup.'

'So tell me. What's a Scottish guy doing living on the Welsh coast?'

Doug refilled his mug again and raised it. 'Ah, the things we do for love.'

Jesse looked intrigued. 'Oh? So ... you met your wife here then?'

'Aye. She was training on an A&E rotation, and I'd gone to hospital with one of the crew as the old skipper was a bit worried about him.'

Jesse was surprised. 'So, you've always been in Castleby?'

Doug nodded. 'It started off as a series of summer jobs, things like lifeguarding and some fishing work on the trawlers. I kept thinking I'll go soon, I'll go soon, but for whatever reason I couldn't go, I just couldn't leave, so I just kept staying.'

'So, you met your wife in A&E?'

Doug leaned back looking relaxed as he remembered. 'Yeah ... she was the one who treated my guy. We waited for ages I remember. I met her. I took one look at her ... She was utterly captivating, dressed in blue scrubs, same colour as her eyes. She had blood all over her, but to me she looked amazing. I was an instant goner.'

'Wow, quick then.'

'Hmmm.'

Jesse looked at Doug and grinned. 'So, just to be clear, this was when you used to be charming? Way back when.'

Doug chuckled. 'I was indeed, if I do say so myself.'

'So how long have you been together then?'

'All in all, nearly twenty years. Married for fifteen.'

'Wow, that's good. You still a team?'

Doug looked out to sea and took a while to reply. He was no longer relaxed; his eyes were darker and there was a muscle pounding in his cheek.

'I thought we were,' he said softly.

The silence was shattered by the insistent ringing of the doorbell of the station.

Jesse got up. 'I'll go.' She headed to the front door and found two children standing at the door. 'Hi guys, are you OK?'

The boy spoke. 'Hi, I'm Jude, and this is Christy. Is our dad here? Mum said he was, she said his car was and he'd be here.'

Jesse turned around, shouting over her shoulder. 'Doug! Your kids are here!' She faced the kids. 'Come on in, guys.'

Doug appeared, looking surprised. 'You alright, guys? What are you doing here?'

'Mum said she had to go to work.'

Christy leaned forward and whispered. 'Dad, Mummy's really cross … she said the F-word.'

Jude nodded emphatically. 'She did. A lot …'

Doug looked at the kids. 'So she's gone off to work, has she, just left you here, without knowing for sure I'd be here.'

Jude said solemnly, 'She said you'd F-word know this if you ever answered your F-word phone. She said she knew you'd be here. You were always here.'

Doug ruffled Jude's hair and gave him a look. 'That's enough of that, thanks.'

Christy snuggled into Doug. 'Daddy, please can we go home? I'm really tired.'

Doug kissed the top of her head.

'Yes, we can. You kids go downstairs, and make sure the lights are off.'

'You guys go – I'll lock up here,' Jesse said.

'It's fine, it's a two-minute job. Come on, I'll drop you home on the way back.'

Jesse shook her head. 'Are you OK to drive?'

'No, but you are. You only had half a mug.'

'Blimey, nothing gets past you,' Jesse said, exasperated.

'Nope, so are you OK to drive, drop us and keep the car till tomorrow?'

Jesse looked nervous.

Doug persisted. 'Aren't you near Trafalgar Road?'

Jesse nodded.

The kids re-appeared smiling at Jesse shyly and Doug ushered them through the doors and locked up. 'We're just around the corner from you, so it's not far.'

Doug unlocked the truck, and the kids climbed in. He handed the keys to Jesse, opened the driver's door and waved her in like she was royalty.

Jesse climbed into the driver's seat nervously. She was sitting way too far back. Doug was in the passenger seat, looking at her. She felt awkward.

'I can't reach the pedals ... how do you ...'

Doug leaned over her. He placed a hand on the edge of the seat next to her thigh.

'Excuse me,' he said wryly and reached down to a lever between her legs. He shunted the seat forward a few notches. He stayed where he was and looked up at her, his hand still pressed firmly up against her thigh.

'Is that close enough?' he asked softly. She found herself unbelievably flustered, and in a weird way she quite liked it.

'It's very close. Yes,' she stammered, trying not to look directly at him.

'I meant can you reach the pedals?' he asked, giving her a quizzical look.

'Oh yes I think so ... yes, that's fine, thank you, God this thing looks complicated – where is everything?' Jesse wriggled in the seat, accidentally leaning on the horn on the steering wheel at the same time, which made her jump and become even more flustered.

Doug grinned. 'Well I think that's got the horn covered,' he said dryly, putting his seatbelt on.

Jesse started the engine and drove slowly through the harbour area. After a while Doug pointed to a road.

'It's just here. This one. On the corner.'

Jesse was surprised; she had no idea he effectively lived at the top of her road.

'Thanks for this and sorry for bullying you into it,' Doug said with a grin.

Jesse pulled up on the drive and Doug and the kids got out. Doug passed the house key to Jude and the kids waved at Jesse and headed inside. Jesse waved back. Doug leant against the truck door.

Jesse turned off the engine and got out.

'I'm gonna walk home, it's only around the corner, never anywhere to park there.'

Doug looked surprised. 'OK, if you're sure.'

'I am. See you tomorrow,' she said, heading off down his drive.

'Wait, I owe you for pizza. Let me give you some cash?' He called.

'Call it my treat.'

'My treat next time then?'

'I'll hold you to that, see you tomorrow.'

CHAPTER 12

The lifeboat station was busy with Easter tourists jostling their way around to get a look at the boat and spend money in the shop. Doug shut himself away in his office but was interrupted by a heavy-set man with a grey crew-cut squeezed into a smart suit.

'Hi Stu, good to see you.' He shook the man's hand warmly. 'Coffee?'

'Christ no, not if you've made it.' Stuart grimaced and took a seat.

'Three guesses what brings you here, boss.'

Stuart raised his eyebrows. 'I needed to see for myself. I couldn't believe it.'

'I thought I'd seen it all, but this …'

Stuart frowned. 'Are you OK? Are the guys OK?'

'Yeah, I think so, I plan to check in with them. These things fester.'

'I'm guessing you haven't had a chance to write this up yet.'

Doug gestured to the paperwork scattered all over his desk. 'In the middle of it.'

'So, tell me how you found it.'

'It was Paul and Ben. It completely totaled Ben's jet ski, could have killed him. They came back to tell us, we went back and took Jesse with us.'

'The new mechanic?'

'Yup. The others got involved once it had been lifted back here to the harbour.'

'Why the harbour?' queried Stuart.

'We wanted to get it open as soon as possible. The harbour yard can be contained easily as it's got one main access.'

'Makes sense. So you think your guys are OK?'

Doug paused. 'I don't know Jesse well enough to call it yet.' He pushed the door closed, turned to Stuart and said quietly. 'Stu, what can you tell me about Jesse? It's all a bit cloak and dagger.'

'What makes you say that?'

'Well, something isn't right. First off, I've been issued with a strict 'no approach' to her previous team. The contract and notification came from higher than you at head office. She's jumpy, you can't surprise her at all. Don't get me wrong, she's fitting in well and we all like her and trust her, but … there's something about her. She seems …' He searched for the word. 'Skittish … yes. A bit skittish.'

Stuart sighed. 'Doug, I only know about the rumour mill from the higher echelons. She was on the south coast, Hastings I think. She was really well liked, the rumours were she had magic hands with any engine. Then one day, she's not at work anymore and spends six months in hospital recovering and trying to walk again.'

Doug looked shocked. 'Recovering from what?'

Stuart kept his voice low. 'Not completely sure, but she never went back to work there.'

'Come on, Stuart. What were the rumours?'

'Mainly that she got really badly beaten and raped by a local gang and left for dead. Another rumour was it was her partner at the time, beat her within an inch of her life. Raped her. Broke both her legs so she couldn't go anywhere. I think that rumour didn't come to anything because he was police himself.'

'Just 'cos someone's a copper that doesn't make them synonymous with good behaviour ...' Doug snapped.

'I know. All I know is she's lucky to be alive.'

Doug sat back in his chair. 'So, did they catch who did it then?'

Stuart shrugged. 'Dunno.'

Doug rubbed his face. 'Christ, that's awful. Might explain a few things, though.'

Stuart leant forward in full gossip mode. 'It's all hush-hush. Her old team were gunning for blood down there, but she never even went back to get the stuff from her locker. You heard none of this from me, OK? As I said it's all rumours. One thing, though, there's a condition about not having any details of her on our station websites or in the press.'

Doug looked thoughtful. 'She was giving the cameras a wide berth yesterday at the scene, I noticed.'

Stuart stood up. 'Well, now you know – some of it anyway. Come on, I've not got a lot of time here today, can we go and look at the scene?'

Doug got up and they walked towards the door. 'So our main concern is that this wasn't the only one and there's more out there floating around.'

'Yeah. I spoke to the coastguard this morning. They've got some local boats out looking, and they'll do some fly-bys of the area. They've got instructions if they spot anything to call it in and whoever's nearest to go and investigate. Now I'd like that to be you guys, but we're entering silly bugger season, so you might be out on another shout, so we'll try and be flexible. The RAF is standing by again with the chopper.'

Doug grabbed a high visibility coat and passed one to Stuart. 'Here, chuck this on, you'll need it down there.'

The two men stood in the busy harbour looking at the container. The news teams had departed but the place was still tightly cordoned off.

Doug was talking Stuart through the recovery when Stuart's phone rang. He answered and turned to Doug. 'Coastguard's seen another one.'

'Jesus! Where?'

'About a mile out to sea from the last one. It's still floating. RAF will lift it out, bring it here and take the other one for storage at the military base.'

'What do they need us to do?'

'Do what you did last time. Watch out for press, they'll be trying to get out in boats now. Sorry this lands on you again, Doug.'

Doug activated the pagers and ran towards the station. He saw Mike approaching, still holding his guitar, followed by Tom still with his pub uniform and Dan in his chef's whites. Paul and Ben arrived with a squeal of tyres, both covered in plaster dust. They all raced into the locker room.

'Listen up, guys. There's another container, still floating. We launch in five.'

In the harbour, the team watched a replay of the previous day. The crowds and news teams had returned. The area was busy with police and ambulance crews. Helen, the childminder, stood at the police cordon waiting to hand the two kids over to Doug.

She saw him and waved. Doug approached, looking surprised. Christy jumped on him for a cuddle, wrapping herself tightly around Doug. Jude's eyes were like saucers trying to see beyond the cordon.

'Christ, Helen, I'm sorry. I lost track of time.'

Helen smiled at him adoringly. Doug could be six hours late and she wouldn't mind. 'It's no problem. Are you OK? This is the second one, isn't it? Anyone alive in there?'

'Not today, no.' He sighed. 'Such a waste. I hope we don't find any more.'

Helen nodded sympathetically, not really listening and instead wondering whether he was ever going to come to his senses and leave that useless cow wife of his.

'So ... is that OK with you then?' Doug was looking at Helen enquiringly.

'Oh God, sorry Doug. I was miles away,' she stammered. 'Is what OK?'

'To have the kids again for the rest of the week? After school? I just can't rely on Claire at the moment with all this going on.'

'Of course, no problem.'

'Superstar,' he said. 'I'd be lost without you. Thanks Helen, see you tomorrow and sorry you had to bring them here.'

Helen batted the air. 'Don't be silly, anytime. I love having them.'

She waved the kids goodbye and watched him walk away, ruffling Jude's hair and still carrying Christy who was limpet like.

Doug steered the children away from the scene and headed back to the station. As he passed by the news team, he overheard part of the broadcast being recorded.

'Today's container found no survivors with police estimating around another fifty victims. Police suspect this is a new wave of trafficking and are keen to establish the nationality of the two critically ill survivors from the first container.'

Doug took the kids into the station kitchen, produced the biscuit jar and put it in front of them.

'Five minutes,' he said, eyeballing them both. 'I'll be back in five and I expect at least some of these to be left ...' He left the kids arguing and went into his office.

He opened a search engine and typed in 'attack, rape, beaten, woman, Hastings'. He struck lucky. There was a local news story that had to be about Jesse. The article was short; police called to an address in Hastings where a woman had been savagely raped and beaten and left for dead. The woman had rung the police and the phone line had been open during the attack. It described life-changing injuries and said police had no immediate suspects. Doug sat for a while thinking about Jesse. If this was her, this would certainly explain a lot.

He could hear the kids arguing and switched off the computer. He went into the kitchen in time to witness the last biscuit being eaten by a triumphant Jude.

'Time to go,' Doug said, holding open the door.

* * *

Bob headed in the main door of the residential home, a newspaper tucked under his arm. He stopped to chat to a nurse who was passing by. She was attractive, in her late fifties with a wide smile.

'Hey Bob. Terrible business that container thing. We did think of you, wasn't there another one today?'

Bob smiled at her, Julie was his favourite nurse at the home. 'Hi Jules. I didn't bring it in, but I was down with it later helping out when they opened it. Awful thing to see. Today's was no better. No survivors at all. Breaks your heart ... So, how is he today?'

Julie frowned. 'He's the same, my love. That boy has something on his mind, and he won't let it go, and you won't like it, not one bit. He's out on the veranda. I'll bring you a cuppa in a minute, OK?'

Bob looked across the room through glass doors and saw Billy out in the fresh air, wrapped up in a blanket.

'Thanks, Jules,' he said.

Billy sat in his wheelchair. As Bob arrived Billy raised a finger in greeting. Bob sat down on a bench next to him. There was a very faint line of dribble on Billy's chin from a corner of his mouth.

'Alright Bill? What've you been up to then?'

Billy struggled to respond. He found it so frustrating to try and talk since his stroke, but his speech therapist said he was making progress.

'This and that,' he mumbled.

Bob said in a falsely jolly voice, 'You hear about those containers? Bet you're glad you weren't on duty. Silver linings, eh?'

Billy shook his head sadly. A tear ran down one cheek.

'Come on Bill,' he says gruffly. 'You'll be better soon. Back at the station. It just takes time ...'

Billy shook his head. 'No!' he said forcefully.

'Bill, I'm not going to listen to you being all maudlin. I've brought the paper, let's see what's been going on this week.'

Billy stared at Bob, his tears slowly falling. Julie appeared with tea in a mug for Bob and in a beaker for Billy.

'Here you go, boys. So, Bob, Billy asked me to help him write you a letter. Now it took us a wee while, didn't it love? But we got there in the end.'

Julie produced the note from her pocket and passed it to Bob. She leant forward to Bob and said quietly, 'I keep trying to talk him out of it. Now you've got to try.'

'Thanks, Julie. What's this then, Bill? Winning lottery numbers?'

Julie touched Billy softly on the arm and retreated back inside.

Bob read the letter, his face changing. His hand began to shake. 'You can't ask me to do this, Bill. It's not fair. You can't give up. I won't let you give up. I want you here. Not gone.'

Billy shook his head. 'Please Bob,' he mumbled.

He leant forward, clutched Billy's hand and said gruffly. 'You're my oldest friend. I won't do it. You can't ask me, it's not fair.'

Billy stared at Bob with a helpless expression. Bob turned away and shook the paper, blinking back the tears.

'So, what's the news? Developers are still trying to build on that bit of land up by the cove ... they'll be bloody lucky – more fancy houses no one can afford.'

99

Billy turned away, watching the evening roll in, a tear rolling down his cheek, while Bob continued to read the paper to him.

* * *

Jesse looked around Dr Marshall's room, noting that there were always fresh flowers on the table. Finally, Emma stepped in and closed the door.

'Jesse, sorry about that, how are you?'

Jesse folded her arms. 'I'm OK.'

'You were involved with the recovery of the container that was found, weren't you?'

'Yup. It's been a pretty horrendous couple of days. It's a sight that will stay with me for a while.'

'I'm happy to go through it if it will help, Jesse.'

Jesse frowned. 'Do you mind if we don't today?'

'That's fine. Tell me about something else. What's good that's happened?'

Jesse smiled. 'Er. What's good? I feel like I've got to know some of the crew a little better. I spent some time with the skipper after the container shout and it was nice to decompress with someone.'

Emma poured herself a glass of water. 'Tell me how do you decompress after something like that?'

'We had a pizza and watched the bay … talked about nothing. It was nice.'

'Nice in what way?'

'Nice in a unwind after a shitty day shared way. With someone that gets it. Nothing else.'

Emma watched Jesse over her glass. 'So, I'm interested, humour me here. Do you find your skipper attractive?'

'What sort of a question is that?' Jesse asked incredulously.

'It's an honest question.'

Jesse looked off into space. 'Umm, I like strong capable men, so I find that element attractive in him. Why are you asking me anyway?'

'Just curious. I thought it was interesting to see whether you'd thought about finding another man attractive.'

'I'd not really thought about it until you mentioned it,' Jesse said tightly. 'I don't want another relationship. Who would want me anyway? I'm too broken,' she said dismissively.

100

'OK. We'll come back to that comment. Tell me, how are the dreams?'

Jesse shrugged. 'Livable.'

'How do you think the other crew will be at coping with the container rescue?'

Jesse spent some time pondering.

'They've been through some fairly horrific stuff over the years, so I think they'll probably be fine.'

'Do you think you'll be fine?'

Jesse exhaled loudly. 'What is it they say? What doesn't break you makes you stronger? It's seeing the bodies come tumbling out – that's what I struggle with, but it's about learning to live with it and that memory will fade.'

'Sounds like you don't need me for this aspect,' Emma observed.

'When you do this job, you accept what you find, or you'd go mad trying to find reason behind why some people live and some die. Could you have done anything more? Got there quicker? Swum faster. So you just have to accept you did the best you could.'

Emma look surprised 'I think that's a very healthy way of looking at it. Very grounded and sensible. Although, I'm unclear as to why you can't be this grounded and sensible about your attack.'

Jesse looked annoyed 'What do you mean?'

'I just mean, to help you accept it a bit more. Know it wasn't necessarily your fault.'

Jesse snorted. 'It was my fault. I went back. Simple as that. I. Was. Stupid.'

'Think about this for a moment. Do you think he'd have attacked you eventually, even if you hadn't gone back that day?'

'Probably. He was too calm about me ending it. Yes, he probably would have.'

'Yet you continue to blame yourself, that somehow this was somehow your fault?'

Frowning, Jesse said. 'Well, ultimately it was my fault. I didn't see the psychopath lurking beneath the façade of a police officer.'

'Are you angry with yourself because you feel you should have seen it?'

'Jesus! Who wouldn't be angry they didn't see something like that? I've heard friends over the years talk about their partners cheating or doing certain things and they always seem to say …why didn't I see it? I've always listened to my gut feeling, you know that sixth sense – the thing that's says, this is gonna go pear-shaped, or don't do that it's going to end badly – but with Chris, I didn't get that sense at all.'

Emma looked surprised. 'You rarely mention him by name. You're normally much less polite in the way you refer to him.'

'I won't forgive him for this, ever. That sounds awful doesn't it? I like to think I'm a pretty decent person. But this? There's too much damage done. It's like these lovely people who have a child murdered or something like that – they're the nicest people you could ever know – but the trauma has ripped a hole in their soul so big, it can't be fixed. Proper broken as my grandad used to say.'

Emma moved to her desk to pick up a notebook. 'So, we need to look at some techniques used for helping people come to terms with their attacks. Now some people get closure from talking openly to their attackers about what they did. Face to face. Sometimes, they start with writing a letter to their attacker being honest about how they feel. Sometimes this letter never gets sent. For some it eventually moves onto meeting their attacker and it sometimes ends in forgiveness and closure, on both sides. Some people find the process very cathartic.'

Emma tapped her notebook against her hand and looked thoughtful. 'There are … err … other ways some people try and cope with attacks such as yours, but for some it can be almost as traumatic as the actual attack itself.'

Jesse looked angry. 'What? These are my options? Jesus Christ, if this is therapy, it sucks'

Emma held up her hands. 'OK, calm down. Let's unpick this a little more. What about if I said you could write a letter to him. How would you feel about that?'

Jesse looked incredulous. 'I'd say no fucking way!'

'Tell me, why not? We could agree never to send it.'

'I just don't want to,' Jesse said sharply.

'Explain to me why, Jesse.'

Jesse's voice cracked. 'Because it would mean I would have to think about it. I don't want to. With every fibre of my being, I don't want to.'

'Do you feel this way about hypnosis for example, tracking back to the attack? Tell me Jesse, are you afraid of what you might feel?'

Jesse stood, hands shaking. 'No. I'm not afraid of what I might feel. I know how I feel … I feel overwhelming rage, I feel like it's going to consume me sometimes. I don't want to open the door on it too much because I'm frightened of the sort of person this could turn me into.'

'Jesse, sit down,' Emma said softly.

Jesse remained standing. 'No. I don't want to talk about this anymore.'

'I really think we need to explore this, Jesse.'

'I can't do this today. I've got to go.'

Jesse walked to the door, her face flushed, slamming it shut behind her.

Emma sighed deeply and started to write notes.

CHAPTER 13

Jesse was upset after her session with Emma. She headed straight to the beach to clear her head. As she walked, she watched two children in the distance playing with a long piece of seaweed on a stalk. The boy was chasing a smaller girl, waving the seaweed around, and she was screaming with laughter. By a stack of large driftwood, a man had his back to the beach as he tried to get a beach fire going.

Jesse watched with amusement; the boy was merciless and the girl was laughing so much she was complaining of a stitch. Brock rushed over to the children. The boy dropped to his knees and made a huge fuss of him. The girl ran up to Jesse.

'Hello, you work with Dad, don't you? You took us home the other night. What's your dog called?'

'Hello. Very impressive memory. He's called Brock.' Jesse said grinning.

Christy stroked Brock. 'Hello, Brockie. I'm OK, are you having sausages with us?'

Jesse looked surprised. 'Err, no … I'm just here walking … Is your mum here?'

Christy turned and looked at her like she was a moron. 'No, Mum's at work, she's always there. Come on! Dad!' She grabbed Jesse's hand, dragging her towards the man by the fire.

'Dad! Look!!'

Doug turned around and stood up.

'Hello!' he said in surprise. 'Have the kids kidnapped you or the dog?' he said looking over Jesse's shoulder towards the dog who was on his back in ecstasy as Jude tickled his stomach.

'Oh, Christ,' he said, remembering the fire and turning back to it, prodding it with a stick.

Jude broke off from tickling the dog and frowned at Doug. 'Come on, Dad, I'm starving.'

Doug rolled his eyes. 'Hold your horses, nearly there.' He nudged Jesse. 'Kids have got no patience these days.'

Jesse was intrigued. 'Is this a regular thing? Cooking on the beach? Trying to light a fire?'

Doug pretended to look affronted. 'Trying? It's lit and yes, it's one of our regular things.'

Jesse watched the kids, playing with the dog, happy on the beach.

'It's nice ... a nice thing to do.'

Christy had sidled up to Doug and hung off his arm. 'Dad ... I'm starving ... can I eat these?' she asked, holding up a bag of marshmallows.

'No!' said Doug, laughing and grabbing the bag. 'Not yet anyway. Get the sausages out, come on, they can go on now.' He turned to Jesse. 'Why don't you stay with us and have a badly cooked hot dog and a sticky stick with marshmallow all over it? Yes? Come on? Who can resist?'

Jesse felt raw and emotional and knew she wouldn't be great company. For a moment, she didn't know what to do, how to say no without looking rude.

'Er, well, I should be getting back ...' she stammered.

Jude weighed in. 'Come on stay, I'm going to play with Brock. Come on Brockie.'

Jude and Christy ran off with the dog, throwing sticks for him.

Doug was scrabbling about in the cool box. 'Looks like the decision's made. Beer?' he asked, offering her a bottle of Moretti. He motioned to the picnic rug.

Jesse sat and leant against a large piece of driftwood. 'Thanks.'

Doug prodded the sausages and busied himself poking the fire. He looked up to see where the kids were and smiled at them off in the distance, playing with the dog.

'Don't expect to see him anytime soon,' said Doug dryly. He turned to Jesse. 'So, how are you after the container shout? Are you OK?'

'I'm OK. I do get some nights when all I can see is those poor people tumbling out, but I think I'm OK.'

She glanced at him. 'Are you OK? You opened it?'

Doug smiled ruefully and looked over her shoulder to see the children. 'Yes, I think I'm the same, when I'm not expecting it it'll creep up on me and I see the same thing.'

Jesse turned and looked out to sea, doing her best to avoid Doug's wolf-like stare. She took a breath and for a moment Doug thought she was talking to herself.

'Stuff like that stays with you for ages, though, doesn't it? It haunts you and sometimes you even think it's your fault. Doesn't matter how much you reason, there's always the doubt, could I have done something differently?'

'Jesse, we couldn't have done anything. You know that, right?' asked Doug frowning.

Jesse sighed. 'Yes, but when the darkness creeps in you think – what if we could have got it open when we found it? Would anyone else be alive now? You can't tell me you're not plagued by thoughts like that?'

Doug picked at the label on his beer bottle. 'I am, but you can't carry that around, it'll eat you alive. You have to get to a point where you think, "Enough, I can't think this anymore". After we lost Jeff and Gavin in the shout it almost drove me mad. It was my fault and I have to live with it. I question my decisions every day. If it wasn't for me, they'd still be alive, it was my fault ultimately.'

He looked away, swigging his beer, blinking furiously.

Jesse didn't miss a trick. This was a big thing for him to come out with and admit to. She said softly, 'I'm sure it wasn't your fault, Doug. I can't honestly see how it would be. Can you tell me what happened that day?'

'And ruin a perfectly good evening, by getting all maudlin and emotional? Another time, perhaps.'

'OK, I'll hold you to that,' she said sipping her beer. 'So, was that the boss at the station the other day?'

'Yup, a rare visit to tick the box and make the right noises. He wanted to make sure everyone was OK, you included.'

Jesse looked surprised. 'He doesn't know me.'

'He knows *of* you. He's just concerned for us, that's all. He'll probably send someone down anyway to have a chat with us all.'

Jesse, extremely uncomfortable at this prospect, refused to meet Doug's eye. 'Really? A chat about what? How we're feeling? Christ, I've had enough chats like that to last me a lifetime.'

Doug passed her another beer. 'What do you mean?'

Jesse hesitated, there was a part of her that felt she could talk to Doug …

Jude ran up, red in the face, closely followed by Christy and the dog. Jude flopped down covering Jesse with sand and wailed. 'Dad! I'm literally wasting away! Are they ready yet?'

Doug rolled his eyes. 'Your capacity for food amazes me, you just don't stop eating.'

'I'm a growing boy, Dad. Need all my strength,' he said, stealing a handful of marshmallows and cramming them into his mouth.

Doug passed the kids a hot dog each, both kids grabbed them and ran straight off with the dog.

Doug shouted at their retreating backs. 'Sit down to eat!' He turned to Jesse. 'God, I don't know why I bother.'

'That's falling on deaf ears, I think.' Jesse said wryly.

Doug laughed, passing Jesse a hot dog. They ate in silence for a while and Jesse said. 'I like the lads. They seem a really good bunch.'

'Do anything for anyone. A good crew. I'm very lucky.'

'I'm doing my best to win Bob over, but it's not going well,' Jesse said, smiling ruefully.

Doug prodded the fire. 'He's so close to Billy. Bob doesn't cope with loss or trauma, he's old school. His lost his wife to a very painful death a few years back and that changed him. Billy helped him through that. He won't talk about Billy. Keeps it all in and just gets mean and nasty. He doesn't like you because you're replacing Billy. He'd have hated whoever it was, so don't take it personally. He refuses to believe that Billy won't get better. He misses him around the station, we all do, it's not the same.'

'It must be difficult for him. Mike told me, Ben and Paul, they lost their uncle in the accident.'

'Yeah, Jeff was their uncle. They're a generation of lifeboat men. Jeff's dad was a lifeboat guy before he died.'

Jesse looked shocked. 'Did he die on a rescue too?'

Doug shook his head. 'He was lost at sea. He was a fisherman. Went out in a storm, never found.'

'Man, that's tough on them. Was that recent?'

Doug helped himself to another beer. 'About 10 years ago.'

'Were you here then? Out looking?'

Doug swigged his beer. 'Everyone was. For days it seemed. But when you work at sea, there's always a small part of you that expects to die at sea. You know it, you must have seen it doing this job. You talk to any fisherman or their family and there's a part of them that expects it. Old school fisherman, you know that have been doing it for years and years, say that if you take from the sea's bounty, she'll ask for something back at some point.'

Jesse nodded. 'I've heard that from the older guys over the years.'

Doug swigged his beer and fixed a marshmallow to a long skewer.

'So, has our resident Casanova, Tom, tried it on with you yet? Don't be afraid to tell him to bugger off.'

Jesse burst out laughing. 'I think I'm a bit old for him!'

Doug chuckled. 'You're female, easy on the eye if you don't mind me saying, and as far as we can see, single.'

Jesse looked angry. 'As far as we can see? Who's been discussing me?'

'Take it as a compliment, people are genuinely interested. We have a station of red-blooded males, most of whom have wives and collectively, they're nosier than a knitting circle when there's a pretty face around.'

Jesse snorted. 'How much time do you spend in knitting circles?'

'Ach, you know what I mean. It's perfectly normal for people to want to know about a new colleague. Especially in this job, where one life depends on another sometimes.'

'Why can't people just accept others and not be so intrusive?'

Doug leant back against a log. 'They're just trying to be friendly, inclusive, welcoming. You should chill out a bit, be less closed-off.'

'Is this you saying that I'm not chilled out or friendly?'

'Nope. I'm just saying let people in a bit, that's all. Share a bit of yourself.'

'I … find that hard to do … I don't want to … I struggle …' She stammered.

Doug handed her a toasted marshmallow. 'Sorry. I didn't mean to upset you.'

'It's fine, I'm just not used to …'

Doug prodded the fire. 'Look, don't worry about it. Where are the kids?'

Jesse scanned the beach. The kids and Brock were playing on the shoreline, with the dog happily retrieving sticks from the water. She munched on her marshmallow and licked her sticky fingers.

'I've been meaning to ask you. Why does one of the crew's pictures in the station have a massive fingerprint drawn on it?'

Doug chuckled. 'That's Mark, he helps out when he can, but he's pretty busy. He tries to come to training Sunday mornings, depends if his wife lets him out. We joke he's got a big thumb print of hers on his forehead.'

Jesse laughed. 'Ahh, suddenly it all becomes clear!'

He presented another marshmallow to Jesse. 'The screaming hordes will be back for the next course of this gastronomic feast in a minute. I'd get in while you can.'

'I like Dan. Poor guy always seems be working, is he a good cook?'

Doug picked bits of ash out of his marshmallow. 'Dan is a top bloke, great cook. He's a chef at that posh place on the hill. He's very unhappy at home, I think, which is why he's either at work or at the station – I guess he's getting away from it.'

Jesse took a breath and said quietly, 'Could the same could be said for you too?'

Doug stared at Jesse. 'Meaning?'

Jesse looked awkward. 'Sorry. I just meant you're at the station more than home, that along with something you said the other night.'

Doug didn't answer. He turned to fiddle with the fire adding more wood and stoking the flames.

'Let's do the kids' theirs,' Doug said brusquely, handing Jesse two skewers. He looked up the beach. 'Jesus Christ, look, they're bloody miles away.'

'It's fine. I'll just call the dog, they'll follow soon enough.'

Jesse whistled for Brock, who stopped instantly and turned, running full pelt back to Jesse, closely followed by the kids.

Doug looked in amazement. 'Can you train my two to do that please?'

As Jesse watched Jude and Christy squabbling over who would get the next marshmallow, she sat back against the log with the dog snuggled up, and, for the first time in a long time, realised she hadn't been scared or worried for the last hour or two.

We see her through the grass on the dunes. We keep low, we can't be seen, but we see her. She's sat with the skipper and his kids. We move around for a better ... a closer look. We need to see. We want to be close. The dog looks our way. She looks our way. It's OK, it's OK. She doesn't notice. She calms the dog. She doesn't know we are watching. We like it like that. We lie and we watch, we've got time ... We've got all the time in the world to watch her.

CHAPTER 14

Jesse ended the call, grabbed her keys and headed out of the door, Brock pushing past to be first out. She opened the car door for him, and he jumped in taking his usual place on the passenger seat. She drove up the coast road, pulling into the car park of a large Victorian house overlooking the bay.

She went into reception, Brock close on her heels, and a nurse appeared.

'Are you Julie?' asked Jesse. We spoke earlier? I've come to see Billy. Is it OK to bring him in?' She gestured to Brock.

'Of course it is. Animals are good for our patients. My, my, now you're a sight for sore eyes. Billy will love to meet you. What a gorgeous dog.'

Jesse looked around. 'So, it's OK to see Billy? I'll try not to upset him. I just want to have a chat with him.'

The nurse patted Jesse's arm. 'It'll be good for him. He just doesn't know it yet. I've told him you're coming. Bob's really the only one that visits these days, so it'll be a nice change for him. He's out on the verandah.'

Julie led the way outside. 'Billy? I've got a visitor for you.'

Billy was looking out to sea, huddled in a blanket against the wind. Jesse moved around in front of Billy where she dropped down to eye level with him.

'Hi Billy. I'm Jesse, this is Brock.' The dog approached and nuzzled Billy's hand. Billy stroked the dogs head gently with a shaky hand.

'So, we've not met before. I'm standing in for you at the station as the mechanic until you're back on your feet.'

Julie placed a hand on Billy's shoulder. 'Now Jesse, Billy mumbles a tiny bit, don't you my love? But you can make him out, so I'm off to get on with things. Any problems, come and get me.'

'Thank you, Julie,' Jesse said watching her go. She turned to Billy. 'She's lovely, isn't she?'

Billy nodded, his eyes wary. Brock rested his head on Billy's lap.

Billy struggled to speak. 'Lovely … dog.'

'He is, isn't he? I couldn't be without him now.'

Billy regarded her suspiciously. 'What … do … you … want?'

'Just a bit of wisdom. You know those engines in the station like the back of your hand and I just wanted to know what the quirks were … let's call it a later in life apprenticeship.'

Billy smiled, his whole face changing. Jesse struck while the iron was hot. 'I wanted to meet you. The boys talk about you a lot. Bob's really cross with me, he's horrified that I'm standing in for you and God forbid I'm a woman.'

Billy chuckled. 'He … is … cross … about everything … always been an idiot about women … at work.'

'It's so good to meet you, Billy. The boys love you and are always telling me tales of your escapades. They told me how brave you were on the night of that awful rescue.'

Billy's face clouded. 'I miss them … they … don't want to see me like this … It frightens them, reminds them they aren't … immortal.' He struggled with the last word.

'Maybe … perhaps it's that, but my grandad had a stroke and people didn't know what to say or how to be with him, so they kept away,' Jesse said remembering.

'Tell … me … about you.'

Jesse smiled. 'Well, normally I don't like to go on about myself at all, but since it's you, I will. I come from the south coast, Hastings. I was there just over ten years. They had a very similar set up to here – almost the same boat except we shore-launched there, same ribs etc – I used to fix the local fisherman's boats too, helped supplement the income and it helped them out a bit too.'

Billy nodded slowly. 'Why here?'

Jesse looked off into the distance, debating whether or not to be honest. 'Oh, you know. Change of scene. Needed to get away …'

Billy grunted and watched her with a beady eye. 'Sounds … like … you … ran … away.'

Jesse looked thoughtful. 'Maybe I did, Billy. Anyway, what's the deal with the small ILB rib engine? She's a cow and runs too rich, doesn't matter what I do I can't get her to run sweet.'

'Its … the … oil,' Billy said conspiratorially.

'I changed the oil!'

Billy waved a gnarly finger at her. 'She's fussy that one. Only … wants … top … quality oil … no cheap stuff …'

'Oh… that little princess. Right, I'll try again.'

'What else?' asked Billy.

Jesse leant forward. 'You know the guy standing in for you before me? Tim?'

Billy nodded.

'Was he any good?'

Billy rolled his eyes. 'He was … as stupid as a … rock. Father was too.'

Jesse whispered. 'He told me he serviced the main boat and had a load of bits left over …'

Billy looked worried. 'Really?'

'Really. So, I have an idea, do you fancy coming down to the station for a couple of hours and helping me out? You'd be doing me a big favour. Telling me what's what? Julie says they can drop you down in the minibus and pick you up again?'

Billy observed her silently, absently stroking the dog's head. 'Got … it … all … planned? Bob's idea?'

Jesse laughed. 'Bob? Jesus no. Bob hates me … really. He can't even bear to be in the same room. I need your help, just cause you're in a chair doesn't mean you can't point, say yes and no or give me some advice? No?'

Billy was quiet for a while.

'Billy, I'm not asking if you'll move in with me,' said Jesse, exasperated. 'I just want to borrow your brain for a few hours with you attached.'

Billy held up a gnarly finger. 'One condition.'

Jesse sighed theatrically. 'OK then, what's the condition?'

Billy gave a crooked smile. 'The dog … comes too.'

Jesse pretended to think.

'Done,' she said.

Julie appeared. 'Sorry to break this up, but Billy's got physio now, alright love?'

'So, Billy's gonna come down to the station and give me a hand – aren't you Billy?'

Billy nodded. 'Seems so.'

Julie stood behind Bill's wheelchair and let the brake off, giving Jesse a huge wink as she did.

'Well, that's great news, we're doing a drop off in town tomorrow at the harbour for some of the other residents for 10 a.m., pick up at 1 p.m. Does that work for you two?'

Jesse looked down at Billy questioningly. 'Works for me. Work for you Billy?'

Billy looked emotional. 'Works for me,' he croaked.

'Great, see you tomorrow then.'

Jesse watched Julie wheel Billy back inside.

'Mission accomplished,' she whispered to Brock.

* * *

Jimmy sat in the Hope and Anchor; he didn't want to go home yet. Marie would just have a go at him, and he'd had enough of that. He sipped the dregs of the pint he'd been eking out over the last hour. His mobile, currently residing in a small puddle of beer, rang loudly.

'Hello?' Jimmy turned away from the bar in an attempt to not be overheard, wiping the phone on his jeans. 'Where's that? When? And I'll be paid, yes? I'm not doing it otherwise. OK. Six o'clock. Yes, I'll have it.'

Jimmy ended the call. Thank God for that, he thought. His money situation was getting dire and he was convinced they were going to be chucked out of the house. He had people chasing him for money he owed too. He placed the glass down on the bar and nodded to Dylan, the local postman, who took the odd shift working behind the bar.

'Cheers mate, see you later.'

Jimmy arrived at his lock-up. He loaded the crates onto the flatbed of the truck, covered them with a tarpaulin and drove off. He swung into a car park, got out and paced about, smoking. He was nervous. He neither liked nor trusted this lot. In truth, they scared the absolute crap out of him, but it was important not to look scared or they'd eat him for breakfast.

Jimmy heard a vehicle in the distance. He straightened up and looked expectantly. A large black Ford van stopped next to Jimmy and a bald muscular man, covered in tattoos, leant out. He had a strong eastern European accent.

'Jimmy?'

Jimmy nodded warily.

'You have something for me?'

Jimmy raised his chin in defiance.

'You have something for me?'

The tattooed man gestured to the back of the truck. 'Once in the truck, then you get.'

Jimmy stepped back, folding his arms. 'No, I'll have it now and then it goes in the truck.'

He gave the tattooed man what he hoped was a hard stare that meant no messing. The tattooed man shook his head.

'Look mate,' Jimmy said roughly. 'Stop dicking me about. I just want to get my money and get rid of this. Get your arse out of there with the cash and this can go in the back and we can go our separate ways.'

The tattooed man regarded Jimmy. He took his time lighting a cigarette and then took an enormous drag and shrugged.

'OK ...'

Jimmy almost dropped to his knees with relief. He was terrified of this crew, but he hoped his approach of acting tough had commanded some sort of respect. The tattooed man chucked a bulky envelope out of the window. Jimmy caught it awkwardly and checked inside. It was full of cash. Jimmy could hardly contain himself. All he wanted to do was take the cash and get home to Marie, but he still wasn't quite sure how he was going to explain how he got it.

The tattooed man gestured with his thumb. 'You put crates in the back.'

Jimmy stuffed the money in his jeans pocket. He shoved the crates in the back of the truck, stood back and nodded to the tattooed man.

'Done?'

'Yes. Only three.'

The tattooed man nodded. 'OK. Alexy pick you up tonight at sea. Same place. 8 p.m. Then we do same again? Yes? We meet here when it's OK?'

'Eight o'clock. I'll be here,' Jimmy said firmly.

The tattooed man regarded Jimmy silently and then grinned widely. 'See you again, my friend. And we can maybe, how you say ... dick about some more? I like that very much.' He laughed loudly, put the truck into gear and drove off.

Jimmy leant against the cab of his truck and exhaled loudly. Christ what a relief, he was sure he was going to be killed at some point by this lot. He got the money out again and inspected it closely. He almost couldn't quite believe his luck. All this cash for a bit of cloak and dagger. He looked at his watch and hurriedly climbed into his truck and drove off, grinning widely and whistling tunelessly.

Jimmy locked the door to the cottage. Marie was at work and wouldn't be home until well after closing time. He checked his watch and headed off to the harbour whistling happily. He had left the money on the kitchen table together with a note that said, *'Got some work tonight in the boat. Be back tomorrow night, so don't go calling anyone! I'll be late – put this somewhere safe ... don't spend it all, love J.'*

CHAPTER 15

Jimmy was sweating despite the cool morning air. This was always the worst bit, the transfer, and the risk of being caught. He stood on deck as the large boat drew up alongside his. A few men appeared from the bowels of the boat, quickly transferred the ten crates onto Jimmy's boat, and retreated below decks again. The large boat powered away in the pre-dawn gloom.

Jimmy watched them go with relief. He busied himself stacking the crates and covered them with an old tarpaulin. He surveyed his work. That would do if he got stopped by anyone, he thought. He started to pull up his lobster pots. He figured he had to at least go back with something that vaguely looked like it came from the sea.

* * *

Doug looked out of his office window. He'd just called Helen the childminder to have the kids after school for the rest of the week. Claire had announced that morning she was unlikely to be around. Despite Doug's best efforts she refused to engage with him. But Doug had not given up. He couldn't forget the night they spent together, how she had been, what they'd talked about.

It was their anniversary in a few days, and he had plans; he'd created a pretext he was on a course that day just to get her to come home. He planned to talk again that night, try to build more bridges.

The landline on Doug's desk rang shrilly. Doug put it on loudspeaker so he could carry on watching for the seal that had been swimming around the station that morning.

'Doug Brodie ...'

A voice came over the speaker, loud and tinny. 'Doug ... It's Stuart. You OK?'

'Aye. What's up?'

'Another container has turned up.'

Doug turned. 'Jesus! How many are we gonna find? Where is it?'

'I know. Pendine Beach this time.'

'Shit. That's a busy old stretch. Do you need us there?'

'No. The RAF are picking it up now and taking it up to an MOD hanger, away from the press. Apparently, it's bigger than the other two. I almost don't want to know what's in there.'

'Do you need us to do anything?'

'Not at the moment. I've heard that the Home Office suits are trying to muscle in, but that's just a rumour. But you know how these rumours become reality. No smoke without fire and all that.'

'Great, all we need are a load of spooks getting involved. OK, keep me in the loop, yes? And I'll put the word out to the local sailors and fisherman to be aware.'

'OK, take it easy, Doug. Speak soon.'

Doug ended the call and rang Steve, the local police inspector, known to everyone locally as Steve the copper. He tutted when it went to answerphone and left a message asking Steve to swing by the station or give him a call.

Doug was juggling a bacon sandwich and the hottest cup of coffee he'd ever had in a takeaway cup, when he almost ran into Steve outside Maggie's beach café.

Steve said wryly, 'That looks hot. You rang?'

Doug smiled at him. 'Do you want anything?' he said, gesturing to the café.

Steve shook his head. 'No time. What's up?'

'Did you hear we had another container found on Pendine this morning?'

'Yup. They've just taken it off to the MOD range.'

'I'm guessing they know what they're going to find. Out of interest, what are you hearing? Boss says the Home Office are getting involved.'

Steve leant forward conspiratorially. 'Yeah, I'm hearing that too. Latest is that the last two containers were full of Albanians, well mainly. Suspected trafficking ring. The young guy you found said they'd been promised work in Bristol, London and Manchester. They genuinely believed that.'

'We thought it had to be something like that.'

Steve checked over his shoulder. 'This is why the spooks are getting involved. I think they might be crapping themselves because they've somehow missed this massive trafficking ring and people are going to start asking why they didn't know about it. Apparently, there's been an increase in some of the larger cities with quite a few Albanians dead; well, suspected to be Albanian or Lithuanian. Unexplained deaths, no ID. All of them a certain look and style to them.'

Doug frowned. 'What is it? Drugs, prostitution?'

Steve sighed. 'And then some. These people are used like a currency. Doesn't bear thinking about.'

'Do you think the latest one is the same?'

Steve shrugged. 'Only exception is that this container was larger than the others. It might mean there's more of them in there. I'll let you know when I hear anything.'

Steve glanced at his watch. 'Sorry, gotta go.'

'OK. Appreciate it, see you later mate.'

Jesse was in the harbour waiting. Brock sat patiently at her heel. She saw a minibus turn into the car park. The driver got out and pulled out a ramp. Jesse waved to Billy as he manoeuvred his electric wheelchair down it.

'Hey Billy. You've got yourself new wheels since yesterday.'

Billy chuckled. 'These are my ... going out wheels ... don't use them that much.'

'Well, you do now. Come on then.'

She turned and strolled around the corner to the station, with Billy following and Brock trotting happily beside him. Jesse opened the door for Billy.

'Billy, are you OK to go down in the lift?'

Billy nodded and Jesse helped him into the lift. Brock had trotted down to the lower levels and was sat by the lift doors waiting for them. Jesse went to clear Billy a space at the end of a workbench. She passed him a box.

'What's this?'

'This is what Tim said he had left over from servicing the main boat.'

Billy stared into the contents of the box horrified. 'All ... of ... this?'

Jesse nodded deadpan. 'Yup ... bad, huh?'

Billy face registered disbelief.

'But they can't ... use the boat ... In case ...' Billy began.

Jesse could contain herself no longer. 'I'm kidding!'

It took Billy a minute and then he started to laugh, setting Jesse off again.

Jesse nudged him. 'I got you ...'

The two spent an enjoyable few hours together, with Jesse quizzing Billy on various things and pretending she needed help on other more complicated things.

'Billy?' a voice exclaimed.

Billy turned and looked delighted to see Doug. 'Doug ... so ... good ... to ... see you.'

Doug grasped Billy's shoulder and looked into the face of his old friend.

'You look good Billy, sorry I've not been up in a while. What are you doing here?'

'I had a visitor at the home yesterday. Some bossy female ... wanted advice. From an expert.'

Jesse interjected. 'That would be me ... the bossy one.'

Billy chortled. 'Also, I wanted to see the dog again ... so I said yes.'

'Seduced by the dog, eh Bill?'

'Something ... like that.'

He clutched Doug's hand, his eyes filling with tears. 'You … are … you OK? You were … in a bad … way? I couldn't … have lost you too … Doug, we'd have looked all night for you.'

Doug looked as if he was going to fill up too and glanced at Jesse, looking embarrassed.

'Aye, I'm fine Billy. Tell me how you've been. It's good to see you here.'

'Things are …' Billy struggled. The shrill of the alarm broke the silence. Doug looked at Billy. 'Sorry mate, gotta go … catch you later.'

Feet clattered on the stairs and Bob appeared in the workshop.

'Billy? What you doing here? What are you doing with her?' he asked, giving Jesse a hostile glare.

Billy smiled gently at him. 'I'm helping out. We're … friends now … aren't we Jesse?' he said winking at her.

'Yes, we are Billy. Are you going out Bob or do you want to stay with Bill – he's due back in the harbour in an hour or so for his bus.'

Bob looked grumpy. 'Of course I'm going to stay with him!'

Jesse ignored Bob. 'Billy, are you OK keeping an eye on Brock? Just leave him down here, he'll be fine. Or do you want to take him back with you and I'll pick him up later?'

Billy stroked the dog's head.

'I'll take him … with me … see you … later then.'

Jesse sprinted upstairs and met the rest of the crew arriving. The alarm for the roller shutter rang out shrilly and the crew got on board and launched the boat.

The station was quiet. Bob turned to Billy and shouted, jabbing a shaking finger at him.

'A week ago you asked me to help you die, and today you're down here getting all chummy with her. What the bloody hell has changed in the last few days that makes you think differently? Why are you friendly with her all of a sudden? What did she do that I didn't, Billy?'

Billy watched his oldest friend. He sighed heavily. 'She saw … me … not the stroke … not the chair … she saw me, Bob. She gave me a … reason to … feel useful … to … want to get … up in the morning.'

Bob looked crushed.

'I'm sorry, Bob … I'm tired … can you help me to the harbour please? They're picking me up soon.'

Bob walked with Billy and Brock around to the harbour and waited until the minibus came. He watched Billy wheel himself up the ramp with Brock at his side and then managed a half wave as the minibus shut its doors and headed off.

He didn't know how to feel about today. He was kicking himself about why he hadn't made him come to the station, and how that girl had managed it instead of him. He shook his head. He was so angry, but he wasn't sure who he was angrier with; Jesse, Billy or himself.

CHAPTER 16

Jesse was less than enthusiastic about seeing Emma again.

'Hello, Jesse, sit please.'

Jesse frowned slightly at Emma's brisk tone and sat down.

'OK, so are things quieter since the container?'

'We found two more, same deal. No one alive this time. I can't bear it. We're trying to work out where they've come from.'

'Any thoughts?'

Jesse shook her head. 'Nope.'

'OK. How are you getting on with the crew?'

'Good. Really good. I really feel like I'm beginning to be part of a team. I'm getting to know some of them really well and that's nice.'

'How does it make you feel?'

Jesse thought for a moment. 'Err ... it makes me feel less ... cast adrift ... a bit more anchored, I think if that's the right word.'

'Are you particularly close to anyone now that a bit more time has passed?'

Jesse smiled 'They're all lovely. I tend to spend more time with Doug mainly because we're the only two that are full time at the station.'

'Doug, the skipper? Is that a good thing?'

'Yes, he's a good guy to be around. He has his own demons to deal with.'

Emma raised an eyebrow. 'How so?'

Jesse shrugged not wanting to share Doug's private life. 'Just issues in his personal life, I think. We had a good night the other night at the beach, quite by accident. He was there with the kids, made me feel welcome, so I stuck around and we had a good chat. It was nice.'

'I saw you there,' Emma said absently.

Jesse looked surprised. 'What? On the beach? I didn't see you.'

'I saw you sitting with a guy by a fire chatting. You looked like you were having fun.'

'Why didn't you come and say hi?'

'Well, I don't tend to because then people have to explain who I am, and it can be difficult.'

'That's weird. I didn't see you, there weren't that many people around.'

'I was running. Easy to blend in with the crowd. Well, that's good to hear. Are you friends? Or … more than friends?'

Jesse frowned. 'He's my skipper and yes, I think he's a friend now.'

'Do you see him as anything more?'

Jesse blushed. 'He's married! He has a family. That's against the rules.'

'Your rules?'

'My rules,' Jesse said firmly.

'OK. I want to focus on the dreams and how you feel about those. Have you had any more?'

'A few. Different though.'

'In what way?'

'In the last dream, I had something in my hand under the covers and when he leaned into talk to me, I hit him with it.'

'Hmm … interesting. That could mean you're feeling more in control. That's your subconscious working. What happened?'

'I woke up.'

'What do you think would have happened if you hadn't woken? Do you think he would have got control and used your weapon against you?'

'I … I don't know.'

'In reality, would that be a likely scenario?'

Jesse sighed heavily. 'Probably. But I don't want to think about it.'

'Why not?'

'Because it frightens me.'

'Ok. I think we need to work more on feeling in control and being less frightened. Tell me, when do you feel frightened these days?'

'Odd times, I think. No real pattern. Umm, maybe when I realise I'm alone in the woods or on the beach. I've had some odd sensations of not being alone. Creepy really. I was in the woods last week, it was a beautiful day and suddenly I felt frightened. I felt like I was being watched. Dog went all funny too. So it's not when I'm at home or at the station. More when I'm out and about, I suppose.'

'So, that's when you feel vulnerable?'

'I guess so.'

'And was there anyone there?'

'I don't know. I got a really strong sense that there was, though. I … think I … saw …'

'What?'

'Nah, being silly.'

'Come on. What did you think you saw?'

'I thought I saw a flash of something, like binoculars or a lens catching the sun … silly really.'

'Maybe. Maybe not. OK, I think we need to spend some time looking at ways to try and move on from the attack. This might help you feel less vulnerable and perhaps reduce the rage you feel.'

'If you're going to suggest writing a letter or something like that again, then forget it. I keep saying no, and you aren't listening,' Jesse said angrily.

'I'm listening, Jesse. But we need to try something otherwise this will rule your life. So please. How about we start with a simple exercise?'

Jesse crossed her arms defensively. 'Depends what it is.'

Emma leant forward. 'I want you to think carefully. On this pad I want you to write down four key words you would use to describe your attacker.'

Jesse said derisively, 'Just four? None of them will be polite. Jesus, what is the point of this?'

Emma held up a hand. 'Let's see where this goes.'

Jesse reluctantly took the pad and pen. 'I don't see what you're going to get out of this,' she said dismissively.

'Humour me, please.'

'I just don't want to go there.'

'You need to go there.'

Jesse wrote quickly and then threw down her pen. 'Done.'

Emma nodded. 'Good. On a different piece of paper, I want you to write four words that are the emotions you feel about the man who attacked you.'

Jesse picked up the pen again and scribbled quickly. 'Done.'

Emma sat back. 'OK. The first four please?'

'Psycho. Unhinged. Violent. Merciless.'

Emma raised her eyebrows. 'And the next four?'

'I couldn't do four, so I decided to use the same two twice. Rage. Anger.'

'OK. Do you feel your attacker robbed you of anything?'

'Yes, he did rob me of something. Something precious.'

'If you could say to him directly, this is what you robbed me of, what would you say?'

Jesse's jaw was set, and her eyes were hard. She folded her arms and stared at the ceiling, willing herself not to cry.

'He robbed me of children. He robbed me of everything I knew. I had to move away. Leave everything I knew and loved. He robbed me of a life.' She glared at Emma.

'Had you discussed having a family together?'

Jesse ran her hands through her hair. 'For fuck's sake, I don't see how that's relevant.'

'Everything is relevant here, Jesse. You haven't answered my question.'

'Yes. We had discussed it. Happy now?'

'You must have loved him a lot, Jesse, to consider starting a family together.'

Jesse looked out of the window. 'Time must be up now, surely?' she said.

Emma handed Jesse an envelope. 'I've got some homework for you. I want you to read this letter and think about the contents. Think you can manage that?'

'What is it? Oh, God. Who's it from?' She held the letter away from her like it was infected.

'Don't worry,' Emma said soothingly.

'It's a letter from another patient of mine. This is the letter she wrote to the man who attacked her. It took her nearly a fortnight to write it.'

'Why are you giving it to me?'

'There isn't anything you could identify her with in here, what I do want is for you to read it and realise how cathartic this can be. She said it was the best thing she ever did. We'll discuss it next time.'

Jesse moved towards the door. 'See you next time then.'

Emma had turned back to her desk by then and said over her shoulder, 'Bye, Jesse.'

Jesse stood for a moment, looking at Emma's back, and then closed the door.

* * *

Doug had been returning from picking up some training gear, and was about to head home, when he realised he'd left some paperwork in his office that he needed. He pulled into his space in the harbour and was about to head off to the station when Lenny, who ran one of the boat hire kiosks, called over to him.

'Doug … you got a minute?'

'You OK, Lenny?'

'Good, thanks. Look I just thought you ought to know I hired a boat to a bunch of idiots earlier.'

Doug chuckled. 'Now that's nothing unusual, is it?'

Lenny looked rueful. 'Umm, this is a stag lot, though. They had more money than sense and bags full of booze. They left about an hour ago, full of beer already, heading towards Kirby. They said they'd be back for six … just letting you know, well, in case, you know.'

Doug rolled his eyes. 'You telling me now in case I've got to go and get them later?' He slapped Lenny on the back.

Lenny looked guilty. 'Sorry, Doug.'

Doug laughed. 'All part of the service, picking up the odd idiot. Let's hope it doesn't come to it!'

Doug gave a small wave and walked off towards the station.

Doug was thoroughly enjoying himself. He'd cooked dinner for one of the brothers, Paul, and his wife Nicky and the kids. He'd given Claire plenty of notice of the event and had even stipulated he would cook. Once again, she'd cancelled blaming an emergency at work. They had eaten and were all sat around the dinner table laughing and joking when Doug felt his pager vibrate. He looked over at Paul, who was dragging his pager out of his pocket. Nicky rolled her eyes.

'Off you go,' she said grinning. 'I'll wait here until you get back, there are other ways to get out of the washing up, you know!'

Both men stood and Doug gave Nicky a quick peck on the cheek as he left. 'Thanks, Nick, you're a superstar.'

Doug drove quickly towards the harbour, stopping to pick up Tom who was running towards the station. Mike and Jesse were already climbing into their gear in the locker room.

Doug struggled into his gear. 'What is it, Mike?'

'It's a group of lads out of fuel in a pleasure boat. Idiots fell asleep and drifted into the fishing fields. Irish trawler called it in.'

'Christ almighty. Lenny told me earlier he'd rented a boat to a bunch of idiots today. How far did they get?'

'About twenty miles out. They've got no running lights – they were nearly mowed down by the trawler. Trawler only spotted it because they were waving their mobiles about.'

'Fuck's sake,' muttered Doug. 'There should be a law against renting boats to idiots. Launch in five.'

The lifeboat's huge spotlights made the small rented boat look like a toy against the massive trawler. The lifeboat blasted its horn twice, and the trawler returned the sound and departed as the lifeboat approached. The lifeboat pulled alongside the motorboat.

Mike murmured to Doug. 'This is definitely Lenny's boat.'

Doug leaned over from the top deck and shouted to the boys. 'Everyone OK? Anyone hurt? What happened?'

One of the young men, stood uncertainly and called up.

'Err, we ran out of fuel and fell asleep.'

Doug turned to the rest of the crew and muttered. 'Christ, is there an end to the stupidity of some people? Mike, Jesse, get these idiots on board, warm them up. We'll tow the boat back for Lenny.'

Doug called down to the small boat where the boys were huddled, shivering.

'We're going to get you on board and tow the boat back in.'

Jesse jumped down onto Lenny's boat with a length of rope and climbed to the front of the boat to secure the tow line, throwing the line back up to Mike who was waiting.

The crew helped the boys onto the larger boat and sent them below decks to warm up. Doug, happy that Lenny's boat was behaving itself and the tow line looked intact, went below deck where the lads were sat shivering wrapped in blankets, with red sunburnt faces.

He stood for a moment looking at them all, his face like thunder.

'I can't even begin to tell you how stupid you've all been today.'

One of the group looked affronted. 'Look ... we were just having—'

Doug pointed a finger at him. 'Shut it. I've not even started with you yet. Now listen up. You took a boat out, you got pissed, had no idea where you were going, left the engine running and then fell asleep and drifted into the fishing fields. How stupid are you? You could have all been killed. If that trawler had hit you, you would have died a horrible death. Your stupidity is staggering, so much so I'm going to send you a bill for coming out to get you tonight and for ruining my evening.'

The lad tried to speak, but Doug held up a hand. 'Don't interrupt me or I'll double it. If nothing else, you'll remember this for the wrong reasons. When we get to the harbour I don't want to see you again except for when you all turn up tomorrow morning to say sorry for being a bunch of stupid twats and to ask how much the bill is. Now let's recap. Who is going to go out on a boat again, get pissed, fall asleep and end up in the fishing lanes?'

The boys looked sheepish and none of them would meet Doug's eye. Doug eyed them all. 'Aye, thought not.'

He turned and went back up to the main deck.

The lifeboat chugged into the harbour and the boys climbed off it handing back their blankets and thanking the crew quietly. Doug looked down at the boys left on the quayside.

'I want to see you all 9.30 tomorrow morning. Lifeboat station, up by the castle. No exceptions.'

The boys nodded.

'Are we clear?' roared Doug, his face like thunder.

The boys looked shocked and mustered a series of 'Yes Sirs' and turned and shuffled back up the hill into town all looking very sunburnt and sore. Doug watched them go, chuckling, and called down to Bob who was at the controls.

'Home please, Bob.'

We've been watching the cottage through the windscreen. We see her arrive back walking along the road with the dog at her heels. She was just called out to a shout. She's back now. We see the dog catch a scent in the air and stand for a minute, ears up. Alert. We scoot down in our seat. She can't see us. We see her look around, talk to the dog softly and rub his ears. She opens the gate and front door and calls the dog in. He's reluctant to go. She stands in the doorway looking around frowning. Has she seen us? We can't be seen. We can watch, though — we can wait. Not for much longer, though, not for much longer.

☐

CHAPTER 17

A small red sports car ignored the call for twenty being plenty, and sped excessively through Lewes high street, screeching to a halt at the entrance to Lewes prison.

Inside the prison visitors' hall, men wearing grey jogging bottoms and grey T-shirts sat waiting. A prison officer unlocked a side door and a line of visitors filed in.

One man sat at a table on his own. He was tall, blond and extremely good looking. Around his arm was a yellow band, whereas many of the other inmates had either red or blue armbands. He appeared relaxed as he scanned the room. His eyes rested on a figure approaching him and he smiled broadly.

'Hello Sis, about bloody time. I'd almost given up on you.'

Dr Emma Marshall pulled the chair out, and sat down carefully, crossing her arms in front of her.

'Christopher. Being on remand agrees with you. You look well.' She studied the room before focusing on Chris, her eyes narrowing. 'Tell me, doesn't a yellow arm band mean you support gay love?'

Chris frowned at her. 'Fuck off, Emma. That's not even funny. Why the fuck haven't you come sooner?'

Emma brushed an imaginary speck of something off her sleeve.

'I'm busy. It's not like it's just around the corner.'

'Not because you couldn't be fucking bothered then is it?'

Emma leant forward and spoke angrily in a low voice. 'Don't push it. I can easily go again. I think you forget, baby brother, I'm doing all this for you.'

'You're doing all this for me, Emma, because I've given you no fucking choice, and we both know why.'

'It takes time. I can't just click my fingers and make it happen.'

Chris snorted. 'You've been doing this shit long enough, Emma. Come on, work the magic on the mind games.'

'This has to be done slowly and carefully. I can't work fucking miracles,' she hissed.

Chris looked around the room, worried about the guards overhearing. He held up his hands to placate her. 'OK. OK. Calm down.'

Emma looked annoyed. 'Why have I had to drag myself all the way down here?'

Chris jabbed a finger at her. 'I want to know how she is.'

Emma sat back in her chair, arms folded and said sarcastically. 'Oh, so despite you instructing me to make her life a living hell, *now* we're concerned about her welfare, are we?'

Chris narrowed his eyes. 'Just because I want her to suffer, it doesn't mean I don't love her. You know that. But she crossed me, so she has to pay and further down the line she'll understand that. I'll make her understand that. The fact of it is, all the time I'm here suffering because of her – she needs to be suffering because of me. Quite simple really.'

Emma watched her brother closely. 'I can assure you it's far from quite simple.'

'Don't be a fucking martyr about this.'

'I'm not,' she snapped. 'Look, it's a process. I have to get her to trust me first. Talk to her about how we can help her. Then I can start the real work. As I said, this is not an overnight job. Christ, you don't have to be a rocket scientist to figure it out.'

With a tremor of nervousness, she noticed the white line that had appeared around his mouth; the muscle jumping in his jaw, the large vein throbbing in his neck. His eyes glittered. These were the signs of one of his white-hot rages starting, rages where he was aware of nothing but hurting, beating, killing.

'You watch your fucking mouth, bitch. Older sister or not, I can still teach you a fucking lesson.'

Emma leant back in her chair, looking angry, but feeling fairly safe in the environment.

'Do you know what? I'm getting to the point where I don't care what you have over me. Threaten me all you like. Speak to me that way again and you can do the fucking job yourself. Oh wait – you can't can you? You're on remand for beating the absolute living shit out of people.'

Chris clenched his fists and banged them down on the table. One of the prison officers stepped forward. Chris held up his hands. 'Sorry, mate. Sorry. Won't happen again.'

He said quietly, 'Of course you care, you stupid bitch. You'd lose everything. The professional community finding out all about Dr Emma Marshall and her checkered past and nasty habits? They'd lock you up and throw away the key and that's just for what you did to William, not to mention the others. So, you'll fucking do what I say because you know I'll fuck you over if you don't. Now. I'm going mad in here. Tell me.'

Emma played with him. 'Tell you what?'

He looked at her murderously. 'Tell me how she is. Tell me *where* she is. Every detail. Every single thing.'

Emma shifted in her seat and inspected a fingernail. 'She's OK. Doing well considering. New crew, new life. All thanks to you. Oh, and she *really* hates you.'

'What's she said about me?'

Emma smirked. 'Umm, where to start? She'd quite like to kill you. She called you a variety of names the other day. What was it now? Oh yes – psycho, unhinged, violent, merciless.'

'So where is she?'

'No no no, dear brother. I think not. I'm not telling you that.'

'Why not?'

'Just because.'

'Do you think she's happy?'

'She's made progress. She's making friends.'

Chris's head snapped up instantly. 'What sort of friends?'

Emma rolled her eyes. 'People she works with, their families.'

Chris took a breath and said dangerously. 'Is she … seeing anyone?'

'I don't think so. She's close to her new skipper but he's married with a family and she won't go there.'

'You asked her?'

'Of course. She said no, it was against the rules.'

Chris nodded. 'Yup. She's always said stuff like that. Massive moral compass.'

He leant forward and jabbed the table. 'So, come on. Tick tock, tick tock. Work the magic. She needs to suffer. I want her to be so frightened she can't function properly. I want her to see me in dark corners everywhere. No one gets me banged up. Last bloke to try it ended up strangled in his cell. She needs to pay for what she did.'

Emma watched her brother. 'I always knew you were ruthless.'

Chris inclined his head as if he were receiving a compliment and said quietly, 'Look, I don't plan on staying in here for any length of time. She could easily put me away if she testifies with the other evidence, and I'm not fucking having that.' His eyes were cold. 'When I escape, Emma, if you've done your job right, my reunion with Jesse will be utterly … delicious.'

'You've already tried to kill her once and failed.'

'Oh, I'm not going to kill her. I want to have some fun with her. Reset the boundaries. Teach her a lesson. I want to break her. In every way possible. I want her so broken she'll never get over it. I want to hurt her like she's never been hurt before. Body and mind. I want to hurt her so much she'll wish she had fucking died. So, hurry the fuck along. It's not a bloody holiday on the Welsh coast you know. It didn't take me practically every fucking favour under the sun to get your name on the list of shrinks they could go to for her.'

'You need to learn to be patient,' Emma snapped. 'Court date yet?'

'That'll be ages away. Don't tell me to learn to be patient. I plan to be out before that if my plans come off.'

Emma leant forward and spoke quietly. 'How are your chats with the shrinks going?'

He lowered his voice. 'OK. I'm saying what you told me – been hamming it up a bit. I think they believe me. I might not need that if I'm getting out anyway.'

'What the hell makes you think you can escape prison?'

He looked at her arrogantly. 'Because I'm me, Emma. I can do anything I fucking want to – it just needs planning, execution and calling in a few favours. But we'll keep the other thing ticking over just in case it goes shit-shaped.'

Emma bit her lip for a moment. 'Whatever you think. If it doesn't look like it's happening, then maybe you need to really start with the other stuff we talked about …'

'I'll think about it.'

'We can't rush this, take your time with it. She'll take me ages anyway, she's a hard nut to crack.' Emma stood abruptly. 'I need to go. I hate these places. Remember what we talked about.'

She took her time to lean across the table and stroke her brother's face tenderly. 'Love you, little brother. Take care now. It'll all come good in the end. Trust me.'

Emma walked over to the prison officer, asked to be let out and left the room without a backwards glance.

CHAPTER 18

The warmth of the late afternoon sun gave the promise of a balmy evening ahead. Claire was perched on the kitchen worktop over the other side of the kitchen, drinking wine and texting.

'Tell me again why I have to come tonight?'

Doug sighed. 'I keep saying you don't "have" to come tonight.'

'What is it, some sort of fundraiser for the boat?'

'Jesus Claire, this is the sixth time you've asked me. People have been buying tickets all week and we'll do a bucket run too. Mainly for the station, but also for the two we pulled out of the container.'

Claire drank her wine. 'Can't I just chuck £20 in the bucket and not go?'

'I've bought a ticket for you anyway. Do you know what though? Do that. If it's that much of an unappealing prospect to come down, listen to some music and enjoy a night out then don't come. I thought it might be nice to do something as a family.'

Claire rolled her eyes. 'I hardly call sitting in a grotty pub, listening to some amateur singers spending quality time with the family. You don't need me there anyway, do you? You'll spend all night boring each other to death anyway about various rescues and you and your cronies won't even notice if I'm there or not.'

Claire continued drinking wine and texting.

'Look, we're going around in circles here, the kids want to go. But if the prospect is that unpleasant, spend the evening with your phone.' Doug said frustrated.

Doug watched her for a moment as she scrutinised her phone, which pinged as a series of texts arrived. She giggled as she read them, replying instantly. Doug tapped on the kitchen window.

'Kids – dinner!'

Both kids dropped what they were doing in the garden and ran in. Doug gave them a bowl of pasta each and a fork and pointed at the table.

Doug offered Claire a small bowl of pasta. She waved it away without a word and left the kitchen, still texting.

Jude piped up. 'Dad? Will Jesse be there tonight? Will she have Brock?'

'I don't know. I think so.'

'I love Brock. He's my favourite dog of all time. I quite like Jesse too,' Christy announced.

Claire re-appeared in the kitchen. 'Who on earth are Jesse and Brock?'

Doug replied. 'New mechanic and dog.'

Claire glanced up from her phone. 'Jesse's a weird name for a man.'

Jude laughed. 'Jesse's not a man, she's a girl!'

Claire's phone pinged again, and she left the kitchen. Jude watched her leave the room.

'Dad. Is Mum coming tonight? It's like she doesn't want to.'

Doug sighed. 'No mate. I don't think she's coming.'

'She never comes out anymore,' Jude said quietly then looked hopeful. 'Mike's playing tonight, isn't he?'

Doug rubbed Jude's arm. 'Yes, he is.'

Jude smiled. 'Dad, can I take the bucket around tonight and do some collecting? I might ask Tom if I can collect some glasses too – I've finished – please can I leave the table and go back outside?'

Doug nodded, amused at Jude's ability to cram a series of questions into a sentence without drawing breath.

Christy finished her dinner and scooted around the table to put her arms around Doug. 'He's upset, Dad,' she whispered. 'He said he doesn't think Mum wants to be with us anymore. I've told him not to be silly. He'd put it in his worry book, and we talked about it this morning. Can I collect with the bucket too please?'

Doug smiled. 'Yes, to buckets, no to glass collecting. Off you go.'

He was loading the dishwasher when Claire appeared in the kitchen again just as the doorbell went. She put her wine glass and phone down on the counter and went to answer it. Her phone pinged. Doug was putting something away in the cupboard above the phone. He looked down and saw the text.

Sounds perfect. I'll see you there. Looking forward to it. F. xx

Claire returned to the kitchen, holding Christy's coat. 'It was Helen, dropping off Christy's coat. She said she'd see you there later, why she couldn't have waited until then I don't know.'

'You had a text.'

Claire grabbed the phone and looked defensive. 'I'm going to meet a friend from work, her husband's away, I don't see her very often.'

Doug raised an eyebrow. 'Why's that?'

'Why's what?'

'Why don't you see her very often if she's at work. You spend more time there than here these days.'

Claire swigged more wine. 'What are you saying?'

Doug said in a tired and resigned way. 'You go. Have a fantastic time. Hope your friend is well.'

He walked over to the garden door. 'Kids! Come and get ready, we're going soon.'

Christy squeaked with excitement and ran in. 'I'm changing Daddy. I want to put my party frock on.'

'Go on then – as long as you don't take hours getting ready!'

Christy skipped off upstairs. Doug turned to Claire, who was texting again.

'Did you want me to come and pick you up later?'

Claire shook her head. 'No. Have a drink tonight. Are you on call?'

'No, the reserves are all on call tonight, the main crew have the night off.'

'So, you all have the night off and you choose to spend it all together anyway? *God*, you lot, you're all as thick as thieves.'

'And you're not doing that then, with your friend from work? When are you on shift again?'

'Not till Monday morning.'

'So … does that mean you'll be home …?'

Christy re-appeared in a pretty dress. She presented Doug with a hairbrush and a hairband.

'Please can I have Iona hair?'

Doug put on a serious face. 'OK. Remind me. Iona hair is the top bit in a band and the rest loose? Isn't that Izzy hair?'

Christy rolled her eyes and giggled. 'Dad … how many more times? Izzy hair is a ponytail on top of my head … Iona hair is this top bit in a band.'

Claire stepped forward putting her phone down. 'I'll do your hair, sweetie.'

Christy turned to her. 'It's OK, Mummy. Dad's very good at hair now. I told him he had to get better at it because you're never here to do it.'

Claire picked up her bag and phone. 'Well, I'm clearly not needed here,' she said tightly. 'So, I'll go.'

'Will you be home tomorrow?'

Ignoring him, Claire went to the back door and shouted to Jude.

'Bye Jude!' Jude made no effort to come and say goodbye, and stayed in the garden with his back to her. Claire shrugged and left, slamming the front door.

Doug watched her go.

Christy said. 'You didn't get a goodbye kiss from Mum, Dad. That's bad luck isn't it? That's what you always used to say.'

Doug gave a rueful smile. 'I did, didn't I? Right! Everyone ready?'

Doug put the kids in the back of the truck, and they set off. The truck trundled down the high street, and in the distance, Doug spied Jesse walking down the road with Brock at her heels. He pulled to a stop next to her. The passenger window was open, and Doug leaned towards it.

'Get in, come on I'll give you a lift.' Doug pushed the passenger door open. Brock jumped in straight away and licked Doug's face.

'Brock! Sorry! I hate it when he does that.'

Doug smiled. 'I'll take what I can get. It's nice that someone is pleased to see me these days.'

The kids chorused. 'Hello Jesse.'

Jesse wrestled the dog into the footwell.

She turned to Doug. 'Thanks for stopping. Is your wife not coming?'

The muscle twitched in Doug's jaw. 'Nope.'

Jesse's lips twitched. 'Ahh. I now know that's the correct code for "We're not discussing it".'

'Yup. You catch on quick. I like that.'

Jesse turned to the kids in the back. 'And how are you two?'

Christy jumped straight in. 'OK, thank you. Do you like my frock?'

'I love your frock. Very good hair too.'

Christy looked pleased. 'Thank you. Daddy did my hair. He's very good at hair.'

Jesse turned to look at Doug and raised an eyebrow. 'Are you wasting your talents? Should you be doing hair instead of rescuing poor souls?'

Dougs lips twitched.

Jude said proudly, 'I'm going to be collecting money and glasses tonight.'

Jesse looked impressed. 'Wow, lot of responsibility tonight then.'

Jude raised his chin. 'I can handle it. I'm old enough now.'

Christy said excitedly, 'We're here!'

Doug parked the truck and they got out, the dog nuzzling Doug's hand. Jesse smiled indulgently.

'He seems to like you a lot.'

'Impeccable taste …'

The four of them walked down towards the harbour, handing their tickets over as they approached the entrance to the music area.

Doug turned to Jesse. 'First things first. What are you drinking?'

'Oh thanks, a beer, whatever they've got.'

'OK, and a Coke for you,' he said, looking at Jude. 'Christy, will you be wanting your usual?'

Christy nodded.

'She has a usual?' asked Jesse.

'Oh yeah. The all-important bag of crisps. Go grab a table?'

Doug queued up at the bar, nodding and chatting to people he knew as he passed by.

Jesse had picked a bench and sat with the dog and the kids. She saw Tom serving customers and waved.

Doug returned with a tray of drinks. Jesse picked up her beer. 'Thanks for this and for the lift.'

'It's no problem. Good to see you here. The lads will be pleased. This is important to them.'

Mike appeared and clapped Doug on the shoulder.

'Hey, skip. How you doing? Jesse, good to see you here.' He turned to the kids. 'Which one of you two is going to give me a big hug?'

Jude shuddered. 'Ugh, not me.'

Christy giggled. 'I'll give you a huggle!'

Mike held out his arms. 'A huggle is a new one on me. Do you think I'll like it?'

'Of course, you will. I'm the best huggler around,' said Christy, giggling.

'How's it going? All set up?' Doug asked.

'Yeah. We're good to go. Couple of other guys doing sets so it should be a good night.' He turned to look at the small stage where a happy looking bald man had stepped up to the microphone to do a sound check.

'Mike to report to the main stage. Repeat … Mike to report to the main stage. Your mum says your tea's ready.'

Mike turned around and gave the finger surreptitiously to the man on stage, who burst out laughing.

After giving Christy a final hug, Mike headed off. Jude, who had disappeared for a moment, re-appeared saying breathlessly, 'Dad, Tom's got the buckets behind the bar so I'm going off to start collecting, is that OK?'

Christy jumped up. 'I want to go too, Dad?'

Doug said firmly. 'OK, listen. Get a bucket each. Do not, repeat, do not leave this area for anything. Keep coming by me so I can see you, OK? Are we clear? The minute that doesn't happen is the minute this stops. Yes?'

The kids nodded solemnly and then ran over to get a bucket from Tom.

Jesse watched them go. 'Those kids of yours are lovely.'

'Umm, they're great. They have their moments though. Jude's pretty upset about Claire today. He thinks she doesn't want to spend any time with him. He wanted her to come tonight.'

Tom appeared at Doug's elbow and placed a drink down for each of them.

'On the house guys – gotta go!'

Both Jesse and Doug looked surprised. 'Cheers mate,' he said.

Jesse called after him. 'Thanks, Tom.' She focused back on Doug. 'So why didn't she come tonight?'

Doug thought for a minute. 'She just didn't want to. Got a better offer it seemed.'

'You OK with that?'

Doug looked thoughtful and picked up his beer. 'I don't know anymore. I'm annoyed more than anything, I think,' he said, taking a mouthful of his drink.

There was a round of applause, cat calls and whoops and Mike stepped out onto the stage, his guitar slung behind him.

'Good evening everyone ...' A very loud wolf whistle cut him off. Mike laughed 'Alright Mum, calm it down.' The crowd laughed.

'As I said, good evening everyone and welcome to the lifeboat fundraiser. We can't thank you enough for buying tickets and coming out tonight to hear some slightly questionable music being played.'

The crowd laughed and whooped again.

'So, we're raising money. Not just for the lifeboat, which keeps you all safe at sea, and comes to get you when you've forgotten about the tide.' He leaned into the microphone. 'You know who you are Mr Davies – but we're also going to try and raise some money for the poor folk we pulled out of the container a few weeks ago. Both of them are still in hospital so we want to be able to at least give them something, as they have nothing at all. So ... without further ado I'd like to introduce you to the best duo in the area ... give it up for Woodface!'

Amid much cheering, the duo appeared and began playing. A couple approached the picnic bench where Jesse and Doug sat and asked if they could share it. Jesse moved around to sit next to Doug, facing the band.

'What did you mean? Just now ... when you said you didn't know any more about Claire.'

'Nothing really.'

'Come on, Doug. What is it you said to me? Share a bit of yourself?'

Doug snorted. 'I'm not really the sharing type.'

Jesse looked over at the band and took a sip of beer. 'Then once again, we have something in common.'

The kids came past Doug shaking their rapidly filling buckets. Doug and Jesse were sat close together so as to be able to speak and hear each other.

After a while Doug said, 'OK. I'm sharing. I'm worried about the kids and whatever this is with Claire.'

'So what worries you with the kids?' Jesse prompted.

'It's just … like … certain comments they make without them thinking about it. I've realised they don't expect Claire to be there for anything these days. That's not right, is it?'

'Have you talked to Claire about it?'

Doug looked away. 'Most of the time, she's never around long enough to have a discussion. She avoids it. We had a great chat the other night and she promised to try and make it home more, but it's like we never discussed it now. She's often gunning for an argument. I get such a strong sense she'd rather be anywhere else but here with us and that fighting is a handy excuse to go. The thing that bothers me, though, is that the kids don't realise how much they've got used to it. It's like they don't seem to miss her being around, it's like they've accepted it. I think that's a bad thing.'

Jesse took another swig of beer and said thoughtfully. 'Surely that depends how you look at it.'

'What do you mean?'

'I mean, think about it this way. Could it be a blessing they feel this way? Because if things are so broken they can't be fixed, and you're just putting off the inevitable end to it all, then it's going to be easier for them in the long run because they've gotten used to it. But then you have to wonder, is this situation a wakeup call for you all to re-assess where you are with the whole setup.'

'The whole setup?' he said dryly.

'You know, you, her, the kids, her never being around. Is it all of you she avoids? Or just you, or just the kids? I mean … how is she with you?' she finished awkwardly.

Doug gave a bark of laughter. 'Jesus … there's sharing and there's sharing …'

'Consider it good therapy …'

Doug thought and said quietly. 'If you'd have asked me a couple of weeks back, I'd have said great. But then, that was based on one evening. If I'm truthful, and I almost don't want to say this out loud because then it makes it real, it's been really different for a while now. This thing we had – it was us against the world, you know? We'd find something funny in almost every situation … we'd know what we were thinking … we were tight, really tight. We've not been that way for a long time now. It's not a sudden thing … it's been a gradual thing, since before the accident.'

Jesse was quiet for a moment. 'Do you think you've been pushing her away or has she or is it a mix of both?'

Doug rubbed his face and sighed deeply. 'It was my fault. It was the accident. Claire had been odd before that, but I think the accident changed how she felt about me. I could see it in her eyes.'

'In what way? Was she scared of losing you?'

Doug shook his head and said wryly. 'Claire's not scared of anything. But it was like she saw me as a different person. I don't know … broken maybe … weak. She'd always been cool with what I did. Now she thinks it's a job for a loser … she thinks it's unimportant and we spend all day helping grannies paddle in the shallows and teenagers on surfboards that have had too much weed.'

Jesse looked affronted. 'That belittles us all then, doesn't it, and the risks we take?'

'No … I think it's just me. I think I'm not the man she wants me to be. But I think she doesn't know what that is. She struggled when I was in hospital; the kids needed her and she found it hard to juggle the two, her job and them.'

'I hear you were in bad shape – really bad shape. Touch and go.'

Doug was quiet for a second.

'Apparently so. I don't remember much of it. I just remember the most almighty pain and then nothing else really. But I remember coming home and Claire being different. It was like she was angry with me for something.'

Jesse frowned. 'Was she frightened she might have come close to losing you?'

'No, I think it was something else, it was like she resented me somehow.'

Doug stopped and looked for the children.

'Resented you for what?'

'I just don't know.'

The band finished their set and announced a short break amidst loud applauding. In the distance the kids were still rattling buckets and looking happy.

Next to the bar, staffed by Tom, Paul was busying himself on a large barbecue borrowed from the lifeboat station, selling burgers and hot dogs. His wife, Nicky, was helping out too, making sure it was all edible. She had been watching Doug since he'd arrived earlier with Jesse and the kids. She was pleased to see Claire hadn't bothered to come, in her view, the bloody woman was never around for anything. Always too busy at work. Never there for her husband and kids, just lived for her job. A selfish cow was how Nicky described her most of the time.

Nicky was pleased to see Jesse and Doug sitting closely together chatting happily and sharing a laugh. It was nice to see Doug smiling and enjoying himself. She nudged Paul who was busy prodding sausages into submission and gestured with her chin towards Jesse and Doug.

'Check it out. Over there.'

Paul looked blank. 'What am I looking at?'

Nicky rolled her eyes. 'Jesse and Doug.'

'Oh, are they here? That's great,' he said, continuing to prod and looking around aimlessly.

'No dopey,' she said, nudging him.

'I meant check it out.' She nodded meaningfully towards the two of them.

Paul frowned. '*What* are you going on about?'

'Jesus Christ, it's a wonder to me how you actually make it through the day sometimes,' she snapped, frustrated by his stupidity. 'I mean look, they're getting on well. They make a good couple, don't they?'

Paul stood staring as the penny finally dropped. He looked at his wife and back to the pair who were sat chatting, oblivious to Paul and Nicky's scrutiny.

'You think? ... What? ... Really? ...' he said disbelievingly. 'No ... Doug wouldn't ... Really?'

Nicky laughed. 'Close your mouth, my love. I'm just saying they make a nice couple, nothing more, nothing less. No one's done anything – I'm just saying what I see.'

Paul closed his mouth and looked back and forth between his wife, and Jesse and Doug. He was thoroughly confused.

Jesse was unsure what to say.

'What d'you think she resented you about?'

Doug's eyes were flat. 'I don't know. I've this sense … you know … in my gut, that something's off – maybe, broken. There's a part of me that won't admit it for the kids' sake.'

'Just for the kids' sake? What about you? Your life and your happiness. You deserve more.'

Doug picked at the label on his beer bottle. 'It's all about the kids for me. They've had such a tough eighteen months, I can't let something else epic happen. I can't do it to them, they've been through enough.'

Jesse tutted at him. 'Why do you blame yourself for everything?'

Doug looked at Jesse. He had suddenly became acutely aware of how close they were sitting, thigh to thigh on the small bench, arms touching. Doug looked away and took a swig of beer, pretending to be looking for the children.

'Come on. I'm depressing you. I've talked way too much about stuff I've no business talking about. Sorry about that.'

Jesse put a hand on his arm. 'But Doug …'

Doug got up looking for the kids, the closeness broken. He stepped out from the bench and said, 'Another beer? Mike's up next, it's always a good set.'

Jesse shook her head. 'No, it's my round, you stay put and save the table.'

She made her way to the bar passing Christy as she went, tickling her lightly as she passed. By the time Jesse returned to the table with their drinks, Doug was sat next to Helen, their childminder.

'Thanks. Jesse, you know Helen, don't you? She helps me out with the kids?'

Helen smiled. 'Hi Jesse. Good to meet you. So how are you finding this motley crew?'

Helen wasn't in the slightest bit interested in how Jesse was. In fact, she was disappointed she had come back to the table so quickly. When she'd seen Jesse stand to go for drinks she'd almost sprinted over to sit in the seat next to Doug, where she was settled now.

Helen gazed at Doug with open adoration as she waited for Jesse to respond, with Doug being completely oblivious to Helen's longing stares.

Still standing as Helen was in her seat, Jesse said, 'Nice to meet you Helen. Yes, I've seen you with the kids. They talk about you a lot. Can I get you a drink?'

Helen shook her head. 'No, I'm fine thanks. I've got one over there. I just stopped by to say hi and check that Doug got what I dropped off earlier.'

Before she could continue, Mike stepped onto the stage, prompting shouting and applause.

Helen stood reluctantly. 'Right, I suppose I'd better go. See you later, Doug, nice to meet you, Jesse.'

'Bye, Helen, good to meet you too,' said Jesse. She didn't miss the adoring look that Helen was giving Doug who was watching the stage and not paying any real attention to Helen's departure. Jesse helped her out. 'Doug, Helen's going.'

Doug looked around. 'Oh, sorry, yeah, bye, Helen, see you Monday.'

Jesse raised her beer in a farewell. Helen walked away looking over her shoulder and smiling at him, Doug was focused on Mike who was strapping on his guitar. He stepped towards the microphone.

A surge of wolf whistles from the crowd rang out as well as some heckling.

Mike laughed. 'OK … OK … calm down, you lot.' He held up his hands. 'OK, seriously, keep that cash coming, there's buckets around to put it in, not your empties. So, without further ado, I'm going to start with an old Squeeze number for anyone that's been a bit tempted.'

Mike started his song and Jesse sat back next to Doug.

'He's got all the chat, hasn't he? I love this song.'

Doug nodded, avoiding eye contact with Jesse. Suddenly he stood. 'Just going to check on where the kids are, and that Jude isn't necking any empties. I'll see you later. OK?'

Doug walked away and Jesse was left at the table feeling confused at his sudden change. Mike's song finished, and the applause was deafening.

The dog slightly spooked by the clapping and sensing Jesse was unsettled jumped up on the bench next to her where Doug had been sitting. She put an arm around the dog and carried on watching Mike's set, unsure what she had said or done to make Doug react so oddly.

We see her. We watch. We wait. We keep out of sight in case someone looks up and sees us. We see her sat on a bench with Doug. Close. Talking closely. We see her look upwards. Too close! We duck down. We can't be seen. We've not been seen. What are they saying? They look close. We don't like it. We feel angry and we don't like that. We want to control this. We need to be patient. We need to watch.

CHAPTER 19

Doug awoke with a start, breathing in air like a drowning man gasping for breath. He'd had the dream again. The awful dream that his arms weren't long enough to reach Jeff and Gav. Weirdly the dream had featured Jesse, who'd been the other side of the hole, fighting someone else off. In the dream, Doug had been torn between helping Jesse or his friends.

He thought back to the previous evening. He felt guilty about how abrupt he had been with Jesse, and the look on her face when he'd got up to leave. He'd seen her with an arm over the dog who had commandeered his seat. He couldn't work out why he'd felt he couldn't talk to her anymore about him and Claire. He was angry with himself for saying too much. It was unprofessional of him. He felt guilty for upsetting her. His thoughts were interrupted by his phone ringing, which he grabbed before it woke the kids.

'Claire.'

'I was going to leave a message. I thought you'd be sleeping off a hangover.'

'I had one beer. I had the kids with me, if you recall. How was your evening?'

'It was good to catch up. Look, she has tickets for the theatre this evening so I was going to stay on and go with her, so I might as well just stay another night and go straight into work tomorrow.'

'Are you asking me or telling me?' he said, tired of these conversations.

'Of course I'm not asking you, I'm keeping you informed. Why do I sense an issue?' asked Claire in a slightly snippy tone.

'I think the kids hoped to see something of you this weekend.'

'Well, I felt like I was surplus to requirements yesterday, so I expect they'll be fine,' Claire said sarcastically.

'Really, Claire? Can't you see it?'

'See what?'

'See they miss you and want you here.'

'I'll see them in the week at some point.'

'I'll be sure to tell them to wait for that then,' Doug snapped. 'Claire, did it occur to you I might have had something on today and needed a hand with the kids?'

Silence came from Claire's end of the phone.

Frustrated, Doug said, 'Claire, look come on, we can't keep doing this. We need to talk … the other day …'

'If you need help with the children today, as you might have something urgent on, although God knows what that could be, I suggest you ask Helen. From what I can see she'd do anything for you. I have to go.' She ended the call abruptly.

Doug swore softly. He felt like his marriage was rapidly approaching car-crash territory and despite his efforts to put the brakes on the situation, nothing was slowing it down. It irked him she constantly made the assumption he had nothing of importance on, and he would be around to look after the kids the whole time, while she did what she wanted. He got off the bed and stomped into the bathroom, slamming the door behind him.

* * *

Jimmy was on another run. He was enjoying the money and wasn't as terrified of the Europeans as he had been. He was pleased that he'd managed to pay off some of the debts he'd had piling up. He might even be able to get his boat fixed up if this carried on. At the last handover he'd even managed to have a bit of a laugh with the big scary looking Russian.

He stood on deck scanning the ocean as the larger boat drew up alongside his. He jumped down and took the ten crates and loaded them onto his boat. Once done, he gave a thumbs up to the skipper and the boat roared off.

Jimmy covered the crates with a tarp and had started to bring in his lobster pots when he saw a black rib coming towards him at high speed. Something in his gut told him this wasn't good. He grabbed a crate and started to load the small tightly wrapped packages into the lobster pots and threw the pots back over the side in an attempt to hide them. The rib was getting closer. He just had one crate left, so he stacked the lobsters on the top of the crates that had the packets of drugs in.

The rib stopped a few metres away, Jimmy's boat rocking wildly in its wake. One of the men, dressed in black with a hard face, shouted in a harsh Irish accent. 'You Jimmy?'

Jimmy turned and chucked the final lobster pot back in the sea, together with the orange float marker which bobbed in the choppy wake.

Jimmy turned back.

'Might be … who are you?'

The men brought their boat next to Jimmy's and one of the men climbed aboard. At well over six foot, he completely dwarfed Jimmy. The man leant forward to Jimmy and said in a broad Irish accent. 'Either you are Jimmy or you're not. Now which is it?'

'What do you want?' Jimmy spluttered.

The large man clapped Jimmy painfully on the shoulder. He said in a pleasantly conversational tone that belied his vice-like grip on Jimmy, 'Well, a little birdy told me you've been helping yourself to stuff that isn't yours, with some new friends. So I've come to give you a little bit of a telling off and take back what you've taken, which I'm sure you'll agree is only right and proper.'

'I … I don't know what you're talking about, mate.'

'Oh, I think you do, don't you Jimmy, mate?'

Jimmy tried to twist out of the painful grasp.

'Look, I don't know who you are, or what you think you're doing, but I'd be really grateful if you'd stop talking bollocks and get the fuck off my boat.'

The large man shook his head.

'Now that's just not polite, is it? I'm here asking nicely for my property back and you go and say that to me. That makes me pretty angry and a tiny bit upset, if I may say so.'

Jimmy tried to front it out. 'Really? I don't know what you're on about, mate. Now I'm politely asking you to get off my boat so I can go home.'

A smaller man with a face that resembled a rat piped up from the rib. 'Why don't you look for it, Connor?'

'Do you know what Fergus? I think I will because we've reached what I like to call an impasse here haven't we, Jimmy?'

Jimmy looked confused. 'A what?'

Connor smiled, squeezing Jimmy's shoulder painfully. 'An impasse. Now, I could spend some time explaining what an impasse is to you, but I think I'm just going to take matters into my own hands here ...'

Jimmy looked nervous. 'And do what?'

Connor looked at Jimmy in a matter-of-fact way and then hit him hard in the face. Jimmy's nose exploded and blood poured down his face. Connor hit him again. Jimmy slumped down onto the deck.

'So, Jimmy, an impasse is where both parties are at a place where neither is going to give in, although I do think you might be rethinking that now, yes?'

Jimmy was lying groaning on the deck of the boat, his nose covered in blood, one of his eyes closing up from the punches.

'Are you rethinking our little impasse? I'm ever so happy to discuss it, you know. I'm known to be a reasonable man when I want to be.'

Connor kicked Jimmy hard in the stomach, then again in the ribs and then a few more times in the head.

Connor asked. 'Are you, Jimmy? Are you rethinking our impasse?'

Jimmy was unconscious. Connor turned around to the two men in the boat. 'Fellas! Jimmy's tired and having a little sleep.'

The two in the boat laughed.

'So, Jimmy, what's you say? That's very nice of you. I'll help myself. My, my, my what do we have here? Oo, lads, I think I've found some things that belong to me. I think we'll have those back – lads, take these.'

Connor busied himself and tipped some lobsters back over the side and handed over the crate to the lads in the boat.

Fergus said, 'Is this all? I thought there would be more – maybe they split it and took it somewhere else.'

Connor grunted. 'Just take what's there."

'What about him?' Rat-faced man asked.

'Leave him,' Connor said, kicking Jimmy a couple more times. He admired his handiwork and then opened the door to the wheelhouse, grabbing a handful of dirty rags from a small compartment. He tossed them on the deck and produced a zippo lighter and set fire to them. He turned and grabbed Jimmy's jacket and some old rope and threw those on the flames too.

Connor turned to the others. 'If this takes then it's curtains for him. If it doesn't, he won't do it again in a hurry.'

He jumped back into the rib and the three men sped off, Jimmy's boat rocking in their wake.

Jimmy lay unconscious on the deck, the fire smoldering a few feet away.

A sailing boat spotted the smoke from a distance and alerted the coastguard before casting anchor a few yards away. The occupant of the boat jumped into the small tender clutching a fire extinguisher. The small dingy headed towards Jimmy's boat and pulled alongside. The man clumsily climbed aboard, pointed the extinguisher at the fire and shouted over to Jimmy. 'Hello? Can you hear me? Hello?'

The extinguisher was no match as the fire had taken hold of a nearby tarpaulin.

The man shouted at Jimmy again. 'Can you hear me? I've called the coastguard. Hey, are you OK?'

Desperate, the man looked around and saw with relief the large Tamar lifeboat approaching at speed in the distance. The sailor turned around and waved.

The lifeboat engines quietened to a throaty burble, as it approached the burning boat slowly.

Doug, who was stood on deck, shouted down to the crew. 'It's Jimmy's boat.' He shouted to the sailor, 'Sir, can you get off the boat please for your own safety? Is that your dinghy?'

The sailor pointed to the deck of the boat. 'There's a guy here, all smashed up. Not moving.'

Doug turned and shouted. 'Bob, I'm jumping across, hold it steady.'

Doug made his way carefully to the end of the lifeboat on the prow of the vessel and jumped down onto Jimmy's boat. In his hand he held a large extinguisher which he pointed at the fire until the flames died down a little.

'I tried to put the fire out. The guy – I couldn't get to him,' the sailor said, climbing into his dinghy.

Doug turned to the crew. 'Get another extinguisher ready and a couple of buckets. Paul, Mike, you OK to come over and help me with Jimmy? Dan, call the coastguard for the chopper to get him away.'

Doug turned to the sailor. 'Thanks for calling us. Where are you headed?'

'I'm heading to Castleby to get some supplies and carry on.'

'OK, look, can you stick around? The police will want a statement from you. Could you call up to the station in a couple of hours maybe?'

The sailor nodded and headed back to his boat.

Doug turned to Paul and Mike. 'Right, get the fire out or under control, then we'll get to Jimmy. I don't like the look of him.'

Paul and Mike focused their efforts on killing the fire, while Doug checked Jimmy and felt his neck for a pulse.

'Jimmy … it's Doug. We're gonna get you off the boat to hospital, mate. We just need to sort the fire.'

Jesse had jumped onto the boat with a foil blanket for Jimmy and was tucking it around him gently.

'Doug, he looks in a bad way. He's taken a right kicking.'

'Question is why and who started the fire?'

Dan shouted up from the depths of the lifeboat. 'Skip. Jimmy's lucky day, chopper is two minutes from here – it was out anyway.'

Doug gave him the thumbs up and within a minute they heard the whisper of the chopper. It hovered overhead, and a stretcher was winched down along with a paramedic, who attached a neck collar to Jimmy. They got him into the stretcher. The paramedic gave the signal, and the pair were winched up.

Paul was pouring buckets of sea water over the boat and Jesse and Doug inspected the damage among the wet debris.

'Fires not breached the hull, but it's badly damaged, I'd say it's fixable. Shall we tow it back? Keep an eye on it?' Jesse asked.

'I don't want to leave it here. Looks like something happened on board, look at this footprint, it's enormous. The police will want to see the boat. Let's get going. Chuck the rest of those lobsters over the side, they get a reprieve today.'

Jesse chucked the rest of the live lobsters over the side and Mike gave her a hand back up to the lifeboat. He attached the tow line and Paul made it safe on the lifeboat.

Mike said quietly, 'What do you reckon happened?'

Doug frowned, looking at the boat. 'Don't know. He was pretty shifty the other day when I spoke to him about leaving the boat and where he was.'

'What d'you think it might be?'

'I know what I think but I don't want to be saying it out loud.'

Mike looked thoughtful. 'That bad?'

Doug grimaced. 'Maybe. Let's make sure we give the boat a once over before we head off tonight. I want to make sure there's no chance of the fire restarting.' Doug hopped back onto the main boat and called to Bob to start towing the boat back to the harbour.

They manoeuvred it in and secured it to the quayside. Doug stayed on the boat with Mike.

'Right, let's check her over.'

The two of them scoured the boat for signs of fire and looked closely at the area where it had started.

Doug pointed. 'Mike, can you just get some water on that, just to be sure you know?'

Mike poured more water onto the burnt area. Doug grabbed Jimmy's phone and keys from the wheelhouse and pulled the door shut.

'All good, let's go. I really need to speak to Marie and let her know about Jimmy.'

Doug and Mike arrived back at the station, and Paul was busy hosing it down, whistling tunelessly. Doug walked into the kitchen to make a drink. He found Jesse leaning against the counter, waiting for the kettle to boil.

'Coffee?' she asked as he appeared. 'What's the verdict with Jimmy's boat?'

'Yes please. I think it's sound, some repairs to be done on the deck, but I reckon between us we could do that for him.'

'I was going to look at the engine for him anyway, since he'll be laid up for a while.'

Jesse handed a mug to Doug. He was silent for a moment and then they both started to speak at the same time.

'Look, about the other—'

'The other night—'

They both stopped. Jesse glanced at Doug.

'You go,' she said.

Doug looked sheepish. 'Look, I just wanted to say sorry, you know, ...I might have ... you know ... upset you ... by going off.' Doug looked relieved he'd got it out.

'Hmm, I was going to say sorry if I got too personal.'

Doug cradled his coffee. 'You didn't upset me, I just ... err ... overshared as the kids say. Sorry.'

Jesse looked confused. 'That's nothing to be sorry about.'

Doug shook his head. 'No,' he said firmly. 'I said too much. Out of order.'

Jesse said wryly, 'Doug, chill out. It was a chat. You told me to open up more and share. You did exactly that. It's all fine.' She left the kitchen, joining in whistling the same song as Paul, just as tunelessly.

CHAPTER 20

Doug bumped into Marie outside Maggie's beach café.

'Hi, Doug, have you got a minute?

'How are you doing, Marie? How's Jimmy?'

Marie sniffed. 'He's out of the woods now, they say. Still in hospital though. Won't work for a while. I wanted to thank you for what you did.'

Doug held up his hands as if to stop her.

'Seriously, Doug, if you hadn't got him off the boat God knows what would have happened.'

'What's he said about it? Who did it?'

Marie sighed. 'He won't talk about it. He just wants to get out of hospital. He won't tell me anything. He won't even let me go and get the pots he left out. He keeps telling me to keep out of it.'

Doug looked thoughtful. 'Have the police spoken to you about it?'

'Both of us. He's told the police he didn't know who it was, they just jumped aboard and gave him a kicking and started the fire. He said he thinks they thought he was someone else. He said there were three of them, but he couldn't remember anything else.'

'That's all he said? Nothing to do with him going off the other day?'

'No, he's not mentioned that.'

Doug looked surprised. 'Not even to you?'

Marie shook her head.

'When does it look like he'll be back home?'

'They reckon another week, then home bed-rest for another week or two. He'll need a lot of physio and they're still worried about his head injury. He's in a right old mess, Doug. He seems frightened. Keeps telling me to make sure I lock the house and all that.'

'Are you worried?'

'I'm worried he's got himself into trouble and he's not going to be able to get himself out of it. Silly bugger.'

'Don't worry. We can do the lobster pots, no problem. How will you get him home, need any help?'

'Mike said he'd get him. His truck has lots of legroom.'

'Give us a call if you're worried about anything?'

Marie nodded, eyes welling up. 'We don't deserve you lot. Thanks, again Doug. See you later,' she said walking away.

Doug watched her go and wondered what the bloody hell Jimmy had got himself into.

Doug was on the upper deck of the lifeboat, telling Jesse about a woman who'd phoned the station asking if she could hire the lifeboat for her daughter's tenth birthday party and whether they could do some tricks on the boat and take all the children out, when the alarm went off.

Doug jumped down and headed into the office, returning with a piece of paper, going straight into the locker room where Jesse was already struggling into her gear. The door banged and Ben and Paul appeared together followed by Dan in his chef's whites and then Bob. Gear on, they gathered on the boat, the roller door opened, and the boat launched, ploughing off at speed.

Doug shouted over the wind. 'Woman called in about her son and husband out fishing in a dingy past Kirby – they aren't back yet, they're a few hours late.'

Bob appeared on deck. 'Call from the coastguard, a small plane saw two people swimming towards the red buoy a few miles off Kirby Point. No boat seen.'

'Let's get looking, we're going to lose the light soon and I don't want another kid lost.' Doug grabbed his binoculars and started scouring the sea.

Visibility was fading fast. The crew were on the top deck using spotlights and powerful torches to scan the ocean in the diminishing light.

Doug shouted, 'Looking for the red buoy here, that's what they were seen swimming towards.'

Jesse turned to Bob. 'Bob, did the coastguard say what time that plane called in seeing those guys?'

Bob pointedly ignored Jesse and turned his back on her. Doug watched the exchange and frowned.

'Bob,' he said sharply.

Bob faced Doug. 'Coastguard says it was just before they got the call reporting them missing.'

'They've been in the water too long…' Doug muttered looking at his watch. 'Do we know how old the kid is?'

Bob shook his head. The crew resumed searching with binoculars shining the lights across the water.

Mike pointed. 'Red Buoy. Over there.'

The spotlights found a red buoy with a small figure perched awkwardly.

The boat gently drew up alongside the buoy, setting it rocking in its wake.

Jesse leaned over the rail to the boy. 'Hey sweetie. We're here to help you. Your mum was worried. I'm Jesse, what's your name?'

The boy turned a tear-streaked face towards Jesse, blinking in the bright light.

'Where's Dad? Have you found Dad?'

Doug came over to the edge of the boat. 'Hello, mate. What's your name?'

'Ryan.'

'Where's your dad then?' Doug asked gently.

Ryan sobbed. 'He said he was going to swim to Kirby. To get help.'

The crew exchanged glances with each other. Jesse leant out towards him a little more.

Jesse smiled at him. 'OK Ryan, we need you on the boat so we can go and find your dad. Now what's that around your waist there?' Ryan sniffed and looked down.

'Dad's belt. He tied me on so I wouldn't fall in, even if I fell asleep.'

'Well, your Dad sounds like a really sensible guy. That's one of the best ideas I've ever seen to keep someone safe.'

Ryan managed to untie the belt, and flung himself off the buoy and onto the boat so quickly that Jesse only just managed to catch him.

'Woah – that was close. Right. Come on let's get you below and get you nice and warm.'

Jesse turned to Mike and spoke quietly. 'Can you radio the coastguard please and say we have Ryan and see whether the dad has turned up yet?'

'No problem.'

Doug appeared at Jesse's side. 'Ryan, I'm Doug.'

'Are you the captain?' he asked shyly.

Doug grinned. 'Sort of. They call me the skipper. We're going to take you down below and get you warm, and then when you've warmed up a bit, you can drive the boat if you'd like? Yes?'

Ryan nodded enthusiastically. Doug ushered him down the steps below deck.

'Ben, can you give him a blanket and get him warm please?'

Ben steered Ryan away. 'Skip.'

Doug turned to the crew on deck. 'Right. We need to find the dad – let's sweep the area from the buoy to the island – it's a long way, but you never know. Once we get to the island, we'll launch the small boat to check the shoreline.'

The lifeboat purred off slowly and the crew resumed the search with their lights. As they neared the rocky shoreline, the small Y boat was launched with Jesse and Ben aboard. They headed off with powerful lights.

They'd been searching for at least two hours since they'd found the boy and Doug had the feeling in his gut that expected the worst. He turned to Dan who was still looking with binoculars and a search light.

'I think we might need to call it a day. We just can't see. The boy said he didn't have a lifejacket on either. I'm going to call the guys back in.'

Doug radioed Jesse and Ben. 'We've gotta call it a day. We aren't going to find him tonight.'

The two returned to the boat and Doug helped them back on deck. Jesse spoke quietly. 'Have you told the boy?'

'I'm going to do it now. Give me a hand? He took to you.'

Jesse and Doug found Ryan curled up on one of the large seats, wrapped in a cosy red blanket.

'So. We've been looking for your dad now and we can't see him anywhere, but we're going to come out again at first light when we can see better. Your mum is at our station house waiting for you, so we're off there now to see her.'

Jesse rubbed Ryan's shoulder and he sobbed and flung his arms around Jesse.

'Where's dad? Where is he?' he said, sobbing.

Jesse sat with him. 'I don't know, sweetie. Hopefully we'll find him in the morning.'

The boat returned to the station where a group of people were gathered with a white-faced woman who looked distraught. Doug jumped out of the boat and went to her immediately.

'I'm Doug, I'm the skipper,' he said, steering her to a corner. 'Ryan is OK. He's below in the boat, the crew will bring him up in a minute.'

She looked relieved and stared over Doug's shoulder.

'Is he OK then? Oh God.' Her face clouded. 'What about Jack? Where's Jack? Is he OK?'

Doug spoke quietly. 'I think we ought to go and sit down. Can I ask your name?'

She looked confused. 'I'm Eve. Why? What's happened? Oh God. What's happened, why aren't they together?' She started to sob.

Doug took her through to the kitchen and sat her down in a chair. He crouched to her eye level. He took her hands gently in his.

'Eve. Jack tied Ryan safely to the buoy and then swam to Kirby Island for help. We've looked for him all around that area, but that doesn't mean to say the worst has happened. We've lost the light. We're going out again at first light and we've put an alert out to fishing boats to be watchful.'

Eve's hand flew to her mouth in shock. 'Oh God … no … so he could have…? Oh God.'

There was a quiet knock on the door and Jesse appeared with Ryan. He ran to embrace his mother and they held each other tightly. Ryan sobbed.

'Dad said he had to go and get help.'

'Dad thought he was doing the best thing. We've got to hope he's OK and can be found. He's a strong swimmer.'

Jesse handed a cup of tea to Eve and a hot chocolate to Ryan.

'Drink up,' she said. 'Ryan, you're probably really cold from the shock and being out for so long. Are you guys going to be OK getting home? Can we call anyone? We won't go out until probably five-ish tomorrow morning, but we'll take your number and call you with any news, soon as we can, but home is the best place for you both.'

'Drink up, Ryan,' said Doug. 'Here, have a biscuit before this lot eat them all. Now, I need you to tell me what your dad was wearing.'

Ryan scrunched his face up as he remembered.

'He had his red fishing T-shirt on and a blue fleece over that.'

'Dark blue like this?' Doug gestured to his RNLI shirt.

Ryan shook his head. 'No, a lighter blue.' He pointed to a mug on the draining board. 'Like that.'

Doug smiled at him. 'OK, good. Well we're going back out to look for him and we'll let you know what we find.'

Eve put her hand on Doug's arm. 'Thank you so much for saving Ryan, and for looking for Jack. I only hope to God he's OK.'

The next morning Mike, Jesse and Doug left the lifeboat station in the smaller inshore rib and motored out towards Kirby Island, just past 5 a.m. None of them spoke, all lost in their own thoughts and mentally preparing themselves for what they would likely find.

As they approached the island Doug said quietly, 'Let's look around the shorelines here in case he did make it and just can't get past some of the rocks. They'd be pretty inaccessible if you were tired from swimming.'

'What was he wearing again?' asked Jesse.

Doug thought for a moment 'Red T-shirt, sky blue fleece.'

Jesse carried on craning her neck to see the rocky inlets. 'Inspired move I thought, tying the kid to the buoy. No way he'd fall off that even if he fell asleep.'

'Saved that boy's life, that idea,' Mike said.

Jesse sighed. 'God, I hope we find the dad alive.'

Doug looked out to sea and said absently. 'It's not that likely. It's still beyond me why adults don't take lifejackets with them when they go out on boats. If he'd had a lifejacket on, he'd be OK I suspect.'

They carried on searching, the sea getting choppier as they neared open sea towards the rear of the island. Large cliffs loomed and birds swooped in and out of cracks on the cliff faces.

Mike said conversationally as they were looking, 'So, Jimmy's coming home soon, did you know? Maybe a week or so?'

Doug nodded. 'I saw Marie yesterday. She said he's coming home soon, but won't be very mobile. She said he was worried about a whole load of stuff. Even worrying about the lobster pots.'

Mike tutted. 'He left his pots out? I'll go and get them for him in the next couple of days when I get a minute.'

'That's nice of you. I'll give you a hand if I'm around.'

'Thanks, that would be great. Jesse, do you reckon his boat is OK to take?'

Jesse said, 'I'm going to get to it this afternoon and see what the engine's doing; apparently he was having trouble with it. Wait, what's that over there?' She pointed.

Mike frowned. 'Where?'

Jesse pointed. 'At the foot of that cliff there, on the rocks. I'm sure I saw a flash of blue.'

Mike carefully drew the boat as near as he could.

Jesse stood. 'I'm going in.'

She dropped over the side and swam to the rocks. She clambered awkwardly over the rocks, her feet slipping on the seaweed, water still breaking in over them in the shallows.

'It's him,' she called.

Jesse looked at the man, her heart full of sadness for him. He was deathly pale, and his lips were blue. She tore her glove off and pressed her hand to his neck. His body was barely warm, and she couldn't feel a pulse. She ran her knuckles hard up his breastbone looking for a response to the pain and saw a flicker in his face.

'Jesus!' She turned and yelled. 'He's alive. Barely'

'Shit!' Mike almost fell out of the boat to go and help Jesse bring him closer to the boat. Doug radioed the coastguard.

'Coastguard this is Castleby inshore lifeboat. We've just found an adult male, potentially hypothermic from the north side of Kirby Island. In need of urgent medical attention. Can you send the chopper? Over.'

Static crackled over the radio. 'Inshore, this is coastguard. Chopper is 20 miles away at another scene. Can you transport to harbour for an ambulance? Over?'

Doug swore loudly before pressing the return button.

'Coastguard, please arrange urgently. Will bring casualty back into main harbour asap. Over.'

Doug threw the radio down and steered as close to the rocks as possible. Jesse and Mike were trying to bring Jack to the boat, but it was difficult over the slippery rocks.

Jesse shouted, 'Doug, can you get closer?'

Doug expertly manoeuvred the boat closer and Jesse made a grab for it. Between them they managed to get Jack onto the boat.

Jesse grabbed a foil blanket and wrapped him in it.

'Jesus. I can't believe we found him. He must have got himself out of the water but was cut off by the rocks.'

Doug steered carefully out of the rocky shallows.

He said quietly, 'Jesse, he's in a bad way. We might not be able to get him back.'

'We've got to tell them. Eve and Ryan as soon as we can. Not knowing is the most awful thing.'

'Soon as we're back, I'll call them.' Doug said.

The boat surged at full throttle towards the harbour. Jack remained unconscious. They arrived back in a matter of minutes to find an ambulance waiting at the slipway, lights flashing. The paramedics ran to the edge of the harbour with the stretcher and took Jack away, the sirens screaming loudly through the narrow streets in the early morning.

Doug sat at his desk and picked up his phone. He exhaled heavily as he heard the phone ringing. It was answered by a breathless Eve.

'Hello?'

Doug paused for a second. 'Eve. It's Doug from the lifeboat.'

He closed his eyes as he heard her shaky intake of breath.

'Oh God. Oh God. Have you found him? Is he...?'

'Eve. Listen. We found him. He's hypothermic. We weren't sure if he was alive when we found him. He had a really faint pulse, but we have no real idea of how long he's been in that state.'

Eve's voice shook. 'Where is he now?'

'He's at the hospital. It's going to be a long road if he pulls through it, but as I said, he was in a bad way.'

Eve was silent for a moment. 'Thank you. For letting me know and for finding him. We'll go to the hospital now.'

'Let me know how he is, yes?'

'OK.'

'Take care now, Eve, regards to the wee man.'

'Thanks, Doug. For everything you did. All of you. Bye.'

Doug replaced the receiver and rubbed his face. He hoped to God that the guy was going to pull through.

CHAPTER 21

On the quayside Jesse looked down at Jimmy's boat. She had worked flat-out, sorting out the engine, the running lights and practically everything else that was busted, even the lock on the wheelhouse door. Ben and Paul had set about fixing the deck and getting under her feet, but they'd worked together well, ending up in the Hope and Anchor for a few too many afterwards. Jesse realised she felt happier than she had in a long time. She also realised she wasn't as frightened when she didn't see Dr Marshall.

She felt guilty when she cancelled her last chat with Emma but hadn't made another, despite Natalie's amusing messages telling her to do so.

She took a last look and walked to the station. Billy was due in soon. Unbeknown to Billy, Jesse and Julie had been in contact, trying to think of ways to get Billy motivated. Today she wanted him to take something apart for her; she knew if he put his mind to it, he'd do it. Billy's physiotherapist was amazed at the progress he was making.

Mike and Doug were on their way to the harbour to get Jimmy's boat, with a detour for coffee from Maggie's. Outside the café, a group of teenage boys milled about, all with matching T-shirts that read 'Youth

Sailing & Outdoor Programme'. A woman with long curly red hair was passing out maps and compasses. She was joking with the boys, who all jostled for her approval. She spotted Doug on the causeway and waved.

'Doug! Mike! Good to see you!'

'Morven. Is it that time again? It's not two minutes since you were here last summer!'

Mike leaned in and gave her a peck on the cheek. 'Hey, Morven. Got a spare evening to come and sing together?'

She laughed. 'Oh, I wish, Mike.' She gestured to the boys. 'We're hiking around to the big point, which will probably take us most of the day if everyone behaves themselves and no one falls off a cliff. Then it's back to the centre, I'm afraid. They're climbing for the rest of the week. We're back on the tall ship soon though, leaving from here. A couple of weeks, so I'll look you up then?'

'Make sure you do,' Mike said firmly.

She turned to the boys who were getting restless. 'Come on you lot, we've got a long way to go today! Let's get started!' She jumped down onto the beach, the boys eagerly following her.

Doug watched them go. 'She gets them eating out of the palm of her hand. How does she do that?' he said to himself as Mike disappeared into the café.

Standing on Jimmy's boat, Mike looked around in amazement. 'Blimey, they did a good job.'

Doug frowned. 'They?'

'Jesse, Ben and Paul, they worked flat out on this so Jimmy can come back to a business.'

'How long did it take them?' said Doug, looking around and hardly seeing any traces of the fire.

'Jesse spent all afternoon and most of last night here, and Paul and Ben hit it hard after work too. They ended up in the pub last night all covered in dust.'

Doug laughed. 'Good of them to give up their time.'

He started the engine which sprang into life immediately.

'Jimmy's not going to know this boat, it's never sounded this good!' Mike exclaimed.

'Magic hands,' Doug muttered.

'What's that?'

'Just something someone said about Jesse.'

'True though,' said Mike with a laugh and they motored out towards Kirby.

Mike shielded his eyes from the sun.

'Marie said he uses the orange buoy so we should look out for that. I hope they've not got broken or been nicked. It's expensive to replace them.'

The two scanned the ocean.

Doug pointed. 'There.'

He steered the boat slowly towards the buoy, and Mike picked up a long grapple hook. Doug cut the engine and moved around to help Mike reel in the rope. The first pot was heaved in. Mike pulled it onto the deck.

'Jesus! How heavy are these? What the bloody hell is in them?'

Doug turned and grabbed a crate. He peered inside, picked a few lobsters out of the pot and chucked them unceremoniously in the crate. Mike peered over his shoulder.

'You know, that looks awfully like ...'

Doug held up a package wrapped in brown tape, about the size of a brick. 'It does, doesn't it?'

'Is it just one?'

'No, there's loads more.' Doug swore under his breath. 'OK. So, we need to get it all in. Jesus Jimmy, what were you thinking?'

The pair emptied the first pot and stacked it in the corner, lobsters in one crate, packets in the other. They hauled up the next pot and repeated the process.

'Shit, how many of these are there?'

Doug looked over the side.

'No idea, mate. This has to be why he got a kicking and was left for dead. Let's get a move on.'

Finally, the last pot was hauled in. Doug surveyed the cluttered deck.

'Look at all this. I'm going to have to call Steve the copper.'

'Well, just hang on a minute, mate. I can't stand drugs. But what if this is the only thing keeping Jimmy or even Marie alive?'

Doug frowned, 'What d'you mean?'

'What if the fact he's hidden it here is the only reason they didn't finish the job?'

Doug thought for a minute. 'Ok. Let's get back. There's an old archway in the harbour wall that Billy used to use to store all the crap he couldn't be bothered to chuck out. No one really knows it's ours. Let's dump this in there and we'll talk to Jimmy. Who are we giving the lobsters to?'

'Fishy John, he takes them from Jimmy, he can owe him.'

Doug started the boat and watched as Mike dragged a tarpaulin over the crates.

'Hang on a minute,' he said, as if remembering something.

'What?'

Doug pointed to the tarpaulin. 'He's done this before. The time he went missing and then I saw him in the harbour, he had a stack of crates he was covering with a tarp … it must have been the same thing.'

'So, you reckon he's been doing this a while?'

'Maybe once or twice, any more and someone would have noticed surely? We need to have a chat with him without Marie. She's got enough to worry about, we don't need to worry her with this. Thing is, there's a lot of it here and someone will be missing it.'

Both men were silent as the boat chugged back to the harbour. Doug pulled out his phone and made a call.

'Jesse? Can you do me a favour? In the workshop, in an old syrup tin on the top shelf there's a bunch of keys, can you grab them and meet us in the harbour in five minutes, please? Cheers.'

The boat steered over towards the far quayside wall. Doug jumped out and tied on, waving at Jesse who appeared with Brock.

'Found them OK?'

'Yup – along with the biggest spider I've ever seen in my life! Ugh. What are they for anyway?'

Doug looked around. 'I'll explain later. Quiet though. Can you give us a hand?'

Jesse looked curious as she approached the boat. Mike handed up the crates, stacking a final crate full of lobsters on top of the crates of the drugs. He left another crate of lobsters on the quayside.

Jesse stood back.

'Wait … are they what I think they are? Jesus!' she hissed, looking around.'

Mike said sharply, 'Keep your voice down. We had no idea. Before we call Steve we just need to be sure that Jimmy or Marie aren't being held to some sort of ransom for them. We don't want them in danger.'

Jesse looked around to see if anyone was watching. There was a dark-haired man with tattooed arms on the other side of the harbour who was looking their way, but he casually looked away when he saw Jesse looking over at him, then walked towards the high street. There were a few families playing on the small beach by the harbour, oblivious to their activities.

Doug picked up a crate. 'Mike's right. Firstly, we need to see what Jimmy knows. So, just for now, we're stashing it in Billy's old shed. If Marie is being threatened because of this, I won't put her safety at risk. Mike let's take all three, Jesse can you chuck a tarp over it when we lift it?'

Mike and Doug lifted the crates one end each and Jesse threw a tarpaulin over them.

Doug turned to Jesse. 'Got those keys?'

The three of them headed over to the lock-up and Jesse unlocked the door.

Doug coughed and wrinkled his nose. 'Christ it smells like someone died in here. Put them here.'

They arranged the crates and stepped back out, locking the doors.

'Right, lobsters to Fishy John and we're done.'

Mike and Doug returned to the dockside, picked up the crates of lobsters and carried them up the small slipway to the fishmongers. Then the three walked back to the lifeboat station, oblivious to being watched from the castle above by the man with the tattooed arms.

* * *

Doug was pleased with his efforts. He'd texted Claire that morning and left a message, saying it was important she came home for dinner. He'd thought a lot about what he was going to say about how they could try and get back on track.

He'd offloaded the kids for the evening, done the shopping and whipped around with the hoover. He'd arranged a bunch of flowers in a glass vase on the table and set about preparing dinner. He put some music on softly, lit a few candles and opened a bottle of wine. A card lay on one of the plates, along with a small, boxed present. He checked the

173

oven, lifted the lid of the pan, then checked his watch again, hoping she was on her way.

Doug sat at the table. It had been two hours since dinner was ready and there had been no word from Claire. He finished his meal, pushing half of it away and drained his glass. He blew out the candles, cleared the plate and turned out the lights, leaving the present and card on the kitchen table, along with the flowers.

CHAPTER 22

The enormous hospital campus loomed large over a new build four-storey block of flats in the morning light. In one of the flats a couple were wriggling about under the duvet giggling. A dark-haired man in his early forties with chiseled Italian looks appeared from under the covers, his hair tousled. He flung back the duvet revealing a blonde-haired woman. The man rested on an arm and looked lovingly at her.

'I like you here, in my bed, in my home.'

Claire giggled. 'I like being in both those places.'

Felix smiled. 'I want you here more.'

Claire looked frustrated. 'We've been through this before, Felix.'

Felix sat up in bed, crossing his arms. 'Seriously C, I want you to move in with me.'

Claire was shocked. 'What?'

'Move in with me. I love you and I want you here.'

'Felix … you have me here …'

'I want you here all the time, not every now and then.'

'I'm here as often as I can be.' She started to get out of bed.

Felix caught her arm. 'Why not? What's stopping you?'

Claire rolled her eyes. 'Felix, it's really not that simple.'

'It's as simple or difficult as you want to make it.'

Claire pushed his hand away. 'Oh, come on.'

Felix looked serious. 'This can be easy or difficult. You decide.'

'Says the man with no ties at all. Have you forgotten I've two children and a husband?'

'No, of course I haven't, but I assume they'd stay with him.'

Claire stood hands on hips. 'Why would you assume that?'

'Because you spend more time here and at the hospital than at home, so I just assumed.'

Claire started grabbing clothes and getting dressed hurriedly. 'It's not for you to assume anything.'

'I'm only calling it as I see it.'

'Well don't. It's none of your business.'

Felix sat up in bed and tried to placate her. 'Jesus, C, don't be so damn touchy.'

'I'm not being touchy. You've as good as made out I don't give a stuff about my kids.'

'I wasn't saying anything like that. I was just saying that things wouldn't be that different if you moved in, because you aren't at home with them much anyway.'

'See, there you go again!'

Felix crossed his arms defensively. 'You're way too oversensitive about this.'

Claire finished dressing and gathered her things.

'I'm leaving … I need to think … I need to get home.'

Felix snorted. 'Balls. You're running away because I struck a raw nerve. You think I think you're a bad mother and suddenly you need to get home, what does that tell me?'

Claire glared at him furiously from the doorway. 'It should tell you to keep your bloody thoughts to yourself.'

She slammed the door to the flat and left. As she got in her car, she looked up and saw Felix standing at the window, looking down at her. She drove off, fuming.

How dare he speak to her like that? Make judgements about her and how she felt?

As she arrived back home she noticed Doug's truck was missing. Probably out saving some idiot, she thought. She unlocked the front door to an unusually silent house.

'Hi, it's me … anyone here?'

She put her head around the lounge door; it was surprisingly neat and tidy, same in the kitchen. The table was still laid from the night before with candles and place settings, the card and present still where Doug had put them. Claire opened the card.

'Shit …'

She unwrapped the small present; a pair of silver droplet earrings. She would have chosen them herself, in an instant. They were perfect and beautiful. She sighed heavily and sat down at the table. She picked up her phone and called Doug, which went straight to answerphone.

'Doug. It's me … where are you guys? I've just got home … let me know where you are, and I'll come and find you. Let me know, OK?'

Claire surveyed the table. He had clearly made an effort last night. She had ignored his texts and messages, convinced he was going to try and talk to her again which she just wasn't ready to do. A part of her loved the other night they'd spent together, it had seemed like old times, but that seemed like a different life when she was at the hospital around Felix.

She got up from the table, threw the card in the bin, picked up her phone and earrings and went upstairs for a shower.

As the sun was beginning to set, Doug and the kids pulled onto the drive, singing along to George Ezra's *Shotgun* loudly. He noticed Claire's car and raised an eyebrow. The kids went running in the front door.

'Mum, Mum!'

Claire was in the kitchen, wine glass in hand. She had a slightly glassy expression, primarily due to the half bottle of wine she had consumed.

'Where have you been?' she asked the kids.

Jude could barely contain himself. 'We've been on a boat all day, we've caught loads of fish. We went out for breakfast too – it was epic!'

Christy piped up. 'I felt a little bit sick but better when I had some crisps. I caught three fish! They feel yucky though.'

Jude appeared with the bucket and thrust it at Claire. 'Look at all the fish!'

Doug came into the kitchen.

'Hello, how long have you been home?'

'I got home this morning. I called you,' Claire said testily.

'I left the mobile in the car. No point taking it out on the boats, no signal after the point anyway. I wasn't on duty, so I didn't bother. We had the radio though.'

'Well, I must have misplaced my crew radio,' she said sarcastically. 'So I've wasted a day here, waiting for you lot to get back.'

'Why is being at home wasting a day? You could have taken some time to chill out a bit.'

The kids jostled past him and dumped the bucket of fish in the sink. He turned to the kids. 'Jude, Christy, wash those fish properly and we'll gut them and get them cooked. I'll go and fire up the barbecue.'

Christy hung on Doug's sleeve. 'Don't forget the corn on the cob.'

Doug and the kids washed the fish, with Jude flapping it in Christy's face. Doug went to the garden and lit the barbecue; Claire followed him out still clutching the wine.

Doug pointed to her glass. 'Any wine left? Looks like you've been at it a while.'

Claire rolled her eyes. Doug sighed. 'I just wondered when you had to go back to work, as you've had a few.'

'Well, I'm on tomorrow morning, so I'll have as much as I like, thanks very much.'

Doug raised his hands as if to surrender. 'OK, OK ...' He called to the kids. 'How are you two doing in there with the fish?'

'Dad, come and do the gross bit ...'

Doug went back inside. Claire watched through the window, hearing shouts about it being gross or disgusting, and laughter from Doug and the kids. Claire drained her glass and appeared at the back door.

'Isn't anyone going to ask me what I'd like for dinner?'

Jude turned around, his hands all bloody and scaly.

'It's fish, Mum, like it or lump it, that's what you used to say when you cooked for us and we didn't like it.'

Claire looked taken aback by his comment.

Christy said in a matter-of fact-voice: 'Daddy bought a French stick on the way home so you can have some of that and some of the corn on the cob, that's what I'm having, and Dad bought us a sticky bun too. I said not to bother getting you one because you'd be at work, but now you're here you can have half of mine.'

Doug disappeared to lay the fish on the barbecue and shouted to the kids. 'Right kids, grab plates, cutlery and drinks please. Fish cooks quickly so we're good to go soon.'

Doug helped himself to a glass of wine and was handing out plates when the house phone rang.

Claire jumped up. 'I'll get it.'

Doug put a fish on her plate and sat down to eat with the kids. He watched her through the window, strolling around the house chatting. By the time the kids finished their meal, she was still on the phone.

Jude eyed up his cake. 'Dad, please can we go and watch some TV with pudding?'

'Go on. Take your plates in.'

Doug took a moment to enjoy the peace and quiet and drank his wine. Claire finally ended the call. She came out into the garden, her glass refilled.

'Who was that?' Doug asked pleasantly.

Claire ignored him and sat down and poked at her fish, pushing it away without touching it.

Doug raised an eyebrow, waiting for an answer.

'Work, nothing important.'

Doug slowly sipped his wine. 'They seem to want to talk to you quite a bit these days,' he observed quietly.

Claire looked defensive and drained her glass in a single gulp.

'Perhaps they want to talk to me because they value me and my work. I do have a fairly important job, you know?'

'I've never said otherwise, Claire.'

Claire picked up his wine and drank it, looking at him with annoyance.

'What is it, Claire? It feels like you're spoiling for a fight.'

'I come home on a rare day off and you're all out for the day without giving me a second thought, it feels like no one's really bothered about me being here at all.'

Doug looked thoughtful. 'What are you trying to say, Claire?'

'I'm not trying to say anything, I'm just telling you I feel completely left out.'

Doug was silent for a moment. 'Well, I'm sorry you feel that way, Claire. You must have known this was a day off though? Surely at 9 a.m. they can't have just sprung it on you? If you'd told us we'd have waited for you.'

Claire blushed furiously and folded her arms defensively. 'Waited? I wouldn't have come fishing if you'd have held a gun to my head!'

'So … what's your point then? That you missed the fishing or that we weren't all sitting at home on the off-chance you might actually make it home for once?'

Claire looked annoyed. 'You never include me in anything.'

Doug laughed. 'Claire … come on! You need to be *here* to be included. You've been at home to sleep, what, three times in the last two weeks? The way I see it is, if you wanted to be here you would make more of an effort to be – simple as that.'

'Are you saying I don't want to be here?'

Doug was beginning to get angry. Why was everything a battle?

'Seems that way to me, Claire. I don't know what's going on with you. You're spoiling for a fight all the time. I sense you don't want to be here, I've known you long enough to know it. I get you have a busy job. You rarely let me know what's going on and when you'll be home, so I have to get on and keep things normal for the kids as much as I can. Have you even thought about that? Did you even hear what Christy said about the cake and not buying one for you?'

Claire looked like she was about to explode. 'I keep this family afloat financially while you fanny about on boats all day and this is what I get?'

Doug leant forward and spoke in a low voice so that the kids wouldn't hear if they came back outside.

'This isn't a fucking competition about earnings. I'm sorry you hold what I do in such low regard, but at the end of the day I'm talking about being here for the kids and not the importance of my career path. You used to strike a happy medium with it and split the time as best you could and I'm OK with doing the lion's share because it's what we agreed. Way back. Remember? We agreed it was best for the kids, but now that's not the case, so what's changed? You? Me?'

Claire sneered at him. 'You know you've changed, the accident changed you.'

'Almost dying does, Claire.' Doug snapped. 'It focuses the mind about what's important. And what about you? Did the accident change you or just the way you felt about me and the kids?'

Claire shot back. 'Damn right it did.'

'Well you need to share that with me at some point then, Claire, because I'm not a fucking mind reader.' Tired of conversations and arguments Doug picked up his wine glass. 'Oh, and by the way, you're welcome for the earrings, they look nice. Happy anniversary.'

Claire got up, grabbed her phone and slammed out of the front door, marching down the road. Doug watched her leave and wondered what the hell was going on with her.

When Claire arrived home the house was in darkness. She crept up the stairs, giggling to herself. She crept into the bedroom, undressed and got into bed beside Doug. She gently started to caress him through his boxers. She kissed his neck and back and he turned over towards her still half asleep. He groaned and opened sleepy eyes.

'I thought I was dreaming,' he murmured, kissing her back.

She giggled and hiccupped. He opened an eye.

'You're hammered, Claire, you reek of booze.'

She pushed him onto his back and straddled him, kissing his neck and running her hands up and down his chest.

Doug was having a hard time concentrating on forming a sentence. He grabbed her hands and gently pushed her away from him.

'Claire. You can't keep being these two different people and expecting me to be OK with it.'

She pulled her hands free and reached for him again. Doug got out of bed to try and get some distance between them.

'Don't you find me attractive anymore?' she said, flicking back the sheet to expose her nakedness in full. Doug raked a hand through his hair as she knelt on the edge of the bed and pulled him towards her.

'Jesus, Claire,' he said, grabbing her arm. 'This doesn't solve anything. I don't know who you are anymore. Nice one minute, a total cow the next. We need to talk this out.'

'All you ever want to do is talk. It's boring. You're boring.' She flopped back down on the bed and drew the sheet back over herself, turning her back on him. 'You've missed your chance.'

'Claire,' Doug said softly, in a resigned way. No sound came from Claire, apart from a small snore. He stood for a moment and looked down at the person he thought he knew. He went downstairs, grabbed a blanket and lay awake in the darkness on the sofa, wondering what the hell he was going to do about this marriage that seemed to be spiralling out of control.

CHAPTER 23

Cold water. Trapped. Panic. Blackness. Can't breathe. Lungs bursting. Muffled sounds, thumping, pushing, no way out. Trapped. Panic. Chest tight. Lungs burning. Pain. Terror. Dying. White Light. Flash. Bursting ... White light ...

Doug woke, bathed in sweat, disorientated. Then he realised he was on the sofa. He lay for a moment, eyes closed, trying to get his racing heart under control. He rubbed a hand over his face and breathed out slowly, calmer. It was early. He wandered into the kitchen on a mission for coffee and noticed Claire's handbag and phone had gone. He looked out of the window and saw her car had gone too. He thought about his rejection of her drunken advances. He felt guilty and rotten for pushing her away when she wanted to be close so rarely. He decided he'd pop in and see her at work, in the hope that she'd be free and he could apologise. Perhaps see if she could make time for dinner. Pleased with his decision he headed to the shower, whistling.

Doug was driving when his phone rang through the truck's hands-free speakers. He pressed receive and Stuart's voice boomed through the truck. Doug winced and turned the volume down.

'Doug. Where are you?'

'Hi Stuart, I'm out picking up some new equipment.'

'How long will you be?'

Doug thought for a second. 'Er, looking at a good hour and a half.'

Stuart sucked in a breath noisily. 'I'm back over in a couple of days. I'll pop in and see you then, I've not got the time to wait today.'

'Anything urgent?'

'Just need to check in with you and the others that found the container, fill in a form. See you in a couple of days.'

'OK, give us a shout when you'll be coming. Bye.'

Doug ended the call and the radio took over playing.

Doug pulled into the hospital and parked up. He clapped a paramedic he knew on the back and they exchanged a few pleasantries as he passed him on his way to the hospital main doors.

He strode purposefully across the huge lobby which was full of people milling about looking up at the numerous screens that called patients to their locations. He'd thought carefully about what he was going to say to Claire, and hoped she'd be pleased he'd made the effort to come and say sorry.

Abruptly he stopped walking. He stopped completely.

Doug felt like the bottom had dropped out of his world. He thought for a terrible moment he was going to throw up.

Claire was dressed in bright blue scrubs, waiting by a lift. Opposite her was a man also dressed in scrubs. Their heads were close together. He looked angry and was gesticulating and she was clearly trying to soothe his anger. She pulled his hand to her chest and lifted her hand to stroke his face. The man kissed her on the lips.

Doug's stomach roiled. He felt like he couldn't breathe properly. For a split second he wondered if this was a bad dream. He stared, stunned at what he saw. He felt dizzy, everything seemed surreal. A woman bumped into him and apologised profusely, and he didn't even notice. He couldn't move or speak.

Claire and the man entered the lift when it arrived. She rubbed his shoulder lovingly as they stepped in, smiling at him. She was oblivious to Doug standing in the lobby, with everything he thought he knew crashing around him. The lift doors closed.

Doug felt overwhelmed with sadness. He looked down at his feet trying to control his emotions. After a while, he inhaled deeply and looked up. His eyes were filled with tears. He turned, walking across the lobby to get out of the hospital.

He reached the truck and got in slowly. Automatically, he started the engine and the radio came on to the strains of Amy Winehouse. Doug leant forward and rested his forehead on the steering wheel, not missing the irony of the song playing. He closed his eyes and listened as Amy sang about love being a losing game.

He drove back to the station almost in a trance. He wondered what to do. How did it get to this? What about the kids? Should he tell her he knew? Did everyone else know?

He felt so stupid. Suddenly it all made sense. Never in a million years would he have thought that Claire would betray him this way. He climbed out of the truck and took an armful of boxes round to the station, dumping them in his office and kicking the door shut. He didn't want to face anyone and hoped there wasn't a shout on the shift.

Mercifully he was left alone for most of the afternoon, with the exception of Jesse poking her head round the door asking if he wanted tea. His reply of 'Nope,' had been met with an instant understanding of him wanting to be left alone, so she had reversed out without saying a word and had left him alone all afternoon. She even quietly stuck a post-it note to the small glass window on his office that read *Bye. See you tomorrow* and quietly left the station. He stewed for a while longer and then left to get the kids.

* * *

Doug was sat at the kitchen table surrounded by the paperwork he was being hassled about by Stuart. The kids were watching TV and bickering. The day had been long, and Doug felt wrung out. He heard Claire's key in the door and his stomach churned; he still hadn't worked out what to say to her. He couldn't decide whether he was bat-shit mad and one step off going into orbit, or whether he was just beyond sad and completely resigned about the whole thing.

He felt helpless. Useless. He missed Gav's counsel so much. Gav would have known what to do. He genuinely couldn't get a handle on how he felt. He'd been trying to unpack it. He couldn't process how she could be intimate with him one moment and then clearly be the same with someone else.

Claire marched into the kitchen, chucking her bag and phone on the worktop. She looked in an incredibly bad mood, a stark contrast to the woman Doug had seen cuddling up to the dark-haired man earlier. She yanked open the fridge door.

'Any food?'

'Hello to you too – how was your day?'

Claire tapped her foot impatiently. 'Fine – is there any food? I'm starving.'

Doug decided he was going to try and be pleasant for the moment.

'Well, as per the norm, I had no idea of whether you were going to come home or not, so I'm sorry but I didn't cook you anything, but—'

'Oh great, thanks for that, really helpful.'

Doug continued patiently, 'I was going to say, before you interrupted me, I did some extra pasta in case you did turn up and it's in the fridge so help yourself. The kids are fine, in case you're wondering, but Jude wants to talk to you.'

Claire marched to the fridge and yanked out a bowl with pasta in it. She sniffed it. 'This looks horrendous. What does he want to talk to me about?'

Doug looked at the woman he thought he knew. 'Well no one's forcing you and you're welcome by the way. I don't know. He's worried.'

Claire slammed the fridge door and turned to Doug. 'Why's he worried? Can't you speak to him about it?'

Doug sighed. 'Jude's worried. He thinks you're never here and you don't want to spend any time with him. I've had a chat to him about it.'

'I bet you have,' Claire sneered.

'Meaning?'

'I bet I'm the villain here.'

'Do you really think so little of me, Claire?'

Claire ignored him and turned to the fridge again. 'Is this really all there is? You really could have made the effort you know.'

'Have your pasta, stop spoiling for a fight. Why can't we ever just have a conversation without it being a battle? What are you so angry about all the time?'

Claire rolled her eyes. 'I'm not angry all the time, I'm just annoyed at you. It's not too much to ask for something to eat when I get in, is it?'

Doug said quietly, 'No Claire. You just let me know when you'll be needing a meal and I'll make every effort to provide one.'

'Now you're being obtuse.'

'I'm not. I'm agreeing to your request. Just tell me when you'll be here, and I'll do what I can.'

'Unless of course you're out on a shout …'

'Nature of the beast, in which case, no one gets fed, it's always been that way. What's this sudden issue with my job? It's never been an issue before.'

Doug got up with his empty wine glass and took a bottle from the fridge. He proffered the bottle to Claire, who declined. He walked to the kitchen door and called to the kids to get ready for bed.

'I just think you could do better,' Claire sneered. 'It's a bit of a joke, isn't it? You rescue people from doing stupid things like walking their dog on the wrong beach.'

'Jesus, Claire. Yes, I do rescue idiots that need help, it's part of the job. There are the stupid ones and there are the unlucky ones. A few weeks ago I pulled a young boy out of the sea, dead, because he'd been swept in while fishing. He was only a few years older than Jude. Seven hours we looked for him. We started off looking for a living boy who had been swept in and finished off looking for a fucking corpse. Every time we go out it's a risk for all of us. A risk we accept, but we do it to help people and some of us have died doing exactly that. So tell me, Claire, why is that so bad?'

Claire just stood looking at him. 'I can't do this anymore. I need a break from all this.'

'A break from "all what" exactly?' he said, gesturing around the room with his wine glass. 'It's not like you're a regular feature here, is it?'

'A break from all of this. You, me, your job, this life, the kids.'

Doug leant forward and said very quietly. 'Look Claire, by all means you "take a break" from me and my job as it seems such a fucking issue, to be honest I won't see much of a difference. But don't you fucking dare tell me you need a break from the kids. They've done nothing to deserve this.'

'I can't be what they want me to be,' Claire said.

'Oh and what's that Claire? A responsible fucking parent?'

'Don't talk to me about responsibilities. I keep this family afloat financially.'

'Bollocks, you just think you do. You have no idea. What else, Claire? What else are you bringing to the table apart from some money. Have the money. We'll manage absolutely fine without your money. I'm assuming you'll be leaving us for the guy you've been seeing for … how many months since the accident?'

As he talked, realisation dawned on Doug's face.

'It was before the accident. Oh God. It was going on before the accident, wasn't it? Were you with him that night? That's why they couldn't get hold of you? It was, wasn't it? Oh my God, how fucking stupid am I? How did I not see it? I thought something was off with you. Then I saw you, earlier, and all this time suddenly made sense. Who is he? Another surgeon? Of course, he is. I bet you've got no issues with what he does for a living.'

Claire looked angry. 'Felix is – wait, what? When did you see us?'

Doug laughed in disbelief. 'Felix?'

'I'm not going to get into this. When did you see us?'

'Not get into what exactly? Not get into how much of a fucking farce the past two years have been? The concerned and supportive wife? I came to see you at the hospital today. To talk, to apologise for rejecting you last night. Oh my God.' He tapped his forehead with the heel of his hand. 'I've got to have been a fucking idiot not to have suspected something sooner.'

He drank some wine, shaking his head at his own stupidity.

'You know, I could understand it if you were spending time with the kids and being a good mum to them, but you've been absent. You really don't give two fucks about them, it's like they're an inconvenience to you. I've been the one mopping up their tears, helping them with their issues and being around for them while you've been off shagging your surgeon boyfriend.' Doug stopped talking as the kitchen door slowly opened and Jude stood in the doorway.

'Dad? What's going on? Why are you two yelling?'

Doug got up and went over to Jude, giving him a hug. 'Mum and Dad are just having a few words, mate. Nothing to worry about, go to bed.'

Jude pushed Doug away and went to stand in front of Claire.

'I heard it, I heard it all. You've got a boyfriend, you don't want Dad anymore and you don't want us! I hate you. I never want to see you again,' he sobbed.

Claire stepped forward to try to embrace Jude. He pushed her away and ran off upstairs, sobbing.

Claire went to go after him.

'Leave it,' said Doug. 'That'll make it worse. I'll go in a minute. I think you need to give him some space.'

'Are you chucking me out of my own home?'

'Don't fucking tempt me, Claire, and don't you dare act the injured party here. I'm thinking about the kids. I think you should give them some space. I'll tell Christy tomorrow. You should at least make an effort to see them yourself in a couple of days.'

Doug moved to go and see Jude. 'I mean it, Claire. Get some things and go. Come and see them in a few days.'

Claire marched towards the foot of the stairs and spoke to Doug's retreating back.

'You can't tell me what to do with my own children, Doug. I'm not going anywhere. I need to tell them myself, I know my children and I need to tell them myself.'

Doug turned and faced Claire. He spoke quietly, trying to control his temper.

'OK … What's Christy been upset about for at least the last week? Full-on tears most mornings before school? No idea? What's her favourite book this term? Who's she having friendship issues with? What about Jude? What are the issues he's got going at school at the moment? Which girl has he got the hots for? No idea? Well Claire, once you've the remotest idea about what's going on in their lives you can lecture me on what you think is best for them – until then, you let me fucking deal with it.'

Claire looked furiously at Doug. 'You bastard. I can do what I like with them, they're my kids. You can't tell me what to do with them.'

Doug thought for a minute. 'OK. Am I misreading this then? Do you want them with you? You have them, take them to school, pick them up, ferry them about.'

Claire sneered. 'You forget I did all that when you were ill, after the accident.'

Doug laughed. 'You fucking didn't. You took advantage of all our friends and Helen too. You used them all and relied on them to have the kids almost all the time, claiming you were busy at work. Don't think I don't know how much you got them to do.'

'You don't have to be like this.'

Doug looked incredulous. 'Be like what? Fucked off beyond belief because I feel the most colossal sense of betrayal from the person who is supposed to be closest to me? Feel completely used and angry because just last night you were doing your level best to fuck me, then go back to fucking your boyfriend today?'

'I'm sorry Doug ... I never meant ...'

'Never meant to what, Claire?'

Claire said quietly, 'I never wanted to hurt you.'

'Bollocks. There's a line, Claire. Every single person is tested with this line in a long relationship. Every single person. This is why some relationships make it and some don't. A bit of harmless flirting is lovely, who doesn't enjoy that? But most people step back from that line when they know it's going to be crossed. They realise they've too much to lose, but you, well, you knew full well you were going to cross it and you went and jumped right in with both feet.'

'Doug ... it didn't happen that way.'

Claire stepped forward towards Doug. He put his hands up as if to ward her off.

'Come on Claire. We've both been there. The difference is, I stepped back from the line at the right moment and you didn't.'

Claire looked angry. 'What? Are you telling me you said no to someone? Who?'

'It was a moment, just a moment and I stepped back. Because all of this ... was too important to me.'

Jude wailed from his bedroom. 'Dad? Can you come up?'

Claire sighed. 'You'd better go up. I'm going to hang on here for a bit. See what he says.'

Doug pushed open the door to Jude's bedroom. Jude was lying face down on the bed sobbing. He lifted his head as Doug walked in, his heart almost breaking at the sight.

'Dad, is Mum really going? I said she was, didn't I? I knew it.'

Doug sat down next to him. 'Yes, Mum's taking a break. But it's from me. Not you guys.'

'Does this mean you and Mum are getting divorced?'

'I don't know if the truth be known. I just don't know.'

Jude sniffed. 'But Mum's not going to live here anymore?'

'No, not for a while anyway. But you'll still see her, so not a lot will change really.'

Jude thought for a minute. He flung himself on Doug and hugged him tightly. 'You're not going anywhere are you, Dad? You're staying here with us?'

Doug hugged him tightly. 'Jude, I'm not going anywhere.'

'Good. I don't want you to leave, Dad. I love you, Dad.'

'Ditto mate …'

Doug tousled his hair. 'Come on. You need to get some sleep now.'

'OK Dad. Can you stay a bit?'

Doug stretched out on the bed next to him. Jude snuggled into the crook of Doug's arm and fell asleep quickly. After a while Doug kissed the top of Jude's head and eased himself away slowly, leaving the room quietly and shutting the door.

Claire was sat in the kitchen with a glass of wine in front of her. She looked up as Doug walked in. 'How is he?'

'Asleep. Worried. Upset.'

'Worried?'

'Worried that I'll go too.'

'What did you say?'

'I told him you were leaving me not them. That they would still see you. That nothing much would change for them.'

Claire touched him on the arm. 'Thank you.'

'I didn't do it for you, I did it for them. They'll realise sooner or later you've walked out on us all without a backward glance.'

Claire frowned. 'Look, I'm on an early tomorrow. I'm going to stay tonight and then leave early before the kids are up. Do you not think we ought to tell them together?'

Doug shook his head. 'Jude will tell Christy and then I'll fill in the blanks. She goes into his room first thing when she wakes up and they chat.'

'How long have they been doing that?'

'Since I came home from the hospital, I think. They have a worry book they write their worries down in and they write answers and solutions together in the mornings.'

'I never knew ...'

Doug raised an eyebrow and took a sip of wine.

'So ... does your boyfriend know you're doing this tonight? Telling us you're leaving?'

'No, no he doesn't,' Claire replied awkwardly

'He's in for a big surprise then,' Doug said deadpan.

Doug's pager went off loudly in the quiet house. Doug jumped up. 'I need to go. I'll try to get out of it if I can and get back. If I have to go then knock next door and tell Nessie when you're going, and she'll come in and sit with the kids. They're more than used to it.'

Claire snapped. 'After everything that's happened tonight, you're going on a shout?'

'I don't have a choice, Claire. Just like when you get called into surgery, you don't have a choice either.'

He grabbed his keys and ran out of the front door.

Doug returned in the early hours. He let himself into the house quietly and went to check on each child and then entered his bedroom, forgetting Claire was there. He stopped in his tracks when he saw Claire asleep in the bed. He closed the door quietly and returned downstairs to sleep on the sofa. Once again, he lay there, wide awake in the darkness, thinking about how everything had changed in the space of a day.

CHAPTER 24

Dr Emma Marshall was fast asleep in bed when her mobile phone interrupted her dream. She woke, fumbled for the offending item, knocking it onto the floor where it stopped ringing instantly. Emma retrieved it from the floor, called the voicemail service and lay back on the bed.

'Hello, this is a message for Emma Marshall. This is the Governor from Lewes Prison here. Please can you call me urgently on this number as soon as you can. Thank you.'

Emma snuggled into her bed further. 'Naughty little brother, what've you been up to?'

She dialled the number the Governor had left. It was answered almost instantly.

'This is Emma Marshall. You've just left a message for me regarding my brother. Is he OK?' She listened for a moment. 'When did this happen? Is he conscious? Right. I'm leaving here shortly. I'm in Wales so I'll be some time. If you could tell him I'm on my way. Thank you.'

She sat on the side of the bed, tapping her phone against her hand thoughtfully.

Hours later, in the early morning, Emma arrived at the prison. She parked her car in her usual brisk fashion, and lightly jogged towards the main door. She went through security and was accompanied into a lobby by a male prison officer.

'He's in here.'

The prison officer ushered Emma into the medical room, where she saw Chris lying in a hospital bed, eyes closed and sleeping. His bandaged wrists lay on top of the blankets and there was a long cut on his neck held together by steri-strips.

Emma approached the bed, taking his hand. 'Hey, little brother. How you doing?'

Chris opened his eyes, smiling weakly in greeting.

'What on earth have you done, my love?' she said, stroking his face.

'Couldn't take it, Sis,' Chris mumbled.

Emma turned and regarded the prison officer. 'Can I have a moment alone please?'

The prison officer shook his head. 'No Madam. Prison rules.'

Emma pulled up a chair nearer to the bed. She took Chris's hand and whispered, 'Well this is quite the development. Have your plans changed? Can you not get out?'

Chris whispered, 'I've got a better chance of getting out of a mental hospital, that's what my guy says. He can help me get out of that.'

Emma called the prison officer over. 'Is the doctor here?'

'Not yet, Madam. He's due in about an hour.'

'I'd like to speak to the doctor please, as soon as he arrives.'

She turned to Chris. 'You can't stay here, they can't cater for your psychological needs. You can't be left alone,' she said loudly, and Chris nodded weakly.

'I can't take it here, Sis. I see them coming for me in the night.'

'Who's coming for you?'

Chris pointed in the corner with a shaky finger. 'Them. They whisper and tell me what to do. I have to do it otherwise they'll hurt me.'

Emma turned to the prison officer. 'How long has he been like this?'

'Since they brought him in.'

'Chris, tell me … who are you seeing?'

'The Whisperers. They're all there. Can't you see them? They're dressed in funny clothes. Tell them to go, Em, they'll listen to you,' he said in anguish.

Emma greeted the prison doctor coolly when he arrived, making a point of looking at her watch.

'Finally. Hello, Doctor. Needless to say, I'm most concerned about my brother. Have you assessed him?'

The doctor was nervous under Emma's uncompromising gaze.

'I have. I've also had my colleague who's his regular psychologist assess him.'

'You should know I'm also a psychiatrist in private practice. What are your conclusions?'

The prison doctor looked uncomfortable. 'Well, it's clear he's undergoing a psychological event, which prompted him to try and take his own life. He's clearly psychotic at the moment and as such, I do believe he's a danger to himself. My colleague concurs. We've recommended he be moved to a secure mental unit that is equipped to deal with this sort of behaviour.'

'And?'

'We have four options location wise. The Governor wanted your opinion as to where we should place him.'

'Where are they?'

He fumbled with paperwork and looked flustered.

'Er, oh here we are. London, Yorkshire, Cornwall or Glamorgan.'

'Well, Glamorgan would be nearer me, which would be better for him, I think. Where in Glamorgan?'

'I'm not sure'

Emma rolled her eyes. 'When is this likely to happen?'

The prison doctor shrugged. 'A few days, we'll keep him sedated here. Let the wounds heal a little and then move him in secure transport.'

Emma frowned. 'When will you tell him?'

'I suggest you tell him.'

Emma looked thoughtful for a moment. 'Were there no early indicators of potential self-harm? What might have been a trigger? Any ideas?'

The prison doctor sighed. 'In this environment, I've no idea. He does need to be moved where he can be monitored more. He's certainly in no condition to stand trial now until he's undergone assessments and treatment and that could take months.'

Emma regarded the doctor silently and then spoke briskly. 'I'll go and tell him we're moving him. How long do we think it will be for?'

'I'd say it's fairly indefinite at the moment.'

Emma raised her eyebrows. 'Thank you, doctor.'

She returned to the hospital ward and sat with Chris. Very quietly, she outlined the plan going forward, all the while looking exactly like the concerned sister.

* * *

Jimmy was crapping himself. The nurse told him he received a visitor, but as it was outside of visiting hours, she refused to allow him in. Despite Jimmy viewing the nurse as a bit of a battle-axe, he seriously considered kissing her when she described the visitor to Jimmy – a tall man with lots of tattoos on his arms and foreign-sounding, perhaps Russian or Polish. Jimmy was terrified and was living on his nerves. All he needed now was the Irish guy who had nearly killed him to come back and finish the job properly.

The Russians were still after the gear he had left down in the pots to hide from the Irish.

He was desperate to get out, get the pots back and try and find a way out of this mess, but he still couldn't think straight, let alone walk straight. He was terrified they would catch up with Marie and hurt her. Or they would come for him again and then he knew it wouldn't go well – whoever came for him.

He contented himself that at least Marie was safe for a while as she was temporarily staying with her mother, who lived nearer the hospital, so she could be closer to Jimmy.

He tried to think. His head felt like it was full of cotton wool. He didn't know who he could ask for help, didn't know how he was going to get out of this mess. He turned over in bed painfully and tried to organise his thoughts, the pure effort of which sent him off to sleep almost instantly.

* * *

The summer holidays were in full swing. It was late afternoon, and the beach was scattered with families. To one side was a large group of people, many in blue RNLI T-shirts. Most of the crew had turned up for the annual summer barbecue, bringing friends and family, kids and dogs.

Someone had started a fire, and it was surrounded by huge pieces of driftwood that various people were perching on or leaning against. People chatted and laughed, catching up with each other. The tide was in and the small inshore lifeboat was pulled up past the shoreline.

Jesse laughed to herself as she spotted them in the distance, even this far away she could see Paul bossing people about as he took over the barbecue. She strolled towards them with Brock at her heels, swinging her cool bag, looking forward to the afternoon. As she strolled, she thought to herself that Emma would say she felt happy and relaxed because she was around people who would look after and protect her. Her stomach contracted at the thought of another appointment; she wasn't ready to face the direct stare of Dr Marshall just yet. She was afraid she would look at her with those green eyes and know exactly how Jesse had started to feel about Doug. Jesse just didn't want to admit it yet.

In the distance she saw Christy waving madly, running along the beach towards her.

'Jesse! I was hoping you'd come,' she said as she flung herself at Jesse for a hug.

Jesse hugged her lightly. 'You look very pretty today.'

'I know. I've been playing with the puppy over there, he's called Mousse after chocolate mousse. He's sweet, isn't he? Look, he's there.' she said, pointing.

Jesse squinted into the distance. 'Oh, he's adorable, isn't he? I'll have to keep an eye on Brock, though, he's a bit grumpy with puppies. He likes to tell them off.'

As they approached the throng of people, Mike and Paul came over.

She looked at them both. 'OK … so who came in the inshore lifeboat?'

Paul raised a hand. 'That would be me. I thought if we get a shout it's a long way back to the station. So, I brought it here, we can drop it back to the harbour later.'

Jesse looked impressed. 'It's a good idea. I like your thinking.'

Mike chuckled. 'Smacks of being a bunch of lazy arses to me, but who am I to criticise?'

Nicky appeared and passed Paul a bottle of beer.

'Hi Jesse, good to see you here,' she said warmly. Paul threw an arm around Nicky's shoulder.

'Thanks love … See? She caters for my every need, don't you love? One in a million here.'

Nicky rolled her eyes. 'Idiot,' she said. 'So, we're gonna start cooking in a bit … no doubt you'll want to come and interfere and pretend you know what you're doing?' She nudged Jesse. 'What is it with men and barbecues? Half the time they couldn't work the cooker if their life depended on it, but the minute you get a barbecue out, suddenly they're all experts?'

Jesse laughed and proffered her cool bag. 'Oh, I've got some stuff that can go on for everyone.' She looked around. 'Is Doug not coming tonight?'

Paul glanced around. 'He is. He was helping Claire move the rest of her gear out of the house, he'll be down later. Right, let me get my barbecue gear on, this is where the magic happens, my friends.'

He produced an apron with a picture of the torso of a muscular man in tiny trunks on the front, and then produced a chef's hat. He gestured to the apron, his face looking ridiculous on top of the muscled torso. 'You know this is based on me, right? I take my cooking here very seriously, you know.'

Dan wandered over and raised an eyebrow at Paul. 'Shit. Why are we letting him cook? He's clueless. If he's in charge, then everything just gets served black.'

Paul looked affronted. 'Hello? I'm here, you know, and I find that a tiny bit offensive. OK. You supervise then. You supposedly know what you're doing.'

Ben appeared, his arm around a very pretty brunette. 'Alright, everyone? Jesus, lads, we're not letting him cook, are we? Dan, for our sake, please step in and supervise. Jesus, Bruv, what are you wearing?'

In the distance, a lifeguard beach buggy came into view, towing a flatbed trailer. Doug was driving the buggy and standing in the trailer was Bob, holding onto Billy in his wheelchair. He stopped the buggy near the fire and the crew helped to remove some ply sheets and laid them on the sand, forming a path to the bonfire for Billy's wheelchair. Bob, Doug and Tom helped Billy down the ramp and got him settled by the chairs around the fire. Jesse went up and kissed him on the cheek.

'You didn't say you were coming, you old rogue. How are you?'

'Hello, lass. I'm good, thanks. I feel wonderful. Where's that dog of yours? I got a treat for him.'

Jesse laughed. 'You only want me for my dog.'

'Probably true,' Billy agreed, his eyes sparkling.

Jesse turned to look for the dog, who was a speck in the distance with Doug's kids. She shielded her eyes.

'He's off with Doug's two. He adores them.'

Billy eyed her. 'He's not the only one, is he?'

Jesse turned, a flush creeping over her face. She felt embarrassed that Billy had seen it.

'Do you want a beer?' she asked, changing the subject. Nicky appeared as if by magic with a beer for Billy.

'Here you go, my sweet. Good to see you, Billy. We miss you.'

She kissed him on the cheek and rubbed his arm. Doug joined the group and nudged Jesse.

'Hello, you. Good to see you here.'

Jesse grinned at him. 'It's good to be here. That's a nice thing you did to bring Billy.'

Doug smiled. 'Ahh, he always loved this barbecue with everyone. One of his favourite things, isn't it Bill?'

Bob was stood off to the side looking out to sea, slightly removed from the group.

Jesse called over to him. 'Bob, can I get you a beer?'

Bob didn't even look at her. 'I can help myself. Don't need you to do it for me.'

Jesse rolled her eyes.

Nicky called. 'Bob! Stop being a miserable old git. Jesse's just being friendly. Now,' she tuned and shouted, 'who's up for a game of rounders?'

There was much whooping from the crowd, and they gathered themselves together, pushing and shoving.

Nicky shouted. 'Girls versus boys?'

Paul was first to bat and missed every ball, which resulted in a lot of name-calling. Mike was up next and hit it right up the beach, with all the dogs racing after it, including Brock.

Jesse laughed. 'Oh Christ, we'll never wrestle the ball off that lot.' The two teams changed over, and Doug was ordered onto last base. Jesse stepped up to bat and ignored all the banter to try and put her off. She hit the ball hard and started running, she was flat out. Dan wrestled the ball off a dog and threw it back to third base just as she passed it.

'Throw it!' screamed Paul.

Ben threw it to Doug just as Jesse approached last base and, in a final push, she hurled herself at the base, landing on it the split second after Doug had launched himself sideways to catch the ball. They crashed into each other, both hitting the ground together, ending up sprawled in a tangle of limbs and sand. They were both breathless and laughing hard.

Paul looked over. 'Oi! Get a room. Come on food's nearly ready.'

Everyone immediately abandoned the game and rushed over to the food. Doug propped himself onto his elbow and looked down at Jesse, both of them were still laughing.

He brushed a piece of seaweed off her cheek gently.

Jesse rubbed her side. 'I think I ran straight into your elbow.'

'Sorry about that. You OK?'

'I'm fine thanks. Really, apart from a bruise the size of your elbow.'

The two stared at each other for a moment too long.

Jude shouted impatiently. 'DAD!'

Doug didn't take his eyes off Jesse. 'Yeah?'

'COME ON, I'm hungry.'

Doug moved away from Jesse slightly and called to Jude. 'Dig in. Help yourself. You don't need me to get it for you.'

Doug stood and put an arm down to help Jesse up. He yanked her up quickly and she fell against him, laughing, and they took a moment to brush the sand off themselves, Doug picked another bit of seaweed from Jesse's hair, while Brock danced around them both.

The day had been full of games, laughter, eating and drinking. As evening fell someone had stoked up the fire and put on some music. While the sky darkened, some of the smaller kids started yawning and were being settled into blankets by the fire. Doug looked at his watch and walked over to Billy.

'Bill, your lift is here in a minute, let's load you back up, mate.'

Doug drove the buggy back to the car park, with Bob holding onto Billy as they went. The crew waved and shouted goodbyes.

Doug and Bob made sure Billy was safely in his minibus and then walked back along the beach.

As they strolled, Doug said quietly to Bob. 'You know, Bob, you should cut Jesse a break.'

Bob raised an eyebrow. 'Why's that?'

'Because if it hadn't been for her, his recovery would be nosediving in the other direction. I know what he asked you to do. He told me he feels bad about it. But he's got a reason to keep going now. Perhaps some acknowledgement of that would be nice.'

Bob shook his head, his face hard. 'Can't do that.'

Doug looked over at him. 'Any reason why not?'

Bob stopped. 'Because I'm angry with her. And him. One minute he's asking me to help him end it and the next it's like it never happened. She waltzes in has a cup of tea with him and he's like a different person.'

'And why do you think that was, Bob?' Doug asked quietly.

Bob huffed. 'I don't know … but it pisses me off. *She* pisses me off.'

Doug tried not to smile. 'God, you're a stubborn old git. Well I don't know what she said, but I think it's because she just saw it a bit differently to how we'd all been seeing it. Makes sense really, she thought just because he was in a chair, it didn't stop him from still helping out and being involved, while we had all been treating him like things were over for him. It's not rocket science. I wish to God we'd thought that way to be honest. Give her a break. I think you're just pissed off because, despite how you felt for him, you didn't think to look at it this way. Nothing wrong with that, sometimes you just need a fresh pair of eyes.'

Bob grunted and shook his head. 'Doesn't mean I've got to speak to her, does it?'

As they arrived back at the fire Bob stomped off to get some food.

Nicky approached Doug. 'There you are! The kids have asked if they can come back for a sleepover. Is that OK with you?'

'You sure? They'd love that. Do you need me to bring anything around?'

'No, you're alright love.' She said. 'They can borrow what they need. I'll text you when they're up tomorrow. You have a night off and enjoy yourself,' she said, looking meaningfully at Jesse.

Oblivious to Nicky's intentions, Doug looked around for the kids.

'Kids!' he yelled.

Jude and Christy came running up to Doug breathless.

Jude grabbed Doug's arm. 'So, can we?'

Doug nodded and Jude punched the air. 'Yes!'

'Best behaviour and all that tonight or there'll be trouble,' Doug called as they ran off.

Some of the crew were gathering up sleepy kids and heading off with various hugs and waves. Paul and Nicky collected up all the kids going home with them and got themselves ready to go. Jude and Christy hugged Doug, and Christy ran over to give Jesse a hug, while Jude hugged Brock.

Doug looked at the two of them. 'Be good and I'll see you tomorrow,' he said sternly.

Paul called back to Doug, 'Doug, are you alright taking the rib back to the shed later?'

'No probs mate.'

Paul threw the keys at Doug and the family headed off. Doug, Tom, Ben, Jesse, Dan and Mike remained around the fire, chatting.

Tom had been watching Doug quietly staring into the fire, sipping a beer.

'Doug, are you OK mate?'

Doug looked surprised. 'I'm fine. Why d'you ask?'

'We heard that Claire left, and Paul mentioned you were helping Claire pack the rest of her stuff ...'

There was an awkward silence.

'Sorry mate ... I didn't mean ...' Tom began.

Doug sighed. 'It's OK. Yup. Claire left nearly a month ago now. I've come to the conclusion that the only person surprised by this seems to be me. She has a new fella. Been going a while. Kids are staying with me.'

Mike shook his head. 'Sorry mate.'

'Yeah, sorry mate,' Ben echoed.

Dan glanced Doug. 'I think in some ways it's a good thing.'

The others looked at Dan in surprise. Doug raised an eyebrow.

'How's that?'

'Seems to me like Claire's been pretty absent for a while, it's like she doesn't want to be part of this … this whole bigger family thing we have, like today. All I'm saying is that, maybe for you, mate, it's a good thing. I mean it's not good for the kids at all, but for you and you being happy. You're not so old you can't meet anyone else.'

'Thanks … I think,' Doug said wryly. 'I'm not sure how I feel about it at the moment. I think it's been on the cards for a while. Hindsight is a wonderful thing, eh? I can't believe I didn't see it. Kids are doing well though. They'd got used to her not being around so it's not a major change for them. That was my biggest worry.'

'They seem good,' Mike said getting to his feet. 'Sorry guys, I'm heading off. I promised to have a drink with some mates. Tom, you coming? Dan?'

Tom nodded and stood, brushing sand off his backside. He hauled Dan up too. Ben got up quickly looking at his watch.

'Shit, I'm in trouble, I've got to pick up her ladyship from Zumba, whatever the bloody hell that is. Laters everyone.' He jogged off down the beach.

'See you later, guys,' said Mike.

Dan and Tom waved as they walked back together.

Doug glanced at Jesse. 'Are you staying a while?'

'I'm not wasting a good fire and a nice bottle of plonk.'

'D'you want some company?' Doug asked. 'I'm footloose and fancy free from the kids all of a sudden.'

'Why not?' she said with a grin.

CHAPTER 25

Doug settled himself by the fire.

'How's your elbow-shaped bruise?'

'I'll live.'

'I'm glad you came today.'

'Me too. I really enjoyed it. Look … I'm sorry about Claire. I've seen you've been a bit off for a while and we just thought it wise to leave you alone. It's not because I – or we – don't care or anything. The boys said to give you some space and you'd share whatever it was when you were ready. Not to push it.'

'Ahhh, hence the wide berth …'

Jesse grimaced. 'Not very supportive, is it though?'

'Ach, it's fine. I've woken up and smelt the coffee as they say. Now I just wonder how I could've been so stupid as not to see it.'

'Nobody thinks that.'

'I do.' He sighed.

'How do you feel now … about it all?'

Doug stared into the fire for a moment.

'How do I feel?' he murmured. '... I feel ... Angry ... Cheated ... Galactically stupid for not seeing it. I thought I was a good judge of character.'

'Sometimes we just don't see what's right there in front of us. Or we just don't want to see it,' Jesse said softly.

'Sounds like the voice of experience. It's not about me anyway, it's about the kids.'

Jesse leant forward. 'The thing is Doug. It is about you. Yes, it's about the kids too. But they're OK. They're great, well-adjusted kids. You matter in all of this too. Your feelings, your future. You can't let this define how you're going to live your life. Trust me.'

They both stared into the fire for a while, lost in thought. Brock was lying against Jesse, snoring gently. Doug leant against the log next to her.

'What happened to you, Jesse? What happened back down south?' He reached out and pointed to the long scar on her face. 'What happened here?'

Jesse sighed shakily, sometimes it still felt too raw.

'I've not really told anyone.'

Doug said softly. 'OK. It'll stay with me.'

Jesse hugged her knees. Brock opened an eye and got comfortable again. She stroked his side.

'I was at the station in Hastings. I was so happy there. Great crew. Really close. Like you and the boys here. We had a shout one day and the local police were involved. That's when I met Chris. We started to go out and got a thing going. It was really good in the beginning ... isn't that what they all say?'

Doug raised an eyebrow. 'So he was a copper then?'

'Yeah, a detective. He was desperate to progress and worked hard, long hours. I got that, understood it, you know? Must have been the same for you and Claire? But then he started getting weird about the shouts and getting possessive. He had real issues about me being the only female in the crew. You know I look back and wonder why I didn't go, why I didn't bail, but it was one of those slow burns, you know? It's only when something terrible happens that you realise you have perspective on what's gone before it and it's only then you realise you can't believe you've ended up in this situation.'

'Totally hear you there,' Doug said softly. 'How long were you with him?'

'Too long – about three years, I think. The first time it happened I should have just gone. But I didn't. I listened to all the excuses and forgave him.'

'How did you hide it from the guys at work?'

'They tried to talk to me about it. One of them knew he had form for it, knew a friend of a friend who'd experienced it. They didn't like him at all. They found hitting women abhorrent. They told me he was no good. Looking back, it was sweet of them. But I ignored it obviously.'

'Did he have family locally? Anyone close to him?'

'He talked about a sister. I think she was a doctor or a dentist or something, she wasn't local, and they hardly saw each other. He was very isolated in that sense. I think he'd had a very bad childhood looking back. No parents I think, in care a lot.'

Jesse helped herself to more wine.

'It was never that predictable, perhaps if it was, I could've avoided it. It was random ... totally random. One time he came home furious because they'd had to let a suspect go because of a technical hitch. We were having dinner and the next thing I knew I was on the floor and he was hitting me with a wine bottle. Going hell for leather. Cracked a couple of ribs that night.' She stared off into the fire, remembering.

'Afterwards he was sorry. Mortified. He didn't remember it, he loved me. All that crap. He was always sorry. Never meant to do it. Then things changed a bit more. One night I'd been out with the crew. Chris was invited but said he couldn't come so I went. It was a great night, a right laugh. All the guys were there and their partners and families. Anyway, one of the guys had driven, as his wife was due to have their baby any minute, so they gave me a lift home. I got home and Chris wasn't there, his car had gone, and I just assumed he was at work. So I went to bed. I was woken up with him standing over me ... you know how sometimes you sense a presence, and you sort of jump awake?'

Doug nodded.

'So it was Chris. He'd been drinking. Turns out he'd followed me to the party, and he'd been watching me all night. He was utterly livid. He really hurt me that night. He was saying that something was going on with the guy who brought me home, that we'd done stuff in the car, even with his heavily pregnant wife in there too ... it was crazy ... just crazy.'

'Jesus, what happened after that?'

'Took me a while to get over that, physically anyway. I decided I couldn't live like it anymore and he had to go. I talked to a couple of the guys and they said they'd stand by to come and help me if things got nasty. So I decided to tell him I was moving out. I had a friend who had a holiday home that was free for the winter and she said I could use it until I was back on my feet. So I went home and packed my gear and loaded the car. He came home. I said I'm going and he said OK. I'm sorry it didn't work out and all that.'

'So you left?'

'Yes and went to my friend's place and carried on. Looking back I thought it was weird that there was no reaction, no ... consequences. Life carried on. I suppose I should have noticed. He'd been following me. I got called out to a shout one night late – some idiot had fallen off the pier while being chased by the police. Chris was there and he was lovely to me. Nice to the lads. He was like the old Chris. His shift was ending so he said let's go for a late coffee which we did. Thinking about it now, I realise how clever he was ... he was being so nice it was almost like all the violence hadn't really happened. There was part of me that started to think maybe I'd overreacted and that maybe I'd over-egged the whole thing ... you know? Was he really that bad after all?'

'Did you go back to him?'

'He asked me to. Talked about starting a family and that. Promised he'd get help with his anger.'

Tears rolled down Jesse's face as she talked. Doug took her hand and held it gently.

'You OK?'

Jesse swiped tears away. 'Yeah.'

'Then what happened?'

'I told him I needed to think about it. And for a couple of weeks we went out on a few dates and it was lovely. Like the old days. Then, stupidly, I went back. I say stupidly now, but at the time it made sense. So I gave up my friend's house and moved back in. Things were good for a while. We went out more, laughed more. Talked about a future, talked about a family. All those normal things.'

207

'I'm almost frightened to ask what happened next.'

'An old friend turned up. I'd known him for years, we were at marine college together. So he turns up and Chris is working, so I call Chris and say that we're going out for dinner and if he finishes up to come down. So … we go out and have a lovely dinner and my mate trots off. Then I get a call from Chris. He says I've just seen you say goodbye to your boyfriend, see you at home. I thought, "Oh shit … he's off on one again." So I decide to head it off. I call him back and say, "Look, you've got it wrong, he's just a mate, I'm with you." Then I said sleep at the station tonight because you're too angry to come home, you'll do something stupid.'

'What did he say then?'

'Nothing. He just hung up. I didn't know what to make of it. So I went home and double-locked the front door. Then about half an hour later he rings me and says, "Are you ready?" I said, "Ready for what?" Then he laughed at me and said, "Are you ready for the overdue beating you need, you fucking bitch?" He sounded crazy … mad … unhinged.'

Doug leant forward. 'Jesus.'

'Then he told me he was going to kill me and enjoy every second of it. So I called the police. I was utterly terrified.'

'Did the police come?' Doug asked softly.

'When they did come, they thought I was dead. I remember vaguely hearing one of them say they didn't think I'd make it.'

'Jesus. What did he do to you?'

Jesse was staring off past Doug, her eyes filling with tears again as she remembered.

'He kicked the absolute shit out of me, literally. He raped me, then went to work with his police baton, just to be sure. I don't remember that much. Apparently, I was pregnant, so that ended that. The kicking was so violent they had to perform a hysterectomy to stop the bleeding. He broke both of my legs, and both arms too. I remember thinking it would be good to die just to put an end to it, all the pain, you know?' She sniffed and wiped her eyes.

Doug put an arm around her and pulled her close to him.

'I was still in hospital when the Professional Standards Department for the police turned up. Nice lady called Leslie. She helped me through it. They'd been looking at Chris for some time for various other issues of violence against suspects and a couple of staff members. After the attack he went missing, turned up at my best friend's house, where they finally arrested him, but not until after he'd beaten the crap out of her trying to find out where I was.'

'Was she OK?'

'She never really got over it. She was a lawyer, she lives in Europe now, couldn't live here anymore, she doesn't contact me either. She says it's too painful. Anyway, he's on remand awaiting trial. Likelihood is that I'll have to testify. He's a slippery bastard. For my safety, they told me I couldn't go back. That I wasn't allowed back for anything. They were fairly sure he or his friends would kill me, or at least try anyway. So, I'm here now. Starting again. Telling you all this.'

Doug's eyes were cold and a muscle pounded in his cheek. He looked angry.

'I want to kill him.'

Jesse sniffed. 'I think you need to get in line for that.'

Doug pulled her closer to him. 'Are you safe? Really safe? Does anyone know where you are?'

'Far as I know, it's OK. They laid a pretty good trail to suggest I'd gone overseas so I think people think that's what happened. I've a person locally I can call if I get into trouble or if I think I'm not safe.'

'You know you can always come to me,' he said, squeezing her gently.

'I know,' she said softly. 'Thanks, Doug. Means a lot.'

She sniffed. 'For ages, I was too scared to go out. I was terrified of everything and everyone. Then one day I thought to myself, is this what he's left me with? Is this my life? Then I thought, No. I'm not going to live like this, so I started trying to rebuild my life. Piece by piece. Take it from someone who knows.' She sighed heavily. 'You do need to think about you Doug and your life. I can guarantee you being happy will mean the kids will be happy.'

'The voice of reason.'

'You know it.'

'I do now.'

She shivered; the fire had died down and the wind had whipped up a little.

'Shall we get this boat back to the shed?'

'Yup. It's getting choppy out there.'

Doug stood and reached a hand down to help Jesse up. He said softly, 'Thank you for telling me all that. I know it must have been hard. I meant what I said. I'm here if you need me.'

Jesse squeezed his hand. 'Thanks.'

He turned to kick the fire out with sand. Jesse put the empties in the bin and whistled for Brock, who ran over and jumped in the boat. They pushed the boat into the shallows and got in. They sped back towards the harbour in the evening light.

Together they heaved the boat onto the boat trolley and dragged it up the ramp. Doug half shut the doors and Jesse started to hose down the boat.

Doug leant against the workbench, arms folded, watching her. 'Did you have a good time tonight?'

Jesse smiled as she hosed. 'I really enjoyed it. They're such a lovely bunch. I felt part of something again. That's not happened for a long time. So good to see Billy there too.'

She was silent for a minute as she hosed.

'Dan didn't upset you with what he said about Claire, did he? In front of the lads?'

Doug snorted. 'Upset me? Hardly.'

'He meant well in what he said. You've not said much about it, to anyone really before tonight.'

Doug inspected the bench to avoid her gaze. 'I know. You know me. Chatty, prone to sharing.'

Jesse pushed it. 'Dan only asked because he just wants you to be happy, that's all. Not a sad, miserable, lonely old Scottish bloke.'

Jesse said this straight-faced to see whether Doug was actually listening. There was a split second where he heard what she said and turned to face her, his face indignant, and she turned the hose on him laughing. He got an unexpected face full of water and made a grab for the hose.

'Oi!'

Jesse was too quick for him. She darted away laughing, flicking him with water again.

Doug chased her around the boat, trying to grab the hose.

'What are you annoyed about? The water or being called sad, lonely, miserable or old?' Jesse whooped with laughter as she made another grab for the hose.

Brock barked, excited by the laughing and chasing.

Doug laughed and lunged for Jesse. He grabbed her arm and hauled her back to him with one arm and with the other reached for the hose which she was holding high and waving about. They were both out of breath and laughing. Being taller than her, Doug grabbed the hose finally. The two were facing each other. Out of breath. Laughing. They looked at each other, frozen in the moment. Both unsure of what to do next. Doug dipped his head and touched his lips to Jesse's hesitantly, unsure of himself.

At that moment Doug's phone rang. Doug pulled away quickly, like he'd been woken from a dream.

He pulled the phone out of his pocket, both of them seeing that the call was from Claire. Jesse stepped away quietly and started to wind up the hose. Doug answered, avoiding looking at Jesse.

'Claire …' He listened for a moment. 'OK. Calm down. Is it urgent? Where are you? … OK … I'll be there, about 20 minutes, I'm walking. Bye.'

He ended the call and turned to Jesse who was rolling up the hose.

'Look … Jesse.'

Jesse talked over her shoulder as she felt awkward. 'You've got to go – it's fine.'

Doug inspected the floor, too embarrassed to look at her; he was horrified that he'd just forgotten himself and almost kissed her.

'An emergency, apparently. Look … Jesse…' He raked his fingers through his hair. 'I want to … just so you know, I don't want to go. I'm … I'm no good at this stuff. I'm sorry … I didn't mean …'

Jesse pretended there was a problem with the hose and bent down to fiddle with it, anything to avoid looking to him.

'It's fine. Leave me the keys. I'll lock up and give them to you tomorrow. Go!'

Doug was in a flat spin. He didn't want to go, but at the same time felt obligated to since Claire had eluded to some sort of emergency. He wasn't sure of how to even say goodbye to Jesse.

'So … See you then. Thanks for locking up.'

211

'No problem, see you tomorrow.' Jesse still had her back to him.

He let himself out and walked around the harbour, shaking his head. Jesse stood in the doorway of the shed, watching him go.

Claire was sat at the kitchen table when Doug arrived home. She had a wine bottle in front of her and she looked agitated.

'What's the emergency? Couldn't find the corkscrew?' he asked, coming in the kitchen and putting his phone on the counter.

Claire smiled and poured him a glass. 'Where were you when I called?'

'Putting the inshore boat away in the harbour.'

Claire thought for a moment, taking a sip of wine. 'Who was helping you? It's a two-man job, isn't it?'

'What, suddenly you're an expert on our equipment? Jesse was helping me. Look, what's this about, Claire?'

'Is she the new girl? Where are the kids?'

'At Paul and Nicky's. Last-minute sleepover.'

Claire looked at Doug for a long moment and burst into tears. Doug was totally thrown. He hadn't been expecting tears. He'd come home expecting yet another argument.

'Jesus. Claire. Why are you upset?'

She continued to sob. Doug sat looking at her expectantly. She sniffed, twirling the wine in the glass, not looking at Doug.

'So I packed the car up tonight, with the last of my stuff. And then I went down to the front to say goodbye and I saw you all, having a great time, laughing, joking. The kids were having a great time, you looked so happy. Part of me wanted to be part of that again … with you.'

The muscle started pounding in Doug's cheek and his eyes were cold. 'But you don't though, do you?'

Claire sniffed, putting her head in her hands. 'I don't know, Doug. I just don't know anymore. I don't know what I want. I saw you laughing with that girl with the dog. I saw you crash into each other. I saw you laughing with her and lying in the sand … I felt … jealous.' She took his hand.

Doug snatched his hand away, shaking his head, his jaw set. 'This is so typically you, Claire.'

'What do you mean?'

212

'This soul searching – it's all about how *you* feel and what *you* want. How do you think I feel about all of this? Hearing you sit there and saying you don't know how you feel about leaving me, when I know you've been lying to me for so long? That you've been sleeping with someone else for, not just a few months, but, what is it? Years? That you slept with me and then went straight back and slept with him. There's a name for people like you.'

'But—'

'But what, Claire?'

He raised his voice, his accent much more pronounced in his anger. 'Did you think I was just going to forget that? Ignore what you've done and welcome you back with open arms?'

Claire tried to interrupt him, but he held up a hand, shaking his head.

'No,' he said forcefully. 'Your dithering about whether to leave or not isn't my problem, it's yours. I'm done here. You'll always be the kids' mum and I will never stop you seeing them, but I won't be with someone who isn't sure whether they want to be with me or not. Life's too short. The accident taught me that. I want to be with someone who knows it's me they want and me alone. I want them to be proud of the man I am and what I do and respect me for it. They need to be all in.' He shrugged. 'Simple.'

Claire looked shocked.

'But I thought—'

'Thought what, Claire? That I'd forgive you and we'd start again?

'I … I don't know…' she stammered.

'Fuck's sake, Claire. Your arrogance astounds me. We're over. The moment I found out. I don't do betrayal. There's no coming back from this. Stop having this wobble and stand by your convictions. Go back and see what's his name.'

Claire's eyes filled with tears. 'I miss you … I miss … this.'

'I miss you too, Claire, more than you'll ever know. I miss how we used to be, us against the world, poking fun at everything. But that's gone now.'

Claire stood slowly. She kissed him gently on the cheek and stroked his face sadly. He flinched, moving his head away. She took a deep breath and left the kitchen.

Doug heard the front door softly close. He sat drinking his wine and wondered how in a few short months everything had changed so quickly. Was it all his fault? Should he have tried to do more to save his marriage? How did he actually feel about Claire? Why had he almost kissed Jesse?

Irritated with himself, he turned off the kitchen light, went into the lounge and put the TV on in the hope it would help him think about something else.

We watch them on the beach. We've missed her. We watch her greet the cripple. She's taken to him. It seems mutual. She seems part of this family now. We like it better when she's alone. No one around. We are unhappy she seems close to the tall blond-haired man. We see them playing the game, there's something there. She's making us angry now. Time is marching on. We stay and watch the exchange on the beach between her and the blond man. They are too close ... too close for comfort ... we don't like it. At all. Something needs to be done.

CHAPTER 26

Jesse had been on a course for a few days, so she'd not seen Doug since the boatshed kiss. She was nervous about going into work and facing him. She was in the kitchen with Mike and Tom, when they heard Doug shouting.

'Mike? You ready?'

Mike appeared from the kitchen followed by Tom and Jesse. Jesse caught Doug's eye and blushed slightly. Tom was eating a bacon sandwich, oblivious to the ketchup dribbling down the front of his T-shirt.

Doug was smiling. 'Eve's just called. Remember Jack and Ryan? Eve said they were picking Jack up from hospital today. He's doing well. She said to say a big thank you.'

Jesse spoke first. 'That's great news!' The others agreed. 'Are you off to get Jimmy?'

She nudged Tom and pointed to his ketchup incident, which he sorted by lifting the T-shirt and licking it off. Jesse rolled her eyes.

'We are. We should be a couple of hours, do you reckon, Mike?'

'Yeah.'

'See you later then.' Doug looked at Jesse directly which made her blush furiously. Tom announced he was off to work and left Jesse alone in the station.

Doug and Mike walked to Mike's truck, got in and drove off.

A dark-haired man with tattooed arms watched their departure while casually leaning against the harbour wall. He strolled nonchalantly towards the entrance to the station, sat on the bench opposite and made a call.

Jesse couldn't focus. When Doug had looked at her earlier, her stomach had done a little lurch. Now she was having an internal debate about not getting involved with your boss, despite him being one of the loveliest guys around. It wasn't fair on him anyway, she reasoned with herself. She was too broken for him. She couldn't make the leap of getting involved again.

She was at her workbench in the bowels of the station with a small propeller laid out on the bench before her and the radio up loud. Brock was in the corner dreaming about rabbits, twitching as he slept. Suddenly he woke and barked loudly, causing her to jump.

'Jesus! You frightened the life out of me! What you barking about?'

He barked again. Jesse looked around puzzled. As she turned, she came face to face with a large dark-haired man covered with tattoos.

'Who the hell are you?'

The dog was inching forward, crouched low, growling and snarling at the man now. Upstairs, a door banged and Bob's voice called out.

'DOUG ... You in here?'

Jesse was rooted to the spot as Bob came thumping down the stairs.

'What's that bloody dog barking at now?'

Bob stopped, seeing Jesse terrified and the dark-haired man standing there. He took control immediately.

'You shouldn't be down here. Dogs not happy with it for a start. Way out is that way mate,' Bob said pleasantly but firmly, strolling casually over towards Jesse.

The man lent forward and said quietly in a strong Russian accent. 'You have something of mine, I think.'

Jesse stared at him. He was enormous and menacing in equal measure.

217

'I don't have anything of yours. I don't know you,' she said indignantly.

He looked at her, his head on one side. 'You're keeping it for Jimmy, I think. I'll return tomorrow night with my truck, and you'll have it ready for me,' he said quietly, but insistently.

Bob stepped forward. 'Time for you to go, mate, before things get nasty here.'

'Tomorrow night. Harbour. Nine p.m. You or the idiot Jimmy. Then no one gets hurt and everyone can …' he trailed off and thought for a moment '… go about their business.'

The man turned and slowly walked up the stairs and out of the building.

Jesse slumped against her workbench.

Bob looked at Jesse, eyes narrowed. 'What did he want with you?'

'It's not me' Jesse stammered. 'It's Jimmy.'

Bob looked angry. 'He's dealing in that shit again, isn't he? First time he went off I knew he was up to no good with those bloody Russians. They're bad news. They'll bloody kill him.'

Jesse stared at Bob in surprise. 'What? How do you know this, Bob?'

Bob scowled. 'The Russians have been nicking the drugs off the Irish who had a good thing going getting it out of Ireland and into the mainland, through the smaller harbours along the coast. The Russians have muscled in, put a load of Irish out of action and are taking over the operation. Now the Irish are back on their feet and aren't having it.'

Jesse looked aghast. Bob sniffed haughtily.

'I hear stuff, good friend of mine is working the case. I keep an ear to the ground. I reckon it was the Irish that put Jimmy in hospital, but the Russians will still want the gear if he has it.'

'You really need to talk to Doug. He found Jimmy's stash the other day. That guy must have seen us.'

Jesse pulled her phone out and made a call. 'It's me. Where are you?' She listened. 'Oh, OK. So we've just had a Russian guy in here saying we have something of his and he's coming back for it. Thankfully Bob turned up and scared him off with his charm … and this guy said we were keeping it for Jimmy and he'd be back. Tomorrow night in the harbour at 9 p.m. Bob says the Russians want Jimmy's stash and Bob thinks it was the Irish that beat the crap out of him and set his boat on fire.' She finished breathlessly. 'I know! That's what I said! He has a friend working the case, so he knows about it. Can you find out from Jimmy if it was the Irish who did him over and whether the stash is the Russians'? Or should we get him to tell Bob's mate all about it?'

Bob touched her arm. 'Tell Doug if Jimmy co-operates with the police now, they'll go a lot easier on him.'

'Did you hear that? OK. Talk to Jimmy. I don't want the guy coming back.' She listened. 'Bob, Doug says can you stick around here until he gets back, please?'

Bob nodded.

'He says it's OK to stay … OK, see you later.'

Jesse turned to Bob. 'Doug and Mike are going to drop Jimmy off and then come here. Sure you don't mind staying?'

'I'll be in Doug's office.'

'Thanks, Bob, I really appreciate it.'

Bob looked grumpy and disappeared off up the stairs. Jesse went back to her workbench, shaking her head that Bob had known all along about Jimmy's involvement with drugs.

* * *

Jimmy was making a right hash of getting into Mike's truck. Both Doug and Mike were trying to help him and his crutches get in. He looked an absolute wreck. His face was still badly bruised, an arm and both legs in casts.

'You OK there, Jim?' Mike asked, worried that Jimmy was looking pale and sweaty. Jimmy grunted and closed his eyes as the effort of getting in the car was too much.

'Thanks for picking me up,' Jimmy managed.

'It's no problem pal. I came because we need to talk to you without Marie around,' Doug said quietly.

Jimmy looked nervous. 'Everything OK?'

'Not really, mate. Me and Mike got your pots in for you.'

Jimmy gave a sharp intake of breath.

'Nice big haul of lobsters that we've given to Fishy John for you, so he owes you for those. But a nice big haul of something else too.'

Jimmy closed his eyes. 'Sorry guys. I didn't want you anywhere near this.'

Doug said in a low, angry voice, 'Well we are now. I've had one of your drug scum turn up just now at my station and threaten a member of my staff.'

Jimmy looked panicked. 'Jesus! Who? Who turned up? How did they know to come to the station? What did he look like?'

'Jesse said it was a Russian sounding guy, said we were looking after something for you.'

Jimmy moaned out loud. 'Oh God, he came to the hospital, said he was gonna hurt Marie if I didn't get him the stash. I told him the Irish took most of it, but he said he wants what was left. Oh fuck. Why's he got you involved?'

'I can only assume he saw us come back in your boat and they've been watching us.'

Jimmy's voice trembled 'Where's the gear now?'

'In an old lock-up of ours.'

'Look, we can't put the station or the crew at risk. You've got to offload the stuff. Bob knows the coppers running the case. They know about you, Jim, they know about the Russians and the Irish, they'll go easy on you if you help them.'

Jimmy looked terrified. 'They'll bloody kill me! If the Russians won't, the fucking Irish will! What about Marie? I can't put her at risk.'

'Too late for that now. Look, before you decide anything come and talk to Bob, see what he says.'

Jimmy looked desperate.

'What time is Marie expecting me?'

'I'll text her and tell her we've been held up, OK?' Mike asked, picking up his phone.

Jimmy looked exhausted. 'Thanks.'

Doug said. 'Bob's at the station, I'll ask him to get in contact with his mate.'

'Oh God, the Russian … he didn't hurt Jesse, did he?'

Doug shook his head. 'No, but she could do without things like that happening, plus you need to keep her sweet, she's fixed your boat for you.'

Mike agreed. 'Man, it runs like a dream now. You won't know it.'

'Fixed my boat? Why would she do that? I can't afford …'

220

Doug patted his shoulder. 'Relax Jimmy, it's what mates do. Ben and Paul fixed the deck and Jesse fixed the engine, so you'd have a business to come back to.'

'Appreciate it,' he said gruffly. 'No one's ever done anything like that for me before for nothing.' He looked out the window, blinking the tears away furiously.

* * *

It was late afternoon by the time Bob and a taller man, Detective Inspector Jerry Reed, who bore more than a passing resemblance to George Clooney, helped Jimmy navigate the path from the lifeboat station around to the harbour car park. They arrived at Mike's truck and once again went through the performance of getting Jimmy inside. Jerry handed him his crutches and leant forward, speaking quietly.

'So remember, we have to get them in possession of it in order to link them to it? I'll be in touch first thing tomorrow and we'll do what we talked about, OK?'

Jimmy nodded.

Jerry said quietly. 'I'm going to do what I can to get your involvement down to something like a suspended sentence – we've been after this crew for so long, they're not going to be that interested in you, but they'll have to do something.'

Jimmy tried to look grateful.

'It'll be fine.' Jerry smiled. 'Oh, and Jimmy? Don't fuck it up tomorrow.'

Jerry closed the door and stood watching as Mike drove off slowly.

Mike stopped the truck outside Jimmy's cottage. The door swung open and Marie rushed out.

'Where have you been?'

Jimmy got out painfully. 'Sorry, love. My fault. Wanted to see the lads and Doug at the station to say thanks for getting me to safety.'

Marie looked at him with a resigned air. 'Let's get you in and settled. You must be shattered.'

'I am. You coming in mate?'

Mike shook his head. 'No, mate. Gotta shoot.'

'Thanks, Mike, really appreciate it,' Marie said gratefully.

Jimmy walked painfully into the house. Marie shut the door gently and helped him to a chair at the kitchen table.

As Jimmy got comfortable, he said to Marie, 'Sit down, love. I need to tell you something.'

Marie sat down looking worried. 'What? Oh God, Jimmy what is it?

Jimmy sighed and started talking.

CHAPTER 27

The day had been long, and Doug felt wrung out as his sleep had been plagued with bad dreams. He was on his way back from the police station, where he'd been giving further details to a visiting suit concerning the container. As expected, a load of 'suits' had appeared and taken over the investigation completely, and Doug had been asked for further information on the retrieval. Doug knew he probably wouldn't be a huge help but had shown willing. He was walking home along the beach path just as Jesse was coming off the beach with Brock. As she reached the top of the path, they came face to face.

'Hello,' said Doug, grinning.

'Hello, you out for a stroll?' she asked.

Doug shook his head. 'Not really, I've just dropped two reluctant kids off at sea cadets for a few hours, plus I had to pop in to see Steve and finish some paperwork about the containers.

'Still think human trafficking?'

'Yup. The Home Office are involved now. I think the scale of it has surprised them.' Doug shifted about and stuffed his hands in his pockets. 'Look, feel free to say no, but I was going to go and have a beer at the Long Beach Bar while the kids are out, do you fancy a drink?'

Jesse shrugged. 'OK.'

They arrived at the pub and found a table in the sun. Brock made himself comfortable on Doug's feet, with a large sigh, as a waitress took their drink order.

Doug gestured to the dog. 'Should I be flattered he chooses my feet to lie on?'

'Not many people get the laying down treatment. Some just get the dribble on the knee.'

Doug stroked Brock's head. The waitress returned with their drinks. Doug picked up his beer and took a sip.

'Look, about the other night, I don't want you to think ...' he began.

'Don't want me to think ...?'

'That I make a habit of, you know ...' he finished awkwardly.

'Wrestling hoses off people?' asked Jesse lightly.

Doug smiled in relief. 'Yeah.'

'What was the emergency, anyway, if I'm allowed to ask?'

Doug rolled his eyes. 'There wasn't an emergency. Claire was just having a wobble. Should she stay or should she go.'

'Oh?'

Doug closed his eyes and tilted his face to the sun.

'Ahh, a golden hour of beer and not being Dad for a bit. I love them, but every now and again it's nice to have a beer without constant interruptions and being asked what's for dinner.'

'How are they coping with Claire going?'

'They're doing better than I thought. They're both very clingy though.'

'Is that just insecurity?' said Jesse, frowning.

'Probably. Somedays it seems to me that Claire hasn't looked back at all since she left. She's hardly seen them.'

'What were you expecting?'

Doug thought for a moment. 'I thought it might be more of a team effort if the truth be known. But then, I'm not sure why I'm surprised.'

They sat in silence for a moment.

Jesse broke it. 'Is Jimmy all set for tonight with Jerry? Hope he'll be OK.'

'Jerry's a top bloke, he'll look after Jimmy.'

'Jimmy's got to be some sort of idiot, getting involved in that.'

'I agree. But he was desperate. Boat needed fixing, couldn't afford to do that, but needed to use the boat for work. Vicious circle really. The life of a fisherman. It's hard. Hand to mouth. My grandfather was a fisherman in Scotland. Life was bloody hard up there.'

'What about your folks? Where are they?'

'My folks are still in Scotland, North Berwick. They moved there to be closer to my brother, but he died in a climbing accident a few years back. They won't leave there now. Too much upheaval. Plus, my mother thinks that anyone this side of Hadrian's Wall is a purse snatcher or a terrorist. Dad won't leave because he thinks the whisky is better up there.'

'I'm so sorry about your brother. He was a keen climber then?'

Doug looked out to sea. 'He loved it. His goal was to climb the Suila Grande, and Everest. He was climbing in Scotland and slipped. He hadn't tied himself on properly. I think he was trying to free climb and it went badly wrong. Mum and Dad were devastated. He was the golden boy, you know? Brilliant career and all that.'

'Did that bother you?'

'No. They were right to be proud of him. He worked hard. I was proud of him. For me, I didn't want all that, I just wanted to do something that mattered.'

'I know what you mean. I've always needed to be by the sea. I needed to do something that mattered. This seemed a natural fit.'

'When he died, he left me everything. His house, investments, everything, he was pretty well off. He left a letter saying how proud he was of what I do for a living. He said it was the most admirable career a fella could have. Lovely really.'

Doug smiled remembering. His phone rang, breaking the comfortable silence.

'She's left and still she calls,' he said quietly. 'Sorry, I just need to get this. Claire?' He rolled his eyes as he spoke. 'Well, we're all out at the moment, but we'll be back in an hour or so … yes if you want. Right. Bye.'

'OK?' Jesse ventured.

'She wants to see the kids.'

225

He looked at his watch, realising the time. 'Shit! Kids will be finished in a minute. I need to go.' He started to leave and then realised he hadn't paid for the drinks.

Jesse waved him away. 'Go! I'll get this.'

Doug protested. 'But it was me that asked you!'

'Go and get the kids.'

'OK, see you tomorrow – drinks are on me next time.'

'Hold you to that.'

Doug stopped and smiled at her. 'I'll look forward to it.'

He left with a wave and Jesse found herself smiling broadly.

* * *

The usually busy harbour was quiet in the evening light. The boats were rocking gently with the lapping of the water as the tide came in. There were a few people out strolling with dogs, but the lower part of the harbour near the sailing club was almost deserted.

Jimmy sat in the bar in the sailing club, nervously sipping a half. His leg twitched constantly, causing a thumping sound due to his plaster cast. He couldn't stop looking at the clock.

Finally, his phone pinged. Jimmy grabbed it and read the message. He finished his half in one enormous swig, stood awkwardly and hobbled to the door.

He sat down to wait on the slipway. A man approached him from behind and said his name softly. Jimmy jumped.

'Jesus! Don't be fucking sneaking up on me like that. You're like a fucking ninja.'

The Russian laughed heartily. 'Ninja, I like that. You've looked better, my friend. You need to keep better company.' He chuckled at his own joke.

'So. You have something for me? I'll perhaps be a little sad if you have as I was looking forward to seeing your lady friend who works on lifeboat. She looked like she would put up quite the fight.'

Jimmy tutted in disgust. 'Well, we don't treat our women like that here. You might want to learn a thing or two.'

'Oh Really? Perhaps I'll pay your wife a visit and she can teach me ...'

Jimmy went white and pointed an angry finger at the Russian. 'You watch your fucking mouth, mate. Just take the shit and go. I want no part of this. You know what the fucking Irish did to me. Nearly killed me and

226

set me on fire. At least I had the sense to hide some of the gear in the pots. So take it. I want no part of it anymore.'

The tattooed man shrugged. 'We will see. It's not up to me. Where is it?'

Jimmy gestured to the sail lock-ups over his shoulder. 'Number 6. Under the blue tarp. It's open. You might wanna bring the truck around.'

The tattooed man sent a quick text and a minute later headlights appeared down the slip road. The van stopped and the driver emerged. The tattooed man gestured to the driver to follow him. Both men entered the lock-up and emerged a few moments later with the crates. They removed the tarpaulin and checked the contents. The tattooed man swung them easily into the back of the truck and then approached Jimmy.

'Is this all there is?'

Jimmy nodded.

The tattooed man leaned into towards him. 'The boss will not be happy. This is not the end for you, I think.'

Jimmy stared at him. 'I don't give a fuck about that.'

He stopped as he noticed another man strolling down the slipway.

'Evening lads. I couldn't help but overhear. But do you know what?' He turned to the Russian. 'I think the boss is going to be really, really, unhappy tonight, because, as they say in this country, mate, you're nicked. Oh, and so is the boss. My officers are there now arresting him while I've the pleasure of arresting you.'

From around the harbour a number of police officers emerged, and Jerry approached the tattooed man and driver, drawing out a pair of handcuffs.

'I'm Detective Inspector Jerry Reed. I'm arresting you, very happily I might add, for a range of offences almost too numerous to mention, but let me have a go – trafficking, intimidation, pirateering, laundering money, intent to distribute, actual distribution, possession … And the list goes on. You do not have to say anything, but it may harm your defence if you do not mention when questioned something which you later rely on in court. Anything you do say may be given in evidence.' Jerry grinned and turned to a uniformed officer. 'Get this pond life out of here.'

The tattooed man hissed at Jerry. 'You're making big mistake.'

'Am I? Good to know. Now you and your mate are going to have a nice cosy ride to my B&B where you'll spend the night before we charge you with all of that list I just reeled off, among a raft of other things. Night Night. Sleep well, be sure to leave a good review on trip advisor won't you, so all your pals can visit?'

The pair were dragged away with the tattooed man trying to spit at Jimmy. He avoided eye contact and tried to light a cigarette, but his hands were shaking too much.

He turned to face Jerry. 'Shit. Did you hear him? He knows about Marie? Do you think he'll hurt her?'

Jerry shook his head. 'Calm down. One of my guys is with her now. You guys should take a break for a couple of weeks. Let things die down here a bit. It'll be fine though. They won't come after you or her. They'll be bailing out as quick as they can now we've got these two and all the other evidence. Well done, Jimmy. Need a lift home?'

Jimmy was white as a sheet. He shook his head. 'No. I've gotta lock up the shed for Doug.'

Jerry looked sympathetic. 'Let me do that, you look in a right state.'

Jimmy shook his head again. 'Thanks, I'll be OK, you get off.'

Jerry looked doubtful. 'If you insist.'

Jimmy mini-saluted as if to say goodbye, then grabbed his crutches and made his way clumsily over to the lock-up. Inside, he leant against the crates, put his head in his hands and sobbed quietly.

CHAPTER 28

Doug waved the kids off as they climbed into the back of the sea cadets' minibus for a night away on Barafundle Bay Beach. He watched with amusement as they trundled off up the steep hill, with the kids pulling faces from the back windows.

He hadn't organised anything to do except the mountain of paperwork piling up on his desk. He sighed heavily at the prospect and headed around to the station.

Doug passed the usual number of tourists in the station admiring the boat and spending money in the shop. He unlocked the privacy gate and headed down into the mess, waving at Nessie who stood at the till in the shop as he disappeared to make a cuppa.

He heard Jesse's radio on loudly in the workshop and was surprised she was in on a day off too. He stepped into the workshop and saw Brock fast asleep on what looked like the old fleece that used to hang over the back of his office chair. He wondered where that had gone the other day and assumed Nessie had put it in a charity shop. Jesse was in the parts store.

He yelled. 'Jesse … cup of tea?'

Jesse's face appeared around the door. 'What are you doing here?' She wiped her hands on a rag as she spoke.

Brock woke and rushed over to sit in front of Doug, his tail wagging. Doug pointed to the fleece Brock had been lying on. 'Is that my old ...?'

Jesse nodded. 'I assumed you gave it to him. He just appeared dragging it the other day. He won't sleep on anything else now.'

Doug looked amused. 'No, I think he just decided to help himself.'

Jesse was mortified. 'Brock. Did you steal Doug's fleece?' she asked sternly.

Brock flattened his ears and trotted back over to the fleece and lay down on it again, sighing loudly.

'Did you want it back?' ventured Jesse.

Doug smiled indulgently. 'How could I? Tea?'

'Yup. Thanks. The kids with Claire?'

'Don't be ridiculous. They're at sea cadet camp with Paul and Nicky for a night. I figured the paperwork wouldn't do itself and I'm at a fairly critical stage with it.'

'You're not in trouble or anything ...?' She trailed off.

'No. There's no more room in the tray. It's gotta be done.'

'You're so rock and roll,' she said, retreating to the cupboard. 'Best crack on with that tea first.'

Doug turned to go back upstairs. 'Cheeky mutt,' he said to Brock affectionately as he passed.

Hours later, the 'done' paperwork pile was significantly bigger than the 'not done' pile. Doug felt like he had made good progress. He'd responded to a load of emails from Stuart too. Doug's phone pinged and he picked it up to see a picture of the kids happily dancing around a beach bonfire with others. Doug grinned; it was from Nicky. A moment later his phone pinged again. A text from Stuart, who said. *What's with all the emails? You been drinking your own coffee?*

Doug carried on, enthused by his progress. A knock at the door interrupted him.

'Coffee?' Jesse asked.

'Please.' He was determined to finish the small pile that was left.

Jesse re-appeared a few minutes later and dumped a mug on his desk, leaving him to it. She laughed to herself as she returned to the workshop. A rare night off and he was doing paperwork while she was sorting out the parts cupboard. What a sad pair.

She was feeling quite unsettled today. She had felt another odd sensation this morning when she'd been out in the woods with the dog, the hairs on the back of her neck standing up like there was an uncomfortable presence nearby. She couldn't place it. So she had come and taken refuge in her safe place.

Doug finished and sat for a while surveying his efforts with a large grin of satisfaction. Brock appeared in the doorway, came in and laid heavily on his feet.

Jesse appeared. 'What's up with him?' asked Doug, pointing to Brock.

'He's sucking up. Don't fall for it.'

'Aww,' said Doug, tickling the dog under the chin.

'Sucker,' Jesse said. 'Right, I'm off. You staying here?'

'No, I'm off. Are you rushing away anywhere?'

'Why? What d'you need?'

'Well, by my count, I owe you not only a pizza, but a beer too. How about I make good on my promises at the Hope?'

Jesse thought for a moment. The loud rumbling of her stomach broke the silence, she shrugged and said, 'Why not?'

They locked the station and strolled up the hill towards the Hope and Anchor, with Brock happily trotting along between them. They went in the front door and were immediately hailed by Tom, behind the bar.

'Skip. You guys been at the station?'

Doug nodded, looked around and spotted a table by the window. He pointed. 'Jesse, jump on that one. I'll get the beers. What's your poison?'

'I'll have a white wine please.'

Doug went to the bar and Tom, who had heard Jesse, held up a bottle of white and whistled. Jesse gave him a thumbs up. Pouring an enormous glass for Jesse and a Guinness for Doug, Tom leaned over the pumps and lowered his voice.

'So, Skip, is this like a date?' he said, winking.

Doug handed over some cash and Tom waved it away. 'On me,' he said.

'Thanks, Tom. It's two work colleagues, having a bite to eat and a drink after a long day.'

'Can't blame a man for asking, Skip,' he said. 'It's just …'

Doug picked up the drinks and looked back at him. 'It's just what?'

Tom grinned. 'Well, you know. Get in there, Claire's gone, you're YFS and RTM.'

Doug raised an eyebrow. 'I'm almost afraid to ask – YFS and RTM?'

'Young free and single and ready to mingle.'

'Dear God,' he said, trying not to laugh. 'Thanks for the drinks, Tom.'

Doug picked his way around various tables and put Jesse's drink down.

'Cheers,' she said, picking it up and sipping. Doug did the same.

'Don't thank me, thank Tom.'

'Oh,' Jesse said looking over Doug's shoulder for Tom to catch his eye. She gave him a thumbs up.

'Pick your feast,' he said, passing her a menu. 'My treat, no arguments.'

'I'm done. I don't mess about. Paella please.'

'Right, you're having paella and so am I. Two secs.'

He went to the bar to order. A moment later his phone pinged with a text and Jesse looked down and saw it was from Claire. Most of the text was visible and read: *'D. You around? Need to talk xx'.*

Doug returned to the table. 'OK?' he asked.

'Your phone pinged, I think,' she said.

Doug picked up his phone and saw the text, putting it back down again.

'I don't mind if you need to make a call or anything?'

'It's fine.' He picked up his drink. 'Cheers.'

Jesse picked up her drink and clinked glasses. She was silent for a moment.

'Doug, what's the deal with you and Claire now?'

Doug frowned over the rim of his glass. 'Deal?'

Jesse twirled her glass unable to meet his probing eyes.

'It's just … well … it's … you said she had a wobble. She's calling you, texting you … I know it's nothing to do with me, but I just wanted to be clear, because of the … you know … the other night …'

Doug felt awful. He couldn't help himself in the boatshed the other night. He had wanted to stay, to kiss her properly. He didn't know what to say, didn't know how to handle it. He wasn't sure how he felt about saying it out loud.

'Jesse,' he began slowly. 'With Claire … the other night, after the boatshed … She saw us all on the beach, saw you and me together and she was jealous, she said. It confused her. She didn't know how she felt anymore about leaving …' He was silent for a moment. 'She said she didn't know how she felt about me …'

Jesse stared at Doug. 'Jesus … what did you say to that?'

'Two paellas?' The waitress appeared with a large dish and two plates which she put down in front of them. 'Plates are very hot so take care. Enjoy.'

Neither of them acknowledged the food in front of them.

Doug spoke softly. 'I said it was over. It was too late. I couldn't be with someone who didn't know if they wanted to be with me or not.' He shrugged. 'I said I wanted to be with someone who wanted me totally, for me, for who I was and what I did. Someone that was all in.'

Jesse was staring at Doug. For a second she wanted to climb onto the table, shove all the food aside and grab him and kiss him senseless, right there in the pub. Instead, she cleared her throat.

'How did she take that?'

Doug picked up cutlery and passed it to Jesse.

'I think deep down she expected me to say it was over.' He took a mouthful of paella. 'Umm this is good, have some.'

'Are you on good terms?' Jesse took a mouthful, desperate to know the answer.

'Oh aye. No point being snippy now, it's all out in the open. I told her she'd always be the kids' mum and I'll never stop that. I'll never stop her seeing them. But us? No way.'

'That's good.' Jesse carried on eating and pretending not to be too bothered about the conversation.

'I just feel …' Doug began softly.

Jesse looked up from her plate as he faltered in what he was saying. He was looking at her with an odd expression; she put a hand out to touch his arm.

'Feel what, Doug?'

He looked towards the ceiling as if annoyed with himself. 'I just feel a bit … out of control, with everything at the moment. A few months ago everything was different and now … everything is different again … and I feel … I feel like I'm struggling to catch up a wee bit.'

Jesse felt like she was going to burst into tears. She had no idea what he was trying to say to her, but she suspected it was all about being left alone and what a mistake the boatshed was.

'It's a cliché, but it's not you, it's me … and I just need to get my head straight … I … you know … want to explore this … with you. Do you understand?'

'Absolutely,' she said. 'Message received and understood.'

She looked away from him and pushed her plate away, with only half the contents eaten.

'Jesse?'

Jesse turned to look at a woman who was standing next to the table.

'Emma?' she said in disbelief.

Emma smiled and turned to Doug. 'Hello,' she said, extending a hand to him in greeting. 'I'm Emma, a friend of Jesse.'

'Doug. Nice to meet you,' he said shaking her hand. 'Do you want to join us?'

'I couldn't possibly intrude upon your evening, besides I was looking for a friend who said he would meet me here, but he's so reliably unreliable, God only knows where he is.' She focused on Jesse. 'How are you Jesse? Long time no see.'

Jesse blushed. 'I'm sorry. I've been a little sidetracked with things.'

Emma eyed Doug appreciatively. 'Mm, I can see that,' she said. 'Perhaps ring me tomorrow and we'll set a date to meet up?'

Jesse nodded.

'Promise?' laughed Emma 'Or I'll just have to resort to turning up every now and again, just so I get to see you!'

'Scouts honour,' said Jesse, wildly uncomfortable at the prospect she might suddenly turn up at any time.

Emma's phone rang loudly, and she pulled it from her pocket.

'Talk of the devil,' she murmured. She turned to Doug and placed a hand on his shoulder. 'Good to meet you, Doug. I've heard a lot about you. Bye, Jesse. Don't you forget to call now.'

Emma turned and left.

234

'She seemed nice,' said Doug, picking at his paella again. 'Is yours not good?' he asked, gesturing to her plate with his fork.

'What? Oh, it's fine, thanks,' she said absently, craning her neck to look out of the window at where Emma had gone.

Doug tried again. 'Jesse, I don't think you got what I was saying ...'

'I got it,' she said, focusing intently on her wine glass.

'Jesse,' he said softly. 'Look at me for a minute.'

Jesse looked up at him, and to her utter horror, her eyes filled with tears.

Doug took her hand. 'Jesse, I don't want to, hurt you. I wasn't saying we shouldn't ... I was saying ... I was saying ...'

Jesse interrupted him. 'Let me do it. Here's how it goes. Jesse, the boatshed, the other night was a mistake. I overstepped the line and all that. I've got a family and responsibilities, I can't get involved with anyone. That about cover it, Doug?'

Doug looked puzzled.

'Jesse, that's not it. At all. You couldn't be further from the truth. I was just saying I need to get my head into a place where ...'

He opened his mouth to say more and his pager went off, closely followed by Jesse's and Tom's. Tom vaulted over the bar.

'Come on, guys.' he said, running out of the door.

The rescue was mercifully quick. A couple of teenagers had got stranded on a ledge, after trying to take a selfie, not noticing the tide approaching and cutting them off. Jesse was below decks in the lifeboat, trying not to chuckle, while Bob lectured the two on the perils of social media and the coastline. They arrived back at the station and Jesse changed quickly and whistled quietly for Brock who had been asleep on Doug's fleece. She slipped out of the side door. She just couldn't have a conversation with Doug tonight.

After consistently refusing a number of requests for selfies, Doug finally said goodbye to the teenagers when their parents came to get them. He changed in the locker room and went down into the workshop looking for Jesse but couldn't find her anywhere. He locked up, turned off the lights and walked around the harbour, heading for home, frustrated she was now thinking the wrong thing completely. He decided that the sooner he could speak to her properly and clear the air to try to explain himself the better.

We see her. We watched her last night at the beach bar. With him. She looked happy. We don't like that. We don't like him. We need him out of the picture. She left the station with him tonight, went to the pub. Then after the shout she looked upset. We were happy about that. We might need to see that more. We like her when she's alone. We want her to be vulnerable and upset. All Alone. We can still wait. Time is getting tight – but we're still watching and waiting.

CHAPTER 29

On his way home, Doug stopped and took a moment to stand and admire the beautiful tall ship moored in the harbour. He remembered that Morven said they would be back in a few weeks with their group of boys for the Youth Sailing Programme.

His mind wandered to Jesse. It was bothering him that he still hadn't managed to talk to her properly since the previous night in the pub, but he had plans to rectify that. He needed to clear the air.

He leant against the wall and took some time to watch the activity on the deck of the tall ship. He saw the teenage boys stood in huddles with coloured arm bands on. They were doing 'Up and Overs' which was where they had to climb up the side of the rigging and down the other side without slipping or losing their nerve because of the height. There were cheers and whoops as the boys climbed and lots of applause when one managed to reach the top or the bottom. He watched Morven's interplay with them and again marveled at how she worked so effectively with what were invariably very troubled teens.

Fishy John from the fishmongers' shack strolled out to join him, to see what the noise was.

'Hello, mate, you off for the day?' he asked Doug.

'I am. How you doing?'

'I'm good. Busy day today. Everyone after crab – you'd think it was going to be made extinct tomorrow, verging on panic buying today.'

Doug chuckled. 'Keeps you in cars, women and beer though, mate?'

John laughed. 'It does.' He gestured to the tall ship. 'Look at this bunch of muppets. Every year, a new bunch of them. Looks like they've got their work cut out, doesn't it?'

'Aye, they do. Gotta be a handful, that many teenage boys. I pity Morven.'

Fishy John rolled his eyes 'There'll be tears before bedtime, you mark my words! See you later.'

'Aye, see you later.'

Doug stood for a few minutes longer. Morven caught his eye and waved enthusiastically. He waved back smiling, climbed into his truck and drove home.

* * *

Emma was in a secure psychiatric hospital, sat around a table with two doctors. The room was decidedly impersonal and the furniture very utilitarian, the walls that odd shade of light green that Emma noticed many older hospitals favoured.

'So in your opinion, he's not mentally fit to stand trial?'

Dr Nunn, a tall dark-haired man with glasses, referred to his notes. As he spoke, he repeatedly pushed his glasses up his nose.

'Yes Dr Marshall. Chris is exhibiting some very typical sociopathic tendencies, and this makes me very concerned.'

'I see,' Emma said shortly.

His colleague, Dr Stevens, shifted in his seat; this woman made him incredibly uncomfortable.

'I agree. Chris doesn't really have a grasp of what's happening to him or where he is at the present. He can't stand trial like this.'

'So what does this actually mean for him?' Emma asked Dr Nunn.

He cleared his throat. 'We'll keep him here and work with him until we see an improvement and he's mentally fit to stand trial. That can take years for some patients. The CPS will then arrange an assessment. Presently, he's in complete denial about his actions and almost catatonic when we press him about it.'

'Tell me Dr Nunn, what are you suggesting as a treatment plan?'

'Err. Well, there are a range of treatments available such as, antipsychotic medicines, psychological therapies, plus some social support when he's ready.'

'What sort of therapies are you thinking of?' Emma interjected.

'Well, if you agree, Dr Stevens, perhaps some cognitive behavioural therapy might show some improvement.'

Dr Stevens agreed enthusiastically. 'We've had some very positive results here with other patients.'

Emma folded her arms and regarded the two doctors. 'I see.'

Dr Nunn began. 'In some cases, hypnosis has been—'

Emma interrupted him. 'Absolutely no hypnosis. I must insist.'

Both doctors glanced at each other, uncertainly. Dr Nunn inclined his head.

'Whatever you're comfortable with Dr Marshall. We'll obviously discuss his treatment plan with you once we have it finalised. Is there any reason why you're so against hypnosis?'

Emma looked uncomfortable. 'Well, Chris had some hypnosis as a child, and we think he was abused by the doctor. Let's just say that this is a lid on a box I'd like to keep on at this stage. God knows what might happen if we open that box up.'

Both doctors raised their eyebrows.

Dr Stevens asked, 'Does your brother have a history of mental illness before this episode?'

Emma shook her head. 'Not specifically, but he's always been quite highly strung and had difficulty controlling his anger. He had a traumatic childhood. Struggled to cope mentally when things got difficult. When do you think you'll have a treatment plan for him?'

Dr Nunn shifted uncomfortably in his chair. 'Certainly within the week, Dr Marshall.'

'Fine. I'd like to see my brother now.'

Dr Stevens stood. 'I've another meeting to go to but Dr Nunn, perhaps you would be kind enough?'

Dr Nunn smiled. 'It would be my pleasure.'

'Dr Marshall. I'll be in touch.' he said, shaking Emma's hand and leaving the room.

Dr Nunn turned to Emma. 'Shall we go?'

'I just need to pop to the ladies?'

'Of course, three doors down on the left.'

Dr Nunn held open the door. Emma nodded her thanks and walked along the corridor. In the room, she looked at herself in the mirror, laughing softly.

'You're exactly where I need you to be, baby brother. Indefinitely. Bunch of fucking idiots.'

She applied more lipstick, opened a button on her blouse and left the room.

Emma and Dr Nunn stopped outside a locked metal door with peeling paint. Through the wire threaded window in the door, Emma could see a plain room, a barred window and Chris, sitting on the bed, slowly rocking. Emma turned to Dr Nunn.

'Is he OK?'

'He's had a mild sedative. He should be fine. I'd like to accompany you inside for your safety.'

'Thank you. I don't think he'd hurt me, but I appreciate it.'

Dr Nunn unlocked the door and Emma entered slowly.

'Chris? Sweetie, it's me ...' she said softly.

Chris didn't acknowledge her, but the rocking stopped as soon as she spoke. He sat completely still. She tried again.

'Chris?'

Chris turned towards Emma, his eyes were unfocused and his head was tilted as if listening intently. He whispered to himself, nodding. 'She's here. You said she'd be here.'

Emma walked over and sat down next to him on the bed.

Chris smiled broadly. 'Hello. You're very pretty. Who are you?'

Emma took his hand. 'Chris, it's me.'

Chris unexpectedly laughed out loud. A maniacal laugh. 'I know, dummy! I'm just playing with you.'

Emma looked relieved. Chris put his head on one side, listening. He whispered to himself again. 'I know she is. Don't say that!' he shouted.

'Sweetie. Who are you talking to?'

Chris turned to her, his eyes gesturing over his shoulder. 'They're there. The whisperers. They're over there.'

Chris turned his back on Emma and shouted at the corner. 'I won't do that!'

Emma leant forward. 'Won't do what, Chris?'

241

Chris stared at Emma's hand on his arm and put his head on one side. 'They want me to teach you a lesson ... show you who's boss here.'

'How are you supposed to do that? Tell me Chris?'

Chris looked uncomfortable and then leant forward to whisper to Emma.

'They want me to touch you,' he said, looking around furtively.

'Where?'

'Here.'

Chris placed his hands on Emma's breasts. Dr Nunn moved and Emma raised a hand to him to reassure him she was OK. She carried on looking at Chris.

His face was flushed and he was glassy eyed. He trailed a hand from her breast to her cleavage where the button was open.

'Here too ...'

Chris took his hand from her cleavage and slid it up Emma's skirt. Dr Nunn stepped forward again.

'Really, I must stop this ...' Dr Nunn began.

Chris was breathing heavily, his hand moving under her skirt.

'Christopher.' She grasped his arm firmly. 'Christopher, I'm your sister.'

Chris shoved Emma down on the bed. He was red in the face and whispered to Emma.

'They say you're not my sister and I should teach you a lesson for lying.'

He straddled her legs and reached down and ripped her blouse open. Dr Nunn hit the alarm strip and stood by the door, shouting for assistance.

'CHRIS! Stop this.' Emma struggled.

Chris raised a hand and punched Emma hard in the side of the face.

'Fucking bitch! Trying to trick me!'

Emma was scrambling to get away, but Chris was strong. He hit her again. Dr Nunn ushered in two male nurses who grabbed an arm each and pulled him off her.

Chris screamed at her. 'Fucking bitch! You did this to me! They said it was you!'

Chris was wrestled to the floor by the nurses. Dr Nunn helped Emma up from the bed.

'Dr Marshall, I'm so sorry. Are you OK?'

Emma was clutching her face and trying to hold her blouse together. She was unusually flustered.

'It's fine. I'm fine.'

The nurses gently picked Chris up. Dr Nunn moved in front of Chris while he was being held.

'Chris. Your behaviour towards your sister is unacceptable. Are you calm, or do I need to sedate you?'

Chris stared at the floor.

'Chris. I need you to acknowledge you hear what I'm saying to you.'

Chris started nodding.

'Chris. Are you aware you have seriously hurt your sister?'

Chris looked at Emma, his eyes full of tears. 'My sister's here? Em? Who did that to your face?'

'Chris. You did that to your sister. Just a moment ago.'

Chris looked horrified. 'Em? Oh, God … Sis' … I'm so sorry.'

Chris tried to step towards Emma and Dr Nunn stepped forward to block him.

Chris whined like a small child. 'I'm sorry. I'm so sorry. Ems? Can I have a hug, Em? Em, please can I have a hug? I need to say sorry. I need it to be OK.'

Tears were rolling down Chris's face.

Dr Nunn turned to Emma, who stepped forward. The two embraced for a while and Chris held her tight. Emma felt Chris shift his position slightly and he moved his lips towards her ear, whispering, 'So, how did I do, Sis' … Oscar worthy?'

CHAPTER 30

Doug leaned against the worktop in his kitchen, staring intently at his mobile. He took a couple of deep breaths and grabbed it, dialled a number and then hung up instantly.

'Jesus Christ. How hard can this be?' he muttered.

He picked up the phone again and took another breath. 'Come on. Man up.' He dialled again and it was answered almost immediately.

'It's Doug ... You OK? ... Good. So, look, feel free to say no, but Mike is playing at the Stowaway tonight and I wondered if you wanted to go and maybe have a bite to eat on the way, maybe at Joe's.' He listened for a moment. 'OK, great. I'll walk past yours and get you on the way then. About 6.30? ... OK. See you later. Bye.'

Doug stood for a moment with his hands on the counter, then left the room shaking his head, talking to himself. 'Sooo out of practice.'

* * *

Jesse had wasted as much time as she could to make herself late for her session with Dr Emma Marshall. She knocked and heard Emma call out, 'Come in.'

'Jesus, what happened to your face?' Jesse exclaimed, seeing the angry bruising on Emma's face.

Emma waved a hand dismissively. 'Oh, a patient got out of control. It's nothing. How have you been? Short session today I see?'

'Umm, sorry about that.' Jesse plonked herself down in one of the chairs she usually favoured.

'It was nice to see you in the pub the other night. You looked like you were enjoying yourself.'

'Doesn't strike me as your sort of place. Aren't you going to ask me if I read the letter you gave me last time?'

Emma raised an eyebrow. 'Jumping straight in today, aren't we? OK. Did you read the letter?'

'I did …'

'And …?'

Jesse shrugged. 'It was her story.'

Emma settled into a chair. 'But how did it make you feel?'

'If the truth be known I felt a bit annoyed with her.'

'How so?'

'Because I felt she was embracing being a victim and not fighting against it.'

Emma looked surprised. 'Is that an important thing to do?'

'Well, yes. Otherwise they've won, haven't they? Hey, I'm not saying I've not felt like a victim. Have there been times when I've been at the mercy of that feeling and it's almost destroyed me? Yes. But you need – or I need – something to get me through that and for me it's anger and rage.'

Emma made a note. 'Do you not think she felt that way?'

Jesse shook her head. 'No, not at all. She wrote to him. Told him how she felt. Why would you do that? Why would you waste time on that piece of shit?'

Emma said wryly, 'She saw it differently, I think. They met. They laid a lot of ghosts to rest.'

'More fool bloody her. She's effectively said to him, "It's OK what you did to me … I forgive you." Tell me, has he done it again?'

'I wouldn't know that.'

Jesse raised her eyebrows. 'Oh, I think you do.'

'As far as I know he hasn't done it again,' Emma said. 'Tell me something, Jesse. What if your attacker, Chris wasn't it? What if he didn't mean to hurt you? What if he couldn't help himself due to something that happened to him?'

Jesse stood up suddenly and paced the room. 'He took pleasure from what he did to me. I was there. I saw it in his face. He's damaged, unhinged and that's what he does to people. He enjoys it. Didn't mean to do it? What a load of utter crap. He needs locking up and the key throwing away.'

Emma persisted. 'You were close once. Do you feel no ounce of empathy for what might have happened to him to make him this way?'

'Seriously? I can't believe I'm hearing this from you.'

'I have to look at things a different way here, Jesse. From all angles. What would you say if you discovered he was sorry and wanted you to forgive him because he still loves you?'

Jesse, who was still pacing, stopped. 'What?'

Emma said soothingly, 'Sit down, Jesse. I'm interested in exploring something. I want you to think carefully. Do you think your actions were a significant trigger for his actions? Do you feel responsible for his actions in any way?

'What?' Jesse looked incredulous.

'Sometimes with patients, it's helpful to really unpick certain scenarios. For example, if you hadn't said something or done something, would he have attacked you anyway? Or were you the trigger? Sometimes it transpires that the victim actually goads the attacker into it.'

'Excuse me?'

'It's a simple enough question.'

'You're asking me if I deliberately goaded Chris into nearly killing me?'

'Yes. Some folk have deep-rooted masochistic tendencies.'

'Why would you even suggest that?'

'Calm down, come and sit down. I was just testing a theory to see how you felt about it. Your reaction tells me a lot.'

'Tells you a lot about what?'

'That you bear no responsibility in any way for the attack apart from the fact that, by your own admission, you went back. Out of interest, Jesse, have you thought about exactly what the triggers were for Chris to attack you? Was it things you might have said or did? Looking back, what might you do differently?'

'I don't want to start thinking about this – having to go through every little detail. Unpicking it. I can't do it. This is achieving nothing.'

'Jesse – wait.'

Jesse marched towards the door.

She turned around. 'Oh, and don't think turning up in the fucking pub again will get me back here either. We're done.'

She wrenched the door open and slammed it behind her.

Emma closed her eyes.

'Fuck.' She muttered.

* * *

Doug left his house and strolled down the road, enjoying the feeling of freedom and the evening sun's warmth. He turned the corner and arrived at Jesse's front door, just as Jesse stepped out, smiling and shutting the door behind her. This was met with an indignant bark.

'See you later,' she called. 'And no barking.'

They walked down to the pizza place and were shown to a table in the corner. Doug looked at Jesse over the top of his menu.

'You look nice,' he said awkwardly. 'You look different.'

'Haircut,' said Jesse. 'Long overdue. I've not been in here before. Is it good? I know how funny and old fashioned you are about pizza.'

Doug raised an eyebrow. The waitress came over and got their order, returning with their glasses of wine promptly.

'It's good. All made here … in there.' He gestured to the open kitchen and leant forward, grinning. 'They're real Italians here, too, and that means nothing on a pizza that shouldn't be.'

Jesse rolled her eyes. 'Where are the kids tonight?'

'They're with Nessie. She asked them in for tea and a movie evening. She makes the most amazing popcorn so they were desperate to go.'

'So Claire doesn't have them much?'

'She tends to come over and spend time with them at home, rather than at her place.'

'Is that not weird for you?'

'Weird how?'

'Weird in the "moving on" kind of way.'

Doug looked thoughtful.

'I've not really thought about it. Well, I have in as much as I don't want the kids meeting her new bloke yet; it's too soon I think, and Jude is way too angry. But she gets it and is happy to keep things as they are and then go home to what's his name.'

'Do you wonder … that it's not so broken it can't be fixed?'

Doug twirled his wine glass. 'Not now. Look, this is what I was trying to say the other night in the pub. It's broken alright, with Claire. Unfixable. If the truth be known, I don't want to fix it, you know? The trust has gone. That's it. Game over. You ran out on me after we picked up the teenagers the other night and I didn't get a chance to explain.'

Jesse waved her hand dismissively, and Doug caught it.

'No. Don't dismiss it or wave it away. What I was trying to say very badly, was I want to explore this thing with you. I just need to get my head straight. So, I wasn't saying I don't want to, I very much want to—'

'Wrestle more hoses?' Jesse provided.

'Exactly,' said Doug softly. 'Lots more wrestling of hoses.'

Jesse exhaled heavily. 'Are you sure, Doug? I mean really sure? I don't want to get in the middle of anything here.'

Doug leant forward across the table, his thumb stroking her wrist, his light wolf eyes boring into hers. 'I'm sure.'

Jesse raised her glass. 'Ok. I'll drink to that. Any news on the containers?'

'Stuart had an audience with the Home Office bods. They think they've stumbled on a massive trafficking racket. They're trying to work out where it would have come from. It's totally out of our hands, we just help with retrieval if any more are found.'

'Do we know how the two we saved are?'

'They're good. As far as Stuart says, they're helping to try and catch the people responsible. From what I hear it was the usual promise of a new life, job, house. Just wait in this container until we can get you on the boat and before you know it, we're pulling them out of the water. One of them thinks they were in the sea for a few days before we found them.'

'A few days being in a container among the dead? My God. How would you ever move on from that?'

'Tough. I guess they'll get loads of help and support.' He focused on her with his direct gaze. 'On that front, how are you doing?'

Jesse pulled a face. 'Hmmm. I'm getting there in some ways. I've got this therapy gig. It's all paid for by the police. Leslie, the lady who helped me with all my evidence and the interviews afterwards, recommended it. Said it would help. At the time, I wasn't keen but I figured it's paid for I might as well use it, plus I felt obligated as she was so good to me.'

'Why doesn't it sound like a good thing?'

'It's the woman who turned up in the pub the other night, Emma. I was seeing her fairly regularly.'

'You were? Past tense? Are you getting anything from it?'

'I don't know. I stormed out today. She's all about forgiveness and all that crap. I'm all for killing him. She wants to explore different techniques which make my blood run cold at the thought. We don't seem to agree.'

'She wants you to forgive him?'

'Apparently that's part of it. It's never gonna happen though.'

'Does she think that will work?'

'Christ knows. It's not going to work for me, I know that much. I physically don't think I have it in me to forgive him. He's robbed me of too much.'

Jesse's eyes suddenly filled with tears. She tried to blink them away and then wiped them quickly with her hands.

'Shit, sorry, don't know where that came from ... just when I think I'm doing OK ...'

'I get that. Don't do it if it's not working for you.'

'I'm pretty close to bailing on it, but then I think, what if it could help? Is this part of the process? Is it supposed to be this difficult and challenging? Tell me, did you talk to anyone after the accident?'

Doug raised an eyebrow. 'Ah, I assume you know all the juicy details about that then?'

'Mike told me the details, but he didn't tell me how it affected you.'

Doug looked across the restaurant as if remembering.

'I didn't talk to anyone, probably should have. It doesn't matter what report I read on the accident or who I talk to, I still blame myself for letting them go down there. So I need to live with that. The accident made me question my judgement, still does. We'd be on a shout and I would start to doubt my own instructions, it was awful. The one place I'd always felt in control, I felt out of control, like I was winging it.'

'And now?' Jesse prompted.

'I doubt myself less and less and rely on my gut feeling more. Listen to your gut. Gav always used to say that. No buts, go with your gut. He was a big loss to the crew.'

'And to you … he was one of your closest friends, wasn't he?'

Doug looked away; he felt his throat closing. He struggled to push the grief back.

'Yup. Miss him … Every day.'

'So, no help coping?'

'No. I think I'm learning to live with it now, more than before anyway.'

'What about physically?'

He shrugged. 'Who needs a spleen anyway?'

'Seriously?' Jesse was surprised.

'Seriously. I'm OK now. It was a bit dicey at the start, but all good now. I do find it amazing how the body repairs itself in this slow methodical way. It's just up here.'

He touched his forehead. 'Where the healing takes a wee bit longer.'

A stressed looking waitress delivered two pizzas to their table.

'Enjoy,' she said. 'Can I get you anything else?'

The two shook their heads and began eating.

Jesse paused. 'Are the kids OK?'

'They're good. Something you said back at the fundraiser has totally rung true. They'd gotten used to Claire not being around so it's not been the upheaval it could have been. So in some ways a gradual absence has probably made the whole thing easier on them. When I look back it wasn't a marriage of any sort really. She's been gone properly a few months now and it seems to me like it's been that way for as long as I can remember.'

'So it's easier on you too?'

'Probably…' he thought for a second longer. 'In fact, definitely.'

Jesse took a breath. 'Do you miss her?'

Doug stared at his wineglass, thinking.

'At first, but that was way, way back. It was the little things I missed. You know, like when you see something amazing or beautiful or funny, you want to share it with the person who'll totally get it. We used to really joke about things like Jude's inability to put the lid back on the toothpaste and Christy's inability to pick anything up from her bedroom floor.'

'And now?'

'I've got used to doing things on my own with the kids, appreciating these things on my own. We're a tight team now. I get flashes of missing her when she's at the house and being with the kids and they're having fun and happy, but then I remember all the lies and the deceit, and I don't miss her at all.'

'And she's living with him permanently now?'

'As opposed to semi-permanently before while she was supposed to be married to me?'

'Sorry, I meant ...'

'I know – me being sarcastic. She is. Who knows whether it's a bed of roses or not. Her choice ... Her bed. Game over.' Doug looked away and drank some wine.

They walked into the Stowaway, spotting Mike immediately. It was a cavernous little bar, made out of a few old sail lofts knocked through together. The floors were uneven and the walls bare brickwork, but the abundance of fairly lights everywhere gave it a slightly magical air. Jesse decided instantly it was one of her new favourite places.

Mike was in the middle of a song and they both raised a hand in greeting. He carried on singing but winked. Doug pointed to a small table and went to get drinks, while Jesse perched on a rickety stool and watched Mike sing.

CHAPTER 31

Mike was doing well in the Stowaway where a big crowd had gathered who were listening and clapping enthusiastically. Doug was making Jesse laugh with his sarcastic observations about the amount of fans who were women. Mike finished his set and waited for the applause to die down before speaking into the microphone.

'Thanks, folks. I'm just going to take a short break.'

Mike made his way over to Jesse and Doug.

'Hey guys. Thanks for coming. Did you come together?'

Doug look at Jesse. 'We did.'

Mike grinned 'About bloody time!'

A girl sidled up behind Mike and tapped him on the shoulder. He turned back to Doug and Jesse.

'Gotta go. Enjoy yourselves.' He winked broadly and was dragged off by the girl.

'He's a dark horse, that one' said Doug, rolling his eyes.

They laughed. Jesse noticed her phone flashing and motioned to Doug she was going outside to answer it.

Doug watched her go and then looked around. The place was busy and, in the corner, Mike was kissing the girl he had been talking to earlier.

Doug picked up his and Jesse's drinks and went outside. Jesse had her back to the door. He caught the end of the conversation.

'Do you need me to come down? … Has he got his phone with him in there? … OK, let me know after they've done it? Let me know if I can do anything … OK, love you. Bye.'

She dropped her head and turned around to see Doug standing behind her. He passed her drink to her.

'Everything OK? People only ring at this time of night for a booty call or an accident.'

'It was my sister. Dad's had a bad fall, broken his hip. They're operating now. I might have to go down for a couple of days. He's probably fine.' She eyed him with amusement. 'Anyway, how often do you get booty calls?'

'Hope springs eternal.'

The two were standing close, next to the harbour wall, Jesse leaning with her back against it. Doug stood in front of her.

'So … about the other night …'

Jesse was nervous at how close he was, but didn't want him to move.

'In the boatshed? That other night?'

'Uh huh. I've been thinking about it. Quite a bit … of thinking in fact.'

Jesse was rooted to the spot as Doug moved closer, almost touching.

'So, I've been thinking …' he continued.

'Awful lot of thinking going on,' she whispered.

Doug bent forward and kissed Jesse's lips lightly. Softly, briefly. He stayed close, lips almost touching.

'So I concluded from my thinking …' he whispered.

Jesse could barely contain herself.

'What did you conclude?'

He took her face in his hands gently and bent his head to kiss her again. As his lips touched hers, his pager went off followed a beat later by her pager.

Doug closed his eyes. 'For the love of God…' he muttered.

Jesse laughed. 'Come on. Never a break, and with all that thinking going on too.'

Mike ran out, yelling over his shoulder.

253

'Come on you two!' The three of them ran around the harbour towards the station.

The lifeboat launched and headed off into the night. Doug, Jesse, Mike, Dan, Paul, Bob and Tom were all aboard.

Doug raised his voice over the wind, 'Bob, what have we got?'

'Tall ship on fire. Youth cruise, it's Morven's. Fire has taken hold. Gonna be bad, Skip. It's been so dry. Hope to god they're ok.'

'Jesus. I saw it in the harbour earlier today. I can't believe it's in trouble already. Right lads, get the fire gear ready, prime that pump and prepare to try and get it under control. Bob, call the coastguard, they might need to get a fireboat out. Keep your heads straight. Take no chances.'

The lifeboat motored powerfully through the night water, the orange glow of a fire on the tall ship could be seen in the distance. Doug's stomach churned. He hated fires on boats, it was about as bad as it could get.

The lifeboat slowed as it approached, and the crew took stock. The boat was ablaze, flames creeping along and catching on whatever they touched. There were people on the deck trying to fight the fire. In an untouched part of the boat, the fire gradually crept up the rigging despite the efforts of the crew to keep the mast and sails wet.

Doug called, 'Bob, call the coastguard. This wind is pushing the fire along. We need a fire & rescue boat. It's not taken hold around the other side. Dan, Paul, Jesse take the Y round there and collect these people on deck.'

Dan disappeared with Paul and Jesse. They launched the Y and headed off to the other side of the tall ship, where Dan manoeuvred the small boat closer and Paul leaned out shouting to the crew.

'We need to get you to safety. How many are there of you?'

The captain approached the side of the tall ship. 'Hi, I'm the Robert – the captain.' He said breathlessly, 'we've got a crew of eight and twelve boys who are in the lifeboats now.'

Paul radioed to Doug. 'Skip. Captain says eight crew and twelve boys in the lifeboat. Over.'

'We've got the lifeboat now and are transferring them onto the main boat. We count ten boys, not twelve. Repeat. Ten boys not twelve, and both youth workers are on board.'

Paul looked over at Robert, worried. 'Skipper says only ten boys in the lifeboat.'

Robert turned and shouted to his crew, 'Two boys missing! Let's find them.' He called to the nearest crew member. 'Amy check down there!'

Jesse watched as Amy headed down into the ship, avoiding the fire as best she could. The larger Tamar lifeboat pulled alongside at a safe distance and the two crews worked together to help control the fire, using fire hoses and extinguishers. Amy re-appeared, breathless and coughing.

'No sign of them at all. The front hold is the only place they could be, surely?'

They heard a creaking sound and a large roll of burning sail dropped onto the deck, narrowly missing Amy. The burning sails now covered the hatch for the hold. Amy looked around frantically as she could hear faint shouting from the hold below.

'I can hear something!'

In the lifeboat, Dan turned to Doug and shouted, 'Skipper. Sails are burning pretty bad here and they've fallen on the cover for the hold, that's where the boys are.'

'OK, hang tight. We're coming over.' He turned. 'Tom, we'll go on and move these sails and get the kids out.'

Doug turned to Bob. 'Bob, bring the boat close to the ship so we can jump across. Then pull back. Keep an eye on that burning rigging.'

The two of them jumped across as soon as the boat was in position. The fire was intense, the smoke thick, swirling around as the various gusts of wind caught it. The heat was staggering, Doug could feel it burning his face. Burning sails floated down like they were doing a mad dance. Doug began heaving the burning sails over the side of the boat and with help from Tom they eventually got the front hold cover exposed. Both men tried to lift the lid of the burning hold and with a struggle it finally came free.

Doug bent down and peered in.

'Hello?' he yelled, coughing from the smoke pouring out. 'Tom, hand me a torch.'

Doug shone the torch into the hold and saw the two boys unconscious on the floor.

'They're here, but they're unconscious. We need to get them out,' Doug called urgently. 'I'm gonna need to jump down and get them with Tom and hand them up to you with the strap.'

Dan shouted to the captain, 'Hey! I need a pair of hands over here!'

Robert and Amy ran over. Doug lowered himself down into the hold, followed by Tom. Dan moved to the edge and lay down looking in.

Inside the hold, the smoke was thick and pouring in, and Doug was overwhelmed with a sense of claustrophobia. He coughed violently and tried to see through the smoke. He found the boys, almost stumbling on one of them, and bent down to check for life signs, struggling to get a glove off so he could feel for a pulse on them both.

'Faint pulse here, can't find one here. This fella's going first,' called Doug, coughing. He hooked a strap under the arms of the first boy and struggled to hoist him up, with Tom helping him. Tom was coughing violently with the acrid smoke.

Dan stretched his arms down.

Doug shouted up, 'No pulse here. Up and out and CPR.'

Dan pulled the boy up by the strap and Amy stepped forward to help get him out. She lay him down and gave CPR to the boy, with the deck all around her still burning.

Doug fixed a strap around the second boy and hoisted him up again with Tom's help.

Doug shouted, 'Weak pulse here.'

The boy was coughing, but his eyes were closed and he was fairly unresponsive.

In the hold, Doug turned to Tom, coughing, 'You're up and out. Come on.'

Doug cupped his hands for Tom to get a leg up and climb out of the hold. As Tom rolled clear, a deafening cracking sound was heard, and part of the mast fell. Its weight hit the deck with an almighty thud, blocking the hold entrance, trapping Doug inside and raining down burning embers into the hold.

Jesse heard the noise and looked over, seeing it happen almost in slow motion. Tom was trying to move the mast, but the flames were too intense. In a panic Jesse clambered across the length of the main deck and ran to Robert who was still trying to fight the fire. She yelled breathlessly.

'Our skipper – he got the boys out, but he's trapped in the front hold. Is there another way in?'

Robert looked worried. 'The only other way is over there, and the fire's too intense. I don't know how to get to him.'

Jesse was beside herself. There had to be another way. She turned to the larger lifeboat, shouting at Bob who was looking over worried.

'Bob!' she yelled. 'Doug is trapped in the hold and we can't get to him. How many axes have we got? Can we go through the deck to get him?'

Bob nodded. He beckoned Mike over to steer the boat and a moment later he was climbing aboard the main ship holding two axes.

'We're going to have to go through here to get to him,' said Jesse grimly. The two swung the axes but it was hard, backbreaking work in the intense heat, with the smoke thick and the hard wood unrelenting.

When they broke through, smoke rushed up through the opening.

Jesse looked horrified at the volume of thick smoke.

'Oh God! Look at that smoke. Doug! Doug – can you hear us?'

Bob and Dan tried to make the hole bigger. Paul appeared with a crowbar and the three worked feverishly. Eventually the hole was big enough and Tom lay down and looked below.

'Jesus, it's thick smoke in here. Jesse get the oxygen off the boat … I see him. He's not conscious … guys, can you lower me down and I can see if I can grab him?'

Jesse ran to get the small oxygen tank, yelling across to Mike to throw it across.

Dan, Bob and Paul all held Tom's legs as he stretched in.

'I've got hold of his jacket. Can you pull us out?' Tom called.

The lads pulled Tom back, and he pulled Doug up through the hole by his jacket. They heaved and struggled, and more of the crew ran over to help. They got him clear of the hole and the fire, and Jesse ran over with the oxygen.

Doug's face was black and there was a large gash on his forehead that was bleeding profusely. Jesse knelt by Doug and loosened his jacket. Tom took control and felt for a pulse. It seemed like an eternity before he spoke.

'Pulse. Not great but good enough. Air on, Jesse.'

Jesse put the oxygen on with shaking hands.

'Doug, Doug! Wake up!' she said urgently, her breath coming in huge sobs, oblivious to the others there. She was filled with panic that he wouldn't make it.

'Let's turn him on his side,' Tom said.

As they turned him, Doug coughed and his eyelids fluttered. He lay, eyes closed, for a few minutes, coughing sporadically. He opened his eyes and smiled weakly at Jesse.

Jesse sat back on her heels and exhaled heavily, her tears streaking her blackened cheeks. She was shaking her head.

'Jesus, you gave me a fright.'

Doug looked in pain. 'Hard to breathe,' he gasped.

They helped him sit up and he dissolved into a coughing fit.

Jesse frowned. 'We need to get him to hospital. How are the other boys, Dan?'

'Not great. Amy's brought hers around and mine's drifting in and out of consciousness. We need to get back quick.'

Bob took charge. 'Get the boys and Doug onto the boat.'

Bob approached the captain. 'Right, everybody off now. We need to go and get these casualties to hospital. I can't leave you here. I can't get a chopper to get these guys off the boat as that will drive the flames.'

Robert started to argue, but Bob shook his head and held up his hand.

'I know you're the captain, but as soon as you sent a mayday you became our problem and I call the shots for everyone's safety. We can't fight this. It has to run its course. Round up your team please. Don't put them at risk.'

He turned and motioned the crew to get the casualties on the main lifeboat and Paul brought the Y back and put it away.

The Tamar's engines roared and the boat surged off towards Castleby. In the bowels of the boat, Doug sat in one of the seats, strapped in with the oxygen mask on. He was struggling to breathe, gasping for air. The two boys were on stretchers on the floor and the rest of the youngsters were sat huddled in blankets, looking sooty and shocked. Jesse appeared from the upper deck and knelt in front of Doug.

'How are you doing? You look dreadful.'

His face registered pain and he was struggling to breathe. Suddenly he lost consciousness. Jesse kept his head upright and yelled,

'Doug's gone again. Hurry up!'

Bob shouted down.

'Two minutes. Get him up on the main deck, I don't care what anyone says, he's off first. There's a rig waiting.'

Bob, Paul and Jesse all lifted Doug to take him to the upper deck. Bob leaned down and helped pull Doug up by the jacket. Mike guided the boat into the harbour as fast as he dared, positioning the boat as near to the ambulance as he could get it. Paramedics Liz and Phil came running with their bags.

'What we got?' asked Phil breathlessly.

Jesse stepped forward. 'It's Doug. He was trapped below decks, thick smoke in there. He's been coughing and slipping in and out of consciousness.'

Phil looked shocked. 'Doug? Jesus. When was he last awake?'

'About five minutes ago.'

Phil said, 'Liz. Get a stretcher can you and the O2 tank. He'll need 100 per cent. How many others?'

'Two teenage boys. One in bad shape. Tom should get checked too.'

'OK.' Phil pulled on a pair of nitrile blue gloves. 'Liz, radio in for another bus while you're there. We'll take Doug and the worst one now.'

Phil worked on Doug for a while, getting him an IV and ensuring he was stable before he nodded to Jesse to help him lift the stretcher into the back of the ambulance. As they were loading him in, Doug came around briefly and opened his eyes. Jesse took his hand.

Doug closed his eyes again, but still held onto her hand firmly. Bob, who had been anxiously watching, stepped forward and placed a hand on Jesse's back.

'You go with Doug. We'll come later, OK? Nessie will sort the kids.'

Jesse looked surprised at Bob. She smiled gratefully, swallowing back the tears that threatened.

'Thanks, Bob.'

He held her arm tightly for a moment, looking into her eyes.

'I can't have anything happen to him. Not again.'

Jesse squeezed his arm. She moved over in the ambulance to allow Phil to slide in the stretcher with one of the boys, who was still unconscious. Amy was accompanying him, looking worried. Liz slammed the doors and the ambulance drove away fast, passing another ambulance on the way in to collect Noah.

Bob gathered the rest of the boys up and motioned them towards the lifeboat station. The subdued and shivering group trailed after him.

The ambulance arrived at the hospital, with sirens blaring and blue lights flashing, the doors were flung open and Doug and the boy were wheeled in on stretchers, followed by Jesse and Amy. A doctor approached the stretcher followed by a nurse, and Jesse grabbed her arm.

'You need to get Dr Claire Brodie in here. This is her husband.'

The nurse took a look at Doug's prone form, turned, and ran off down the corridor.

Doug had an oxygen mask on and was connected to a drip. Various machines beeped quietly. He had a row of stiches on his forehead, but he was quiet. Asleep. Next to him, in the hospital chair, was Jesse, fast asleep. Her face, neck and hands were still smeared with soot from the fire.

The door opened quietly, and Claire stepped in. She inspected the machines Doug was connected to and grabbed his chart from the end of the bed. She adjusted his drip and oxygen levels and shook her head as she looked at him. She reached out and pushed back his hair from his head wound, her hand staying on his face too long.

'Jesus, Doug … what have you done to yourself this time?'

A figure stood at the door watching Claire touch Doug's face through the small window. The door opened again quietly, and Felix stepped in.

'How's he doing?' he said softly.

Claire turned at his voice.

'Early days. Lungs are in bad shape as he inhaled so much smoke. Any longer in there and that would have been it. He needs oxygen and steroids and a bit of luck and he should be OK, but next twelve hours are crucial.'

Felix stood behind Claire, rubbing her shoulders as Claire watched Doug sleep.

'It's funny, isn't it?' she said quietly. 'This is the thing you least expect these guys to come into contact with.'

'What?'

'Fire … you know, you expect these guys to have been in the water too long, hypothermia or exposure, being hit by boat debris or whatever, but not fire. Doug's always said that fire is about the single worst thing that can happen on a boat.' Her eyes filled with tears.

Felix looked over and gestured to Jesse, still asleep in the chair. 'Who's that?'

'She's one of the crew. Look at the gear. One of them will always stay, they all have this weird bond. It's like they need someone here to watch over them. Let her sleep. It sounds like it was a bad shout.'

'Where are you going now?'

'I need to go and see the kids, they'll be worried. I'll call you. OK?'

Felix nodded.

She kissed him on the cheek and walked down the corridor, quickly texting on her phone.

In intensive care, the two boys who had been stuck in the hold were both sedated. One was attached to a ventilator and the other was on oxygen and a drip. The nurses moved about quietly and efficiently, checking machines and making notes on charts. Morven was on the phone at the nurse's desk, trying to reach the parents of the boys.

Dawn had come and gone, and the sun streamed into Doug's hospital room, shining directly onto Jesse's sleeping face. Doug was awake and watching Jesse sleep.

She woke slowly, blinking at the bright light and stretched, seeing Doug watching her.

'You snore … a lot,' Doug said in a croaky voice that was barely above a whisper.

Jesse smiled. 'Liar. How are you feeling?'

Doug went to reply, but coughed, which looked like it caused him pain.

Jesse jumped up from her chair.

'Do you want some water?'

Doug nodded, and Jesse fetched him a beaker of water from the bedside table and gave it to him. He took a sip, then lay back looking exhausted.

'How do you feel?' she asked.

Doug struggled to talk. 'Like I have a dead weight lying on my chest.'

Talking made him cough more and one of the machines started a small beeping alarm. A nurse entered, pressing the reset button on the machine. She tutted and placed the oxygen mask back over Doug's face.

'Keep it on,' she scolded.

'Yes boss,' Doug replied sheepishly.

The nurse winked and left the room.

Jesse perched on the edge of the bed.

'So, Doc says they think you'll probably be OK. Quite a bit of lung damage from the smoke but they think the steroids and oxygen are working. They've threatened to put you in a bariatric chamber for a while if it doesn't improve … so best behaviour, I think.'

Doug lifted the oxygen mask. 'I just remember the mast falling and the hatch filled up with burning sails.'

Jesse said triumphantly, 'We smashed through the deck with axes to get you out.'

Doug rolled his eyes. 'Jesus. Bet the captain was pleased.'

Jesse snorted. 'He was fighting a losing battle. A wooden tall ship after a dry period? It went up like a tinder box. Bob ended up ordering him off and they had to let it burn. Coastguard sent a fire boat which damped down the worst of it, but all that's really left is the hull, which is in OK shape. Still floating at least.'

As she spoke there was a knock at the door, and it swung open revealing the crew who were all jostling to get in. Dan got in first followed by Paul, Ben, Mike, Bob and Tom. They all gathered around the bed and greeted Doug warmly. Doug started coughing as he tried to speak, and the nurse came back in and ushered the crew out.

'Come on lads,' she said briskly 'You can see he's OK, but he can't be coughing this much.'

The crew shuffled out of the room, looking sheepish. The door opened again, and Mike beckoned Jesse outside. He was stood with Amy and Morven, along with Steve the copper, and a younger constable who looked slightly too small for his uniform. Mike rested a hand on Jesse shoulder.

'Steve's after finding out how the fire started. Any ideas from anything you saw Amy?' Mike prompted. 'Did you see anything suspicious, anything that could have caused the fire?'

Amy shook her head. 'Absolutely not. We're paranoid about that sort of thing as it's a wooden boat.'

As they were talking quietly, a nurse walked along the corridor holding a small clear bag.

'Sorry to interrupt,' she began hesitantly. 'I've been meaning to come and see you, but here you are. I found this in one of the boy's pockets. Thought it might be helpful.'

She passed the bag to Steve, who opened it.

'It's a spliff. You know what this means, don't you? It's not definitive, but it's a fairly good suggestion of what could have happened. What sort of shape are the boys in?'

The nurse looked glum. 'Not great. One of them can't breathe on his own at the moment, the other one is stronger. We've got them heavily sedated, though, so it'll be a few hours before they'll be able to form a sentence I should think.'

'OK. I'll come back later,' Steve said. 'Morven will you still be here? Does anyone need a lift back?'

Both Jesse and Mike nodded.

'Thanks, Steve, I just need to pop in and tell Doug we're off,' said Jesse.

She ducked back into Doug's room to find him fast sleep again; not wanting to disturb him, she collected her gear quietly, kissed his cheek gently, opened the door and crept out.

Finally, we see her. We've been worried. The fire was all over the news so we knew she must be involved. We've been frantic trying to find her. The crew have come this morning. They are never far away. She looks tired. She looks worried. We duck down as they approach the car. The skipper is nowhere to be seen. We like that. Perhaps something's happened to him. We are hopeful. We can't be seen. We hear her say she's coming back later. We'll wait. We need to see her.

CHAPTER 32

Doug was leaving hospital after a week and Jesse was picking him up to bring him home. She spoke to Brock firmly as he sat in the passenger seat, ruffling his ears and shutting the car door, after dropping the windows a few inches. She jogged around the side of the hospital and in through the main doors.

Doug was sat on his bed, dressed. The door opened and Claire appeared dressed in scrubs.

'How are you feeling?'

'OK. Apart from the coughing. Chest a wee bit tight, but that should go, right?'

Claire pulled a face. 'Depends.' She consulted his chart.

'Depends on?'

'Steroids. Rest. Recovery ... the last two you're not particularly good at if I recall.'

Doug rolled his eyes. 'Kids OK?'

'Fine. Looking forward to you being home.'

She removed her stethoscope from around her neck and tugged up his T-shirt. She listened and tipped him forward to listen to his back.

'Breathe deeply,' she said absently. 'Normally.'

She pursed her lips and tugged his T-shirt back down, hooking the stethoscope around her neck.

'Nessie says she's loaded up the fridge and she'll be around. Do you want me to come and stay? It's no problem.'

'I'll be fine. Thanks for sorting them out. I appreciate the offer, but I'll be fighting Nessie off.'

'No need to thank me. They're my children too if you remember. How are you getting home?'

'One of the crew is coming.'

Claire rolled her eyes. 'Of course one of the crew is coming. Stupid Claire. If you're not all joined at the hip for more than a minute, surely the world will fall apart. That one that came in with you – the nurses had to practically force her to leave, poor thing. She must have been shattered, sleeping in that chair. She refused to leave until she knew 100 per cent you were out of the woods.'

Doug looked surprised. 'I don't remember much about it.'

Claire handed over a paper bag of medicine.

'You need to carry on taking these for a week. No booze. And use this inhaler for when you have a bad coughing fit. OK? Call me if you're worried about anything and back to see the lung nurse in a week for further tests, OK?'

Doug nodded.

Claire's pager went off; she looked down and tutted. 'Gotta go. I'll call you later. Look after yourself. Doctor's orders!'

She kissed him on the cheek and touched his face lightly with her hand.

Jesse was walking along the hospital corridor, juggling two very hot coffees. At the door to Doug's room she faltered slightly as she saw Claire bending down to kiss Doug and place a hand on his cheek. Jesse moved away from the door, turning her back to it as she saw Claire approach. For some inexplicable reason she couldn't face the woman yet.

The door opened and Claire walked out and off down the corridor. Jesse watched her go. Then she pushed the door open with her shoulder. Despite being confused at Claire's intimate gesture, she plastered a cheerful smile on her face as she entered the room.

'Morning!' she said.

Doug looked pleased to see her. 'Hey! Good to see you. Are you getting me out of here?'

'I'm busting you out as they say. Are you OK to go?'

'Yup. Just been dismissed and issued with medicine.'

Jesse handed him a coffee. 'Your drug of choice, M'lord.'

'Oh contraband! The coffee in here is unrecognisable. I'm having withdrawal symptoms from a lack of caffeine.'

Jesse gestured to the bag on the bed. 'That everything?'

He nodded, sipping the coffee.

'Christ, that's hot,' he said, putting it down quickly.

'When you're up to it we can go.'

Doug sat on the bed, and looked at Jesse, a little embarrassed. 'Look. They said … they said you were here for hours … that you stayed here until I got over the worst of it.'

Jesse looked defensive. 'Well, I wasn't going to leave until I knew you were alright.'

'I don't remember much of it at all. But thank you.'

Jesse blushed and shrugged dismissively, picking up Doug's bag. 'It's OK. No big deal.'

She walked to the door and held it open, gesturing for Doug to walk through it.

'Come on, I've been told I'm to take you straight home.'

'Do I even get a say in anything?'

'Nope,' Jesse said with a grin.

'Are we not discussing it then?' Doug asked innocently.

'Nope,' Jesse said briskly. 'You catch on quick. I like that. Come on.'

Doug could vaguely hear someone calling his name. Slowly he opened his eyes and realised he must have fallen asleep on the way home from the hospital as the truck was now parked in his driveway. Jesse was gently trying to wake him up.

'You OK?' she said, looking concerned. 'You were out for the count. I stopped and checked for a pulse at one point.'

Doug felt dreadful. He tried to wake up properly. Jesse came around to the passenger side and opened the door. Brock jumped out first and sat waiting for Doug, who climbed out slowly, coughing.

'Come on, let's get you inside.'

'DAD!' The kids ran out of the front door. Christy threw herself at him. Jude also joined in the hug. Jesse picked up his bag and walked towards the front door.

'Come on, you lot. Let's get your dad in; he needs loads of rest.'

Doug and the kids walked slowly into the house, still hugging. Jesse closed the front door behind them. The kids dragged Doug towards the kitchen where there was a unanimous 'Surprise!' from the crew. Doug looked really pleased to see them and tried to say something but ended up coughing. Mike guided him to a chair and gave him a glass of water and the crew spent time greeting Doug and giving him bloke hugs.

Jesse observed all of this smiling, touched by how much they felt for Doug and what a part of the team he was. He was the glue that held them together and made them what they were. She leant against the door jamb smiling; Doug caught her eye and winked.

Jesse was loading plates into the dishwasher when Mike came in.

'That's it now. Everyone's gone. I've sent the kids up for a bath.'

'You're very domesticated, you'd make someone a lovely wife.'

Mike chuckled. 'Doug's out for the count on the sofa. You OK here? I've gotta go. Hot date tonight.'

Jesse waved him off. 'You go, Casanova, I'll do the last of it. Thanks for helping.'

Mike kissed her cheek. 'No probs. See you later.'

'Have a good night!'

She finished clearing up and went to tuck Christy in and read her a story, telling her to wake Jude if she was worried or needed anything. Jesse then went and knocked on the door to Jude's room.

'Jude?' She stuck her head around the door. 'I've said to Christy to come and wake you if she's worried about anything. OK?'

'OK.'

'I'll stay for a bit and then Nessie's coming in to sleep in the den later just so there is someone here," said Jesse. 'Read for a bit, then lights out. OK?

Jude nodded; Jesse winked at him and went downstairs.

She crept into the lounge, seeing Doug still fast asleep. Brock was snoring at his feet. She picked a blanket off a chair and laid it over him gently. She turned out the lights in the lounge, called the dog softly and shut the door quietly, going to the kitchen to wait for Nessie.

* * *

Jesse had been on the beach with Brock, who had succeeded in knocking her over twice by taking out her legs with his stick trick. She was annoyed, had a wet backside and was covered in sand, but he was delighted with his efforts.

The two of them walked up the hill, with Jesse planning to pass Doug's house to check on them. She hadn't planned to go in, she just wanted to see it was OK. As she arrived, the kids were leaving the house to get into the car of Helen, the childminder. Christy came running over.

'Hi, Jesse! Hello, Brockie,' she crooned and seeing them, Jude dumped his schoolbag on the drive and rushed over.

'Looking cool today, that a new haircut?' Jesse teased.

Jude looked embarrassed. 'You like it?'

'Very much.' Jesse winked at him.

Jude went bright red but looked very pleased with himself. Helen walked over to Jesse. She'd just had a lovely ten minutes clucking around Doug and gazing at him adoringly, and was genuinely one step away from offering to move in with him until he was fully recovered. She couldn't work out if this woman and Doug were friends, colleagues, or something more.

'Hi Jesse, how are you?' she asked.

'Good, thanks. You taking these two off to school?'

Helen nodded. 'I thought Doug could do with the break and rest up a bit, I think he's doing too much.'

'That's so nice of you.' Jesse turned to the children. 'Kids. Is Dad OK today?'

'Yes. He made pancakes this morning,' Christy announced.

Jesse pretended to look horrified. 'Pancakes? With maple syrup?'

Christy nodded. 'Mm, although I quite like them with Marmite.'

Jesse thought for a moment. 'Pancakes are my absolute favourite, but with maple syrup, not Marmite. Did you save me any?'

Christy giggled and shook her head. 'Jude had four helpings.'

Jesse turned to Jude. 'Four helpings, Jude?'

Jude looked indignant. 'I'm a growing boy. I need to keep my strength up.'

269

Helen touched the kids' shoulders. 'Come on you two, time for school.'

She ushered them into the car and tooted as she drove off. Jesse gave them a wave and turned to see Doug standing at the front door leaning against the frame, watching with a smile and waving at the kids. He looked good, in an old T-shirt and shorts, like he'd just stepped off the beach.

'Hello,' he said. 'There's some pancake batter left if you want one? I'll chuck in a coffee?'

'Well, who can resist an offer like that in the morning? How are you feeling?'

'Good … still mortified I fell asleep at my welcome home party. I'm guessing it was you who cleared up and tucked me in?'

'Mike helped but had to leave for a hot date. He was on a promise, I think.'

She followed him into the house, Brock trotting at her heels.

Jesse sat herself at the kitchen table and was handed a mug and a cafetiere by Doug; she helped herself.

Doug moved around the kitchen slowly, coughing occasionally. 'Are two pancakes OK?'

'Bring it on.'

Doug passed her a plate and moved the maple syrup over her way.

'Dig in.'

'Ta very much.' Jesse wolfed down the first pancake. 'Mm, God these are good. No end to your domestic talents, is there? Good hair doing according to Christy, excellent pancake making … what, I wonder, is the next surprise from Doug Brodie?'

'I do a mean garlic roast chicken … perhaps I'll tempt you one of these days.'

'Promises, promises …'

Jesse's phone rang shrilly in the kitchen. She saw the display.

'Do you mind if I take this?'

'Go ahead,' he said and busied himself clearing up.

Jesse answered. 'Hello.'

'Jesse. It's Emma Marshall. How are you?'

'OK thanks, can I call you back?'

Emma pressed on. 'No need. Look, I just wanted to say I'm sorry I upset you in our last session. I really want to make amends. I promise I'll try not to upset you. Can we book in a session?'

'Err, I'm not sure.' Jesse felt cornered.

'Come on – second chances and all that. How about later today about 5 p.m?'

Jesse would have agreed to anything to get her off the phone. 'Err, OK, I think we need to get this sorted.'

Emma was delighted. 'Great! See you then Jesse.' She ended the call before Jesse could change her mind.

Jesse put the phone down on the counter. Doug met her eyes over the rim of his coffee cup.

'OK?'

'Yup. Shrink. Remember I told you about it? I got a bit shouty last time and stormed out. She's trying to lure me back.'

Doug raised his eyebrows. 'Don't you want to go back?'

'She was pushing me to think about something I didn't want to ... still don't want to.'

'Facing up to the attack?'

Jesse looked defensive. 'Facing up?'

'I meant, reliving it or something – pushing you too much. By your response I'm guessing that's the case.'

Jesse hung her head. 'Sorry. Yes, she was. She called to apologise. Asked me to come in.'

'You going?'

'I am. If nothing else than to say I don't think it's working for me if we're going to go down this current route. I can't do it, Doug. I just can't go there. Re-live it. I just can't. It'll break me.'

She looked up and her eyes were full of tears. Doug looked sympathetic.

'Hey come on ...' He leant forward across the counter-top and took her hand. 'See what she says and then make a decision. Don't be forced into doing anything. But remember, at some point, you'll have to revisit it, just for your own mental health. Perhaps, now just isn't the time.'

Jesse took a deep breath.

'You know you can talk to me anytime about this?'

Jesse rolled her eyes. 'Then you'll know precisely how unhinged I am. You'll run for the hills.'

Doug shrugged. 'It's OK. In good company and all that. I promise I won't run.'

Jesse took her plate over to the sink and washed it up. She looked at his clock on the wall.

'I need to get going. Billy's in today for a bit. I said I'd meet him. Thanks for that. Pancakes, coffee ... The list of your abilities just gets longer and more impressive.'

'Anytime – for any of it,' Doug said softly.

'Thanks, Doug. Get some rest. You look better. See you later,' she said over her shoulder as she let herself out.

* * *

If Jesse could have come up with a good excuse not to go to Emma's office, she would have used it. However, despite her efforts, she hadn't been able to think of anything.

'Thanks for coming, Jesse.'

Jesse sat down on a sofa. Emma took her usual chair.

'Once again, I'm sorry about the last session. I pushed too much.'

Hmm, it seems an odd sort of therapy to me. To make me feel worse rather than better,' Jesse said grumpily.

'Well, I'm certainly not trying to do that, although the road to better mental health does get rocky and you'll have to face things you'd perhaps rather not. For now, let's keep it light. You look well.' Emma scrutinised Jesse. 'Very well, in fact ... What's new?'

Jesse pulled a face. 'Nothing much. I feel good though.'

'What's the secret?'

'Nothing. I'm just feeling good at the moment. Like I'm part of something again. Part of a team ... with the things that matter.'

'Feeling needed?' Emma suggested.

'Uh huh, feeling needed and feeling I play a role. We had a rescue, a tall ship on fire. You probably saw it on the local news.'

'I did. I was glued to it. I thought about you. Wasn't it a youth sailing programme or something?'

'It was. Anyway, there was a bad fire. A fire on a boat is always bad. A fire on a wooden boat after a long dry spell is even worse.'

'Was anyone hurt?'

272

'The two boys who we think started the fire were badly hurt. Doug too. He was trapped in a hold after getting them both out. We had to smash through the deck to get him out.'

Emma leant forward. 'I met Doug in the pub didn't I? Is he OK?'

'He wasn't. He came out of hospital a few days ago. We were all so worried. He's such a big part of the team. His lungs were badly damaged but he's on the mend now.'

'And the boys?'

'One is OK. The other has lung damage and pneumonia. Looks pretty bad for him.'

'Nasty rescue then. So, you feel closer to the crew?'

'Yes, I feel part of that family now. It's good.'

Emma picked at a loose thread on her chair. 'Isn't Doug married? His wife must have been very worried.'

'She was. She's a surgeon at the hospital.'

Emma smiled. 'So all is good at the moment. No more weird sensations or not feeling safe?'

'The woods again … when I was there with Brock the other day, but I couldn't see anything to explain it.'

'Any more dreams?'

'Not the usual dreams. Last couple have been the fire on the tall ship and not being able to get Doug out.'

'That's suggests Doug is very important to you.'

Jesse folded her arms defensively. 'He's my friend. My boss. He's important to all of us.'

'He seemed very nice when I met him in the pub. Has anything developed between you two?'

'Nothing that warrants any discussion here, I don't think.'

'OK. I think we should start to talk about a way forward.'

'I don't want a way forward to be writing a letter or trying to forgive Chris.'

'OK. I think we've established that. I think we need to perhaps think about some sort of hypnosis, perhaps some regression therapy.'

Jesse folded her arms. 'What would that achieve?'

'That depends entirely on you, Jesse. I'm still really concerned about your anger and rage … your words, yes? There's almost a red mist element to it. Plus, you are, in your own words, too frightened to push this sensation and examine how you feel in a more deep-rooted sense. Jesse, you just can't carry that around, it will eat you alive from the inside out.'

'What do you suggest I do?'

'Well, I can help you with the therapies I've suggested, but I think we'll be waking that sleeping lion up properly and saying hello, rather than just poking at him. You'll have to go places and think about things you'd rather not think about.'

Jesse took a deep breath and looked out of the window; tears were threatening just at the mention of it.

'I don't know if I can do that,' she said in a small voice.

Emma lent forward. 'What's stopping you, Jesse?'

'I just can't … I'm afraid … OK?'

'What are you afraid of?'

Jesse lent forward and put her head in her hands.

'I'm afraid to go there again. I'm afraid that in my mind, I won't be me when I come back. I'm frightened part of me will just shut down if I go back there, and I won't be me.'

She stood abruptly. 'I need to think about this. I'm not ready … I don't think I'll ever be ready.'

Emma raised a calming hand. 'Jesse, calm down, sit down … we can take this slowly. I'll help you.'

Jesse paced around the office, running her hands through her hair.

'I'm doing OK. Why would I go back to thinking about that? I need to go. Sorry.'

Jesse ran to the door and wrenched it open, running out. Emma watched her retreating back and sighed deeply.

* * *

Jesse had suffered a restless night. She was trying to unpick why she ran out whenever the conversation with Emma got difficult. To her, it was clear – she was unable to face it. But then she fretted about whether that was a healthy way to be, mentally. *Probably not*, she thought ruefully. She had thought about Doug too. Endlessly. How he was and what he was doing. How he had been with her just before they got the call to the tall ship fire. Perhaps this was the start of something new.

She decided to walk Brock somewhere different and drove to some pine woods a few miles away. The sun was out and streaming through the pines, casting rays across the forest floor. Jesse stuck in her headphones and Brock capered along happily, picking up sticks, trying to catch her on the back of the legs. She was feeling better already; she was enjoying the music and was singing along softly to a Passenger track called "Survivors". She smiled. She loved this song and boy could she relate.

Suddenly the dog stopped dead in his tracks and dropped the stick. Over Jesse's shoulder a twig snapped and the dog crouched, listening hard. Jesse was oblivious. Without warning the dog launched himself into the bushes and barked, chasing a squirrel.

Jesse laughed at his antics. 'Brock! Leave the poor squirrels alone.'

She completed the long circuit of the woods and ended up at the car. She opened the boot, grabbing a bowl and a bottle of water to put down for the dog. As she sat in the open boot while Brock drank, she had another strange sensation of being watched. The hairs on the back of her neck stood up and she shivered slightly. Brock seemed very alert and kept stopping his drinking to look around. Jesse checked her surroundings carefully. She caught a flash of something reflective in the distance, but then heard a car so she assumed it must have been that. Brock finished drinking and jumped into the boot of the car, looking at her expectantly. She stood for a moment longer, still feeling uncomfortable, and looked around frowning and then shook her head at her paranoia.

As she drove home, her phone rang, but she let the call go to voice mail.

When she pulled into the harbour car park, she played the message.

Jesse. It's Emma. I'm sorry. Look, I just wanted to say I think we're really making progress. Yesterday you told me you were too frightened, but I think I can help you with that. I don't think you realise quite how far you have come. You just need to keep the faith. Can we please talk about it? Call me when you get a minute please?'

Jesse strolled up to Doug's to drop off some fish that Fishy John had given her for him. Jude was playing out at the front of the house and captured the dog as soon as Jesse approached the house, telling Jesse to go on in. She walked in softly, in case Doug was sleeping. She heard laughter from the lounge and rounded the corner to see him on the sofa.

Claire was perched next to him, listening to his chest carefully. Doug's T-shirt was off, and they were chuckling about something. Claire ran a familiar hand from his chest around to his back and tipped him forward. She moved the stethoscope around his back. She playfully slapped his arm out of the way and they both laughed.

'Sounds good, tiny bit of a rattle, but not too bad. When do you see the lung nurse?' she said, hooking the stethoscope back around her neck.

'Tomorrow.'

'Better keep off the fags until then.' Claire said dryly.

Doug picked up his T-shirt. He spotted Jesse in the doorway and said, 'Oh hey, come on in.'

Jesse wanted to run. Fast. Away. Now. But she entered the room, slightly hesitantly and looking embarrassed. She waved the carrier bag.

'Sorry, Jude was out front, he said to come in and drop this off ...'

Claire was looking at her, head tilted to one side.

'Jesse, isn't it?' she asked briskly before Doug could get a word in.

Doug put his T-shirt back on.

'It is. Look, I can see you're really busy. I'll come back another time. This is from Fishy John. I'll leave it in the kitchen. See you later.'

She left hurriedly, shutting the door behind her. She jogged out of the front door and whistled for Brock, waving to Jude who looked confused at her sudden departure.

Jesse walked fast down the road, tears stinging in her eyes. *Jesus! What the hell was that? Why am I so upset?* She shook her head and talked to herself.

'Stupid, stupid, stupid.'

She got to her front door, went in and slammed it behind her loudly. Ten minutes later her trainers were on and she was on the beach, the dog beside her. She was running full pelt, upset and angry. She stopped and bent over, hands on thighs, and breathed deeply. The dog ran around her in circles. Her phone rang and Jesse saw it was Doug calling. She looked for a moment, declined the call and set off running again.

Doug was frustrated. He couldn't get hold of Jesse and wanted to talk to her. He wasn't sure why she left so abruptly; something was odd about her expression and he was clueless as to what it was.

He was sure it couldn't have been because Claire was there, because Jesse knew how he felt about Claire now. Either way, he was confused and felt like he had upset her somehow and the feeling unsettled him.

For the millionth time in the last month he wished for the counsel of his best friend, Gavin. He'd know what to do, what to say. He tried her phone again, frustrated as it went straight to voicemail.

She's in the woods. She's laughing at the dog. He's chasing something. Stupid thing. She looks happy as she wanders along. We like it when she's alone. What would she say if she saw us? What would she do if she knew how we felt about her? She's no idea we see her, we could do anything. Surely, she knows she's not safe here alone? We need to be careful, we don't want her to see us. We know he is better now. We don't like this at all. It makes us angry. We'll take some action. We need to be careful though ...

CHAPTER 33

After ten days of twiddling his thumbs, Doug was finally back at work. He sat at his desk, with his feet up, chatting on the phone.

'Ach, I'm fine. Yes, I've got the all clear. Lungs of a 25-year-old, I'm told.' He laughed. 'Yes, back on light duties.' He rolled his eyes. 'Well I don't plan on spending too much time underwater if I can help it. Jesus, you're nagging me more since you left than you did when we were together. Yes, the kids are OK. They're looking forward to seeing you at the weekend. OK ... take care. Bye.'

Doug hung up and removed his feet from the desk. He was just about to see who wanted a cup of tea when the alarm went off for a shout. He headed to the locker room and Tom appeared with a sheet of paper.

'Dog walker cut off by the tide. Can't swim.' He rolled his eyes.

'OK, let's take the inshore, no point in taking the big boat.'

'Yeah, but aren't you supposed to be on desk duties, Skip?'

Doug gave him a look and Tom shrugged.

'OK, good to have you along. Missed you,' he said, clapping Doug on the back.

Thirty minutes later, the inshore lifeboat chugged back into the harbour with an elderly man and a black Labrador on board.

'There you go, Mr Davies, all safe and sound. Look after yourself now, won't you? See you in another couple of weeks.'

The old man grunted, and headed off up the harbour hill, with the dog trailing after him.

Tom watched him go. 'When will he ever learn? That's what? The sixth time?'

Doug made a rueful face. 'He won't change. Give me a hand in with the boat and I'll hose it down. You guys can get off.'

The boys helped Doug hoist the boat up the ramp, then headed back to the station. Doug pulled open the doors to the boat shed and looked in surprise at Jesse, who was already in there.

'Hello,' he said in surprise. 'I've been trying to get hold of you.'

'I've been here. I'm looking for something Billy said might be here.'

'What are you looking for?'

'Why? You wouldn't know what it was anyway.'

Doug frowned at her tone. 'Humour me?'

Jesse rolled her eyes. 'A flexible four-inch diameter marine clamp coupling.'

'Ah one of those!' Doug grinned. 'You're absolutely right, I've no idea.'

Jesse turned her back on Doug and carried on sorting through boxes. Doug came and stood behind her, putting a hand on her arm.

'Jesse,' he said softly. 'I've been calling you. I wanted to talk about the other day. With Claire. You didn't need to go.'

Jesse couldn't bring herself to turn around. 'Oh, I think I did.'

'You're angry with me, you need to tell me why.'

Jesse grabbed a box and left the shed, pushing past Doug.

He called out after her. 'Jesse, come on. Talk to me.'

Jesse walked away quickly, refusing to look at him. Doug stood looking after her, a resigned look crossing his face as he grabbed the hose and started to blast the boat with water.

Jesse opened her front door and shut it behind her with her foot. She pondered on what she considered to be a shitty day. There was a knock at the front door and Brock barked loudly. Jesse opened the door, surprised to see Emma standing there.

'What are you doing here?'

Emma stood at the door awkwardly.

'Look, sorry to just stop by. I've been leaving messages. I was worried about you. I wanted to check you were OK.'

Jesse leant against the doorjamb.

'I did get your messages. How do you know where I live?'

'You filled in some forms when we started remember? Address is on there.'

'Weird, I don't recall filling in a form. Look, I'll sort out another session soon. I just need to decide whether I want to wake the lion or leave him sleeping.'

'I'll get Nat to call you tomorrow.' Emma suggested. 'Come for another session and I can lay out the exact approach and how it works, might make the decision a little easier? We could even try some very light hypnosis, see how you feel? We don't have to go near the lion unless you want to.'

Jesse looked awkward and glanced at her watch.

'Look, I'm sorry. I must seem rude. I'm running late, otherwise I'd ask you in.'

Emma held her hands up and backed away. 'It's fine, it's fine. OK, let's use the next slot to outline the different approaches, then you can give it some thought. Off anywhere nice? Can I give you lift?'

'No thanks. Few of us going to dinner. It'll be nice.'

'Right. I won't hold you up then. I'll get Nat to call tomorrow – first thing.'

Jesse frowned slightly; Emma seemed desperate, which struck her as odd.

Emma turned and walked away calling over her shoulder. 'Bye then.'

Jesse shut the door and leant against it.

'Weird,' she said to herself. She glanced at her watch, rushed upstairs, and scrubbed her face and changed. She clattered back down the stairs, rushed into the kitchen for a bottle of wine and left the house.

Emma sat in her car watching Jesse leave the house. Only when Jesse was out of sight did she start the engine and drive off in the opposite direction.

* * *

It was dark when Jesse left Paul and Nicky's house. The air was cold, and Jesse shivered, wishing she had brought a jacket with her. Paul was hugging everyone and saying goodbye, and Nicky was busy prising him off everyone as he was very worse for wear on red wine. Jesse started walking along the road and Doug fell into step beside her.

'You cold?' Doug asked.

'A bit. Look you don't need to walk me home.'

'Here, have my jacket, and I'm not necessarily walking you home. I'm just walking and you happen to be next to me.'

'Won't you be cold?'

'I'm Scottish, remember? What you southerners consider to be cold, we consider to be positively balmy. Take it.'

Jesse took the coat and snuggled into it. It smelt of Doug and she found it strangely comforting.

'Thanks. It was good tonight. You looked like you were on good form, enjoying yourself. Can't believe how drunk Paul gets on red wine.'

'I know, he's normally not allowed it. I did enjoy myself. You still aren't speaking me to though,' he said, giving her a sideways glance.

'I am.' Jesse was defensive.

'I mean, really speaking.'

Doug stopped and took Jesse's elbow, pulling her closer to him.

'Come on, Jesse, what gives?' he said softly. 'Everything has been weird since the other day when Claire was at the house. What's changed?'

Jesse raised her chin defiantly. 'I have. It's all on me. I woke up and smelt the coffee, to use one of your phrases.'

Doug frowned. 'Whatever you think you saw with Claire, you couldn't be more wrong.'

'I know what I saw, Doug. I saw something that isn't going to end well for me if this … this thing we have' – she waved her arms expansively – 'carries on. You don't want to get involved with me anyway, I'm too broken. And you … you have way too much unresolved stuff with Claire to deal with. I can see it!'

Doug was angry, the tell-tale muscle pounding in his cheek.

'Fuck's sake!' he snapped. 'I've said it. I'm done with Claire. Black and white to me. Nothing unresolved there.'

She glared at him. 'Certainly didn't look like it to me, with you two getting all cosy.'

Doug ran his fingers through his hair and looked at Jesse angrily. 'Jesus. Would it make you feel better if I told you again? I don't want Claire, *at all?*'

Jesse faltered. 'I ...'

'Would it make you feel better?' he demanded.

She nodded, not looking at him.

'Then feel better.' He turned and leant on the railing, breathing heavily.

Jesse looked at him, biting her lip. She'd not seen him this angry. He turned to her.

'Jesse, I'm doing my best here. Me and Claire. I don't feel that way about her anymore. I thought you knew that?'

'You can't just chuck away over a decade together.'

'I didn't chuck it away. She did. That's it, no going back for me. I'm trying to move on. Make a new start. Just like you.'

Jesse looked frustrated 'I don't know ...'

'What else can I say ... or do?' He started to walk away and turned back. 'I think you need to give it a bit more thought and then let me know how you feel. I know how I feel, and I couldn't be any fucking clearer about it. It's on you now. Night, Jesse.'

Doug walked away, looking angry.

Jesse watched him go, half of her wanting to run after him and the other half being just as angry with him.

She called after him. 'What about your jacket?'

'Keep it,' he shouted over his shoulder. He strode off up the road shaking his head, leaving Jesse standing by the railings.

Jesse was tired after a sleepless night. She was nervous about facing Doug as she didn't know what she was going to say to him or how he was going to be with her after being so angry last night.

She'd shut herself away for the majority of the day in the workshop, with the radio on and she was humming softly, once again replaying the argument in her head. Her phone rang, making her jump and answered it, glad for the distraction.

'Hey Nat, how are you?' She wiped her hands as she spoke. 'Yes, I know she did. I'll come and see her. I need to understand where we would go from here, how it would work or, between you and me, whether I should bail on this for a while. Can I pop in tomorrow first thing?' She listened. 'OK. See you then. Bye.'

* * *

Emma sat at her desk on the phone, playing with a glass paperweight as she listened.

'I understand that Dr Nunn. But I must insist he has more time before the CPS assess him. He's only been with you a short while – not nearly enough time for you to have undertaken a prolonged clinical assessment of him. Tell me, is he still saying he can see the whisperers?' She rolled the glass paperweight between both hands.

'As I said, it's just far too soon. Do we have any say in delaying their visit? Can I talk to anyone myself?'

She listened as she jotted down a note on her notepad and then tutted.

'I'll put that in the diary then. If you could confirm the time via email, I'd be grateful. Thank you, Dr Nunn … Goodbye.'

She replaced the receiver and sat for a moment. There was a light knock, and Nat stuck her head around the door.

'I've just spoken to Jesse. She says she's coming in first thing tomorrow. I get the impression that part of her wants to bail, though.'

Emma frowned. 'Bail on tomorrow, you mean?'

'No. Bail on the sessions altogether.'

Emma smiled tightly at Nat. 'Thank you, Nat. Put it in the diary please.'

'No worries.'

The door closed and Emma leaned back in her chair and closed her eyes.

'FUCK!' she screamed, hurling the glass paperweight across the room.

She stood up, put her jacket on, collected her handbag and walked through to the reception area as Nat was ending a call.

'Nat. I have to go out. I won't be back today,' she said briskly. 'Can you cancel my afternoon appointments please?'

Nat looked surprised. 'You OK, what was that crash?'

'Fine. I dropped a paperweight in there. The glass needs clearing up. See you tomorrow.'

* * *

Jesse jogged up the stairs from the lower level, her hands oily. She was wiping them on a rag and was just about to knock on Doug's office door when he opened it and she almost fell into him.

'Oh!' she said, surprised.

'I was just coming to see you,' Doug said.

'And I was just coming to see you,' she said awkwardly.

Doug raised an eyebrow. 'About?'

'Oh … er, I wondered if I could borrow the truck?'

'Where are you off to?' Doug asked, all business.

'To get a part. One of the boat's main caterpillar engines is in bits and I need to get it and put her back together in case we have a shout that the inshore boat can't manage. Is that OK? What did you need me for?'

'I've just had a call that we've got to pick up some new gear from some place near the docks at Pembroke. I said I'd pick it up, but Stuart's just called, so would you mind getting it for me? I've gotta get something out for him tonight, it's the final paperwork on all the containers we found.'

'OK, I'll pick up the gear for you along the way.'

'Read my mind. Hang on.' He disappeared into his office and re-appeared with the keys to the truck and a piece of paper, which he handed to her.

'Chuck it in the sat nav. Middle of nowhere it looks like. Some industrial unit. Some woman called Jane called and told me it was ready for us and they'd leave it outside if we got there after they closed.'

'OK. It's kind of on the way back. Do you want the keys back later? I don't know how long I'll be – I'll come back here and fix the boat till it's done. Am I stopping anything happening by having the truck until later?'

'Nope. It won't affect my rock-and-roll lifestyle. Text me when you're back and we'll decide what's easier later … OK?'

Jesse turned to go and then stopped herself. 'I've still got your jacket,' she said quietly.

Doug nodded, his wolf like eyes probing Jesse's.

He said, disarmingly softly, 'Hang on to it. Then you can use it as a real excuse to come and talk to me about things properly.'

Jesse looked uncomfortable.

He shrugged. 'Your call. Unless of course it takes you so long that winter will be upon us. Obviously then I'll freeze to death without it.'

He turned and went back into his office. 'See you later,' he said over his shoulder.

CHAPTER 34

Darkness was falling. Jesse was driving the truck and swearing like a scaffolder. She was trying to hold on to a large box on the passenger seat that was sliding around when she went round corners. She was also fairly convinced she was lost. The sat nav was in a spooling tantrum and she was trying to drive and look at the map on her phone. Finally, she turned into an industrial unit that was in darkness. Jesse wished for a moment she hadn't dropped Brock off at home and she had his comforting presence. She climbed out of the truck. There was no sign of boxes left out. She banged on the door, but no one came. She made a call, rolling her eyes when it went to voicemail.

'Doug. I'm here at that unit. There's no sign of anyone and nothing's left out. I'm heading back to start on the boat. I'll maybe see you later.'

She climbed in the truck. As she went to turn back down the way she came, she noticed a car parked in the middle of the road, with no one behind the wheel. She leant on the horn for a while in the hope that someone would appear, but the car sat unmoving. She tutted and consulted the map on her phone. The only way out appeared to be to follow the long narrow lane that ran next to the cliffs. She drove slowly out of the yard. Through gaps in the hedge she could just make out the edge of the cliffs.

Jesse heard the roar of an engine and saw full-beam headlights coming up quickly behind her in the rearview mirror.

'Jesus,' she muttered to herself. 'Get in the back why don't you?'

The car behind Jesse lurched closer, and suddenly slammed into the back of the truck.

'SHIT!'

Jesse fought to stay on the road, managing to straighten up. She was petrified. The car behind held back and then rammed her again without warning; this time pushing the truck off the track and through the hedge. Jesse struggled with the wheel, her heart thumping so loudly she thought it would burst out of her chest. With one final ram from the car behind, her truck burst through the fence and hedge. She screamed and held onto the wheel tightly as she rolled, gouging out tracks in the field, and landed heavily on the passenger side rocking gently.

Everything was quiet. Jesse moaned. Her head hurt. She pushed the airbag away from her face, coughing painfully from the dust. Blood was running down the side of her face and she felt dizzy and sick. She could smell diesel too. She tried to get her bearings in the truck.

She tried to think. Get help. She needed to get help.

She fumbled in her jacket pocket for her phone. Sighing with relief, she saw that the screen was cracked but it was still working. She dialled 999 with a shaky hand.

'Police and fire … Hi … my name's Jesse Stevens. I've just been run off the road. I'm near an industrial estate on the other side of Pembroke Dock on a single-track road … I think it's Mill Back or something? I'm in an RNLI truck and I'm pretty close to the cliff edge and I can smell petrol.' She touched her head as they asked her questions. 'My head hurts and my side too. Yes, I'm bleeding … I …'

Suddenly the truck was filled with bright light and she heard the car approaching again, coming straight for her across the field. She screamed and tried to move but the seatbelt was pulled tight. She felt the truck rock as the car hit, trying to push it nearer the cliff edge. She felt the truck lose traction and slide sideways. It slid into something and then stopped. Jesse craned her neck and was terrified to see how close the cliff edge was. She scrabbled to try and loosen herself from the seat belt which was still pulled tight across her in the position she had ended up in.

Jesse was so focused on releasing the seat belt she didn't register the car reversing again and revving loudly; then she heard it roaring towards the truck where it slammed into the side pushing it, so it rolled off the side of the cliff. Jesse grabbed the side of the door and then everything went black.

* * *

Jesse felt dreadful. She had been semi-awake for a while, listening to the hospital come to life in the early morning. She felt much better if she kept her eyes closed. If she moved too much or breathed too deeply, her side hurt.

The nurses had been fussing about with steri-strips on her head, drips and various other things. She lay with her eyes closed as the nurse made an adjustment to her drip and then left the room.

The door swung open and Doug barrelled in.

'Jesus Christ,' he muttered.

Jesse continued to lie still, her eyes shut. Doug moved towards the bed, picking up one of Jesse's hands and looking at her intently. Still with her eyes closed, Jesse murmured.

'On a scale of 1 to 10, how pissed off are you about the truck?'

Doug breathed a sigh of relief. 'Fuck's sake. Forget the truck. Are you alright?'

Jesse opened one eye and squinted at Doug.

'Who rang you?'

'Steve the copper. It was my truck, remember? He said you reported you'd been run off the road? What the bloody hell happened?'

'I don't really know. I went to that place to get your gear. There was no one around at all. Nothing left out, so I left. Out of nowhere this car suddenly appeared behind me, forces me off the road and kept trying to push me off the cliff.'

'It did push you half off the cliff. Did you recognise the type of car?'

Jesse shook her head. 'I just saw two headlights.'

'Is it too early for a joke about women drivers?'

'Little bit.'

'Steve said he'll be by for a statement soon.'

'When can I go home?'

'Nurse said they want to keep you in for another night as you've had a bang to the head. You've also got two cracked ribs. Do I need to call anyone for you?'

Jesse thought for a moment. 'Can you take Brock for me? He'll be desperate to go out, and probably starving? Can you also call that shrink for me? I'm supposed to see her this morning. Just say I'll reschedule when I'm out? She's in the book – Dr Marshall. Is that OK?'

'No probs. I'll take him to mine? Kids would love it. I'll call that shrink too.'

Jesse pointed to the bedside table. 'There's the keys. You sure you don't mind having him?

'Ach, stop fretting. It'll be fine. I'll take care of the dog, ring the shrink, be back to get you tomorrow. OK? Right. Get some kip. See you tomorrow.'

Doug leant over and kissed her gently, just as Steve the copper walked in.

'Enough of that, this is a key witness,' he said, grinning.

Doug turned to Steve. 'I'm just off. You ...' – he gestured to Steve – '... be nice to her.'

Steve look surprised. 'I'm always nice, what do you mean?'

'See you later.'

Doug walked along the corridor, googling Dr Marshall on his phone. The call went to voicemail.

'Hi, this is a message for Dr Marshall. Jesse Stevens asked me to call you about her appointment this morning. This is Doug Brodie, her Skipper. She's been in an accident and is in hospital. She'll reschedule when she can. Thanks.'

As Doug was climbing into a cab his mobile rang.

'Doug Brodie.'

'It's Dr Emma Marshall. You left a message on my phone about Jesse. Is she OK?'

Doug covered the mouthpiece and gave the driver Jesse's address.

'She's had a big bang on the head and has cracked a few ribs. She should be out tomorrow night.'

'Why are they keeping her in?' Emma sounded desperate for news.

'She was sick a few times after the bump on the head, she was unconscious for a while too.'

'Was it a rescue?'

'No. She was in my truck over near Pembroke Dock picking some stuff up for me and someone ran her half off the cliff. She was very lucky.'

'Give her my best, won't you? Bye now.'

Abruptly Emma ended the call. She sat thinking for a moment and then, in a fit of rage, screamed and threw her phone at the wall.

Doug was looking forward to seeing Jesse. He'd got up early, walked the dog, sorted the kids out and felt very efficient. He whistled to himself as he walked along the corridor to Jesse's room. He pushed the door open gently as he could see through the window she was on the phone. She had her back to the door and didn't see him.

It's fine,' she said impatiently, and Doug knew she was rolling her eyes. 'Stop fretting, it was only a couple of ribs. You've done more than enough recently, looking after Dad after his op … Look, I've got to go, my lift is coming in a minute and I'm going home. OK. I'll call you tomorrow. Bye.'

She turned, noticing Doug leaning against the wall.

'I'm your lift apparently, here to pick you up,' he said wryly.

Jesse grinned. 'Well, you know what they say. Never tell anyone anything they don't need to know. If I'd told her it was you picking me up, I'd have had a 45-minute grilling and she'd have booked a church and reception. Trust me it's best left alone.'

She stood and put her coat on slowly.

'How did you get here? I trashed the truck?'

Doug picked up her bag. 'HQ has come good with another truck until I'm allowed a new one. We travel in style.'

He opened the door and they walked along the corridor together, with Doug lightly holding Jesse's elbow in support. As they walked through the main lobby of the hospital, they passed the coffee shop just as Claire and Felix emerged laughing together.

'Douglas. What are you doing here? Oh hello, it's Jesse isn't it?'

Jesse nodded.

Doug placed a hand on Jesse's shoulder.

'I'm picking up this one here, she was run off the road yesterday in my truck, got pretty banged up.'

Claire turned to Jesse.

'Oh my goodness. Run off the road? How awful for you. Yes. Jesse, I remember seeing you at our house and at the hospital after the boat fire. You were here for a couple of days fairly constantly if I recall.'

Felix shuffled uncomfortably and coughed gently. Claire turned to him.

'Oh, how rude of me, Douglas, Jesse, this is Felix. Felix, Jesse is one of Doug's lifeboat crew.'

Doug hesitated for a moment and then held out his hand to Felix. Felix shook Doug's hand briefly and Doug had the cold lupine eyes out for his benefit. Jesse suppressed a smile.

'We're just on the way back now, so we ought to get going. See you again.'

He guided Jesse away with a hand in the small of her back.

Claire came after Doug.

'Douglas! Hold up a second! Jesse isn't it?'

Jesse didn't like games like this. 'Still Jesse, yes, not changed in the last two minutes.'

Claire inclined her head. 'Could you give us a minute please?'

'I'll go over there and grab us a coffee, Doug.'

Doug looked uncomfortable.

'Yup, get it to go though. I won't be long.'

He turned to Claire, who stood hands on hips.

'What the hell was that?' she demanded.

Doug looked perplexed. 'What was what?'

'The way you were with Felix.'

'Excuse me?' Doug was angry now.

'You were rude and unfriendly.'

'Seriously? And here's me thinking I was charm personified to the man who's been sleeping with my wife for the past two years behind my back.'

'You were rude. You didn't need to be.'

'I shook the guy's hand. Played nice. You're lucky I didn't punch him in the face.'

'Don't be ridiculous. You wouldn't have done that ... would you?' Claire asked, horrified at the prospect of that happening in the hospital lobby.

Doug snorted. 'Look, I'll be pleasant and shake his hand, but we won't be cosying up with a bottle of prosecco and a few nibbles like besties.'

'I'm just saying I think you could have been nicer. Felix looked uncomfortable.'

'He's a big boy. He'll get over it.'

He turned and walked away, with Claire calling after him.

'Oh, of course, the crew takes priority over everything, doesn't it?'

'It certainly takes priority over discussions about your boyfriend's feelings, yes,' Doug said over his shoulder.

Jesse approached him, carrying two coffees. 'Err ... do you need another minute?'

'We're done here. See you, Claire.'

Doug turned and guided Jesse by the arm to the door.

'She's pissed off. What was that about?'

'I was being rude and unfriendly apparently.'

Jesse burst out laughing. 'Oh? Very unlike you.'

Doug pulled the truck to a stop outside Jesse's house. He helped her into the house with her bag.

'Are you sure you're OK here on your own? You're welcome to come and stay with me.'

'I'll be fine, honestly. I just want to sleep. Where's Brock?'

'Bob's got him. Him and Billy are spending the day with him. I said I'd get him when I took Billy home.'

'Lovely. Thanks, Doug. Do you want to take the spare key in case I'm asleep when you come back?'

'Sure.'

Jesse picked it off the hook and passed it to Doug.

'Thanks for picking me up. I really appreciate it.'

'All part of the service. Go and sleep. Do you need any food?'

'I'm OK, thanks. Not that hungry.'

'I'll bring you some food by later when I drop the dog off. Can't have you wasting away.'

'Thanks. Look, about the other day ... I was planning to give you your jacket back ... before I ended up being run off the road.'

Doug looked surprised. 'Oh? Is that code for wanting to talk?'

'Stay and keep me company for a bit later maybe?'

'No probs. I'll let myself in later then, yes?'

At the front door he turned and pointed to the stairs.

'Go. Sleep. Recover.'

'Yes boss.' Jesse saluted and shut the door.

We've hurt her! We didn't mean to. We wanted to hurt HIM. We've frightened her, hurt her. Because we love her. Because we couldn't control our anger. He was getting in the way. It's all his fault. We want her to get better. To be her again. We need to see her. Just to check she's OK. Time is running out now. We can still do it though. Once she realises ... she'll be so happy.

CHAPTER 35

Dr Nunn escorted Emma along the corridor, her high heels the only sound in the quiet corridor. He stopped abruptly outside a door and pushed it open, gesturing for her to enter.

The door opened into a large meeting room, which smelt vaguely musty with a whiff of cabbage buried in the aroma. Along the top table, Dr Stevens was seated already and on the opposite side sat two individuals, male and female both in dark suits. The table opposite the two in suits was empty. Dr Nunn steered her towards Dr Stevens.

'You remember Dr Stevens?'

Emma smiled.

Dr Stevens stood. 'Dr Marshall. So nice to see you.' He gestured across the room. 'Can I introduce you to Maxine Ward and David Young. They are working with the Crown Prosecution Service.'

They both shook Emma's hand.

'Dr Marshall …' Dr Stevens gestured to a chair next to him.

As she sat, Emma took a moment to inspect the two people. The woman was in her late forties, tall with blonde curly hair that was cut in a bob. The man had a pleasant face, but fairly blank expression.

Dr Nunn cleared his throat.

'So, Maxine and David. You requested a discussion about the accused and his mental state prior to you undertaking your own questions and assessments of him. I—'

Emma interrupted. 'Before we start, I'd like to say I don't believe we should even be having this meeting. There simply hasn't been enough time to assess his mental state for you to decide whether he's fit for trial.' She folded her arms defensively.

Maxine leant forward. She spoke loudly and precisely, with a broad Yorkshire accent. 'Dr Marshall.'

'Please call me Emma …'

Maxine shook her head. 'I won't, if it's all the same. Thank you for your comment. The timing, though, is decided by me. Now, Dr Marshall, had you been aware of your brother's mental issues prior to him being arrested? And if so, what measures did you put in place to help him get treatment?'

Emma shifted uncomfortably in her chair. 'I'm not sure I like what you're suggesting, Maxine.'

Maxine held up her hand. 'If we could stick to "Ms Ward" please.'

'OK. Ms Ward. I'm not sure I like what you're suggesting here.'

Maxine shrugged. 'I'm waiting for a response, Dr Marshall.'

'I've been at the opposite end of the country for years due to work commitments. I'd no idea that Chris had the issues he had.'

'Were you not in contact?'

'When you speak on the phone or catch up by email, it's hardly enough exposure to someone to be able to diagnose them with mental illness. Now do you want to get to the main point of your question, Ms Ward, or shall we continue to dance around the subject?'

Maxine looked surprised. 'I was merely enquiring whether there had been a history of mental issues you were aware of.'

'Not to my knowledge. The only thing I suspected at one point was depression, but I think he managed to get through that.'

'I saw the footage of your recent incident with him. What did you make of it?'

'Personally, or as a psychiatrist?'

'Either.'

Emma cleared her throat and took a sip of coffee.

'It's clear he underwent a psychotic episode. He attacked me not consciously being aware I was his sister and not being aware of the unwritten boundaries we all adhere to. I think there's some significant work needed to help him through this.'

Maxine regarded Emma, as if silently assessing her. Then she smiled and said brightly, 'So! As you know, we're here to ascertain whether or not we, let's use the word "believe", that Christopher isn't fit to stand trial for his crimes. And on that note, I'm very interested to know what your view is, Dr Marshall.'

'My view?'

Maxine raised an eyebrow. 'Yes. Your view. Am I not being clear enough? I'll re-phrase. Do you think he's pretending or not? He wouldn't be the first to try this on, and I pride myself on my reputation for getting to the bottom of these things.'

Emma shifted in her seat again and took another drink.

'I'm extremely concerned about my brother's mental health. He's not well. I strongly believe that this is the best setting for him at the moment until he's properly assessed and has received treatment.'

Maxine nodded. 'I see.'

She looked through the door and beckoned to someone outside. Chris was brought into the room, looking calm and smiling at everyone. A tall male nurse sat him down at the empty table and moved to stand behind him.

Maxine addressed him directly. 'Christopher. I'm Ms Ward and this is my colleague, Mr Young. We're here to assess you. Thank you for joining us. I was just asking your sister what she thought about you staying here or standing trial.'

Chris focused intently on Maxine, not speaking to her.

'Christopher. Did you hear me?'

Chris laughed madly.

Dr Nunn frowned and spoke to Chris. 'Hello, Chris.'

Chris turned to Dr Nunn. 'Oh hello, Doctor.'

Dr Nunn smiled.

'Chris, have you noticed who else is here?' He looked pointedly at Emma sat next to him.

Chris looked agitated. He shifted about in his seat and started to sob quietly.

Emma leant forward. 'Chris?'

Tears rolled down his face. 'Ems. Sorry I hurt you. I didn't mean to. They told me to do it.'

Chris started to rock gently. He whispered to himself. 'I know, I know. Who is she?' he said, pointing at Maxine. 'They don't like her. Not one bit.'

Maxine leant forward. 'Why not, Christopher?'

Chris was smiling, his head on one side. 'Because you want to lock me up and throw away the key. You want to try and get them out of here.' He tapped his forehead and leant forward. 'They're not going anywhere.'

'That may be so, Christopher,' said Maxine briskly, 'But I want you to get better so you can come to court and explain to a judge and jury why you think it's OK to viciously beat, rape and attempt to kill people.'

Chris pointed at Maxine with a shaking finger. 'No, no, NO! I didn't do any of that. They made me.'

'So you say. I think some of your victims may say differently. What about Jesse Stevens for example? You told her you were going to kill her and, let me get this right …' she consulted her notes, '… enjoy every single second of it.'

Chris wrapped his arms around himself and rocked gently, smiling.

'I love Jesse. That wasn't me that did that. I still love her. I want to be with Jesse. I would never hurt her. I love her. She'll come back to me.'

'But you beat her half to death and left her to die, Christopher,' Maxine said loudly.

'No, no, no … that wasn't me. She did need to be taught a lesson though. I want to get better so I can see Jesse again.'

'I expect she wants nothing to do with you. I expect she would like you to remain in prison indefinitely.'

Chris shook his head at Maxine. 'She would understand it wasn't really me,' he said dangerously. 'She would forgive me. Jesse loves me.'

'You delude yourself. I've seen the photographs, Christopher. I've also seen what you did to your sister the last time she was here.'

Chris's leg started jigging. He nodded as if agreeing with himself.

Emma raised her hands. 'OK. Ms Ward, I think you're trying to provoke my brother.'

Chris's leg got faster and his nodding became more intense. He muttered to himself. 'Yes. Yes. I know!' he shouted. 'I know.'

He stood suddenly, knocking over the chair behind him and pointed to Maxine, snarling. 'She needs to learn some fucking respect, and I'll be the one to fucking do it.'

The male nurse standing behind Chris, took his shoulders and pushed him to sit. Chris sat looking triumphant and sneered at Maxine. His head was on one side again and he nodded.

'Yes. Yes. I've just said that ...' he said impatiently.

Maxine leant forward, scrutinising Chris intently. 'So, how will you teach me some respect, Christopher?'

He leant forward and whispered to her, 'You're trying to get me into trouble, bitch. I know you. You're EVIL. You'll get what's coming.' He carried on in a sing-song voice. 'Don't forget to look behind you now ... there's danger everywhere ...'

Emma interrupted again in a snippy tone. 'This is getting us nowhere, Ms Ward. Look, I'm of the opinion that my brother is not fit to stand trial and should be kept in this secure environment undergoing treatment until he's in a fit state mentally, and then we'll reconvene. But I've no assessment of when that might be.'

'For him to be able to stand trial?' Maxine clarified in an equally snippy tone.

'If that's what you're pushing for, Ms Ward,' Emma replied coolly.

'That is why we're here. Your brother will stand trial for the crimes he's committed, whether it be now or in ten years' time.'

Emma raised an eyebrow. 'And if you still don't decide he's mentally fit then...?'

'Then he'll remain here indefinitely. Under lock and key,' Maxine said firmly.

She flicked through her papers. 'So, to continue. Out of interest, when he attacked you, what did he say to you when he embraced you?'

'Excuse me?'

'I said, what did he whisper to you after the attack, Dr Marshall?'

'Oh ... er ... I'm not sure he said anything to me.' Emma shifted uncomfortably in her seat.

'Oh, I can assure you he did. On the footage I saw his lips moving. No matter, I'll get my lip readers to have a look. They usually come up trumps.' She smiled at Emma. 'We'll see what he said.'

Chris stared at Maxine with clear malevolence. 'Emma!' Chris snapped. 'What the fuck is this bitch saying?'

Emma turned her attention to Chris. 'They're deciding whether you're fit to stand trial. We think you aren't, so you need to stay here to have treatment to get better.'

'I'll have some treatment here and then come home with you, where you can treat me,' Chris said firmly.

Dr Nunn interjected. 'No, Chris. You're too ill to be released into the community. You need to be in a secure environment where we can help you to get better and then you might have a clearer sense of what you've done.'

Maxine added. 'And then when that occurs, we'll put you on trial for your crimes.'

Chris shook his head. 'No! You'll treat me here and then release me into the care of my psychiatrist sister. I'll come back for treatment if and when I need it.'

Maxine sat up in her chair slightly. She leant forward slightly, listening intently, totally focused on Chris.

'I'm interested, Christopher. What makes you think you can go from being on remand for serious crimes committed against another human being to being let out to go and live with your sister?'

'I'm not well. I need treatment. My sister will give me treatment,' he said in an authoritarian tone.

Maxine smiled triumphantly. 'Oh yes. That would be good, wouldn't it, Christopher? Release you into the care of your sister for treatment, then we don't see you for dust. You must think we were born yesterday. You either stay here in a nice comfy padded cell and lots of comforting drugs or be back on remand for your crimes, where you'll probably end up being someone's new "girlfriend" for the foreseeable future.'

Chris snarled. 'You watch your fucking mouth, bitch.'

Dr Nunn leaned forward. 'Really, I do protest …'

Maxine held up a hand to silence Dr Nunn. She got up and strolled around the room towards Chris.

'So, Christopher. Was all the acting worth it? You so nearly got there, didn't you? Play the idiot brother with mental issues. Hear voices, all of that. I bet they all fell for it. The attack on your sister, that was excellent. A stroke of genius in fact. You almost had me – until you whispered something to her at the end. Hell, I wouldn't mind betting your caring sister was in on it too. Certify him insane, tell him what to say. Leave him here and he'll slip through the net one day, hey presto. No trial, no prison … Scot-free.'

Emma looked furious. 'How dare you? Who the hell do you think you are?'

Maxine whirled around to Emma. 'I represent justice. I'm here to see through bullshit like this. I'm going to recommend your brother goes back to prison to face trial. Immediately.'

Chris's face was white with anger. He launched himself over the table and punched Maxine in the face, ducking the grab by the male nurse. He threw another punch, but Maxine dodged the blow.

Chris screamed at Maxine. 'I'll fucking kill you! Who the FUCK do you think you are? Get off me. GET OFF ME.'

He struggled as the male nurse grabbed his arms behind his back, the door opened and more staff appeared to help pin him down. Chris turned his anger on Emma, he snarled at her, his face distorted with rage as he struggled against his captors.

'You said this would fucking work. I knew you'd fuck this up. Can't get anything right, can you? Useless fucking idiot. Always have been. You'll pay and you'll be sorry you fucked this up. I'll come for you.'

The male nurse injected Chris and he slumped in the hold of the nurses as they dragged him unceremoniously from the room.

Maxine moved back to her place at the table and sat down. She had a red welt on her face and a smear of blood. She pulled some paperwork from the file and signed it, giving it to her colleague to counter sign. She looked up at the rest of the room who sat looking shocked. She directed a look to Emma and said cheerfully, 'Excellent. Always get there in the end. Nearly got us though. Dr Nunn, I'll recommend that the patient rejoins his remand centre back in Lewes and awaits trial as soon as possible.'

Dr Nunn nodded slowly, as if struggling to comprehend. 'Right … I see.'

Maxine began to pack away her paperwork.

'Don't look so shocked, this happens more often than you think. He was quite a tough nut to crack. Dr Marshall, I'll be discussing your involvement with the CPS to see whether they want to press charges.

Perversion of the course of justice comes to mind. If I had my way, I'd throw the book at you, but hey, we can't have everything we want to in one day, can we? So, I'll bid you all farewell. It really *has* been an absolute pleasure today.'

She left the room, her colleague shutting the door quietly behind him.

* * *

Jesse was fast asleep on her bed. She'd showered and washed her hair to rid herself of the hospital smell. She then laid down on her bed and not known another thing. She was vaguely aware of a blanket being laid over her, but it didn't permeate her consciousness enough for her to wake up.

Downstairs there was activity. Candles were being lit, a bunch of flowers hastily arranged, a bottle of wine and two glasses placed carefully on the table. The smell of cooking drifted through the house.

Jesse woke slowly and winced slightly, snuggling herself under the blanket. She opened her eyes as she became aware of the warm blanket and the smell of cooking. She smiled, the thought of Doug downstairs cooking for her made her ridiculously happy.

She sat up and ran her hands through her hair, rubbing her eyes. She stood for a moment, slightly wobbly and pulled on a jumper. She walked lightly along landing and as she went down the stairs she called out.

'Something smells amazing!'

She walked slowly through the house, admiring the candles, which were flickering gently and casting a low glow. She approached the kitchen expectantly, wondering for a brief moment why Brock hadn't rushed up to see her.

Doug thought he was doing well. He was dropping the kids off at Paul and Nicky's.

Paul, who was in the front garden, approached, opening the truck door. He picked up the kids' bags and ushered them towards the house.

Doug called. 'Kids. Behave. See you in the morning. Have a good time.'

Christy blew him a kiss, while Jude waved from the doorway. Paul leant against the truck and looked at Doug with concern.

'Alright mate? How's Jesse doing? Nicky said she was going to swing by tomorrow and check on her. Is she at home?'

'Yup. She's OK, got back earlier. A bit banged up, broken ribs and a bang on the head. I'm dropping the dog back and taking her some dinner in a bit.'

Paul tittered. 'Proper Florence Nightingale you are.'

'Hardly,' Doug said wryly. Gotta go, mate, I'm running late taking Billy home. Ring me with any problems with those two, OK? Thanks again, mate.'

Doug collected Billy and dropped him off at the home. Brock now sat on the front seat of the truck. Doug's phone rang shrilly and he answered the call on speakerphone.

'Doug. It's Steve. Sorry to call. I need you to come and see something. Like now. I'm in Appleby.'

'What's in Appleby that's so urgent?'

Steve exhaled loudly. 'Can you come, please? Ferrybridge Road. Look for my car outside. Trust me, you really need to see this. This is serious.'

Doug grimaced at his watch. 'OK. Give me ten minutes. See you there.'

He turned the car round and drove off as fast as he dared, knowing that at least one local police officer was otherwise engaged and wouldn't nick him for speeding.

Doug arrived at Ferrybridge Road and parked outside a pretty Victorian house with Steve's car in the driveway.

Doug pushed the door open and stepped inside, calling for Steve. 'You in there, mate?'

Steve appeared, wearing blue nitrile gloves.

'Doug.'

Doug frowned. 'What the hell is going on here?'

Steve lowered his voice. 'The neighbours thought there was a robbery or something going on, they'd heard lots of crashing, banging and screaming, saw the door wide open and called us. So I come on in and look around and see nothing and then I come in here and, Jesus Christ, Then I called you. Don't touch anything.'

As he talked, he was moving along the corridor. He opened the door just as he finished his sentence. Doug stopped in the doorway and stared.

'Jesus fucking Christ,' Doug said quietly.

Doug felt like the breath had been pulled out of him. He couldn't believe what he was seeing for a moment. Couldn't believe the scale of what he saw. Panic washed over him, like an icy wave. Everything was there. Everyone was there. He stood looking, not believing what he was seeing. Not wanting to believe it.

The room was full of photographs of Jesse, the crew and of him too. They covered every inch of all four walls. In many of them his face had been scrubbed or scribbled out. There were photos of everything; the beach fire with Jesse and the kids; the rounders game. Jesse and the dog on the beach. Jesse leaving the station, working on Jimmy's boat. Jesse going into her house. Jesse at the table in the pub. Jesse wearing Doug's jacket.

'In the garage there's a smashed-up car with scratches of white paint all over the bodywork,' Steve said. 'We'll do a paint match to your truck. I'd lay money this is who ran Jesse off the road, mate.'

Doug's face was pale and his breathing was choppy, 'Whose house is this?' he managed.

'A Dr Emma Marshall's. Some sort of shrink in town – small practice, new to the area.'

'Jesus,' said Doug quietly, clutching the door frame for support. 'I've met her. I've spoken to her! JESUS! She evens knows where Jesse lives! Where is this fucking woman now?'

Steve looked alarmed. 'How do you know she knows where Jesse lives?'

'Because Jesse said she was there the other day, she just called in. Jesse said it was weird. I need to call her,' Doug said desperately. He tried calling Jesse's phone, it just rang and rang with no answer.

Steve threw the photographs down on the desk and walked towards the front door.

'We need to get to Jesse's house. Follow me. I'll stick the sirens on. Where is she?'

'Twelve Trafalgar Road.'

Steve roared off, sirens and lights on, with Doug driving fast behind him, his RNLI truck emergency lights on.

Doug was shaking so much he could barely drive straight. He couldn't understand it. Who was the woman? Why did she have so many photographs of Jesse? Had she actually tried to kill him and accidentally hurt Jesse instead? His mind was reeling. He tried calling her again and stabbed at the phone, almost dialling Joe's Pizza House with his shaking hands. Jesse's phone rang.

'Pick up, Jesse ... pick up ... PICK UP!' he yelled.

The phone rang and rang again, with no answer.

'FUCK!'

He clenched both hands into fists around the wheel. He had to get to Jesse.

CHAPTER 36

Jesse walked through the house, smiling at the candles as she approached the kitchen.

'This is so lovely. Perhaps we should add patient care to your long list of domestic attributes.'

Jesse stopped dead.

Emma sat at the kitchen table with a glass of wine.

'Hello, sleepyhead! How are you feeling? You look terrible.'

Jesse felt something shift primevally in her gut, warning her of danger. She had experienced that feeling once before and had almost lost her life. Her mouth went dry, and she struggled to breathe, only managing small shallow gasps. She sat shakily down in a chair on the other side of the kitchen. Jesse sensed that this woman, whom she thought she knew, was highly unstable and very dangerous. She reminded Jesse of someone … but she couldn't place who. She managed a small smile.

'Emma. What are you doing here? Did Doug let you in?'

Emma looked intently at Jesse and smirked. 'Good old Doug. He just won't go away will he?'

Jesse was confused but felt she should try to keep things on an even keel. Deep down she was terrified, but she knew she couldn't show it.

'How did you get in, Emma?'

Emma stood and walked over to Jesse.

'Come and sit down at the table. Have some wine.'

She held out a hand and when Jesse didn't respond straight away, she impatiently clicked her fingers. Jesse allowed herself to pulled up and steered to a chair at the dinner table. Emma gave her a glass of wine and raised a glass herself.

'Cheers Jesse. Here's to your good health. Go on, drink and relax. You look like you need it.'

Jesse took a small sip of wine and put her glass down.

'Thank you, Emma,' she said robotically.

Emma got up from the table. She opened the oven door, made an appreciative noise and then picked up a knife and started to chop lettuce. She turned to Jesse with a stunning smile.

'Dinner won't be long. I wanted to make something nice for you. I feel terrible you were in an accident.'

Jesse rubbed her forehead and shook her head. She took another drink of wine.

'Emma, it's very nice to see you, but I'm a little confused. I'm not really up to company.'

Emma smiled. 'I did knock but the door was open. I came in and found you sleeping. Covered you up with a blanket. By the way it's not a good idea to fall asleep with wet hair, not good for you at all. So I started dinner and waited for you to wake up and here we are. Hope you're hungry. I've made a pie.'

Jesse was struggling to comprehend Emma's statements.

'How did you know I'd been in an accident?'

'Doug rang and cancelled your appointment. Needless to say, I was really worried that my favourite patient was hurt. I care about you, Jesse.'

Jesse looked surprised. 'Oh ... thank you.'

Emma frowned at her, knife in the air. 'No. I don't think you're hearing me properly. I care about you, Jesse. Very much indeed.'

Jesse cleared her throat. 'Emma, you don't know me ...'

Emma smiled at Jesse indulgently. 'Oh, but I do, Jesse. Much better than you think.'

Jesse was struggling to stay awake and the world was suddenly a little fuzzy around the edges.

'Emma, this is lovely of you. But could we do this another day? I feel a bit odd, probably shouldn't have had the wine.'

Emma looked at Jesse sideways. 'Don't you want to be my friend?'

Emma stopped chopping the lettuce and absently ran the point of the blade against her leg, not seeming to notice it, while she stood looking at Jesse questioningly.

Jesse was feeling worse, nothing made sense.

'Emma, I just … I just want to talk to you when I can think clearly. We're not allowed to be friends are we? As patient and doctor?'

Jesse watched as Emma forced the point of the blade into her own skin, through the trousers she was wearing. She didn't even flinch as blood trickled down her leg, staining through the fabric.

Jesse tried to focus.

'Emma. You're hurting yourself.'

'Oh, I think I'm beyond that, Jesse.'

Jesse's phone rang and Emma inspected it.

'Oh look. It's Doug. What is it with you two?'

'Nothing Emma, I'm just part of the crew, that's all. He treats everyone like that.'

Emma gave a derisory laugh. 'I certainly don't think he treats everyone like he treats you. I don't think he kisses people in the boat shed or outside the bar, does he?'

Jesse looked shocked. 'Have you been following me, Emma?'

Emma pointed the knife at Jesse, her hand shaking.

'I've seen you! You tell me you're just workmates and all the time you two are getting involved. Kissing…'

Jesse stared at her in disbelief. 'Emma. Come on. Please.'

Jesse was holding out her hands to try and calm Emma down. Emma looked murderous for a moment and took a vicious swipe at one of Jesse's hands with the knife, cutting her palm deeply.

'No! You have no idea what I've done for you. The depth of my love for you. The risks I've taken. All for you. You're *so* ungrateful. How could I love you as much as I do?'

Jesse's hand was bleeding badly. She stared at it in shock and grabbed a napkin wrapping her hand in it, the blood soaking through the crisp white linen quickly.

'Emma. What are you talking about? What have you done? What risks?'

Emma's eyes were bright, glassy. 'It was all for Chris. But now – I've betrayed him. He'll kill me.'

Jesse stood suddenly, knocking her chair over in her unsteadiness. She stumbled backwards from Emma, shaking her head at her, looking around, terrified.

'Chris? What about Chris?'

Emma said triumphantly, 'He's my brother.'

Jesse felt something slide into place. She saw Chris's face in Emma's face. Why had she never seen it? She felt a tidal wave of emotions pass through her, disbelief, shock, anger. She clutched the wall for support. Black spots danced in her eyes and she was frightened she was going to pass out.

Emma approached Jesse, holding the knife.

'Don't go getting on your high horse with me. I tried to get him locked him up for good, tried to make them think he was insane.'

'He is insane.'

Emma laughed delightedly. 'This is what I love about you, Jesse. Of course he isn't insane! He just thoroughly enjoys brutalising women.'

Jesse shook her head in disbelief.

'I can't believe I'm hearing this. How did you ever get to be my shrink?'

Emma laughed again. 'We don't share the same last name. Not much to tie us together, why would they even think to check? He pulled a few strings, called in some favours in the force, you know how incestuous it all is. And hey presto, Dr Emma Marshall is a reputable shrink in the same area as the one you're relocated to. If I recall Jesse, you selected me from the list!'

Jesse leant against the kitchen wall, grateful for its support.

'Where is he now?'

Emma stepped forward towards Jesse and waved the knife in front of her.

'Well, there's quite the story. He was on remand, but I just couldn't risk a court case, not with his contacts. I wanted him somewhere where he'd not be able to escape or, worse, get off. So after a lot of work on my part, he was tucked up in a very secure psychiatric unit, safe and warm with plans to be there indefinitely and I'd worked hard to get him to think that was the best place for him. I'd convinced him he'd be released into my care eventually.'

Jesse whispered, 'Why did you?'

'Because, my darling damaged Jesse, he wanted me to make you suffer, make your life hell until he could get out and make you suffer himself. He loves you, but he'll make you pay, trust me, he will. He blackmailed me to do it. I didn't want to, but then I met you. And then I decided I wanted you all to myself. I can't explain it. There's something about you that's quite … addictive, an air of fragility about you, but at the same time there's something else …'

She tried to stroke Jesse's face, but Jesse flinched and moved away.

'I don't know what it is. It's delicious though. I realised I didn't want that brute anywhere near you, that he would be safer put away properly. So, after lots of work on my part, he was considered no longer fit to stand trial. He would have been locked up indefinitely if that interfering bitch from the CPS hadn't turned up. A few hours ago they realised he was completely sane and sent him back to remand.'

'Why would you do that … all this time …?'

Emma looked angry and waved the knife at Jesse.

'Are you not listening? I said I wanted you all to myself. I love you, Jesse, and I want to be with you. We can be together now, without Chris. He'll be in the court system for years now.'

Jesse struggled to process what was being said.

'You don't know me. I … I don't feel that way about you.'

Emma rounded on Jesse, furious. 'NO! I don't want to hear that from you, Jesse. You're in shock and you don't know what you're saying! After everything I've done for you, you won't dismiss me like that. I won't let you.'

Jesse looked confused. 'Emma, what do you mean, after everything you've done?'

Emma looked agitated, she started to tap the knife against her leg again.

Jesse stared at the blood, struggling to focus.

'Emma, come on. Stop that.'

Emma looked away from Jesse, and the knife continued to draw blood as she carved into her leg without seeming to notice. She stared at Jesse with tears in her eyes.

'I'm sorry. I didn't mean to hurt you. I didn't mean to do it. I was just trying to clear the way for us.'

Jesse sat down. 'What are you talking about? What have you done?'

'I didn't mean to run you off the road, Jesse. I would never have done it if I'd known it was you. I thought it was Doug. It was meant to be Doug. He needs to go. I wanted him to go over the cliff,' she said absently.

Jesse looked horrified. 'That was you? Oh my God. Why would you want to hurt Doug?'

Emma turned to Jesse, her eyes angry. 'To get him out of the way!' She rolled her eyes. 'God! Catch up, Jesse. You were getting involved. Developing feelings for him. I could see it in your face.'

The phone rang again, and Emma looked down at the display.

'Talk of the devil. Persistent isn't he? Let's turn this off.'

Emma's demeanor changed suddenly. She placed the knife carefully on the kitchen worktop and looked down at the cuts on her leg and tutted, shaking her head. The eyes she looked at Jesse with, were too wide and too bright.

'We should have dinner. You must be starving, darling.'

Emma got the food from the oven, put it on the table and fetched the salad she had made. She took a plate from in front of Jesse and dished her up a helping of the pie.

'Help yourself to salad,' she said, smiling.

Jesse sat at the table with the food in front of her. Despite the fact she felt she was going to pass out she knew she had to play along with the bizarre charade. She took a deep breath and smiled at Emma as brightly as she could.

'Emma. This looks so nice, but I'm just not hungry. I don't feel well, I just want to go back to bed.'

Emma was tucking into the food and making appreciative noises. She looked at Jesse in surprise.

'What? Don't you like it?'

'I do like it. I'm just not very hungry. I feel a bit weird.'

'That'll be the sedative I put in your wine, didn't want you running off now, did I? Now come on, have something to eat, you'll waste away if you're not careful,' she said in a motherly tone.

Jesse stared at Emma in disbelief, something had snapped inside her and all she felt was anger, which was difficult to control with the edges of everything being fuzzy.

'A sedative? I can't really believe this is happening. Emma, it's not OK to break into my home, do you see that?'

Emma waved her fork around. 'Err ... the door *was* open.'

Jesse ignored her and continued, 'You broke into my home, drugged me, tried to kill me.'

Emma interrupted. 'Err, your boyfriend actually, if we're splitting hairs, I tried to kill your boyfriend, not you.'

'Emma, you can't surely think this is normal behaviour?'

Emma carried on eating.

'Of course it is! I came round to a friend's house, found her door open and cooked her dinner, helped her take her medication, looked after her ... what's not normal about that?'

Jesse got up from the table a little unsteadily.

'Emma,' she said firmly. 'I need you to leave please. Now.'

Emma looked frustrated and leant over to pick up the kitchen knife again. She frowned.

'Jesse. I can't believe you're ruining a nice dinner. After everything I've done. I'm beginning to think that sometimes Chris was right, you need to remember your place.'

Jesse swallowed, her skin crawling at the mention of Chris.

'My place?'

'Yes. He did say you were very argumentative and disobedient sometimes.'

Jesse stepped towards Emma, clutching the edge of the worktop to steady herself.

'Emma, I'm going to ask you again. Please leave now.'

Emma rose from her chair, spun Jesse and forced her face-first against the wall. Jesse cried out as Emma knocked into her painful ribs. Emma traced the blade of the knife carefully down the scar on Jesse's face and snarled.

'You need to be less rude to people who are trying to help you, although in some ways it's a weird turn on. Chris said that was sexy about you.'

Jesse strained to get away. 'Get off me!' she yelled into Emma's face.

Outside there was the screeching of tyres and the sound of a siren. Jesse's heart leapt. Perhaps this was help of some kind.

She said bravely, 'They're onto you.'

Emma smirked. 'Nice try, they've gotta get in first.'

Jesse said defiantly, 'Doug has a key.'

Emma made a guttural noise and hit Jesse hard on the back of the head with the handle of the knife. Jesse slumped to the floor and Emma came to stand over her.

'Jesse, Jesse, Jesse. So wonderfully broken ... so fragile. I feel like I should give you something to remember me by.'

She heard the metal gate clang. Emma knelt and grabbed Jesse's face and inspected it closely.

'Um ... I think here.'

She ran the knife down the side of Jesse's face with the scar, and carefully drew a new deep cut alongside the old scar. She stepped back to admire her work.

'Lovely. I'll be back for you, Jesse. I love you.'

She bent and kissed Jesse firmly on the lips.

Doug was frantic in his need to get to Jesse and keep her safe. Steve's car stopped so quickly that Doug almost slammed into the back of him. Steve was out of the car and running towards Jesse's house, shouting over his shoulder.

'I'll kick it in,' he yelled.

Doug shouted. 'Wait!' He threw his key towards Steve as he ran towards the house.

Steve deftly caught the key and inserted it in the lock just as Doug arrived. Steve pushed the door quietly, but it stuck as the security chain was on. He motioned to Doug to be quiet as he listened. After a few seconds, he shrugged and kicked the door in.

Both men moved through Jesse's house. In the kitchen they found Jesse on the floor and the back door wide open.

'Jesus!' said Doug, dropping to his knees and looking at the blood pooling out of her face and hand. 'Jesse, can you hear me?'

Steve was checking the rest of the house and returned breathless. 'All clear.'

He called for an ambulance and police support, while Doug tried to stem the bleeding from the cut on her face. Jesse moaned and opened her eyes wide in panic.

'Emma ...'

Doug held her hand. 'She's not here. How do you feel?'

'Awful. Where...?'

'She was here?' asked Steve.

Jesse nodded. 'I thought you were here, and it was her,' she sobbed.

Doug frowned. 'What the hell did she want with you, Jesse?'

Jesse sobbed. 'She's Chris's sister ...'

Emma ran down the road at full speed, rounded a corner and stopped to get her phone out. She made a call and listened as it went straight to voicemail.

'Jesse. Just ringing to say sorry I have to run, especially during the middle of dinner. But I'll come back for you. I just wanted you to know. I'll only be away a little while and then I'll be back. Try not to miss me. I did leave a little tiny reminder, hope you like it. See you soon.'

As she talked she crossed the road; she was so focused on leaving Jesse a message she didn't see the white van that was driving too fast around the corner until it hit her full on. There was a screeching of brakes and Emma's phone flew up into the air smashing into pieces as it hit the road.

Emma lay in the road, a pool of blood surrounding her head like a red halo.

* * *

It was after nine when Doug pulled into the driveway. He jumped out, moving quickly around to the passenger side. He helped Jesse out of the car, Brock jumping out after her and staying close. Jesse looked pale and had a large dressing down the side of her face. Her head and hand were bandaged, and she looked exhausted.

315

Doug helped her towards the front door, which had been opened as soon as Doug's truck appeared. Nessie was standing there, wringing her hands with worry.

'Now you rest up, Jesse. I'm off, everything's ready for you. See you tomorrow.'

She picked up her capacious knitting bag and squeezed Doug's shoulder before letting herself out.

Doug looked at Jesse. 'Sit. I'm going to get you something to eat.'

Jesse shook her head. 'Don't go to any trouble, Doug. I'm not that hungry.'

'How about some soup?'

'OK, thanks. Where do you think she is, Doug?'

'Don't know, but I don't want you worrying about it.'

There was a soft knocking at the front door and Brock was wagging his tail. Doug opened the door and found Steve on the doorstep.

'Hello, mate. I thought you ought to know. Emma Marshall got hit by a van tonight. Driver said she was on the phone at the time, didn't know a thing about it until it was too late.'

'Jesus. Did she make it?'

'She's in ICU. I don't think she's going anywhere soon. Can you give this to Jesse? We've finished with it. There's a message for Jesse on it, we think it's the one she was leaving when she got hit.'

Doug took the plastic bag containing Jesse's phone. 'Thanks, Steve. For everything.'

'No problem. I've gotta get back to the nick.'

'See you mate.'

Doug shut the door and returned to the lounge.

'That was Steve. Emma's been hit by a van. She was making a call when it happened and wasn't concentrating. Apparently, there's a message from her on your phone.'

Jesse looked at her phone nervously.

'Is she …?'

'She's in ICU, pretty bad.'

Jesse played the message on speaker. Doug stood by listening.

Emma's voice rang out clearly over the speakerphone.

'What's the tiny reminder she mentions?' asked Doug.

Jesse pointed to the scar on her face. 'This. Jesus. All that time. All the things I said.'

Doug sat down on the coffee table opposite Jesse and took her hands.

'Jesse, I think you had a lucky escape. Christ, you should have seen the room at her house … all these photos of you, us, the crew … all of us. I just can't believe she's Chris's sister and no one knew. That the police recommended her as a therapist. It's just beyond me.'

'She's as insane as he was, she just hid it better. Steve said he was going to contact Leslie, the DS who was with me and collected my evidence, to try and work out how Emma could have got involved. I have to admit, he wasn't that surprised she slipped through the net though.'

'He'll work it out.' Doug touched Jesse's arm. 'Right. Soup. Be two tics.'

Doug and Jesse were in the kitchen. Doug was washing up.

'I feel a bit useless and a bit of a wimp for crashing here tonight. I just can't go home yet. I want the locks changed and some bolts and stuff fitted. Stupid I know but it'll make me feel better.'

'Stay as long as you like. The brothers are changing the locks and making it super safe for you as we speak. You might re-think staying in the morning when the kids are up and making loads of racket.'

'Well, I'm really grateful. Really. I'm taking the sofa though, no arguments.'

Doug shook his head. 'Not ever gonna happen.'

'Come on. I'm not turfing you out of your bed,' Jesse protested.

'I've said. Not gonna happen.'

'Can we at least discuss this?'

'Nope. Go and sit down, you look done in.'

Jesse went into the lounge and sat on the sofa, leaning back closing her eyes.

Doug came and sat gently next to her cradling a coffee.

'So, what happened at your place with Emma? You want to talk about it?'

Jesse sighed. 'It was like one of those dreams you can't quite get a handle on. In her mind, she'd clearly justified it as being perfectly normal. There she was cooking dinner, lighting candles.' She shuddered. 'When I

317

woke up, I thought it was you downstairs. Then I went into the kitchen and she's there, like she comes around every day and cooks for me.'

'What did she say?'

'She told me Chris had blackmailed her to see me and make my life hell. Make me suffer, mentally, psychologically, until he could escape and do it himself. But then she decided she wanted to be with me and made a plan to put him away for as long as she could. And it was her who ran me off the road, thinking it was you. She thought you stood in the way and you needed to be got rid of.'

'Steve said that. Lucky escape in more ways than one. It must feel awful you talked to her and shared stuff with her.'

'I think in some weird way, it helped me think through some things. Helped me be clearer about how I felt. I don't think I'll ever be able to pick it all apart though, I'm still too frightened. I just want to be free of the pair of them though. They're both too dangerous, too ... insane.'

Jesse yawned widely.

'God, sorry! I'm shattered.'

Doug stood and held out a hand. 'Right bed. Come on. I'll show you to your boudoir. No arguments.'

He headed off up the stairs and Jesse followed. Brock had taken up residence by the front door.

Doug opened a door, showed Jesse in and handed her a couple of towels.

'Bathroom's through there. Mon casa, Su casa, as they say. Help yourself.'

Jesse smiled gratefully. 'Thanks, Doug.'

'No problem. I'll be downstairs, OK? Holler if you need anything.'

Jesse was wide awake. The house was quiet. She was snuggled underneath the covers in Doug's bed, while Doug was on the sofa downstairs, fast asleep. There was a light growl from Brock, and suddenly alert he ran growling to the front door. He barked loudly and whined, hearing the sound of running footsteps.

Doug woke and fell off the sofa in his confusion and then emerged from the lounge and calmed the dog down before his barking woke the children up. He opened the front door and Brock rushed out barking. Doug looked around, called him in and calmed him down again. Doug went upstairs and checked on the kids, and then opened his bedroom door slowly. Jesse sat up in bed.

'Why is Brock barking? Oh God, what it is?'

Doug stepped into the room and whispered, 'It's fine. I've checked around, everything is fine. He's taken up residence by the front door. Hey, you're shaking … come on, it's OK.'

Doug sat on the edge of the bed and put an arm around her and, without warning, Jesse sobbed.

'God. Sorry. Can't seem to hold it together at the moment.'

'It's OK,' Doug soothed, using his best voice for calming the kids down, hoping it would work on Jesse.

Jesse felt calmer with Doug around. She felt wired, though, despite being exhausted. She said in a small voice, 'Could you stick around and just talk to me for bit? I'm so tired, but I just can't sleep.'

Doug stretched out on top of the duvet.

'I'll stick around for a while. My sparkling conversation is bound to send you to sleep anyway.'

Jesse giggled. 'Stop it. What was out there? He only kicks off if it's the postman or someone putting something through the letter box.'

'Nothing there. I went out to check. It's all fine. Stop fretting.'

Jesse yawned again and said, 'This is nice. How was Billy today?'

Doug told her about Billy and how he had been that day and waited for a response. But Jesse was asleep. She turned in the bed, and, still asleep, placed her hand on his chest. Doug thought that the frantic thumping of his heart would wake her, but she slept through, oblivious to the effect she was having on him. The weight of her arm on his chest felt so good that, despite his best intentions to sleep on the sofa that night, he fell asleep shortly after Jesse.

Doug awoke the next morning with the sensation he was being watched. He opened an eye expecting to see one of the kids next to the bed and instead came face to face with a black and white fluffy face. Brock was staring at him, making very small noises in his throat, his tail thumping on the floor. Doug looked over at Jesse, who was sleeping soundly and eased himself off the bed gently. Doug left the bedroom and got the children up, asking them to get dressed quietly. He showered quickly after letting Brock out and put some coffee on. There was a quiet knock on the back door and Nessie appeared with a huge plate of pancakes.

'Here you go,' she said. 'Special request from the kids last night as they know Jesse loves pancakes.' She handed over the steaming plate.

'Nice you've got company of a female nature,' she said smiling broadly and left Doug stood holding the plate. 'See you later,' she said winking, leaving Doug looking vaguely embarrassed and at a loss for something to say.

CHAPTER 37

Jesse had spent ten minutes dithering over what to wear. Most of her wardrobe was in a heap on the bed. She settled for a lightweight jumper and jeans. She grabbed a bottle of wine and a large bag she had put by the door. She told Brock not to bark, shut the door and strolled up the road.

Doug had surprised her a few days ago when he'd asked her if she'd like to come for dinner.

'A proper dinner,' he clarified. 'Not a bowl of soup dinner.'

'Ooh, a proper dinner,' she teased. 'Who can possibly refuse?'

Outside Doug's house, she picked up a soaking-wet teddy from the porch as she rang the bell.

Doug appeared as she was wringing it out.

'What did that poor thing ever do to you?' he asked. He leant forward and kissed her cheek.

Jesse handed him the teddy.

'It was making a run for it on the porch. Something smells amazing.'

Doug propped the teddy on the hall radiator.

'So do you, if I may say so. Give me your jacket. As you know, I'm a man of many domestic talents ...'

Jesse shrugged off her jacket and handed it to him.

'Where are the kids?'

'They're with Claire overnight. Felix is away, so she felt it would be good for them to see where she lives, without meeting him yet.'

'Wow … an evening off for you.'

'Absolutely. Drink?'

'Mm, lovely. I've got some wine here.'

They walked into the kitchen. The table was laid and there was a candle lit in the middle. Music played softly in the background.

Jesse looked around. 'This is nice.'

Doug gestured to the bag. 'What's in there?'

'This,' she said pointedly, 'is your jacket being returned.'

Doug raised an eyebrow. 'Wow. Wasn't sure if I was going to see that again.' He folded his arms and leant against the worktop, grinning. 'So, you returning my jacket … Are we going to have a proper discussion about things now?'

Jesse blushed. 'I was unfair. I let me being scared affect how I saw things. Despite what you said, all the assurances you gave me … I was still scared.'

'You thought I still felt a certain way, and you thought it would be you that got hurt.'

'Uh huh.'

Doug handed her some wine. 'So … what do we conclude from this?'

Jesse smiled. 'That I need to have more faith in you.'

'Excellent plan. I like it. Right … You hungry?'

'Starving.'

Doug busied himself with plates and Jesse wandered over to look out of the window into the garden.

'Have you seen Steve lately, what's it been? A couple of weeks now? Is there any news on Emma?'

'I saw him in passing earlier, he said no change. When she was first admitted they induced a coma for a while. She's stronger, breathing on her own now. Just won't wake up. The brother is back in prison. So I'd say you're safe.'

After dinner they sat at the table, in low candlelight. Doug emptied the last of the bottle of wine into Jesse's glass and went to get another from the counter.

'More wine?'

'Why not? Life's short, enjoy it while you can.'

'Don't we know it.' He opened the wine and topped up Jesse's glass. As he sat he asked, 'How are you finding it, not going to that shrink and off-loading?'

Jesse pulled a face. 'I hate to admit it, but despite her agenda, she had sort of got me to a point where I knew I had to decide something pretty crucial.'

Doug frowned. 'What d'you mean?'

Jesse looked into her glass, swirling the contents around.

'Whether I want to open Pandora's box or whether I try and deal with what happened without having to re-live it and face it.'

Doug nodded absently, thinking. 'It's about facing up to your worst fears, isn't it?' he said softly. 'Facing the demons and wondering whether you'll make it through and still be the same person. Whether you can get past it and still be you and not lose yourself along the way.'

Jesse stared at Doug. 'That's exactly it. My grandad used to call it kicking the hornet's nest and staying for the show, rather than running away. I'm so terrified of going there because I'm scared that my mind might completely shut down … you know?'

'I know. God, I know exactly. You'll get through it though. But you have to be ready to go there and take that step, I think. Do it when you feel you can cope with whatever might be in the box.' He paused. 'Look at it the other way. Take a moment and look behind you. See the distance you've come from it. You're looking forward now and actually in a place where you're thinking, "I'm never going to be able to get past this and deal with it," but take a while to realise how far you've come from when it happened.'

'When did you get so insightful?'

Doug picked up the plates, embarrassed.

'It's not insight. I spent months that way. Add in a healthy dose of self-blame and it all adds up to something that needs to be dealt with. I still struggle with it. It's never going to go away.'

'So how did you deal with it in the end?'

Doug put the plates in the dishwasher.

'It's by no means dealt with. It's more about accepting things. I did make myself think about it, revisit it, and I'm glad I did. I'm better now. More confident about my abilities, especially in a rescue. But it took me ages to know I was ready to go there.'

'How did you know you were ready?'

'I'm not sure you ever really know, you just have to go with your gut. Gav's old mantra. Go with your gut – no buts.'

'Wise man.'

Doug swallowed hard. 'Yup. Have you had enough to eat?'

'Yes, thanks. That was lovely … a few more things to add to that domestic goddess list of yours.'

'You'll be calling me Nigella next. You want some coffee?'

'Umm, please.'

Doug pointed to the lounge. 'Go and crash out. I'll bring it in.'

Jesse wandered into the lounge and got comfy at one end of the sofa.

Doug appeared with the cafetière and mugs.

'Comfy?' he said, grinning.

'Yup. Now tell me. How are the kids doing? Jude was really off the other day at the station when I saw him. What's up?'

Doug looked rueful. 'It's a mix of raging hormones and wanting his mum, and not wanting her because he's so upset she's left.'

'Is he talking to you about it?'

'Yup. He is. All the time that's happening, it's OK.'

'And Christy?'

Doug smiled. 'She's fine. Just gets on with it all. Her primary focus this week is turning her bedroom into a pet salon. I keep finding wet teddies in the bathroom, apparently they're waiting to dry and be groomed and then they can go home.

'Ahh hence the one trying to escape on the porch. Perhaps I should drop the dog off.'

'At your own peril, I think.'

He poured Jesse a coffee. She took it and snuggled down in the sofa.

'Mm, this is nice.'

'The coffee?'

'Coffee, dinner, all this …' She gestured with her coffee cup and it sloshed out all over the arm of her jumper.

'Shit! That's hot. Shit!'

She jumped up, pulling her arm out of her sleeve and taking the dripping arm into the kitchen. Doug followed her.

'Run that arm under cold water.'

Jesse ran her arm under the tap, the jumper arm hanging loosely, gently dripping onto the floor.

'Give me the jumper and I'll get that off it.'

Jesse turned around to Doug and bit her lip. 'Err, I haven't got a lot on underneath it ...'

Doug held up a tea towel. His face was dead pan.

Jesse laughed. 'Stop it. Have you got a T-shirt?'

'I have, yes thanks. Lots.'

Doug stepped forward and pulled the jumper over Jesse's head, leaving her in just her bra. He looked down at her appraisingly.

'See? You do have something on underneath. That passes for more than enough clothes. In fact, it might actually be a few too many.'

He turned off the tap and took Jesse's face in his hands, kissing her gently. She turned around and kissed him back.

'God, you smell nice,' he murmured.

Doug's phone buzzed insistently on the kitchen counter.

'Are you going to get that?' Jesse murmured, kissing his neck.

'Nope,' he said, looking at the display. 'It's Steve. He'll leave a message.'

Doug kissed her again and moved to lift her onto the counter. He stood between her thighs and took her face in his hands.

'You OK? With this?' he whispered.

Jesse nodded and kissed him passionately. As Doug slid one of her bra straps down her arm, Jesse shivered.

'Are you cold?'

'Far from it,' she murmured.

'Did you get any coffee on your jeans?'

Jesse giggled. 'Why? Are they coming off too?'

Doug chuckled. Jesse's hands were exploring inside Doug's shirt, she felt scar tissue underneath the scattering of hairs on his chest. She hooked her legs around Doug's back and pulled him closer.

He wrapped his arms around her tightly and kissed her deeply.

I'm thinking so clearly now. I don't have HIM thinking with me. I can't hear his voice any more. I've never felt so free. It's better without HIM.

I've found her. The scar is healing well; a lovely reminder of me every time she looks in the mirror. That's love. She's at his house. Drinking wine, eating and laughing. She looks happy. This is NOT part of the plan. She needs to be with me. She'll want to be with me when she comes to her senses. I'll tell her I'm the one she is supposed to be with. She'll understand and after a while she'll accept it. It's meant to be. She'll realise all I've done for her and she'll know that this is the only way. He's kissed her. Again. She's taking clothes off. No No NO ... She should be with ME. This needs to stop. This needs to end. I will kill him and make her watch and then she'll understand. She'll understand the depth of my love. She'll want to be with me.

CHAPTER 38

Emma stood in the garden, watching them, shivering in the thin hospital scrubs she had stolen. She ached all over, and her chest hurt to breathe. She had been coughing up blood and unbeknown to her it was smeared across her cheek. She didn't have much time; she needed to do it, then take Jesse and go.

She watched Doug lift Jesse onto the worktop and kiss her. She felt rage bubbling up, pressure building, the sensation so strong she felt her chest was going to burst open. She opened her mouth and screamed, her hands covering her mouth. She couldn't let them hear her. She shuffled closer to the tree to lean against it, sobbing quietly.

She watched Doug take Jesse's hand and lead her out of the kitchen. She watched him lead Jesse upstairs and saw a soft light come on in the room above.

Emma stopped crying, snapping back to reality. She was sure she heard Jesse laughing. She felt her rage build again. What if they were laughing at her? She looked at her hands and saw they were shaking. She wouldn't succumb to the rage. She had to use it. She stared into the kitchen window, not seeing the reflection of a wild-haired mad-eyed woman, with blood around her mouth.

She had a plan. It was a good one. He would die, but Jesse would be OK. Jesse was a survivor. Part of Chris's legacy had made her that way. She could survive anything, she was special and protected. Untouchable. Emma shuffled around to the kitchen door and stepped in awkwardly, doing her best to be quiet.

She walked to the sink and opened the cabinet door below, scrutinising the cupboard, finally seeing what she wanted. She grabbed it, placed it on the worktop and started to go through the kitchen drawers for the next thing.

Upstairs, Jesse was kissing Doug's chest and tracing his scars, running her hands across his chest and back.

Suddenly from downstairs Doug's phone rang shrilly through the quiet house. Doug looked towards the door.

'Shit. Who the bloody hell is that?'

'Leave it …' she said quietly. 'Let it go to voicemail.'

'What if it's about the kids?' he said, torn.

Jesse kissed his neck and traced her hand around the waistband of his jeans, unbuckling his belt.

'Then Claire will cope.'

'OK.' Doug carried on his journey of kissing her neck and the top of her breasts, sliding her bra straps off her shoulders. He nudged her to the edge of the bed where pushed her back gently onto the bed.

She grabbed his hand and pulled him down beside her.

'Now, about those jeans coming off …' he murmured.

'What sort of girl do you think I am?' she said with a giggle.

'My sort.' He kissed her neck. 'Definitely my sort.'

The phone rang again.

'Fuck's sake,' said Doug. 'No one ever rings me this much, not even when I'm at bloody work.'

Jesse leant on her elbows and looked at him. 'Are you going to get it?'

Doug was torn. 'What if it's about the kids.'

Jesse pinged open the buttons of his jeans. 'Yeah, what if …'

He rolled his eyes. 'Sod it,' he said. 'Claire can cope. Now about these jeans of yours, they seem to be still on.'

Emma was pleased with her efforts. She squirted more barbecue lighter fuel onto the fire, which immediately burnt brighter and higher. She was transfixed. The heat was intense and warmed her. To her it looked like the orange tendrils were reaching out to her and she put a hand out to touch them, not feeling them burn her.

'So beautiful ...' she murmured as she caressed them. 'Let's go and find our girl.'

She walked around the kitchen and opened the door, turning to squirt more of the fluid behind her and the fire snaked after her.

'Come on, my beautiful dragon,' she murmured as her mind turned the flames into a faithful follower. 'We've got work to do ...'

The sound of the smoke alarm made Doug sit up.

'What the hell is going on tonight? Is someone trying to tell us something?' He looked over at Jesse in frustration as he marched towards the door, wearing just his underwear. He flung the door open and a thick wave of acrid smoke forced him back in the room.

'Jesus!' he slammed the door. 'Get dressed,' he barked at Jesse, who was hurriedly climbing into her jeans. Doug strode over to his wardrobe and pulled out a shirt, chucking it at Jesse. He yanked on jeans and a T-shirt.

'We need to get out. Go to the bathroom and wet a couple of towels.'

Jesse ran to the bathroom, grabbing the towels and wetting them as best she could. She wrung them out and passed one to Doug, wrapping the other around her face, leaving her eyes free.

Doug did the same and opened the bedroom door slowly. Flames licked the edges of the door frame. He slammed the door and turned to Jesse.

'Too close, can't get out that way.' He gasped and ripped the towel from his face and laid it along the bottom of the door.

'Is there a phone up here?' Jesse asked desperately.

Doug shook his head. 'We have to hope someone's called the fire brigade,' he said, running over to the window.

He threw it open and leaned out. In the distance, he heard a siren and hoped it was for them. He turned to Jesse who was frantically stuffing the towels around the door more firmly. The smoke was pouring in around them and the room was rapidly filling with smoke.

'The door's getting hot. I can feel it!' she coughed.

'Jesse.' He beckoned her over. She leaned out of the window and took a deep breath of fresh air, coughing.

She peered downwards. 'It's too high to jump, isn't it?'

'We will if we have to. I reckon we can probably get the mattress out of the window, then we can at least land on that if we have to jump.'

He turned back to the window at the sound of the siren and saw with relief it was coming up the road, as the houses opposite were bathed in blue light.

The smoke was filling the room quickly and being sucked out towards the window.

'Get on the floor,' shouted Doug.

Jesse lay down on the floor, where the smoke was slightly less dense.

Doug was hanging out of the window shouting and waving his arms at the fire crews.

Jesse pulled him down next to her. Doug moved to cover Jesse as best he could.

'It'll be OK, it'll be OK,' he whispered, holding her tightly.

Emma and the dragon were like one. She marveled at how it could shape itself. Its beauty. They were dancing together in a beautiful duet. The dragon followed her wherever she went, she called to it and beckoned it as she made her way through the house. She used the last of the liquid on the door to the bedroom, and marveled at the dragon, trying to get into the room to Jesse. At the top of the stairs, she stumbled on something and fell. As she lay, the dragon reared up above her.

'So beautiful …' she murmured, stretching a hand up to its face. 'So beautiful … my beautiful dragon … Go and get my beautiful girl.'

In the early morning light, two fire engines and an ambulance were parked in the large driveway at Doug's house. The scent of smoke hung heavy in the air. A fireman walked out of the house carrying a body in a bag, laid it gently on a stretcher and walked back into the house. A car pulled into the drive and Claire climbed slowly out, her face a picture of utter disbelief. She broke into a run towards the house, shouting over her shoulder.

'Stay there.'

'Doug!' she screamed, seeing the body bag on a stretcher and running towards it. She clutched the side of the stretcher and bowed her head, shoulders heaving as she stretched a shaking hand out to the bag.

Doug and Jesse sat on the back step of the ambulance with sooty faces and blankets around their shoulders. Doug squeezed Jesse's shoulder and walked over to Claire.

'Claire.' Doug touched her gently on the shoulder. 'Claire … I'm OK.'

Claire spun around.

'Oh God.' She held him tightly and sobbed into his shoulder. 'I thought for a second … I thought I'd lost you and I didn't have a chance to …'

'To what, Claire?' he asked gently.

'To tell you I was sorry.'

Doug gave her another hug. 'Come on. Don't be a numpty.'

She wiped her eyes and pointed to the body bag on the stretcher. 'Who's that poor soul?'

'No idea at all. We're waiting for Steve to turn up. He's on his way. Thinking about it, he was trying to call me last night.'

The kids ignored Claire's instruction to stay in the car and ran over to hug Doug, wide-eyed and upset at the state of the house.

'Has Mum told you?' Jude asked him.

'Told me what, mate?' asked Doug, ruffling his hair.

Claire gasped. 'Oh God. I'm so sorry. That's why we're here. Doug, your dad's been trying to call you, your mobile, all last night. He couldn't get hold of you, so he rang me. Your mum, she's in ICU, she's had a heart attack. He needs you up there. You need to go to Scotland. There's not a lot of time.'

Jesse had seen Claire arrive and fling herself at Doug, followed by the children. She watched as Doug's face suddenly changed as he took a step backwards, shaking his head in disbelief. She watched him run his hands through his hair and look around, confused.

Frowning, she walked over to him.

'Doug? What's happened?'

'I … I don't know what to do,' he said, looking around at the house. 'I need to go,' he added quietly. 'Mum's in ICU, heart attack. Bad. Dad needs me up there. Not much time.'

'Jesus,' Jesse murmured. 'You have to go.'

Claire walked over to the firefighter chief and had a discussion. He nodded and turned to a colleague who shrugged out of a coat and hat. Claire took them and walked over to Doug and said authoritatively, 'Go in and find the spare keys for the truck, they're in the desk drawer in the den. Put a few clothes in a bag. They'll only smell of smoke, the fire chief said the fire didn't reach the bedroom. You can go in accompanied, they'll make sure you're safe. Go on.'

Claire held out the fireman's coat and he put it on; she placed the hat on his head and stood back.

'It's a good look for you,' she said tugging the collar of his coat straight. 'Go on.'

Doug turned and walked towards the house. One of the firemen had brought out a few things that were untouched by the fire and placed them on the drive. Doug stopped next to the small pile. He picked up a denim jacket and turned to call Jesse.

'Jesse. Your coat's over here.'

He held it out to her as she walked towards him. She took it and pointed to the bag that she had bought with her earlier that contained Dougs jacket.

'Look at that … untouched,' she said.

'It's a sign,' said Doug. He held out the bag to her. 'Take it. Look after it for me.'

'A sign of what?' She took the bag from him. He looked at her in a way that made her stomach lurch.

'A sign that says we're not done discussing it … At all.'

Jesse looked at the bag and smiled.

'So, this means we'll carry on discussing it then?' she asked quietly.

Doug looked at her. 'Absolutely. Soon as we can. Lots and lots more discussions to be had,' he said softly, running his thumb down her face.

'I'll look forward to that.' She murmured.

As he walked away she called out.

'Hey Doug.'

'What?'

'Claire's right you know.'

Doug looked confused. 'About what?'

'That's a good look on you … See if you can hang onto the hat.' She raised an eyebrow. Doug grinned.

'Will do. Gotta go.'

'Take care. Keep in touch,' she said softly.

He nodded and tapped the hat.

'I'll see what I can do.' He winked and turned, going into the house flanked by two firemen.

* * *

Chris sat with his handcuffed hands in his lap, with his usual air of insolence. The Governor, used to dealing with pond life, ignored the attitude and removed a file from his desk drawer.

'I'm sorry to tell you your sister died in a fire a few days ago. We understand it was her that started the fire. Pending a review of your behaviour, you'll be allowed to attend the memorial or funeral, but you'll be accompanied at all times. As soon as I hear when that will be, I'll inform you. Any questions?'

Chris looked at the man and wondered if he had enough time to climb across the desk and strangle him, or at least punch him in the face before the prison officers caught him. He shrugged.

'Back to the cells,' said the Governor unceremoniously. The officers dragged Chris out and returned him to his cell.

Chris lay in his bunk, trying to work out how he felt about Emma's death. Frustration appeared to be the overriding emotion, he decided. Fucking woman couldn't even be trusted to get this little job right for him. Ended up dying like some fucking idiot.

He lay with his hands behind his head. Clearly, if a job needed doing, he'd just have to do it himself. He scowled. He'd find her. He had contacts. He would spend time making her suffer. Make her appreciate him a little more. He wasn't planning on staying in prison for any length of time, particularly now he had a funeral to attend. He just needed to get his ducks in a row.

Contented, he closed his eyes and started planning.

He had time. He would make her suffer. Oh, how she would suffer.

The End

ACKNOWLEDGEMENTS

With any fairly epic undertaking there are always people hidden in the wings that deserve to step into the spotlight and receive huge applause and heartfelt thanks.

Thank you to Nikki Brice, who in the early days, helped me shape what was 'The Crew' to 'Sea State' from extremely clunky script to book.

Huge gratitude and thanks go to the lovely Heather Fitt for picking up the editing baton and running with it so brilliantly. Thanks for your patience with my extremely bad habits. Your 'we can make it work' mantra is always music to my ears.

Immeasurable, heartfelt love and thanks go to the hotly contested 'Crew's biggest fan' posse. You were my 'first' readers. Thanks for your honesty, your criticism, your enthusiasm and support, and your continuing deep love of the characters. You never fail to inspire me to want to write more. You know who you are.

To the wonderful Jane Bateup. Thank you for your deep love of Castleby and everyone in it. There will always be a reserved seat, front and centre, just for you.

Finally - thanks to 'My Crew.'

My two rescue Border Collies; Brock (Yes he does exist!) aka Max and Merlin, who sit at my feet for hours while I write and accompany me on walks where I work out my plots.

My gorgeous, loving and wonderfully supportive Sis' for being such an enthusiastic reader, critic and debater and for having such a deep and long-lasting affection for Jimmy and all his disastrous ways. He stayed in just for you.

Thanks to my two beautiful girls who before my eyes have morphed into gorgeous young women who sneak into my office and read the bits they can get their hands on and tell me what they think. Their love of the characters and Castleby, inspires me every day to write more to make them proud.

For my wonderful (and occasionally irritating) husband who regularly professes (grumpily) to "hate reading" but pushes on anyway to read my efforts. Thank you for letting me retreat into my head and live in my own world for what must seem like weeks on end. Thank you for always being positive, encouraging, supportive, having my back and being my "cell mate". Thanks to you and our girls for continuing to indulge my deep-seated love of our special place that first inspired Castleby.

I am truly lost at sea without you all next to me.

Printed in Great Britain
by Amazon

18263159R00193